BLINDING BEAUTY: A RETELLING OF THE PRINCESS AND THE GLASS HILL

THE BECOMING BEAUTY TRILOGY, BOOK 2

BRITTANY FICHTER

WANT FREE STORIES?

Sign up for a free no-spam newsletter with coupons, free short stories, exclusive secret chapters, and sneak peeks at books before they're published.

Details at the end of this book.

To my big little brother, Danny, for always protecting your big sister and threatening to break the legs of any man who broke my heart. I forgive you for stealing my dolls and eating my cookies before I was able to finish decorating them. I now laugh in your general direction for calling me a nerd in high school. Engineers forfeit all rights to call other human beings nerds. Keep on truckin' and protect that big brain of yours because one day it might just save the world.

CHAPTER I

THIS QUEEN

Isa's weapon lay uselessly on the ground just a few feet away. She threw her hands up to protect her face, but it was too late. The blue flame from Ever's sword hit her head-on, knocking her across the floor. Her head slammed against the stone tiles with a sharp crack.

Sheathing his sword, Ever was at her side before the ever worrisome servants could make it to the center of the training room's large floor. "I'm sorry," he groaned, gently lifting her head and examining the spot that had struck the ground. "I didn't mean to make that one so strong."

His wife gave him a weak smile, but winced when his fingers found the spot they were looking for, buried at the base of her thick, auburn braid. Pulling off his right glove, Ever placed his hand over the bump that had already begun to rise, releasing just enough power to draw the swelling down. As the blue light rolled back and forth between the knot and his palm, Isa's breathing evened and she let out a gust of air.

"I truly am sorry," he said again. Isa gave him a genuine smile this time, and as they often did, her large eyes caught him off guard, holding him captive in their midnight depths.

"It was my fault." She shook her head and accepted his help in standing. After dusting her clothes off, she went to retrieve her sword. "I don't know why I keep missing that attack. I see you coming, but I'm too slow to parry."

"Your wrist is too stiff." He moved to stand just behind her so he could put his hand over hers where she gripped the sword's hilt to show her the proper form.

Instead of fixing her stance as he demonstrated, however, she turned and leaned back for a kiss, and Ever couldn't help himself as he bent his head to meet her soft lips. Somewhere behind him, he heard the sound of retreating footsteps, and he smothered a laugh.

Before his wedding and coronation, the crowd that gathered to watch Ever's combat practices had generally been large. In those days, as their then-prince took on single, double, even seven or eight opponents sometimes, his spectators would watch in awe. Fathers would point out specific moves to their sons, and the women would whisper about how graceful and strong he was. Everyone agreed they had never seen the like.

Since his wedding and coronation, however, though he still practiced with his soldiers, the spectators had learned quickly that their king was not shy about flirting with his wife.

Even during weapons practice.

"I don't know what else they think they're going to see," Ever had once overheard Garin, the Fortress steward, remark with a chuckle. "It's only been five months since the wedding. They would do well to let the love birds be."

But in truth, Garin and Ever both knew what the spectators wanted to see from their new queen. And as time went on, everyone, Ever included, grew more anxious when it didn't appear. Today had been no exception, and the flirting wasn't to blame.

"That's enough practice for one day."

Ever cringed as Gigi's sharp words drenched the warm

moment like a bucket of melted snow. He should have known the exiting footsteps had belonged to one of the kitchen mistress's spies. Grudgingly he stepped back to allow Gigi to examine Isa more thoroughly.

"I thought we discussed this," Gigi scolded him, lowering her gray brows when she found a rather large bruise on the back of one of Isa's arms. "What if she were with child? How could this possibly benefit any of you?"

At this, Isa let out a huff. "We *have* been through this, and I am *not* with child. Ever is right. I'm still not very good at defending myself."

"Well, you're done for the day," the older woman clucked, taking Isa's sword and handing it to Ever as though it were a dead serpent. "We have to fit you for new gowns."

"More? What in the heavens for?"

"I'll tell you on the way. Speaking of which, Ever, Garin needs to see you."

Looking defeated, Isa let the matronly woman lead her away, and Ever turned to find his steward smirking at him.

"You may be king, but that woman orders you about more by the day."

"She doesn't do it in front of the servants." Ever sheathed his sword. "I can't see any harm."

Garin didn't argue. Gigi had been more of a mother to Ever than Queen Louise had. Certain liberties were hers for the taking. She had earned them.

"How was practice?"

"I thought she would be more in control by now. But she just stagnates." Ever let out a gusty breath. "She's so unsure of herself as it is. I just don't know how to help her."

"I remember the day you first discovered your strength." Garin waved his hand at the servants to open the doors to the king's study. "You certainly never hesitated to use it." The glint in his steward's eye told Ever that he was remembering all the tricks Ever had played on the Fortress staff as a small boy. "You were quite imaginative, if I may say so."

"It came so naturally." Ever shook his head as the doors closed behind them. "I never had the problems she's having."

"There is quite a difference between discovering the Fortress's strength as a child and discovering it as an adult," Garin said as he lifted a stack of parchments from Ever's desk and began rifling through it. "Children accept life as they see it. But Isa has had to face an enormous amount of self-doubt and adversity. Her confidence is still shaky at best. I know you do not want to hear it, but give her time, Ever. The Fortress knows what it's doing."

Ever placed his hands on his desk and let his head sag, something he never allowed any of his other subjects to see, or even his wife, for that matter.

"In truth, did any of the other queens struggle this much with their powers?"

Garin's eyes grew very old, as they always did when talking about the Fortress's past. "Let me remind you that many of the queens never even gained the Fortress's strength at all. The Fortress never saw them fit to carry its power. As for those who did receive and master it, I've found it best not to compare. The Fortress will teach her in its own time. Her heart must be ready. Now, for other things to talk of." He handed the stack of parchments to Ever. "I think you'll find some of today's reports quite interesting."

Ever grinned a bit when he took the papers and noticed their broken wax seals. It was nothing new to Ever for his steward to read his messages first, but Isa's younger brother, Launce, had once seen it and gawked.

"When you've overseen the Fortress business for a few centuries, you too may read the king's messages," Ever had told him when he had seen the young man's astonishment.

Today, Ever glanced at the first few reports, mostly numbers on taxes and regional crop production. But when he saw the letter from the Lingean king, his heart beat uneasily, and as he read it, he found his gut instinct was right to be worried.

Everard,

I fear I have no pleasant tidings to bring you this day. Though you know me as the sort to keep order in my own realm, I have had reports of a most heinous crime committed along our northern border. Indeed, it was so outrageous I would not give it heed until I had seen it with my own eyes.

Ten of our region's priests were journeying to a small town that has recently been taken with a terrible illness. It is my understanding that their intentions were to assist the healers. They never reached the town, though. The day after they should have arrived in the village, a shepherd found their bodies strewn about in a nearby field.

I regret requesting your assistance, as it is three days' journey from your home, but I cannot fathom what kind of monster the murderer must be to cut down ten men appointed by the Maker himself. If you are at all willing, I implore you to help me solve this mystery. My people are more afraid by the day.

Your friend and ally,
  Leon Tungsvara of Lingea

"I want a military contingent to escort two of the Fortress healers to Lingea at once. Have them examine the bodies and bring their findings back to me."

"I thought you would find that odd." Garin's voice was tight.

"Ten holy men murdered in one day goes far beyond odd." No wonder his northern neighbor had reached out to him. No such atrocity had been reported in decades. Garin nodded and went to relay the order as Ever read the next parchment hoping to find better news. Garin walked back in just as he finished.

"This one *is* truly odd." He waved it at Garin. So that was why Gigi had wanted new dresses for Isa. "Since when do the Cobriens allow outsiders to compete to be the royal successor?"

"Since now, I suppose." Garin frowned slightly before smoothing his face. "Does that mean you're going to find out?"

"It does. Apparently, we're going to Cobren."

CHAPTER 2
FIT FOR A QUEEN

Remove the sleeves up to the shoulder," Gigi instructed the seamstress. "Now replace them with this." She held up a white roll of sheer lace.

Isa eyed it suspiciously. "That's showing quite a bit of skin for a wedding betrothal, isn't it?"

"I know you don't think so, but may I remind you that you are the most powerful queen in the northern kingdoms. It's only appropriate for the others to see that you are not like the other women." Gigi nodded once to the seamstress as she pinned the new fabric into place over Isa's bare arms.

Isa looked down at her new dress, and in spite of Gigi's confidence in the daring design, felt all the more self-conscious. To be fair, Isa was a far cry from the crippled woman with a bad ankle and crooked wrist who had hobbled up the Fortress steps the year before. She now stood tall and proud as her etiquette instructors had taught her to. Her once lame wrist and ankle, now healed by the Fortress's great power, no longer hindered her. But that didn't mean she was quite ready to be put on display.

After being healed, Isa had reveled in her new body. She had spent long hours out riding with her husband, practicing archery, learning swordplay, and trying to better understand her new powers as Ever had insisted she do.

"While being a ruler of the Fortress does provide special strength," he had told Isa when he had handed her a crossbow for the first time, "it also means many people will see your power. And there will be others that covet it as well. I need to know you won't be helpless when the time comes that someone tries to test you, to see how far you can be pushed."

Happily, Isa had agreed. And in truth, she had enjoyed the training. She just hadn't noticed until now how tan and hard her lean arms had grown during her many hours in the sun. This new gown made her look almost fierce, and she wasn't sure she liked it. Gigi, however, seemed delighted, despite her great disdain for all of Ever's *activities*.

When the seamstress was finally finished, Isa donned a plainer dress and cloak, and using what little control she had over her powers, she made sure no one saw her as she made her way down to Soudain.

Destin was full of many cities, but none were as impressive as its capital. Or at least, that's what Ever said. There were no dirt roads, as Isa heard other cities and villages had. Instead, every street was covered in cobblestones or wooden planks. Lamp posts lit every corner at night, lighted by small boys who ran from corner to corner with tiny flames on long poles.

Isa inhaled the scent of fresh bread and newly picked herbs as she passed through Soudain's largest square. People milled about, most moving from stall to stall while others called out their wares to the passersby, but nearly everyone looked content. Since Isa and Ever had broken the Fortress's curse, harvests were turning out to be more plentiful than ever, which meant full markets and happy citizens. Isa felt herself relax a little in the familiarity of the setting. It was almost the same sense of belonging she'd had here at one time.

True nostalgia was impossible, however, for she was suddenly aware of the two guards that flanked her. They weren't supposed to be visible in their commoners' clothing, but Isa knew her husband would never truly let her go into town alone anymore. She sighed a little. Perhaps she hadn't been as stealthy in her exit as she'd thought, just another reminder of how unreliable her powers were becoming. But as she finally reached her destination, she mustered up a smile before walking through the door of the corner mercantile.

"Isa!" Deline wiped her hands on her work apron and drew her daughter into a strong hug. "I didn't expect to see you here today. Megane, take over for me while I speak with your sister."

They moved through the back door behind the store counter into the main room of the house. Isa exhaled deeply as she sank down onto the long bench beside the table and watched her mother stir whatever was in the kettle over the fire. It was here, with her mother close by and her guards outside where she couldn't see them, that Isa could truly rest.

"So," Deline turned and sat beside Isa, "what is it that you want to tell me?" Isa gave her a wry smile, and her mother laughed. "I know you, love. What's bothering you?"

"I'm not sure if *bother* is the right word . . ." Isa said slowly, tracing the grain lines in the wooden bench with her finger. "We will soon be setting out for a betrothal ceremony in Cobren. Gigi says the travel itself will take two days, and the festivities could last up to a week, or even longer. Apparently, something about this betrothal ceremony is different from their traditional ones of years past. It will be a lengthy trip." To her surprise, Isa looked up to see a smile on her mother's face.

"Isa, this is exactly what you and your husband need."

"Truly?" Isa blinked. "I thought you would be upset. It's so far away."

"I am not saying that I won't miss you, but I trust your husband to keep you as safe as anyone."

At this, Isa had to smile and nod. Ever's strength wasn't only known throughout Destin, but all of the northern kingdoms. And he took her safety more seriously than anything else. The guards outside were proof of that. She wouldn't have been shocked if more were milling about, unseen as well.

"You need to get away though, and have some fun," Deline continued, pulling a lump of bread dough from a basket and beginning to knead it. "You and Ever have been so busy since the wedding, I think some time together will be good for you. You may be king and queen, but you are also newlyweds. The strains on marriage don't disregard couples just because they're royal."

"I have to admit, it will be nice not to hear the Fortress gossips for a few weeks." Isa stood up and took the lump of dough from her mother and began to knead it. Sometimes it was nice to have something to pound. They never let her knead dough in the Fortress kitchens.

"With that, I can't help you." Deline let out a short laugh. "All I can tell you is that when the good Maker intends for you to have a child, He will give you one."

"You wouldn't think that from the way people whisper," Isa grumbled, hitting the dough a little harder than necessary. "You would think it has been five years instead of just five months!"

Deline stopped stirring the kettle and took Isa's hands in hers, pulling them away from the bread dough. "What else is wrong?"

Isa took a deep breath. It was hard to talk with her family about the special strength the Fortress bestowed upon its monarchs. The way it flowed from her soul felt so natural, such a part of her that she didn't really have words to express what it truly felt like. Or didn't, as of late.

"I practiced with Ever today, and it didn't go well." She shook her head and glared at the floor. "He doesn't say anything, but I can tell he's worried. I just cannot understand what's wrong with me. It felt like everything fell into place at the wedding, but now I can't seem to do anything right. I feel like an impostor, like I'm just holding the throne until the true queen appears. I haven't produced an heir, and my strength refuses to grow, and there seems to be nothing I can do about it!"

Deline drew her into a tight hug. Isa held on, clinging to her mother like a small child.

"I know not what to tell you, but just to trust the Maker. The Fortress acts on His will, and the Maker never makes a mistake. The Fortress chose *you*, and no one else. That has to mean something, as do these." She pulled back and touched just below Isa's eyes, which Isa could feel burning with the rings of blue flame she'd received with her powers. Just then, Isa's younger brother walked in.

"Launce," Deline said, not looking away from her daughter. "Isa will be going to Cobren soon."

Launce stared at them for a long moment, his mouth full of the bread he'd just shoved in, before swallowing loudly. "Whatever for?"

Isa had to smile. It was no secret that Launce detested everything royal. It didn't help that Ever, with good intentions of course, was determined to make him into a respectable member of the court.

"We're attending a betrothal ceremony for Princess Olivia."

"I'm sorry." He shook his head and grabbed another piece of bread. "Being around all those snobbish royals sounds terrible."

Isa had to agree with that. She hadn't met many of the other royals since her own wedding. And while their introductions and smiles had been polite, many of them had seemed less than genuine, particularly those of the women. When Isa had asked her lady-in-waiting, Cerise, about this, Cerise had admitted sheepishly, "Most of the women were either vying for your husband's hand just last year, or trying to obtain it for their daughters."

Isa had immediately understood the rest of what Cerise was *not* saying. Not only had their efforts been in vain, but to add insult to injury, Ever had married a commoner. For women who had been primped and primed to do nothing less than marry a king, losing a conquest to a nameless peasant was unthinkable. And while the opinions of others didn't seem to bother Ever in the slightest, Isa found herself dreading the trip once again.

As Launce continued around the room, gathering whatever food he could find to feed his voracious appetite, Isa had an idea. "Launce . . ."

He looked up at her, suspicion in his eyes. "What?"

Isa hopped over to her brother and threw her arms around him. "I am going to ask you something, and I need you to *please* listen before you say no."

He stared at her for a minute before his eyes bulged, and he tried to pry her arms off of his waist. "No. No! Absolutely not!"

"Launce, at least listen to what your sister wants."

"I know what she wants! And I am *not* going to Cobren!"

"Launce," Isa whined, "you said so yourself! I'm going to be miserable up there as the only commoner! You're going to leave me alone with all of *them*?"

"You'll be with King—"

"Launce!" Deline cut him off. "I told you I don't want to hear that word in this house! And be respectful. Your brother-in-law is still your king."

Launce scowled. "It's still your fault," he grumbled. "You didn't have to marry him."

"You know that's not true. Besides, I love him." Isa sighed. "I just don't love everything else that comes with being queen."

Launce glared at her for a long time before huffing.

"Fine! I'll accompany you in your misery." Then an evil grin stretched out on his face. "But you still have to convince your husband to take me. I doubt he'll like it any better than I do."

"Leave that to me." Isa smiled as she stood up, suddenly ready to return to the Fortress.

"YOUR BROTHER HATES COURT AFFAIRS." Ever frowned. "Why in the world would he want to come along on this one?"

Isa shifted uncomfortably. It had been easy to assure her family that Ever would accept Launce's company, but it was another matter entirely to actually secure that acceptance.

"I might have asked him," she finally admitted. Her husband's gray eyes widened in surprise, and she thought she detected a small amount of hurt in them before he smoothed his features over.

"I thought we would have the time to ourselves," he said.

"We will!" she hurried to assure him. "I *want* the time with you! It's just that you tend to get rather . . . occupied during official visits."

Ever exhaled heavily and gave her an unhappy look. Isa escaped his frown by moving over to stare out the window near their bed. It was one of her favorite spots, affording a view that stretched up the mountain side that the Fortress sat upon. From the balcony, it was possible to see almost all the way up to the summit.

"You'll have the court ladies to get to know," he finally said in a more subdued voice. "As queen of the Fortress, it's imperative to become familiar with all—"

"I will. But a week is a long time." She picked at a loose thread in her gown. "It gets lonely being the only commoner." In response, Isa felt him walk up to where she stood and gently lift her face up to his. Her breath caught as his fingers brushed behind her ear.

"You are no commoner." His deep voice was unusually soft. "You never were. The Fortress chose you before birth to be one of its keepers. Don't ever forget that."

"True as that may be, it doesn't guarantee that anyone will agree with you once we're there. Please," she searched his face for a sign of resignation, "don't make me do this alone."

"I wish you could see the truth about your place for what it is," he said. After taking another deep breath, he sighed. "But if it will make you feel better, your brother may come."

Isa put her head on his broad chest. "Thank you."

They stayed in the embrace for a long, rare moment. Isa wished she could keep him there forever, away from dignitaries, councils, and wars. Too soon, however, he gently pulled away and kissed the top of her head before lifting a stack of parchments from the table nearby, and sinking into a chair to peruse their contents.

"You know I don't dislike Launce, but life would be easier for both of us if he would just trust me."

Isa let out a short burst of laughter. "Can you blame him?"

"Actually," Ever drew his eyebrows together, "yes, I can. He should trust your judgment in marrying me."

"To be perfectly honest, he thinks you have me under a spell." Isa couldn't quite hide her bemused smile as Ever's head snapped up from his papers with a horrified look. She walked over and sat on the edge of his chair. "Try to see it from his perspective," she said. "He blames himself for allowing me come here in the first place. He didn't see all the months of change in you that I did as we broke the spell. All he knew was that you threatened to kill his family in the autumn, and then you married his sister the next spring. You know I'm trying, but it will take time for him to really know *you*."

"If he loathes me so much," Ever scowled, "then why does he insist on spending so much time here?"

"You never had a brother or sister." Isa shook her head

affectionately, wrapping her arms around his shoulders where he sat. "The ties are . . . inexplicable. My brother is a part of me, and he always will be, whether I like it or not. He wants to protect me."

"How does he honestly expect to do that? He can barely lift a sword without injuring himself."

"You were powerless against Nevina," Isa reminded him quietly. "Yet you still tried to save me."

Ever stopped trying to read the parchments and stared listlessly out the window. He didn't like talking about the part he had played in the Fortress's curse, particularly not the last night, when the greedy Tumenian princess had nearly caused Isa's death.

"He stays because he loves me," Isa said. "Isn't that worthy of some respect?"

Ever stared at her for a long time before his eyes softened. "Yes, I suppose it is."

CHAPTER 3
FLAT SIDE OF THE BLADE

I don't want to do it," Launce frowned at his sister. "I am not a member of the court. There is no reason for me to know swordplay." Launce *had* been enjoying the second day of their ride east. They were traveling through an exotic canyon with walls made of red sandstone and small scrub brush bushes at the bottom. A river snaked down the canyon floor, filling the air with a constant rushing sound of busyness. Admiring the scenery and watching for rattlesnakes in this strange little canyon had done everything Launce had needed it to and more to help distract him from the thoughts that constantly plagued him back in the city these days.

That was, until Everard had announced to Launce that they were practicing swordplay that night.

Isa stared at her hands as she fingered her left wrist the way she always did when distraught. "I told you, he's just trying to help."

"Look, I don't want to! What is so hard to understand about that? Why do you always have to take *his* side?"

"I am not trying to take sides! I love both of you!"

A movement from the camp caught their attention when

Cerise, Isa's lady-in-waiting, glanced at them in concern before meeting their eyes and quickly looking away. Isa took a deep breath before lowering her voice and speaking again. "I need both of you. I just happen to think he's right in this instance. It would be safer if you learned—"

"Why did you even bring me out here if you were just going to side with him?" Launce glared at her through the quickly thickening darkness of the evening.

"I wanted to see you." Then, in a smaller voice, she added, "You've been avoiding me lately."

"I've been busy with Blanchette." He folded his arms and stared out into the blue, orange, and red layered depths of the skies, hoping she wouldn't call his bluff.

"No, you haven't!" Then her tone softened as she looked up at him with a pitying expression that was annoyingly close to their mother's, something he'd seen all too often as of late.

"And how do you know that?"

"Mother told me . . ." her voice trailed off as she fingered her red riding dress. "All I want to do is spend time like we used to. I know things are different now—"

"Different is an understatement, Isa. He's done nothing but make you miserable your whole life! First he ruined your ankle and wrist. Then he threatened to kill all of us if you didn't come live with him all alone—"

"The servants were there."

"We didn't know that! He kept you there for months without so much as a message to let us know you weren't dead, or worse! And then you married him!" Launce didn't realize he was shouting until Everard looked up from where he was talking with his guards and stood. Launce thought he might lose his mind if he had to face his brother-in-law at that moment, but Isa shook her head at her husband. The king hesitantly sat down again, but not without glaring pointedly at Launce, a look Launce did his best to ignore.

"I've told you, it's hard to explain, but he's different now. And I didn't bring you along to talk about this. I want to talk to *you*. I miss you," she finished in a quiet voice that threatened to soften his heart.

"Well, that's too bad." Launce turned away from his sister's pleading eyes and began to walk away. "Because you made your choice." Part of him felt terrible as he left his sister standing alone. But he was too angry to apologize for his words. They sounded cruel, but they'd made perfect sense the countless times he'd practiced telling her exactly what he thought. He had waited five months to tell her what he thought of her marriage, so when the opportunity came, the words had spilled out of him like a bowl with too much broth, haphazardly and without order.

As he stomped over to his horse and pulled the waterskin from his pack, Isa silently returned to Cerise and picked up a set of knitting needles, which she began to use in exaggerated, dangerous motions. Everyone else seemed suddenly very interested in their own pursuits. The servants cooked supper over a large fire, the guards swapped what Launce guessed to be embellished feats of victory, and Everard was already examining his sword, a sign of the dreaded practice sure to soon come.

It was difficult for Launce to look at the king without suppressing the desire to sneer at him. And as far as Launce could tell, the feeling was mutual.

Everard had approached him the day before, just before their party had set out for Cobren. Though it had still been dark out at the time, the servants were already running about like frenzied ants to make sure the king and queen were well prepared for their journey, and Isa was busy exchanging goodbyes with their parents and little sister when the king had pulled him aside.

"I gather that joining us on this journey was not your idea."

Everard had given him a hard look. "You're coming because Isa asked you to?"

"Yes," Launce had answered him evenly, trying to match Everard's unmoving expression.

"If it will make her feel more comfortable, then I am grateful for your help. But—" The king had fixed his burning eyes on Launce in such a way that Launce had to fight the need to squirm. "I need your word that you will obey me without question should the need arise."

It had galled Launce that his brother-in-law would treat him so. Launce wanted to reply that what he did was his own business, but he'd bitten his tongue just in time. Relative or not, Everard was still the king, something Launce's father reminded him often. The Maker had seen fit to make it that way, although Launce often found himself wondering why.

"If you need an incentive," Everard's words had been low and dangerous, "and you are not to repeat this to a soul, not even your sister, something is amiss in Cobren. I'm allowing you to come because I know you care for Isa, and I need to know someone is watching out for her when I'm not around. Can you swear to me that you will obey me for your sister's sake?"

The words had surprised Launce so much, he'd nearly let his mouth fall open. Everard had never given him a secret before. And though he still hated being ordered around like a child, he'd finally nodded, a sliver of unease rippling through his body at the disquiet in Everard's voice. If being near Isa might keep her safe somehow from whatever had the king on edge, Launce would endure it for her sake.

But that did not mean he had to like it.

While the others waited for supper to finish cooking, Launce walked past the clearing they had camped at to stand on a wide bank just beside the small, swift river they were following through the chasm. Everard was no longer watching him, talking quietly instead with his personal guard, Norbert, and Isa was still intent on stabbing the life out of whatever she was knitting. Launce almost felt guilty for making her so angry. She hated knitting.

As he stared up at the stars that were slowly appearing in the twilight sky, Launce had to wonder again at Everard's choice to use him to help protect Isa. Launce had seen the king's skill with the sword, as with other weapons, and he had to admit that no one he'd ever seen could compare. The only thing Launce could imagine himself doing to remotely protect Isa was saving her from herself. Of course, that alone would be no easy task.

Of course, a small, annoying voice in his head prodded, *it might be easier if you admitted you were just a bit jealous as well.*

Nonsense. Nothing could serve to make him jealous of his sister. And yet, the hole Blanchette's missing company had created was most assuredly there. Had she still lived in Soudain, he would have asked to bring her, too. Launce could imagine her sitting beside him, raising her head toward the blackening sky, saying all the right things, flipping her goldenrod hair from her face in that adorable way she did.

But she wasn't coming back, and Launce didn't even know where she was or what she was doing, aside from what the note had said. He was tempted to take it out of his pocket and read it again. It wouldn't do any good though. He already had it memorized.

Launce,

Blanchette is safe, but you need to know that my daughter is no longer to be your concern. You are living a new life now, but it is not the life best for her. Do not search for us. We have begun our own new life, and Blanchette is to be married in a week's time. He is the son of an old friend, and she is happy. Please do not dash her happiness by searching. You would only cause her heartache.

. . .

John Guerin

LAUNCE KNEW that John couldn't read or write, so the letter had to have been written by Blanchette, which made it all the more painful. Launce had taught her to read and write, so reading the letter in her hand was like hearing the words directly from her. She could have written anything, and her father wouldn't have known. She could have given him some hint as to where she was or that she didn't want to be married. And yet she hadn't, so after two years of courtship he had naught to show for it but the yellow, wrinkled letter.

"Supper is finished," one of the servants called. Soon, everyone except the two guards on watch was huddled around the fire. Launce ate his supper quietly as he listened to the group's hushed conversations, which seemed to have recovered from his argument with his sister. Only Isa still looked unsettled. After finally giving up on her knitting, she'd snuggled up against Everard with his cloak drawn about her, exhaustion heavy on her face.

The savory food Launce had been enjoying felt dry as he swallowed. His intention hadn't been to make his sister unhappy. But just knowing that it was Everard she had chosen, who had caused her fourteen years of pain, felt like a stab in the back.

"Alright, Isa." Everard stood and looked down at his wife. "Let's have a round before we turn in for the night." A nervous smile lit Isa's face as he helped her stand. Launce groaned inwardly. He had been dreading this activity since they'd set off. His brother-in-law seemed incapable of missing a practice session no matter where they were . . . or who wanted to participate.

They had gone through such practice the night before, so Launce knew what to expect. It would begin with Isa, who no matter how tired she was, couldn't resist anything involving movement since her ankle and wrist had been healed. It would end, however, with everyone but the servants, and sometimes even them, having a round with the king. Launce had managed to edge his way out the night before, but he was sure Everard wouldn't let him off the hook tonight.

Everyone settled in to watch as the king and queen faced off. As they moved, Everard gave instructions, praises, and critiques. Isa began the match with the same look of weariness she'd worn since the argument, but as she got deeper into the movements, the fire in her eyes grew brighter, and she focused more. She was improving in form to be sure, but Launce couldn't help noticing that there was no blue light tonight that flowed from her hands. He wondered whether that was by choice, or if she simply didn't have any to give this time.

It wasn't a secret that Isa's power was flailing instead of growing as it should have been, but it was a topic that wasn't widely discussed either. Everard made sure to silence all idle tongues in his court when it came to Isa's abilities, and commoners in general didn't discuss their monarchs' power at all. Still, somehow, everyone knew that the queen was struggling. It didn't trouble Launce much, if he were honest. In fact, it made her seem a little more like the sister he knew. But she was obviously bothered by it.

"That will be enough for tonight. You did better on the second form this time," Everard announced. Launce watched incredulously as Isa beamed at Ever, in spite of his stern tone. How could she stand to be treated so callously? He didn't have much time to wonder at his sister's madness, however, because Everard was suddenly looking at him.

"Launce, it's your turn." Everard held out one of the practice swords. Launce had the urge to slap it away, but knew better than to even fully entertain that thought.

"I'll just watch today."

"Come now." Everard held the sword out even farther. "All young men of the court are expected to learn."

Launce felt rage bubble up inside his gut. He wasn't a member of the court, and he never had been. But Everard was the king, and he had promised to obey. Still, he and Everard shared a long look before Launce unhappily accepted the sword.

The weapon felt large and clumsy in his hands as he moved into the clearing they had made for the practice. Everard's body melted into a ready position, like a snake coiled to strike. Launce tried to mimic him, feeling foolish. How much humiliation would Everard heap upon him tonight?

Norbert declared match begun. Neither of them moved, however. When Everard stayed still for far too long, Launce realized that the king was allowing him the first attack. Raising the weapon high, he lunged. The king lifted his sword just enough to block the exaggerated movement, then touched Launce's back with the flat side of his blade. It didn't hurt, but if it had been a real fight, Launce would already be dead.

"You communicate your intentions with your whole body," Everard said in a tense voice. "Don't waste your energy on such full movements. Keep them short."

Launce had no desire to do anything his brother-in-law told him to do. It was bad enough that he'd ordered him out in front of everyone just to embarrass him. Everard knew well how Launce struggled with the sword. Countless forced rounds at the Fortress had already proven that. Anger coursed through Launce's body as he threw himself in for another attack. Again, it seemed Everard hardly flicked his wrist before disarming Launce completely.

"Slow your breathing!" Everard said as he circled a weapon-less Launce. "You'll pass out before the fight is half done."

Launce just stood there, hoping the torture would be over soon. His hopes of being left alone, however, were dashed as Everard pointed with his sword at Launce's blade where it had landed in the sand across the clearing. Launce glared at him a moment more, but Everard's stone face never moved. With a huff, Launce slowly went to pick up his sword, wishing the whole time that his sister had not married the king. The punishment for trying to bloody his brother-in-law's nose would have been less severe. For now, Launce could only fantasize.

It didn't matter how many times he suffered defeat. Familiar shame filled him as everyone watched him fight once more without so much as ruffling the king's fine golden hair. How many times would his brother-in-law insist on humiliating him this way before he stopped demanding Launce's obedience and participation? How many times would Launce be able to stand there as everyone watched him flail about helplessly like a clumsy child? He didn't know if he could take it very much longer.

One more desperate attack, and one more infuriating stumble later, and Launce refused to stand or raise his sword any more. He crouched in the dirt where Everard had left him, pebbles cutting into his palms and knees. Only the fact that his sister and her maid were watching them kept him from turning and throwing himself at Everard in anger, the way he would have at any other man who would dare to treat him in such a way.

"Ever." Isa's voice broke through the tension that had suddenly filled the clearing. Everard didn't move, however, as Launce tried to calm himself. When he didn't respond at first, Isa called her husband's name again, warning thick in her voice this time. "That's enough." A moment later, the king stood before him, offering his hand to help Launce up. Launce looked up at him, but the gallantry of the act was overridden by the disgust written all over the king's face.

Launce stood on his own, ignoring Everard's outstretched hand, but Everard grabbed and pulled him in as if congratulating him. In Launce's ear, however, he whispered, "Acting like a child will do you no good. Try to learn something once in a while." When Everard finally released him, Launce shoved away from the king, perhaps a little too hard.

"I believe it's my turn for a beating." Edgar was quick to pop off the rock he had been seated on. As he walked between Everard and Launce, he good-naturedly tapped Launce's sword with his own. Launce nodded his thanks before going to sit by himself at the edge of the circle.

Eventually they all had their turns, and everyone was seated again as they stared into the embers of the fire. It was high time everyone was in bed, but the chill of autumn made it cold enough that no one wanted to get up and actually lie down. So instead, they sat around the fire passing around wine and ale, telling stories.

"I propose a toast." Norbert raised his wineskin. "In honor of our queen's first official outing. May she strike the ladies with jealousy and the kings with admiration, and then find it all terribly boorish and want to return home as soon as possible."

"I'll drink to that," someone chuckled. Even Everard cracked a smile and looked down at Isa, who was curled up at his side, with an expression that nearly convinced Launce that the king truly did love his sister.

Nearly.

CHAPTER 4

A BROTHER NEVER FORGETS

It had taken a good deal of Ever's self-control for him not to march over to Isa's brother and strangle him when she'd returned from their argument with tears in her eyes. He'd restrained himself, however, because he knew she would have been even more upset if he'd interfered. So instead, as he had listened to them argue, Ever had contented himself with imagining how miserable he would make Launce during the sword practice he'd planned for later that evening.

Isa's relationship with her family was a mystery to Ever. She was different when she was around them, more like a child, more comfortable with who she was. And for that reason, a part of Ever balked whenever she wanted to spend time with them. They were so cohesive. Everyone, from the father to the youngest daughter, had a place and a function. They squabbled and laughed and teased each other continually. And yet, part of him relished the chance to study her among the people that had produced such an unusual creature as his wife.

Though it had been five months since the wedding, and the curse on the Fortress had kept them together for the entire winter before that, Ever felt uncomfortable sometimes when he realized how little he truly knew Isa. And it wasn't for a lack of trying on her part.

Just a few weeks before, Isa had waltzed into his study with two goblets of wine and a basket of fruit and sweets. "I spoke with Garin, and I know your afternoon is free of politics, councils, and hearings." She had raised her eyebrows, daring him to challenge her. "We are going on a picnic, and Garin is not to disturb us unless the Fortress itself is on fire."

Ever had walked around his desk to properly greet his wife, chuckling at her scheming. "You've had this planned for a while, haven't you?" he'd asked, peeking under the basket to see his favorite meat pies. As she beamed at him, he noticed that she wore a new dress. Its midnight blue matched her eyes, just as the jewels in her curled hair matched their sparkle. The pink of her lips suddenly had him wishing it were proper to scoop her up and escape the Fortress entirely as fast as his legs could carry them.

"When you leave on all of these diplomatic visits, it does give me some time to think." Isa's tone was just a touch reproachful. Smiling, Ever had leaned down to indulge himself with a kiss, but she'd grabbed his right hand instead and thrust the basket into his other hand.

"We're going *now*, before Destin finds some other way to fall apart and desperately need you."

Laughing, Ever had allowed her to drag him toward the door. Just as they'd reached it, however, a knock sounded. Isa's face went white, and Ever had inwardly groaned as his favorite general stepped in.

"Your Highnesses." Acelet bobbed a bow at both of them. "I —" He stopped short, though, when he saw the basket Ever carried. "I am so sorry," he said in a soft voice, "but I fear I must interrupt."

"What is it?" Ever had growled in an attempt not to moan

like a spoiled child, which was exactly what he had wanted to do at that moment.

General Acelet held up his hands apologetically. "The king of Siamji is here, demanding to speak with you."

Ever had felt his eyes nearly pop as he stared at his general and then at Isa. He knew what was coming.

Acelet looked at the ground again. "I honestly am sorry, Your Highness," he spoke, this time to Isa. It was exactly what she had predicted. "But you know how he is . . ."

"Let's just go." Ever had handed the basket back to Isa and stormed out the door. "The sooner we see him, the sooner he will leave."

And so their lovely escape had turned into an afternoon and then an evening of listening to the whiny king pontificate about how another king had slighted him, and Ever had been forced to sit across from his dutiful wife, watching her as she fought the tears she deserved to cry.

Ever was adamant that his marriage not end up like his parents', but finding that balance was proving to be a much greater struggle than he'd anticipated. He had desperately hoped this trip would give them a chance to step away from their normal duties, to simply enjoy one another. Then she had asked to bring Launce along.

His immediate reaction had been to tell her no. This trip was supposed to be for them. True, they would bring along a few servants and guards, but that was to be expected. Ever hadn't planned on bringing the insolent young man who seemed intent on provoking him every chance he got.

Still, he'd wondered if having Launce along might not open new doors to Isa's true self. It wasn't as if he thought she was hiding anything from him purposefully. But Ever sensed that deep down, there was much more to her that she had buried, perhaps even unbeknownst to her. And although Ever didn't like to admit it, there was something about being around her brother that brought down her walls. Perhaps, if Ever learned how to find the true way to Isa's soul, she might find her full powers and her peace. And if nothing else, having one more set of eyes on Isa couldn't be a bad thing, particularly when her powers at present were so unpredictable.

So far, however, no good had come of Launce's presence. After their long exchange, Isa had hardly spoken a word all evening. She didn't even attempt to use her strength during their practice. Every time he glanced at her now, snuggled up against his arm with the fire's shadows flickering on and off her face, it became more apparent how upset she really was. His attempt at using this journey as a time to break down her walls was off to a dismal start.

"Launce," Norbert said in his song-song fashion, interrupting Ever's musings, "queens like ours do not learn bravery overnight. Surely you must have a tale about your sister from when she was young." Ever kept his face smooth, but was immediately grateful to his eldest guard for the suggestion.

Launce hesitated as the others looked at him eagerly, his eyes flicking to his sister and then Ever. Ever made sure his nod was grave enough that the young man wouldn't think him desperate. Isa didn't look at him at all, just stared straight ahead into the flames as they licked the cool night air.

"Come now, lad," Norbert prodded. "Give us a tale for sweet dreams." Launce looked once more at Ever before finally nodding in consent.

"After the accident …" Launce started.

Ever's jaw tightened at the mention of the *accident*, as they called it, though Isa's fourteen years of pain had been wholly his own fault. "My father wanted to give Isa a way to get around. We had an old mare, but Father used her for business, so he and Mother decided they would buy Isa her own horse.

"Father worked extra hard that year, driving bargains he'd never dared to before, and Mother went without a new dress that winter. Gifts were small on that Sacred Star Day, but we didn't mind. By spring, Isa had her horse."

Everyone sat, spellbound, as Launce spoke. Only Isa wore a distant look. Suddenly, Ever was uncomfortable. Something told him this wouldn't be a tale with a happy ending.

"Isa changed after the accident," Launce said quietly. "The other children used to wait for her at first, but when they realized she wasn't going to get any faster, they usually left her behind. Sometimes she would follow along—"

"Launce." Isa interrupted him, her voice unusually sharp. "You can skip that part." They shared a long look before Launce finally nodded. Ever suddenly wanted desperately to know what her brother had been about to say, but Isa seemed adamant, so Launce continued.

"Father got the horse from a neighbor who was moving to Bas Riviere. It was a spindly, brown thing named Doux, and he and Isa were inseparable. When she and Doux were together," he whispered, "they were invincible. She stopped worrying about keeping up or looking like everyone else . . ." He paused, then shook his head as if to clear it.

"Sometimes I would ride along on the family's old mare. I couldn't keep up when she galloped, but at least we had a way to go places together. We were out one summer . . . I think I was about eight, so she would have been twelve. It was late afternoon, and we were riding through an orange grove, one of those just north of the city. Isa decided to go for one more sprint when we reached the road. Doux kicked up a trail of dust, and the last I saw of them was when they rounded the corner.

"It took me a few minutes to catch up. The road wraps around the mountain so that it's impossible to see around the bend until one makes the turn."

Ever knew exactly the spot Launce spoke of, and by the looks on the faces around him, so did everyone else. It wasn't a good place for any young girl to be riding alone.

"Isa had come to a complete stop, and she was facing two large men on the ground. One held a bow, the arrow already nocked and pointed right at Isa. The other held a sword. He stood a bit closer to Isa, close enough to reach her with the sword. They both had light, thick hair, and when they spoke, had accents from the north.

"'Two horses!' the one with the sword called back with a smile. 'I told you the gods have smiled upon us!' The one with the bow didn't answer, just frowned more deeply and stretched his bow a bit tighter. 'Boy, I will tell you what I told the girl. Give us the horse, and you're free to go.'" Launce shook his head, his eyes full of wonder as he stared into the fire. "I trembled so that I nearly fell off my horse. But Isa just held their gaze, didn't even blink. Instead, she told me not to move. The two men stared at her in shock, and the one with the bow finally spoke. He said, 'You will get off those horses, or I will get you off myself.'

"'No, you won't,' Isa answered him. She was as calm as a breeze. The one with the sword chuckled. 'And why the blazes not?'

"'Because the Fortress is just a short ways up this mountain,' she said, 'and the king is there at this moment. If you kill me, the king will know, and he will hunt you down like the dogs you are. And believe me when I say his treatment of you will be anything but merciful.'"

Ever couldn't help but look down at his wife. She was a bit taller than most women, and since he had been training her, she'd certainly grown stronger than she had been before. But even now, in the light of the fire, she looked anything but fierce, with her shoulders slumped forward and her head against his arm. He suddenly burned with anger as he imagined anyone threatening to kill her. Launce's voice pulled him back into the story, however, before he had time to linger.

"The one with the sword stared at her as if she were mad.

'And how would a girl know such a thing?' he asked. 'I know,' she replied lifting her skirts just enough to show her ankle, 'because the power that flows from the king is the same power that crippled me.'"

Ever looked up to see Launce looking directly at him, and he knew why. Though all had been forgiven between Ever and his wife, shame still filled him with a sickly warmth. All along, the story had been for him. Isa's brother might be terrible with a sword, but he knew exactly how to use his words like a dagger in Ever's ribs, slowly carving his way to the heart.

"The thief with the sword seemed a bit taken aback, but the one with the bow immediately turned and pointed it at me," Launce continued, not bothering to break eye contact with Ever as he spoke. "'How about this,' he asked her. 'You get off your horses, or I'll kill the boy.' Without another word, Isa pulled herself off the horse. She landed on her bad ankle, as she didn't have a step to help her like we did at home."

Ever closed his eyes as he imagined Isa, the crippled child, trying to get off the horse by herself. The remorse that filled him was nearly painful.

"We walked home that night, Isa leaning on my arm. Father had to borrow a neighbor's horse to come looking for us. He didn't find us until it was almost sunrise." Launce shrugged. "That's the story. Isa nearly came to blows with two horse thieves, and she couldn't even walk."

Ever tried not to look as miserable as he felt. Launce was indeed skilled with words. He had pierced his king's heart in one of the only places it hadn't yet healed.

"How old are you, boy?" Norbert asked, rubbing his silver whiskers.

"Twenty," Launce replied.

"I think I remember those two." Norbert looked at Ever thoughtfully. Ever struggled to pull himself together so he could somewhat intelligently answer whatever his guard was about to ask. "We had gotten several complaints from the people in Soudain in just two days. Weren't you leading the contingent to find them?"

"It was the first contingent my father allowed me to lead on my own." Ever's voice felt tight as he answered, like a rope strained too far. The two horse thieves had been foreigners, unfamiliar with the Fortress monarchs' unusual abilities. He had simply had them chained and returned to the Fortress for his father to deal with. It was nothing too exciting, but now he found himself wishing he'd made them much more miserable first.

Everyone sat in an uncomfortable silence after Launce finished, not sure what they should do. It had certainly been a story that exemplified Isa's bravery, but it left a bitter taste, and whether he wanted them to or not, everyone knew why. Ever had been the one to injure Isa, and if it hadn't been for Ever, Isa never would have been threatened by such evil. It always came back to him, no matter what he did. Sometimes, it felt as though Ever would never be allowed peace with his wife. There was always the past of his actions to haunt them.

As they settled into their tents for the night, Ever looked at Isa as she began to slip into deeper breathing. The moon was covered by the clouds that had rolled in, but the fire was still burning, and he could just barely see the contour of her face. Her expression was finally peaceful as she slept, and Ever found himself wishing greatly to keep it just as peaceful when she awoke. One thing he knew for sure, however, was that no matter the past, it was now his duty to keep her safe.

No matter what the cost.

CHAPTER 5
COMMONER

Would you hold still?" Cerise sighed as she readjusted Isa's sash for the third time. Instead of tugging on her sash, Isa decided to fiddle nervously with her jeweled necklace as she stared into the rose-tinted mirror that hung on the wall of her new chambers.

"Are you sure about this?" She touched the piles of curls that Cerise had heaped on top of her head. They felt unusually heavy in their precarious perch.

"Gigi gave me strict instructions." Cerise's own honey-colored curls bobbed as she finished braiding the sash into Isa's bodice. "She even made me practice on some of the other servants until I had it just right. Now," Cerise finally took Isa by the shoulders and looked her in the eyes, "*what* is the matter?"

Isa placed one of her hands on Cerise's and squeezed, glad to have her childhood friend with her.

Choosing Cerise as her head lady-in-waiting had caused no small uproar in the Fortress court. Unwittingly, Isa had offended the noble candidates who should have been her first choices when she'd requested Cerise as her lady-in-waiting, rather than choosing a traditional high-born lady-in-waiting.

Ever, of course, hadn't given it a second thought when he'd said yes. As usual, he didn't care a wit about which of his odious cousins were offended, particularly if it made Isa happy.

"Have you seen those women? They're beautiful! All of them!"

"And?" Cerise pressed.

"They've been raised for moments like this! While they spent time learning which utensil to touch first, I was selling grain in my father's store." Isa shook her head, her massive pile of curls exaggerating her motions. "I don't want to shame my husband," she said quietly.

Before Cerise could respond, the door was unlocked, and Ever stepped through. The silver wolf stitched masterfully into his clothing glittered from his chest as he turned. His thick, midnight blue robe, cut to distinguish his broad shoulders and muscled arms, was drawn together by a thin silver belt that encircled his waist. A black cloak flowed behind him, accentuating the grace with which he moved. In his short, wheat-colored hair, he wore a thin silver circlet with flecks of gold.

It was moments like this, when he looked more imposing than ever, that Isa still sometimes found it difficult to believe he was the same man she'd fallen in love with while he was under the curse. Hoping to do at least some justice to their joined titles, she stood a little straighter as Cerise pulled her gown out so it draped properly. The silver shimmered every time the gown moved, and while it was excessively pretty, Isa had asked Gigi before they left if it wasn't too gaudy.

"I don't think you understand what a high rank you hold, my dear." Gigi had shaken her head as she'd looked at Isa. "It is no longer just about your husband. The law says that you are just as much a ruler of the Fortress as he is. The first night will be essential to showing all of the northern kingdoms that you, too, are a force to be reckoned with, that you're worthy of respect. No gown or ornament will be too much for that first banquet."

But as Isa stared into the mirror, the queen that everyone expected and the queen that now hid beneath the shimmering silver dress suddenly felt like two very different people.

"We need to be going," Ever announced as he rubbed his sword with his cloak. "They will be announcing us soon." Another wave of nausea hit Isa as he turned and looked her up and down with an appraising look, the same look he gave his soldiers during inspections. Then, with a cursory nod, he offered his arm. Just before she took it, Cerise cried out.

"Wait, Your Highness!" Running to the back of the room, Cerise thrust her arm to the bottom of a bag and pulled out a small red velvet pouch. She loosened the drawstrings and pulled out a delicate silver laurel wreath. Leaves were woven in and out of one another with such grace that Isa gasped as Cerise brought it closer. Just as she was placing it on Isa's head, Isa caught a glimpse of sapphires the size of rose seeds sprinkled all over it.

"There." Cerise beamed at Ever. "She's ready."

"That she is." Ever nodded.

"I'm confused," Isa whispered as they left their chambers. "Shouldn't we be showing deference to the hosting king and queen? I feel a bit . . . conspicuous."

"If we were at home, we would be in our ceremonial attire," Ever said, inclining his head at a bowing stranger. Isa envied the ease and comfort with which he accepted the attention that made her want to cringe. "We are, however, to be the guests of honor here. Seven years ago, my father and I helped King Rafael quell a rebellion that threatened to tear the kingdom in half."

"So many wars . . ." Isa couldn't help wondering aloud.

"There would have been many more had the Fortress not given us the ability to intervene," Ever said in a low voice as they walked. "Tumen is not the only kingdom that tends to test boundaries. It's important that the other monarchs see we are watching. Evil persists when unchecked."

As they rounded the corner and turned down another low-hanging hallway, she prayed that Launce would be ready by the time they reached his chambers. Ever had commissioned the Fortress tailor to create new, appropriate clothes for her brother before they'd gone, and Isa wasn't sure if Launce would know how all of the fancy pieces would fit together. And from the look on Ever's face, he wasn't in any mood to wait for a boy who couldn't dress himself. So when Launce came to the door disgruntled, but all in one piece, Isa sent up a prayer of thanks.

"You look very handsome," she whispered back to him as the three of them made their way toward the ballroom.

"I feel like a fop," he said, daring a glance at Ever. Ever's mouth tightened just a bit, but he said nothing in response. To Isa's relief and horror, they arrived at the end of the hall just then. The hall ended in a balcony, which looked out over a great ballroom, and on it stood a lanky herald dressed in what Isa guessed to be the Cobriens' colors, fire orange and red. He stood with a large pole, which he pounded upon the floor twice before declaring in a loud voice, "Welcoming His Royal Highnesses, King Rafael and Queen Monica's guests of honor, the venerable King Everard Perrin Auguste Fortier of Destin, Queen Isabelle Fortier, and Her Highness's brother, Launce Marchand."

Isa felt her face warm at the shortness of her name, and her heart went out to Launce when she saw a few people snicker at the common surname. Thankfully, after the assembly bowed and curtsied and the pole had been pounded twice more, they were able to make their way down the front staircase and into the crowd. Ever led them directly toward the thrones on the right side of the large room.

As they walked, Isa was struck by how very beautiful the smooth red floor stones were, and how carefully they must have been laid. *Head up*, she reminded herself, fighting the sudden desire to study the floor. Instead, she strained to hold her head with completely unfounded confidence as her etiquette tutors had taught her to do, smiling benevolently at those around her who bowed as the crowd parted for them so they could reach the thrones.

When paying homage to the kings and queens of other countries in their own lands, the shrill voice of her etiquette tutor echoed in her head, *you will curtsy, but only so much. Keep your head up so others will know your station. You are showing them respect, not subservience, for you are not their subjects. You are their peers. Head up, now. You're not a commoner any longer, Your Highness.*

"Ah, Everard." King Rafael stood and held his hands out to greet Ever as they stepped up onto the large, round dais. Ever took them both in his own and gave them one firm shake. "It is good to have you back under more joyous circumstances." He then turned to look at Isa, taking her hand and bowing to kiss it. Isa forced the most confident smile she could muster, inclining her head in return. "Your bride is even lovelier than the rumors here suggested." He raised a bushy brow at Ever. "I find it hard to believe she was ever a commoner." Isa felt her face grow hot, and glanced sideways at Ever, unsure of whether or not she had just been insulted.

"The Fortress chooses those who are worthy." Ever's voice was velvet and dangerous. "It does not see commoners and royalty."

"Of course," the other king said quickly. "I only meant that she is striking. Please," he gestured with a meaty hand at the empty places closest to thrones. "Do stay near. We will be beginning the banquet shortly." Ever once again nodded, and Isa and Launce dropped a quick curtsy and bow before moving over to the right of the throne. The men and women standing near the spot he'd gestured to spread out even further so that the three Destinians were nearly alone, despite the sea of nobles and royals that filled the great hall.

As they stood waiting for the rest of the guests to be announced, Isa used the time to discreetly study the two women on the king's left side. Both shared the same lovely complexion as most of the people around them, fair skin kissed by the sun with just a tinge of olive. Queen Monica sat, but Princess Olivia stood. Neither of them were as tall as Isa, but both more fully proportioned. The deep-set hickory eyes of the queen appeared distant and somewhat preoccupied, but the princess looked the way Isa felt, her eyes wide and her face paler than the rest of her skin. Isa could only imagine her fears, knowing she would unknowingly meet her future husband that night.

The princess's prospects were mixed from what Isa could see. There was a large number of unaccompanied men present, and quite a few were a great deal older than the princess, some even older than King Rafael himself. Isa suddenly felt mildly repulsed for the princess's sake, and hoped she would be won by someone more fitting for her age at least, if nothing else.

The pole sounded three times, quieting the crowd, and the king stood and raised his hands.

"Let us adjourn to the banquet hall, where each of you has had a special place prepared." After the king, queen, and princess stood and began walking down the dais, Ever stepped into line and followed them. Isa found herself very glad that etiquette required her to hold his arm. She would have been terribly lost among the great throng of people, had she been left by herself. Launce walked behind them, and following him, the servants placed the people in the correct order, Isa guessed, so from greatest rank to the least. It was unnerving to think that she wouldn't have even qualified to stand at the end of the line just the year before.

King Rafael led the procession through a tall arched opening into a long room filled with a cedar table that stretched from one end of the room to the other. Isa followed Ever's lead, continuing to stand even when they had been brought to their places on the long bench on their side of the table. It was astounding how many people would have to crowd into the room, despite its enormous length.

The walls in this room were whitewashed just like the rest of the palace walls were, with great timber beams crisscrossing the low ceilings. Each wall had one large arched fireplace in the center, as only one wouldn't have been able to heat the entire room. Intricate murals were painted on the walls around each hearth, large images of women dancing in twirling skirts the colors of strawberries and limes and oranges and lemons. Each of the painted women had the same deep-set hickory eyes as the queen, and each wore a smile as she performed.

Isa's musings were interrupted when everyone was finally in the dining hall, and the king sat, gesturing for everyone else to do so as well. Ever was seated on the king's right hand while Queen Monica sat on his left, the princess sitting to her left, just across from Isa. Isa wished desperately that she could have sat beside the princess, for they seemed to be suffering from the same set of nerves. Launce also looked about the table with wide eyes, but said nothing, and Isa wondered if he was regretting his decision to come with her. She didn't have time to ask, because a holy man was brought to the room and asked to thank the Maker.

The first course followed the prayer, and Isa was very grateful to have something to do with her hands besides twist them nervously under the table. She was aware of the eyes of a number of men and even more women upon her as she began to eat, and she hoped her hands didn't shake too visibly as they watched her.

"So, I want to welcome you back from your rendezvous with the Maker," King Rafael was saying to Ever. Isa studied her salted fish with renewed vigor as she waited to hear what Ever would say. While the encounter between the Fortress and its once wayward prince had ended well, it was still a somewhat intimate matter.

Fully explaining to others what had gone on there during the curse, the way the Maker, through the Fortress, had brought about change in both of them, was next to impossible. Only Launce, to Isa's knowledge, had come even close to understanding it, and that was most likely due to the nature of their relationship. Her brother had always been able to read her. Not that any of that would matter to the curious King Rafael.

"Thank you." Ever's deep voice was steady, but Isa detected a note of caution in it. "It is good to be traveling again."

"I must ask, what were you doing all that time, cooped up in that great citadel?" The king took a great bite of his fish before leaning so close to Ever that Isa could hardly hear his next words. "Rumor has it that Nevina had put you under some sort of curse?" Isa glanced at her husband to see his jaw tighten slightly at the name of the Tumenians' late princess.

"You should know better than to believe in rumors, Rafael. They will get you nothing but trouble."

"How will I know what to believe then if no one tells me otherwise?" the other king pressed. His voice was polite, but his brown eyes gleamed with interest.

"Suffice it to say that when the Maker gives you a great deal of power, and you choose to use it unwisely, his servants, such as the Fortress, will have no choice other than to show you the error of your ways," Ever responded as he looked the king straight in the eye. His blue fiery gaze was so stern that the king held it only for a moment before looking down at his food again and changing the topic.

Isa lost interest in the men's conversation after that, something about a recent excess of rabbits in farmlands, and she began to listen to see what the other royals and nobles were doing without the attention of their host king. The cacophony of voices was lively, many of the others deep into various conversations by now. As she watched, she caught other eyes watching her as well. Most of the men smiled, as well as some of the women, but a few simply stared, no inkling of friendliness in their tight lips, despite Isa's attempt at smiling. One in particular did nothing to hide her displeasure, glowering openly at Isa so intensely that Isa felt her smile falter upon meeting the stranger's eyes.

Isa had noticed the woman earlier, and she was nearly as tall as Isa, maybe even taller. Her delicate white skin, fiery red hair, and green eyes made it obvious she wasn't from Cobren. Her oval-shaped face would have been lovely, filled with almond eyes and rosy cheeks, had it not been so full of wrath. Isa wondered if this was one of Ever's serious contenders at his own betrothal ball, the one that had ended in a war with Nevina. The hate in the woman's eyes made Isa long to shrivel behind her husband. It was also at that moment that Isa realized her ridiculous pile of curls was beginning to give her a headache.

"Did that woman eat a wolverine?" Launce leaned over and whispered in Isa's ear. Isa nearly choked on the bite of potato she'd just put in her mouth. As soon as Isa laughed, the red-haired woman scowled even deeper before turning to the woman next to her and whispering in her ear.

"This is why I wanted you to come," Isa muttered to her brother. "It's going to take me a while to get used to this." Launce's response was cut off when the second course was announced, candied beets with nuts and sprigs of mint garnishing the plate. Isa turned her focus back to using the correct utensils, and as she did, King Rafael's voice caught her attention once again.

"About time we found a new path to choosing a successor." He sounded proud as he dug into the beets.

"How were successors chosen before?" Isa asked.

"Like your Fortress, a child of either sex can inherit the

throne here in Cobren," Rafael said, a piece of food falling out of his mouth as he spoke. "I don't know if you are aware of it, Isabelle, but our two kingdoms are the only ones in the northern realm that allow daughters to be crowned as sovereigns." When Isa nodded, he continued. "Anyhow, the hopeful successors, mostly royals, second born and such from other kingdoms, and nobles from our own court, would face a series of interviews, tests run by the king, queen, and their advisors. All tedious, trifling affairs, I can assure you."

"What changed?"

The king leaned forward eagerly, this time speaking again to Ever. "As much respect as I have for you, my old friend," he whispered gleefully, "the Fortress and its inhabitants are no longer the main instruments the Maker will be using in the world." Then, leaning in even closer, he said, "The Maker has sent us a special holy man to divinely appoint this heir." Alarm shot through Isa's body as the king sat back and grinned, although she wasn't sure why. Ever had frozen completely, the rings of fire in his eyes burning more intensely than Isa had seen since the Fortress curse had broken. Even Launce's jaw had dropped. It took a moment, but Ever was the first to recover his voice.

"And how is this new method to take place?"

"Ah, you'll have to wait to find out," the king answered mischievously. "The same as everyone else." Then the king's gaze fell upon Launce. "You should try though, lad! Anyone can enter." Launce sent a petrified look to Isa and then Ever, and Isa almost dropped her spoon when Ever responded that they would think about it.

As she looked in shock at her husband, Isa sensed that he was keeping something from her, something important, and she resolved immediately to find out what.

CHAPTER 6

WHAT MEN WILL DO

By the time the king declared everyone should dance, Isa's head throbbed as though a mason had laid a stack of bricks upon it. Ever offered her his arm, but his eyes were distant. Launce looked sick, though Isa guessed that was due to the many piles of rich food he had just consumed, and not the dancing itself.

Despite her party's current state of mind, Isa was relieved to have reached the final part of the opening ball. In secret, she had looked forward to it, relishing the anticipation of dancing with her husband. Her desire to dance with him grew even stronger when she noticed just how many women's eyes were trained on his fine form. And though she often struggled to harness the strength from the Fortress within her, it was so strong now that she had to flex her hands a few times to keep it hidden, heat building, threatening to burst from them as many of the ladies openly gawked. Frightening them with a little display would do little to improve their opinion of her, she chided herself . . . even if they did deserve it.

Ever led Isa and Launce over to the far center of the throne room, the same one they had been introduced in. From the front of the crowd, near the two golden thrones, they had a good view of the dance floor, which had been cleared for the ceremony.

A large group of musicians set in a corner began to play, a melody of sweetness and sorrow. As the music began, the king led his daughter out into the center of the floor. The smile the princess gave her father was lovely, her dark eyes gazing into her father's face. Isa noticed for the first time that the princess's skirt was a bright salmon color, and unlike her own complicated gown, looked as though it had simply been made to twirl. With each step, the fabric fanned out gracefully, making the princess resemble a flower in bloom. A movement to Isa's side made her realize Launce was watching, too, his eyes more unguarded than she'd seen them in a long time, and it made her smile.

The sweet dance was over soon, and Isa's stomach fluttered with excitement as she looked up at her own dance partner. The night before, as Ever had explained the order of events to Isa, he'd made it clear that this was to be an important dance.

"As we are the guests of honor, the second dance will be for the king and queen and us," he'd said.

"Everyone else will be watching?"

"It doesn't matter." Ever had smiled and tapped her on the nose. "Surely you've had enough practice." At that, she'd blushed a bit, and he'd gone on to explain. "This is the first chance most of our peers and their nobles will have to see us together. It's important for them to see a united front, and that you are truly the queen the Fortress has chosen."

When she looked up at him now, Ever seemed completely unaware that the people around him were staring. Even the musicians hesitated, waiting for the guests of honor to join the king and queen on the dance floor.

"Ever," she whispered, tugging discreetly on his arm. After a moment, his eyes finally rested upon her, and he gave her a polite smile as he seemed to realize what they were supposed to be doing. Even when they were out on the dance floor, however, as soon as the music began, his eyes resumed their search of the crowd.

The dance was slow, one Isa knew well, but it failed to bring the feelings of peace she'd look so forward to. His calloused hand held hers loosely, and his movements were just slightly behind the music, not enough for the spectators to notice, but Isa could tell. As they turned, she watched his face miserably, wishing with all her heart that he might look down at her just once. His fiery eyes were occupied, however, and his jaw was set tightly in a line Isa knew well.

For all Ever's talk of showing everyone the Fortress's chosen queen, it suddenly appeared to be of little importance. Isa didn't even bother to glance at her feet, for she could feel that no blue fire whirled around them now, though from her husband's lack of attention or her lack of ability, she couldn't tell.

As soon as the dance was finished, Ever didn't hesitate, but immediately led them off the floor. The crowd began to rearrange itself, some people going to dance while others formed clumps. Somehow, Ever found the very group of women that had stared at her during supper.

"Isabelle."

Isa nearly cringed as he used her full name. She hated that royals didn't use nicknames in public.

"This is Lady Beata, Lady Jadzia, and Princess Damira." He slightly bowed to the three colorfully adorned women. Each woman curtsied in turn. The one who had glowered at Isa earlier responded to the name of Jadzia, and her eyes never left Ever's face as he spoke, not even when he introduced his wife.

"I would like for you ladies to become acquainted with my wife. Isabelle, I have some business to attend to. Please enjoy yourself." Isa watched him incredulously as he stalked away. Was he really leaving her alone with them?

"Queen Isabelle," the one named Princes Damira began. Her hair was the color of acorns, and it was worn long and straight with jeweled pins scattered throughout it. Isa envied the princess as her own head throbbed worse than ever with the weight of her hair. "It is wonderful to finally meet the lucky queen."

"Luck had nothing to do with it," Lady Jadzia reminded her companion. "She was chosen." Lady Jadzia's pale eyes glittered as she spoke, and her ruby lips pulled up at one corner.

"How is your family doing?" Isa did her best to ignore the jab by looking at Lady Beata, suddenly very grateful that her tutor had forced her not only to memorize all of the royal and noble names of their neighboring lands, but their current affairs as well. "Has your family repaired the damaged wing of your home yet?" The young woman looked as though Isa's personal question had surprised her.

"They've started . . ." she began, her composure melting away a bit. "The fire did more damage than we had originally thought though."

"So how have you and Everard been spending your time since the wedding?" Jadzia asked. Isa noticed the woman eyeing her shoulders, and was immediately very aware of her own suntanned arms which, thanks to Gigi, were on display for the entire ball to see through her thin sleeves.

"We have both been kept busy," she began, wondering at the woman's audacity. Even her commoner parents had taught her such questions were beyond rude. But before she could finish her answer, however, a movement caught Isa's eye, and she realized she'd been unconsciously searching the crowd for her husband. Launce was off in a corner hiding behind a platter of dried fruits, but it took her a moment to find Ever, and when she did, she felt her heart beat unevenly.

He was talking animatedly to a woman in the clothing of one of the southern kingdoms. If her dress hadn't given it away, her appearance would have. The woman held a proud posture, the fine curve to her neck and straightness of her back exactly what Isa's tutors had been trying to teach her for the last five months. The woman's skin was the color of almonds, and her eyes were alight as she listened carefully to whatever Isa's husband was saying. As Isa was studying them, however, the woman's gaze shifted directly to Isa.

Immediately, Isa wanted nothing more than to hide, suddenly unable to add anything to the pointless conversation she was now a part of. She might have had the energy to handle the catty women that morning. But seeing the excitement on Ever's face as he spoke to the woman, whoever she was, was too much. He hadn't spent that much time talking with her in over a month. Besides, her head felt as though someone were beating it from the inside with a mallet.

"I am going to get a drink," she excused herself in a weak voice, not waiting long enough to remember that royals did not get their own drinks, but raised their hands for them instead. And at the moment, her faux pas didn't matter. She just needed to get away.

After grabbing a drink off the first servant's tray that she could find, Isa took a long sip and sighed. The wine was exceptionally good, and a rebellious part of her wanted to grab another goblet and just run back to her chambers with it. But she ignored that desire with the shred of self-control which she still possessed, and began trudging back to the group of women. As she moved through the crowd of wide skirts and swishing capes, she could hear the women before she rejoined them, and what she heard made her stop in her tracks.

"Did you see how little attention he paid her even during the dance?" Princess Damira's voice had an amused edge to it.

"He made his choice. Now he has to abide by it," Lady Jadzia said. She took a sip of her own wine, no doubt acquired through appropriate means.

"You don't think she broke the curse?" Lady Beata asked.

Lady Jadzia gave a delicate snort. "I've heard rumor that she doesn't possess any of that special power, if that's what you mean. It's really a pity."

"Why did he marry her then? I thought Everard wanted his queen to be something special."

Lady Jadzia's reply was icy. "I heard that the man was imprisoned in a building alone for months, according to my sister. It's amazing what lonely men will promise to anything with a pretty face." Then Lady Jadzia stopped and placed her hand over her upper chest. "Good gracious," she said in a faint voice. "I . . . I feel quite awful just now."

"Perhaps it was the beets," Lady Beata said, her brows knitting together in concern. "Take some more wine for your stomach."

"No. No, it's not that. I feel—" But before she could finish answering, Lady Jadzia broke down in tears. "I just feel terrible, as though a great weight has been placed upon my soul!" she sobbed. "Please make it stop!"

A strange sensation had come over Isa, but she didn't know what it was until someone cried out and pointed to her hand that clutched the goblet. Looking down, she realized bright blue flame was coming from her hand. People scrambled to back away, yet all Isa could do was stare stupidly at the fire in her own hand as her head pounded harder than ever, and treacherous tears threatened to spill down her face. All the while, Jadzia continued to blubber about how wretched she felt.

The blue fire began to climb, and was almost higher than the rim of the cup when two cool hands took hold of hers. It wasn't until Isa looked up that she realized Ever was standing before her, gripping her hands and saying her name out loud.

The woman he'd been speaking with stood behind him, her eyes troubled as she watched.

"What are you doing?" Ever's voice finally drew her into focus. It took another long moment for Isa to find her voice and the words with which to reply. Finally, under his steady gaze and cool hands, Isa's head cleared enough to respond.

"I . . . I don't know . . ." her voice trailed off as she looked around to see the entire court watching her with wary eyes. Princess Damira, Lady Beata, and Lady Jadzia were all huddled in a group, staring as though she'd turned into a monster. Seeing them made Isa remember why she'd been upset in the first place, and once more, briefly, power pulsed through her. Ever's eyes widened as he felt it move, and quickly followed her eyes as they settled on the women he'd left her with.

"Isabelle," he said in a low voice. "What happened?" Isa looked into his eyes, but to her shock, where she had expected to see comfort and concern, she saw frustration and impatience. Suddenly, it was all Isa could do not to burst into tears herself, or shout at the top of her lungs that her head hurt, and this entire ball was a waste of time, and that Ever was in no position to judge her after leaving her alone with such vipers.

"Everard," the woman behind him said chidingly, her low voice melodic. "Your wife obviously is not feeling well." As she drew closer, Isa realized with a start that she sensed power seeping from the woman as well. Much to Isa's relief and annoyance, her husband finally looked concerned.

"Is it true?" he asked her in an even softer voice, his gray eyes searching her face. Almost too angry to speak, Isa could only bring herself to nod. She was fully aware that the people around them were still watching.

"I don't know why my power—"

"Not here," he whispered urgently. "You never know who might be listening." He pried the silver goblet from her hands and held it out to the nearest servant. "Launce," he called. There was no need, for her brother was already there. "Take your sister back to our chambers, then return here to me." As Launce took her arm, Ever leaned in once more and whispered, "I will join you soon. Try to get some sleep."

As Launce led her away, the music began to play again, and people chatted once more, but the sister and brother were given a wide berth as they made their way to the closest hallway.

"King Everard and Queen Isabelle's chambers?" Launce asked a nearby servant uncertainly. As they followed the servant back through winding halls and many turns, Isa felt herself relax against her brother's steady arm. She could feel him studying her as they walked.

"I'll be fine, I promise," she said. "It's this confounded hair that's been giving me a headache. I never knew I had this much hair." To her relief, they had finally reached the familiar arched door of the room she and Ever had been given.

"Something else is wrong," he said, crossing his arms and staring down at her after the servant had gone. "This isn't just a headache. What happened back there with your power?"

Isa sighed. "I don't know, Launce. I really just want to go to bed—"

"You drag me down here to this blasted ball, then you won't tell me anything—"

"I promise!" Isa's threw her hands up to her aching head. "I will tell you later! Just let me go to bed!" She felt a stab of remorse though as his face fell and he looked at the floor. For a moment, he looked just like the little boy that had once faithfully followed her about on her horse. "I'm sorry." She reached out and grabbed his sleeve. He looked back, his eyes injured, and she sighed. "I really do have a headache, and it's hard to explain. I just don't have the words right now." At that, her brother looked slightly mollified, and he nodded once before leaving.

As soon as Isa was back in her room, Cerise was hovering

over her, trying to pull the pins out of her hair. Apparently, news traveled just as fast in King Rafael's palace as in her own. Isa counted it a blessing though in this instance. In less than ten minutes, Cerise had changed her out of her silver gown, shoved a cup of tea into her hands, and had her in bed, Isa's long hair free and spread out wildly around her.

It would have felt lovely, had Isa not been so angry with her husband. After treating her like a soldier waiting for an inspection, then ignoring her their entire dance, he had left her with the cruelest women alive, all so he could search out the stranger from the south and speak to her . . . without Isa. And it was only because of the woman that he had noticed she was in distress at all.

And he hadn't even bothered to escort her back to their chambers himself.

CHAPTER 7

THE KING'S MEAD

"Y ou should go to her," Kartek murmured as they watched Launce lead Isa away. Her voice was kind, but there was a reprimand buried in the soft words.

"I need to talk with Rafael first. He's having his third round of mead now. Then I'll see how she's doing," Ever said, although he knew deep down that he was trying to convince himself as much as he was trying to convince his friend.

Kartek nodded thoughtfully, the large golden hoops in her ears jangling melodically. "I am surprised Rafael invited me at all," she said as they watched the couples on the dance floor twirl about. "Rafael rarely bothers to meddle in the affairs of the south."

"I'm glad he did, although I can't say I'm surprised from the tenor of his invitation. It seems he wants the whole world to know about this contest. I suppose he hoped you would spread the word to the rest of the southern kingdoms."

At this, Kartek raised her chin and snorted delicately. "If that was his desire, he shall be disappointed. I did not speak a word of his invitation to my neighbors. I could not see a reason to share such foolishness until I had seen it for myself." She shook her head at the king as he raised his goblet a fourth time. "Look at him. Have you ever seen him like this?"

"He's worse than I thought." Ever shook his head. "Someone else has a hand in this, but what I cannot work out is who might want to alter his temperament so greatly."

"Do you think dark power is involved?" This question was whispered, but Ever still glanced about to make sure prying ears weren't nearby. Kartek continued, "I can't feel any, but your senses were always stronger than mine."

"Not yet." Ever unhappily studied Rafael once more as he laughed raucously with one of his nobles. "But empty praise can do just as much damage as dark strength. And I fear we might have both at play."

"Here comes your younger brother."

As Launce made his way over to them, she lowered her voice even more and leaned in close, the scent of dates hitting Ever as she did. "I am serious though when I say you need to take care of your wife, Everard. You are right to be mindful of whatever is at stake here, but do not forget the woman the Fortress gave you. Something tells me she is not as delicate as you think."

"You saw how tonight went," he groaned quietly. "She may never want to come out in society again."

"And it would not be her fault." The southern queen arched a dark brow. "You threw her to the wolves without even an apology." She turned to shoot a glare at the three women that stood not far behind them, keeping eye contact long enough to make even Lady Jadzia look away. "The red-haired minx has not looked away from you since you arrived. It is as if she does not count you married."

"I know, I know," Ever said. "Isa's come so far . . . I was hoping that speaking with her in person would convince Jadzia to leave the matter be. I didn't expect that—"

"She has a headache, but she refuses tell me what else is wrong," Launce announced as he joined them. Though his voice was quiet, the resentment in it was obvious, and for once Ever couldn't blame him. Still, he wished Launce would at least attempt to follow formalities in the company of other royals, if not in his own palace.

"Queen Kartek." Ever frowned hard at his brother-in-law, willing him to remember even a vestige of his manners. "This is Isabelle's brother, Launce Marchand. Launce, this is Queen Kartek, ruler of the southern kingdom, Hedjet." Launce had the sense to at least color when he realized his rudeness before the queen. To Ever's surprise, however, she graced the young man with one of her rare wide smiles.

"You care much for your sister, do you not?"

"I do, Your Majesty," Launce mumbled, still clearly embarrassed. The queen took the young man's chin gently in her right hand and turned his face from side to side, examining him closely. Launce seemed surprised, but didn't resist. Whatever she was looking for, however, she seemed to find, for when she eventually let go of him, she nodded once to herself and smiled again.

"You . . . you have the strength as well!" Launce whispered.

Ever felt his own surprise reflected on the queen's face at the boy's statement.

"You can tell?"

"I'm around Isa—Isabelle—enough that I know what it feels like," Launce mumbled again, this time looking at the ground.

"Do not underestimate this one either, Everard." She turned to him. "He may be wild, but his love for his sister strengthens him." Then to Launce she said, "Yes, I am gifted by the Maker as well. My power is not nearly as strong as your family's though. Now, I must speak with my guard. Both of you take care. I will see you tomorrow." And with that, she turned to go, her colorful skirt creating its own breeze as she moved gracefully away. Launce finally turned back to Ever, his eyes full of wonder.

"I will explain later," Ever said. "For now, I need your help with the king."

"The king?"

"I need you to accept his invitation to compete for the princess's hand in the contest."

Launce's eyes looked as if they might pop. "I'm not a royal! I—"

"Anyone can compete. Besides, I'm not expecting you to *win*. I just need eyes in that stable. I need to know more of what is going on." He didn't miss the scowl Launce sent him when he mentioned his lack of expectations for the boy, but he ignored it and continued in a lower voice. "Isa has enough to worry about with controlling her power and adjusting to her place as queen. If you do this, we will be sparing her one more worry."

Launce held his gaze unhappily for a few long moments before slowly nodding his assent. With that, Ever turned and led them up to the platform where the king lounged in his throne, his wife sitting stiffly at his side. Rafael was holding out his goblet for yet another round of mead when they approached him.

"It's a sweet variety, Everard!" Rafael raised his drink to his friend, nearly falling out of his chair in the process.

"It should be," Ever answered dryly as he helped right the king. "I brought it." At this, Rafael's eyes grew wide and even more joyous.

"Just one more reason you're my guest of honor!" He laughed and took another swig. Ever felt almost guilty for knowingly taking advantage of his old comrade in such a way, but in light of the change that had come over Rafael, exploiting his greatest weakness seemed the only way to save him from himself. Ever had packed the barrels of his best mead as a gift for the celebration, one he knew the king wouldn't be able to turn down. And he had been right.

"Launce has something he wants to tell you," Ever said,

deftly moving to block the king's view of a young servant woman as she refilled the king's empty vessel. In his right mind, Rafael would never have considered such a conquest, but he seemed drunker tonight than Ever had seen before. Queen Monica sent Ever a grateful look as he gave Launce a slight shove forward.

"And what would that be, lad? I'm in the mood to grant all sorts of boons." Rafael laughed, his flushed face shiny with sweat.

Launce glanced at Ever warily before stepping closer to the king. "I would like to join the contest for your daughter's hand, Sire."

"Ah, that's fine! That's fine, boy!" The king leaned forward and surprised Launce by slapping him on the back. "My servants will bring your things down to the stables immediately!"

"He won't be sleeping in his chambers then?" Ever asked. Isa wouldn't be pleased.

"No, no. The contestants share quarters in the stables." He gave them a drooly smile and then gestured for Ever to come closer. As he leaned in, Ever had to keep his face straight as he was hit with the king's rancid breath. "That's what the holy man said they should do! So he could keep an eye on them!" Ever nearly smiled when the king uttered the words he'd been waiting for all night.

"So when did this holy man come to give you such good news?" he asked casually.

"The storm was so great the night he came!" The king held his hands out above his head unevenly to show the size of the storm, nearly falling over again in the process. "*Boom* went the lightning! I've never seen the like of it!" He stopped and rubbed his head before proceeding. "He says that the Maker told him He was watching the quarrels of the land, and it is this holy man's job to mend it!"

"If you're speaking of the rebellion in your own land," Ever frowned, "we ended that years ago." But the king waved his hand as though he were slapping away a gnat.

"Fa! Disloyal subjects and spies stay on. You know that!" His words were beginning to slur so badly that Ever had to work to understand them. He wagged his finger wildly at Ever with a rebellious smile. "You will see soon that our holy man's power rivals even yours." Then he laughed, as though he'd said something quite funny. "The holy man alone carries the plans for the great structure. And the Maker gave him the power alone to create it!"

"Plans for a structure?" Ever pressed, hoping Rafael wasn't uttering the gibberish some drunkards were accustomed to doing. Still, a part of him wished the king's chilling words were nonsense.

"Yes! For the trials!" Rafael moved closer, sending his foul breath toward Ever once more. "The impossible trial will be for only the one who miraculously receives the means to pass it! And only the holy man will know who the Maker chooses!" His eyes grew wide and he stretched his arms to indicate the size of the crowd present. "It could be anyone! Even a commoner!" He pointed at Launce in awe with a dramatic jab of his finger. "Even you!" Launce's jaw twitched in annoyance, but to Ever's relief, he said nothing.

After such a revelation, Ever knew they would get nothing else coherent out of the king. He politely bid the king and queen goodnight, pitying the queen and princess as they stayed behind with Rafael, not missing the look of disgust Princess Olivia was giving her father as he yelled for another goblet of drink.

"How long have you known him?" Launce asked when they were well on their way back to their chambers.

"All my life. He and my father were like brothers."

"Does he do that often?"

"No," Ever answered grimly. "Though he's always had a weakness for wine, he has generally been careful to guard himself." He shook his head. "Someone has been manipulating him, and I intend to find out whom. Now," they stopped before Launce's chambers, "the king will not remember to call a servant to show you to the stables, so call one yourself, and if the stable master does not allow you to bunk there, direct him to me." Launce nodded unhappily before opening his door.

"And remember . . ." Ever stopped the door just before it closed. "This is for Isa."

"I wouldn't be doing it if it weren't," came Launce's reply. Ever itched to remind the boy that he had promised to obey him, whether he liked it or not, but for the sake of peace, chose to let it go. Allowing the door to shut, he turned toward his own chambers, suddenly more than just a little apprehensive of what he would find there.

CHAPTER 8
APOLOGIES

A single candle still glowed on the nightstand between the window and Isa's side of the bed when Ever returned, although the large floor mirror made it look as if two candles shone throughout the room. He immediately felt a stab of shame as his eyes adjusted to the dark, and he took in Isa's sleeping form. It was as far from his side of the bed as possible. Her auburn hair flowed around her like a sea of dark amber, and her face looked sad. Ever rubbed his eyes, guilt gnawing at him from deep inside. He hadn't meant to stay out so late.

As quietly as he could, he changed out of his ball clothes and slipped into the bed beside her. As he did, he could hear her stir. Ever paused, waiting to hear her breathing return to normal. Instead, he heard sniffles.

"Isa?" Reaching out, he gathered her hair away from her face, not entirely sure what to say. He hadn't expected her to cry, and wanted to kick himself for it. "Isa, please, tell me what's wrong."

The sniffling only grew louder. Then, after a pause, she asked in a shaky voice, "Don't you mean *Isabelle*?"

Ever closed his eyes in frustration. He'd known she was upset, but nothing to this extent.

"Isa, I'm sorry." He drew a deep breath. "I should have paid more attention. It's just been a long night—"

"You've had a long night?" At this, Isa sat up, angrily shaking her wavy hair out of her face. "You seemed to be just fine, spending our entire dance looking for whoever she was, before dumping me with that brood of vipers! And then, when I needed you most, you sent me to my room like an unruly pet!" Ever was speechless as she put her head in her heads and moaned. "And this blasted headache is *still* here!"

Thankful for something he *could* fix, Ever drew her drooping form toward him. She didn't curl into him like usual, but she did allow him to place his hands on her head. As he did, whorls of blue danced briefly over her, and he felt her body relax into his, as if being healed had taken the last ounce of energy she had. He shifted her into a more comfortable sitting position in his lap and held her there tightly with his left arm while stroking her hair gently with his right hand.

"Isa, you forget," he said into her hair, "being attentive to other people's feelings isn't—it isn't what I excel at. I truly am sorry for not noticing you were feeling distressed." He paused. "Can you forgive me?"

"Who was she?" The hollowness in her voice broke his heart, and for the first time, it occurred to Ever that Isa actually thought he was considering being unfaithful. This mortified him more than he could bear to ponder.

"Kartek is the closest thing I ever had to a sister," he said. "She, too, has been gifted by the Maker. Her power isn't as strong as ours, but as a child, she was one of the few people I knew who understood me. I haven't seen her in a while, as she is from the southern kingdoms. I only hurried to her because I needed to ask her something before I spoke with Rafael."

It was a moment before Isa responded, but she finally nodded, seeming at least slightly pacified for the time being.

"If it makes you feel better," he added, "she is married as well, and she and her husband are nearly ten years my senior. Now," he shifted the topic, hoping his wife's worries had lessened, "I know Jadzia and Damira are rather unpleasant, but you can't take anything they say—"

"They called me a whore." Isa's voice broke into a sob.

Ever felt as though his blood had frozen in his veins before melting into dangerous heat, and it was suddenly a good thing that his arms were wrapped around his wife, and he was not free to take off down the hall and right the matter himself.

"That woman's father will hear of this," he growled, but Isa stopped him, shaking her head.

"That won't do any good, Ever."

"But they cannot be allowed to speak of you that way!"

Isa pulled away to look at him, a tremulous smile on her lips. "Women do not make amends through rules and by force of righteous indignation, love." She paused before saying in a quiet voice, "But I have to wonder if they were right, at least in part."

"About what?" Had she lost her mind?

"I don't belong in this world." She shrugged helplessly. "All these rules and proprieties I am to pay heed to . . . Even just last year, had Lady Jadzia come to the Fortress and visited the city, she would not have been required to pay me notice. What has changed so greatly in me since then? What does that say about my ability to be . . . to be this?" She gestured at the deep purple sleeping gown she wore. Ever's eyes lingered on the way it fit her graceful curves before realizing she was still talking. "And that power in my hands tonight? I haven't even the slightest inclination as to where that came from! I never meant to hurt anyone!"

"Jadzia will be fine." He briefly smiled. "I'm not sure how

you managed it, but it seemed to me that somehow, you helped her to feel the appropriate emotions that should have shamed her after she said such dreadful things. Your power surfaced because you knew they were lying." He gathered her in his arms once more, wishing he could smooth the lines of pain from her face with just the touch of his hands in the same way he'd banished her headache. "You knew the Fortress had chosen you, that this is your rightful place."

"Then why do I feel so wretched?" Isa's voice broke once more.

"I don't know," Ever whispered, wishing desperately that he knew what to do. Scheming kings, he could handle. Battles, he could fight. But this helpless feeling that filled him, the inability to fix whatever had broken inside of his wife was far beyond his ability or understanding.

"Can you sing to me?" Isa asked pitifully. Ever gave a small sigh of relief and thanked the Maker. That, he could do.

And so, as he gently laid her head back down on the pillow and pulled the covers over her once more, Ever began to sing, and he didn't stop until her breaths were deep and even, and a serene smile lay on her lips.

CHAPTER 9

SLEEPING STABLES

This is where you'll be staying." The stable master pointed at a bottom bunk in the corner of the already overflowing stable. Launce quickly thanked him and dropped his bag onto the rough, narrow mattress. Sitting upon it, though, revealed that it was stuffed with very stiff hay, and one look up at the bunk above had Launce praying the thin wooden slats holding his bunk partner wouldn't break during the night. "Breakfast at first light in front of the stables," the stable master grunted. "Better come as soon as the bell is sounded. This bunch doesn't leave much for the tardy."

Just as the stable master turned to go, Launce caught his sleeve once more. "When are the trials to begin?"

"Day after tomorrow." He looked back at Launce's small bag of belongings. "Have you got some armor of your own? The king won't be—"

"King Everard will be sending some," Launce assured him, hoping his brother-in-law had brought something that would fit his thinner frame.

"Good. And mind you, King Rafael doesn't want the patrons of the contestants snooping around here. That goes for King

Everard too." Launce nodded once more that he understood, although Launce's very presence in the stables was, in fact, Everard's form of spying.

When the stable master moved on, Launce simply sat, watching the others warily. A number of the contestants were still back in the ballroom, late as it was, so it was surprising that so many men were still awake in the stables. Exhaustion had him ready to sleep, but the torches within the stables were still alight, so instead of laying down, Launce studied his new surroundings.

The stable, though nearly as large as the Fortress dining hall, was already filled with men, and it smelled just so. From the looks of those milling around, Launce appeared to be on the younger end of the spectrum, and for that, he pitied Princess Olivia. Isa had told him that her marriage to Everard was somewhat unusual, that many of the male royals were quite a bit older than their wives. And though King Rafael claimed anyone was allowed to compete, it didn't appear as though any commoners were aware of this. Nearly everyone in the stable wore velvet or silk with gold rings and silver buttons. His own clothes, while hardly poor, were nothing as fine. Ever would not only have provided nicer dressings, had he requested some, but would have been overjoyed to make him look proper. But, Launce had told himself and his sister, it was pointless to pretend to be something you were not. You would only disappoint others when they found out the truth.

Had Blanchette been disappointed? Had she thought his new connections would change him?

He could see through the open stable doors that a large number of the men stood outside. Some, like him, were returning from the festivities, but others appeared to still be arriving from the road, looking weary from their travels.

Although patrons weren't allowed in the stables, servants were not in short supply. Many of the finely dressed men had their own pages scurrying after them. One caught his attention as his voice rose in pitch. It was a tall, thin man, one who made Launce look hefty by comparison.

"This is not the saddle I wanted! Boy, what good are you? If I—"

"You!"

Launce was jolted from his musings when a heavy bag was thrown into his lap. Shocked, he looked up to see who had tossed it. A burly man, probably at least a few years older than he, was staring down at him expectantly. He was dressed in red velvet with large puffy sleeves, and wore no small look of self-importance. "Ask your master how much it would cost to borrow you. My page is ill, and I need a new one for the contest." His wide face went from an expression of annoyance to one of outrage as Launce shoved the bag onto the floor and stood to face him, exhaustion forgotten.

"I am no one's servant."

The man cocked a thick eyebrow at him as though Launce were daft.

"Well, who are you then, to act so high and mighty?"

"I'm Queen Isabelle's brother." They were nearly equal in height, although the man had him beat soundly in weight. Everything about him was muscled.

"So you're the commoner," the man muttered, his voice smug.

"And what of it?" For a moment, Launce thought the stranger might throw a punch, but after a moment of intense study, the man just smirked instead as he bent to pick his bag up again, shaking his head with a small, mean smile on his mouth.

"Nothing."

Launce glared at his back as he walked away. Deep down, he knew he should be grateful. If it had come to blows, there would have been no doubt as to whom the winner would have been, but instead of relief, this only filled him with annoyance. He could hear Everard's voice inside his head, telling him repeatedly how important it was that he learn to fight. It was in this foul mood that the servant found him.

"Might you be Launce Marchand?" Launce turned to give a terse reply, but found himself staring into one of the friendliest faces he'd ever seen. The man was older, probably older than Launce's father, and he had deep, permanent smile lines etched into his face. His graying hair had large curls sticking out in every which way, and his eyes were a pale blue. In spite of his bad mood, Launce found himself grinning back at the man.

"Yes, sir. That would be me."

"Ah, good then. If you'll allow me, I have a gift for you from King Everard."

When Launce nodded, the servant turned to go back out front. For lack of a friendlier face in the stable, Launce followed him. Outside was a horse, and though it was dark, there was just enough moonlight to see that it was one of Everard's finest. Upon the horse was a variety of items, from clothing with the green and blue colors of the Fortress, to weapons, to even a suit of armor. Launce swallowed hard when he saw the size of the pile.

"What's your name?" Launce asked as the servant began to unpack the horse.

"Call me Brokk." The lines in the man's face deepened as he smiled again, seeming pleased that Launce had cared to ask. "Forgive me if I'm being too forward, but are you not the brother of the lovely Queen Isabelle?"

"I am."

The man puffed a little as he struggled to lift one of the heavier pieces of armor off of the horse. Without thinking, Launce reached out to aid him. Together, they were able to get everything off the horse without damaging anything. It intrigued Launce that the man allowed him to help without protesting as the Fortress servants would have.

"I must admit, I have been curious to meet you and your sister. Word travels far of her great deeds, what with breaking the Fortress curse and all. And I thank you," Brokk said as they finished. "Most of these men wouldn't so much as look at me unless I accidentally scratched their property."

"It is my pleasure." This time, Launce's smile was genuine. "And my sister would be grateful to hear you say as such." He lowered his voice a bit, the memory of her face that night sinking his spirits. "She is in need of such encouragement at the moment."

"I can only guess that moving from your father's home to this . . ." He gestured at the royal bustle going on around them. "It must have been quite a transition." After a moment, he lowered his head with a look of slight worry on his face. "I apologize, sir. I say too much. It is not my place to speak of the personal lives of those above my station."

"No, please think nothing of it," Launce hurried to assure him. "I will admit that I don't feel anything at home in this place. I can only guess my sister feels the same." He studied the scuffs on his boots as he spoke again. "I cannot imagine what it must be like for her to *live* like this. I'm only here because she wanted me to come along."

"What, a young man like you has no sweetheart at home?" The servant gave a chuckle. "I find that hard to believe."

"I *had* one," Launce gave him a wry smile.

"Ah, I see."

They were silent for a moment, watching the goings-on around them as men continued to stream into the stables.

"Well, I suppose I should be off. It is getting to be *more* than a bit late." The short man straightened his green work vest and dusted off his brown trousers as he turned to go. "But please, let me know if there is anything I can do for you."

"Thank you," Launce said, truly meaning it. "And the same for me as well. I have enjoyed some honest conversation." With another deep smile, the older man gave a short, quick bow and left the stableyard. Launce found himself in a somewhat better mood as a bell sounded from somewhere in the distance.

The men that loitered outside began to gather their belongings in a hurry before suddenly streaming into the stable. Curious, Launce found himself at the edges of the throng that was trying to fit itself into the stable doors all at once. He allowed himself to be jostled and carried along with the crowd.

"With all the dignitaries attending, you would think Rafael have hosted something a bit more appropriate," a man to Launce's left grumbled. "If I'd known we were to be housed and fed like animals, I would have brought my own caravan."

"He wouldn't have let you stay in it and compete," another said as they shuffled forward, although Launce couldn't see the speaker. "I heard him say the visiting holy man wants us all in the same place to see which one the Maker considers worthy."

"I think he's lost his mind," the first speaker, a short, solid man, said mildly.

"Why are you here then?" Launce realized as the words left his mouth that they sounded rather impertinent, but he was genuinely curious as to why such self-important men would stoop to live in what they considered squalor.

"The same reason you are," the man said with more than a hint of annoyance. Lance sincerely doubted that, but he pressed no further. Eventually, after being pushed and stepped on more times than he could count, Launce finally made it back to his bunk. As moments passed, the men still trying to find their own beds, many of whom were more than a bit drunk, began to move at a more frenzied pace.

"What's wrong with them?" Launce asked a servant boy who standing nearby him.

"You must be new." The boy looked him up and down

curiously."

Launce nodded.

"Midnight has come," the boy said, as if that explained it.

"So?"

"Just after midnight, something awful happens outside." The boy, probably twelve or thirteen, looked unruffled, but there was a slight tremor to his warbling voice that gave him away. "How long have you been here?"

"I arrived today."

"Then you have only been to the ball," the boy said. "The other nights, before you got here, were different." He smirked proudly. "My master arrived a week ago."

"But what happened?" Launce pressed, glancing around as they spoke to realize the men were running even faster to finish whatever they were doing.

"Every night, the king stations a guard outside to make sure the competitors don't sneak out. Since we arrived, we've found each night guard on the ground in the morning, dead as they come, pounded to death. I've never seen so much blood." The boy shivered, his brown curls shaking just slightly with him.

"No one hears anything?" Launce asked incredulously. These men were certainly not Everard, but he found it hard to believe that seven men could be pounded to death without the company of men in the stable hearing a thing.

The boy just shook his head.

"But what does the king say about the men who have died?" Launce felt a warm bit of unease slither through his body.

The boy shrugged, glancing over his shoulder as he began to fidget.

"But what if it's dark forces at work?" Launce prodded.

"Someone suggested that, but the king said that if one of you is going to be king, he'd better know how to deal with such anyway. Look now, my master will be angry if I'm not back with him soon."

Thanking him, Launce let the nervous boy go and settled into his own bunk. Before he could wonder at such a strange turn of events, however, his eyes grew heavy, and the bed was suddenly much more comfortable than he'd first thought. As though sharing his sudden exhaustion, a chorus of snores erupted throughout the stable. It was as though all work and bustling had come to a complete halt, and no one cared any longer if their personal chores were attended to.

This struck him as odd, but Launce had just decided he would be better fit to search for the reason in the morning, when he felt the bed tremor lightly beneath him. And then again.

Surprised at his sudden lack of will to get out of bed, Launce did his best to flip over, fighting the crushing drowsiness with all his strength. The competitors' snoring continued for the most part, although Launce did hear someone get up and relieve himself outside. Or at least that's what it sounded like. Try as he might, though, it was all Launce could do to keep his eyelids slitted open.

The tremors began to come faster and harder, and through his nearly closed eyes, Launce saw a strange dust floating around in the air, but only for a moment. The ground was now quaking so violently, Launce felt as though he might be thrown from his bunk. Fear gripped him as he tried desperately to free himself from the grasp of whatever force held him in the state of severe sluggishness, and the strange shaking only made it worse.

As the earthquake grew in strength, Launce could no longer see the room as his teeth jarred and his body slammed into the wall repeatedly. Terror gripped him as he realized someone had left candles upright on the table, but as he prayed to the Maker to keep them from falling, sleep kept him from finishing even that.

CHAPTER 10
BRITTLE HINTS

Launce wanted to cringe as Everard studied him with that infuriating, unreadable expression. Since Launce had awakened that morning, he'd been dreading the scolding he was sure to hear for allowing sleep to take him during the night's quaking. The pastries Everard had brought did lessen the sting, but Launce was a bit suspicious as to how his brother-in-law had known he would be hungry. He didn't ask though. It was best not to expect too much from the king, even on the best days.

To Launce's surprise, however, his brother-in-law slowly nodded.

"I believe you are right, particularly since no one here in the palace felt the quakes, and many servants were awake much past midnight without a problem."

Launce nearly allowed himself to gape, but managed to keep his mouth shut and his sarcastic comment in as well. Everard's agreement had been the last thing he'd expected when his brother-in-law had sent a note early that morning, telling Launce to meet him in the south corner of the outer palace walk.

"I just wish we knew where this power was coming from," Everard mused, turning to stare at the distant seashore that glistened a pearly white in the distance.

"One of the men said the king wants the competitors in one place so the holy man can see them and judge whom is worthy."

"Have you noticed anyone who stands out?"

"Just self-important royals and nobles and their servants."

"From the way you inhaled the pastries," Everard frowned, "I'm supposing they're the same self-important coxcombs who kept you from getting a decent breakfast this morning too." He let out a gusty breath and ran his hand through his short hair. "If you would just wear the Fortress colors I sent, they would treat you with more respect."

"I won't pretend to be someone I'm not." Launce kept his eyes on the hills behind Everard.

"Whether you like it or not," Everard's words were nearly a growl, "you are now attached to the Fortress. It would be easier on everyone if you simply accepted it."

"I am well aware of my attachments!" Launce spat out. His sweetheart's father had said as much.

Everard fixed his burning eyes back on Launce. "We don't have time for this. Isa will be awake soon. Today, I want you to look for any signs of power. See if you can find any residue from last night. Look in the food, the hay, even on the horses. Someone does not want you to see whatever happens to those guards during the earthquakes."

On his way back to the stables, Launce swore to himself that after this, he was done being Everard's errand boy. Being summoned and sent on whim left a bitter taste in his mouth. He would go home, help his father with the shop, find a completely ordinary wife, and leave Fortress matters be.

But then, that still left Isa alone with *him*.

The stables were separated from the main palace, but not

far enough to fit Launce's taste. The palace, with its red clay roof tiles and whitewashed walls, spread out in twists and turns in such a complicated manner that Launce still wasn't even sure that they resembled any sort of organized thought. The stables, though, were simply long rectangular structures, single rooms with double bunks built into each wall across from the horses.

As he entered the main stable, where all the competitors were staying, he tried to slip in unseen. It wasn't hard, considering most of the men were otherwise occupied. Some napped, while others dueled or engaged in political discussions. He found the horse Everard had sent for him and began to groom him. Launce needed to think, and brushing the animal was relaxing, something familiar. As he found a brush and began to groom the horse, he couldn't help but notice how striking the creature was. As far as Everard could push him toward insanity, Launce couldn't fault the man's taste in horses.

"Fine charger you have there."

Launce turned to find the friendly servant from the previous night standing behind him. Ease washed through him as he returned the man's grin.

"It belongs to King Everard." Launce put down the brush and ran a hand down the animal's shiny coat. "But he is a fine one."

The servant held out a cloth bag. "I figured this lot," he waved at the crowd of competitors and whispered, "wouldn't leave you much to eat. Hungry?" Launce had inhaled the three sweet rolls Everard had brought him, but then again, Launce was always hungry. They moved outside to sit on a log at the fringe of the stable shuffle, where there was a bit more space for Launce to dive greedily into the bag of eggs, bread, and cheese.

"I have to admit," Launce said between bites of the bread, which was still warm, "while I'm truly grateful, I am a bit confused as to why you've shown me so much kindness."

Brokk smiled wanly. "I have a confession of my own to make, I'm afraid. I haven't been a servant for King Rafael for very long. I traveled before that, and I've seen more than I would like to recall." His smile melted into a fleeting distant look. But just as soon as it had fallen, he was smiling once again. "As soon as I learned of what your sister did at the Fortress, I wanted badly to meet her. I'm sorry if it seems I've used you . . ." The older man pursed his lips and stared at the ground.

"I'm sure my sister would be delighted to meet you." Launce tried to give the man an encouraging smile. "And I never turn down food." When he said this, Brokk's eyes crinkled up pleasantly, and Launce had to feel pleased himself.

As he finished the eggs, Launce suddenly found himself very curious. "If you don't mind me asking, where are you from, if not here?" Indeed, the more he studied Brokk, the more the servant stood out against the others. Where most of the native Cobriens had olive skin and dark eyes, this man's hair had once been red, or at least had carried traces of it. His eyes were a pale blue, and his skin lacked the hardy warmth of the Cobriens.

"North," Brokk answered, pulling an apple from his pocket and studying it. "I doubt you would know of it."

"What made you decide to leave?" Launce tried to keep from sounding too curious, but there was something different about the man, something knowledgeable. He couldn't explain why, but this servant seemed as though he knew much, much more than what many of the men surrounding them knew combined.

The older man looked down at his scuffed boots and then out at the distant sea to the south. "Sometimes decisions are made for us, lad," Brokk said in a soft voice. The sadness in his voice silenced any further questions Launce was tempted to ask.

They stared out at the ocean for a bit until in a more cheery voice, Brokk asked what Launce planned to do with the afternoon. As he started to answer, Launce paused, unsure of how much he should tell others about his errand from Everard.

"Have you heard of the murders outside the stables every night?" Launce asked cautiously, trying to guess at what the unusual little man knew.

"The servants talk of nothing else."

"I thought I would try and poke around." Launce tried to sound casual as he folded the empty bag, afraid that he looked at Brokk directly, his nerves would give him away.

"May I give you a piece of advice then?"

Surprised, Launce looked at his new friend. The older man's eyes were thoughtful as he gazed back. When Launce nodded, Brokk's smile nearly became a smirk. "Try looking from a different perspective."

"What do you mean?"

"Have any of them tried looking?" Brokk waved his arm at the men milling about the stables.

"I heard some of them whispering about it, but no one seems to do much more than that." Launce frowned as he realized this group, more than any, should have been avidly pursuing justice. The contest was full of knights, princes, and even kings, all raring to show the princess their might. And yet, last night they had cowered in their beds. "What do you know of it?"

"Oh, as little as you, is my guess. But," he leaned in and whispered, "take it from someone who has seen a big world and many peoples. I've been watching this bunch, and I knew as soon as I saw you that you are different." He nodded once and stood, gathering Launce's empty bread linens.

As soon as Brokk had excused himself to return to his duties, Launce decided to try searching for the magic. He had been unsure before, but comforted by Brokk's kind words, he walked purposefully toward the stables, ignoring as best as he could the looks of disdain others cast his way. He considered putting on the tunic that Everard had given him, but imagining the look of satisfaction he would see on Everard's smug face was enough to keep it tucked under the straw mattress and safely out of sight.

Considering Brokk's words, Launce decided to begin at the bottom, with the floor. He must look addled, he thought to himself, bending down just inches from the ground to stare at it. But it was all he could think to do. What was he even looking for? He'd convinced himself he would be able to sense it, the way he could sense Isa's power when she was nearby. When he was near his sister, it felt as if the air was charged, as though lightning had just struck, and everything around him stood on edge. Surely it would be the same way, or at least, similar in sense.

"It's kind of you to offer so readily. My boots do need to be shined."

Launce looked up to see the man from the day before, the one who had mistaken him for a servant. Launce's face flushed with indignation, but before he could respond, a new voice called out from behind him.

"Leave him be, Absalom."

The new speaker was somewhat shorter than average, but everything he lacked in height was made up for in muscle. Visible even beneath his fine tunic, the man had one of the broadest chests Launce had ever seen.

"Stay out of my affairs, Randolph."

"Do you think it really wise to provoke King Everard's kin?" The strong man, Randolph, stood beside Launce and crossed his arms. "You're being a fool. I am merely trying to keep you alive." He grimaced. "Our own king will have my head if I return without you."

Absalom glared down at Launce, who returned the expression. In the end, however, he said nothing more, simply stalked away as he muttered. Not waiting to be acknowledged, Randolph gave Launce a curt nod before moving on himself.

How did Isa stand living around these people? As he returned to searching the floor for he knew not what, Launce vowed again to himself that this was the last time she talked him into accompanying her anywhere.

Two hours later, Launce was hungry again, his eyes were sore from getting dust and dirt kicked in them, and he was no closer to finding an answer. Everard would just have to sneak into the stables against the king's wishes and search for it himself. Just as Launce stood and stepped into the afternoon sunlight, however, a sparkle caught his eye. Leaning down, where he'd seen it, he searched again, this time with gusto.

The particle of shine was so small he nearly missed it, and he had to search to find it again. Lifting up a small handful of the dirt, Launce examined it in the light. This time, not one but dozens of minuscule sparkles glittered as he turned his hand in the light. It looked almost like glass. When he rubbed the dust between his fingers, however, all doubt fled, and he knew he'd found exactly what he had been looking for.

A slight shudder moved through him as the power of the glass rippled out. It was small but strong. Another sparkle caught his eye on his shirt. And his trousers. And in his boots. The more he searched, the more he realized he was coated in the powdery glass. Rushing back inside, he yanked his bag from the wall and held it up to the window beside his bunk. Sure enough, it was covered as well.

How had he missed something that covered every inch of the stables?

It was only then that Launce remembered the footsteps from the night before. What if it hadn't been a contestant going to relieve himself? What if it had been someone else? Launce nearly broke into a run to find Everard, but stopped himself just before leaving the stable.

No. He would do this alone. Then, for once, maybe he would escape that self-righteous look Everard always gave before he barked out more orders.

Launce spent the rest of the afternoon planning. His greatest concern was with positioning. Where could he go that wouldn't be covered with the glass dust? Based on what Everard had said, the dust must have been what was putting everyone into such a deep sleep.

Try looking from a different perspective, Brokk had said. It had worked to help Launce find the dust. Now he needed some way to escape it.

But of course. The roof! He would just have to make sure no one else saw him take his place after night fell.

FINISHING the day felt like an eternity without someone to talk to, but finally evening came. There was no ball tonight, only a simple supper served outside the stables. Once he'd pushed his way through the supper line, and inhaled what little food he did get, Launce made his escape.

Shimmying up the side of the stables didn't take him long. The roof was sloped, but not enough to make it impossible to lay upon. To his relief, there was no dust. Only once he was up, however, did it occur to Launce that he probably should have brought some sort of weapon. Not that he would have known how to do much good with it.

It wasn't long before the guard arrived. As twilight faded, however, into the warmth of a lazy early autumn evening, with singing cicadas and croaking toads nearby, Launce had to shake himself often. His hiding position wasn't very comfortable, nor was it ideal for rousing oneself, as he laid flat against the red tile shingles with his body on a decline and his hands clinging to their edges. Launce had hoped it would keep him hidden, but if he fell asleep, he wouldn't be doing anyone any good.

A movement caught his eye. It was too dark to see much, but it looked as though someone had come through the same side door as the one Launce had noticed opening the night before. He had little time to concentrate on it, however, because out of the corner of his eye, the largest creature he'd ever seen in his life was charging straight for him.

CHAPTER II

TEA AND TEMPERS

Y ou could call on Queen Monica," Ever suggested after he returned from his early morning errand.

"Do I have an official invitation?"

"Well no, but it would convey Destin's good will," Ever said as he scratched his head. But Isa could see right through him.

"If my presence is not officially requested anywhere this morning," Isa replied firmly, "then I'm not going." And nothing Ever said could change her mind. Isa could see that her determination to hide in their chambers confused her husband, but her decision was simply something he would have to accept.

Being in public was easy for Ever, so easy that Isa often envied him the way it buoyed his spirits and seemed to fill him with even more of his endless energy. Explaining her need for quiet was impossible. She had tried. He just couldn't comprehend how exhausted she became by being surrounded by so many people, even when her unpredictable fire wasn't upsetting her fellow guests. But after her upset of the night before, going out to socialize, as Ever called it, was asking too much. She needed time to think.

Sleep had come a little easier once Ever had assured her that the beautiful woman he'd spoken with was like a sister to him. Still, Isa knew there was something her husband was hiding. If the southern queen had her own version of strength, then there was a good chance they had been speaking of Rafael's strange behavior. Ever was more unruffled than he had been since the Fortress curse had been broken. But why wasn't he telling her? Isa might be struggling with her strength, but she was still the queen.

And so Isa spent the day with Cerise, laughing about their childhood pranks and hiding behind the thick wooden door as they sipped tea, trying to ignore the absence of her husband. As she had expected, however, he was up before sunrise, and spent the entire day running about the palace, interrogating whatever poor courtiers he thought might aid his cause, and muttering about how base it was for Rafael to give himself such a hangover that he couldn't attend to his subjects. During one of his many quick stops back at their chambers for this parchment or that gift for a dignitary, she had asked where Launce was. His response that Launce was assisting him surprised her, but Isa decided to simply leave them be. If the two men were somehow getting along, she wouldn't stand in the way.

Everard's determination to help her enjoy the company of her fellow royals couldn't stay dormant for long though. Isa cringed immediately when he waltzed in that afternoon with a sealed note from Queen Monica, and a triumphant smile on his face.

Isa glared at him while she broke the seal, half expecting to find his handwriting inside. Written on the finest of parchment in a scrawling hand that was most decidedly not her husband's, however, the note read:

QUEEN ISABELLE OF DESTIN,

. . .

QUEEN MONICA REQUESTS your presence at her tea on the morrow upon the ninth hour. Your addition to the queen's company will be most welcome, where our circle finds itself eager to know you more.

IN THE MAKER'S BLESSINGS,
   Queen Monica

"YOU PUT HER UP TO THIS," Isa said upon reading the note.

But Ever held his hands up above his head, a look of utter innocence on his face. "Upon my honor, I did not." He tried, unsuccessfully, to hide a smile as she read the note again in dismay. "Believe it or not, some women do actually meet together to become friends. Not every woman interprets tea invitations as insults."

"Not every woman has the ability to accidentally frighten her peers after they insult her," Isa said, scowling.

"Isa, it would be an insult not to—"

"I will go, Ever! But that doesn't mean I have to enjoy myself."

And so Isa awoke the next morning with no small amount of fluttering in her stomach. Memories of the crowd's faces at the ball as she struggled to put out her flame haunted her as she ordered herself several times to get out of bed. It was a good thing Ever had gone so early. There would have been no happy smile to greet him today.

"Which dress will it be today?" Cerise held the wardrobe open as she and Isa leaned in to scrutinize the mountain of dresses Gigi had sent. Isa bit her lip for a moment before annoyance and disgust from the ball's events made up her mind for her.

"Ladies Beata and Jadzia and Princess Damira will be there. Pick the most stuffy, uncomfortable, insensible dress you can find." Isa turned sharply and moved to the full-length mirror to criticize her reflection as Cerise rummaged through the wardrobe. She tried to avoid, however, looking directly at her eyes. She didn't need to see them to know their fire wasn't any brighter than it had been the day before when she had checked. Or the days or weeks before that. It had been her hope that after the incident with the ball, perhaps they might glow a little brighter. But it was not to be. They were as dull as ever.

"Those women must have done something awful to merit such a gown from you." Cerise's voice was muffled, but Isa could hear a smile in it. So Isa told her friend what the women had said.

"What?" Cerise popped her head out of the clothing, gray eyes flashing.

With a sigh, Isa related the ball's events again. The awful ordeal still didn't sound much better, but at least she could speak of it without weeping this time. No. Now she was angry.

When she finished, Cerise shook her head in disbelief. Then her eyes lit up. Hurrying over to a trunk in the corner, Cerise pulled out a small wooden box.

"Gigi gave these to me for the final ball, but I don't think it would hurt to use a few of them today." She opened the box to reveal a pile of hairpins with bright blue jewels at the top. Cerise scooped out a small handful and began to pin them into Isa's hair. Usually, Isa protested such finery. It still felt strange to wear jewels to daily occasions such as tea. There would be no complaining this time, however, as Cerise expertly pinned the baubles into the curls of her hair.

Not long after, a servant knocked on the door to escort the two women to the queen's tea room. Isa was disappointed to know that Cerise would be leaving her once she was properly settled in with the queen's party, but she was grateful that her friend could at least accompany her there.

Isa came to a stop just outside Queen Monica's tea room, and as she waited for the servant to announce her arrival, she wondered about the women inside. If Everard didn't believe in her, why should they?

The queen's tea room was an airy, lavish space filled with sunlight and flowers of every kind. Despite the lateness of the season, bright red and orange petals seemed to cover each surface, and upon a quick peek, Isa realized they were actually growing right in the room, rather than being cut and placed in vases. Sleek, curved chairs carved of a pale wood were placed in a large circle to accommodate the number of women already present. Sofas for lounging edged the room, one placed every few windows. The windows were tall, reaching nearly to the ceiling, and the floor was covered in red stone tiles, like the rest of the palace seemed to be. The furnishings, though, seemed different in taste. Her astounding variety held pieces from a vast number of lands, including a vase made by none other than one of Isa's old neighbors in Soudain.

Nearly a dozen women and girls were already seated in the circle with small tables of treats displayed between each individual. Most of the other women wore lighter gowns than Isa did, but that was fine. The dark blue Isa wore matched her mood. She painted a smile on, however, as she broke into the circle just between Lady Jadzia and another woman, whom she didn't know.

The servant led Isa to the chair directly to the left of Queen Monica's seat; it was an honor to be seated so close to the host. Isa curtsied to the queen, careful to keep her head up. Once she was settled in her own chair, Isa took a deep breath and nodded to Cerise, who curtsied formally before leaving Isa both surrounded and all alone.

"I want to thank you, Queen Isabelle, for joining us on such short notice this morning." Queen Monica's words were formal, but her voice had a quiet cadence to it that Isa found relaxing. "Please, allow me to introduce you to the rest of our company." She gestured, and as she said their names, each woman nodded her head in turn. "My daughter, Olivia, whom you met yesterday. Lady Carlita of Giova, Queen Zineta of Anbin, Princess Damira and Lady Jadzia of Staroz, Lady Beata of Vaksam, Queen Kartek of Hedjet, and Queen Anna and her daughter, Princess Daphne of Ashland." Isa smiled at each, hoping she wouldn't insult one of them by forgetting which name belonged to which face. At least half of them would be easy. Queen Monica, Princess Olivia, and Queen Kartek she knew. Unfortunately, Princess Damira, Lady Jadzia, and Lady Beata's faces would be carved into her memory forever as well.

"I must admit," Queen Monica continued as a servant handed Isa a delicate porcelain cup with tiny painted green leaves, "that I was unaware Everard had married until after the wedding had already passed. I apologize for the oversight." Isa noted the familiarity with which the queen talked about Ever, and for some reason, it made her feel good.

"There is nothing to forgive," Isa said. "Everard told me you were in Giova when it happened. The wedding itself was quick." Isa thought she heard a titter to her left, but she sipped her tea and kept her face on Queen Monica. The queen looked as if she were about to say something else, but Lady Jadzia spoke instead.

"You are looking well, Queen Isabelle."

"Thank you," Isa said hesitantly. What an odd thing to say.

"Most women do not look as lively or keep their figures so well as you have in your fifth month."

Isa nearly dropped her tea.

"Lady Jadzia, whatever do you mean?" It was Princess Olivia who had spoken, but all of the other ladies looked as appalled as Isa felt.

Unabashed, Lady Jadzia widened her eyes. "I apologize if I was mistaken. It was only my impression that the queens of the Fortress always conceive within the first month of their marriage." The other women exchanged glances but said nothing as they waited for Isa's response. If there had been any doubt as to how much this woman had wanted to marry Ever, it was all gone now. She had managed to learn more about the queenship than most Destinians ever knew in their lifetimes.

Isa took a deep breath. "It is the tradition."

"I see. I had only assumed—"

"I think you will find, Lady Jadzia, that I am anything but traditional." Isa's voice was hard. She held Lady Jadzia's gaze until propriety forced the other woman to look away, her orange curls falling over her face to cover her eyes.

Suddenly, Isa was thankful she and Cerise had chosen such an uncomfortable dress. The stiff blue material kept her back perfectly straight, itching her if she slouched at all. She could not have looked defeated in that dress even if she tried.

"Queen Isabelle," Queen Kartek spoke up, throwing a withering glance at Lady Jadzia, who was suddenly too busy smoothing out her flawless silk skirt to notice. "Is your family well?"

"They are, thank you."

"What lands do they hold?" Lady Beata asked. "I've ridden through your countryside a few times in my life, but I've never seen any lands by the name of Marchand."

Isa didn't miss the trap. She hesitated just a moment before answering. Their determination was shocking, but Isa wasn't about to let them frighten her off. "My father is a man of trade," she finally managed to answer in a cool voice, taking another sip of her tea. "He and my mother own a store in the marketplace in our capital city, Soudain, where they sell goods and care for their children and personal livestock."

"Goodness! Are you telling us you have actually milked a

cow?" Lady Jadzia placed her tea back on its saucer with a loud *clink*. Some of it sloshed onto her ivory gown, but she seemed too delighted in Isa's past to notice.

"Lady Jadzia!" Queen Monica began.

"It is quite alright, Your Highness," Isa said, before fixing her gaze on Lady Jadzia. "Yes, I have milked cows. I have also hauled grain, sold goods, groomed horses, and sewn dresses. I have worked alongside my parents until my hands bled so that we could eat. It is a good thing too, as they are strong and ready, now that my husband has decided that I should learn the art of war." Out of the corner of her eye, Isa saw Queen Kartek's sly smile. Princess Olivia made a poor attempt at smothering her giggles before being silenced by her mother's sharp look. The rest of the women fidgeted, however, and nervously nibbled the pastries set out for them. Lady Jadzia's red lips parted, but it was a moment before anything came out.

"I see. It's just that Everard was always so like his father. I had only assumed he would—"

"What my husband and I choose to do with our lives and our kingdom and our family is our business, and ours alone. I will be sure to make you privy to such information, however, when it is in your best interest to know."

"And that," Queen Monica spoke before Lady Jadzia could respond, "will be enough of that. Lady Jadzia, you have insulted my guest in my home more than I should like to admit today, and I will not have it. You may take leave of this company for the time being until you gain control of your tongue."

The blush in Lady Jadzia's pale cheeks and the humble nod she gave seemed to show for the first time that she realized she had indeed gone too far. Mumbling an apology, she dipped a quick curtsy to Queen Monica and the princess before fleeing the room.

As Lady Jadzia passed her, Isa was struck again with the realization that the noblewoman would have been very beautiful had it not been for her mouth. She had lovely curves, more than Isa could ever dream of having, and her skin was flawless. Isa was instantly glad that she hadn't been present for Ever's first betrothal ball. Watching Lady Jadzia throw herself at him would have been torture.

The rest of the tea continued without excitement, something which Isa more than welcomed. Queen Monica was an expert at asking each guest exactly the right question to elicit a response, and Isa began to learn a bit more about other women there. She decided right away that she would like to be friends with the queen and princess of Ashland. The lady of Giova was rather dry, and spent most of the time stuffing her mouth with scones. The others answered in turn, but offered little information worth knowing, Princess Damira and Lady Beata in particular. Queen Kartek was quiet, but sometimes took over asking questions, Isa noticed, so Queen Monica could sip her tea and eat. Princess Olivia, though she spoke little, seemed to Isa like she might be a lot of fun. Of course, she also seemed as though she could be a lot of trouble if she ever had the mind for it. In person, she seemed far different from the shy princess King Rafael had presented the night before.

The remainder of the tea was enjoyable, but Isa ultimately found herself rather tired after her encounter with Lady Jadzia. Not physically, but rather she felt as though her heart had been spent. Relief washed over her when Queen Monica finally declared it time for her to oversee the preparations for that night's supper. Isa stood and curtsied, murmuring her well-wishes to each in the circle until it was Princess Olivia's turn. Rather than curtsying, as everyone else had, however, the princess surprised her by pulling her into an embrace.

"Do not allow Jadzia to ruin your day," she whispered into Isa's ear. "Rumor has it that she emptied her father's coffers on fineries to catch your husband's eye at that ball." The princess released her, only to step back and take Isa's hands in her own as if they were already the best of friends. "But look who has him now," she added with a smirk. Isa felt herself smiling back. It was impossible to be unaffected by the young woman's spirit. And, Isa grinned to herself as she met Cerise in the hall, the princess was right.

Ever was hers.

CHAPTER 12

ESCAPING THOUGHTS

Cerise eyed Isa's leather skirt and trousers suspiciously as Isa dug both the clothes and her sword belt out of the wardrobe.

The combat wardrobe had been Ever's idea. As soon as they were married, he'd ordered the tailor to make her clothes practical for swordplay and riding. No good could come of anyone trying to move about in such stuffy gowns, he'd told the reluctant Gigi.

Isa hadn't been sure of the new clothing, though, until she had tried it on. The top of the set was a long-sleeved tunic made of supple red leather. The tunic was long enough to look like a short skirt that ended just above the knees of her trousers, which were made of the same thin leather but brown. The boots were similar to those she'd worn when she was crippled — strong with good support for her ankles. Though she felt scandalous for thinking it, there was such freedom in trousers! Of course, she would never admit such sentiments to her mother.

"I need some space," Isa answered Cerise's unspoken question. "The streets here are too crowded for a good ride, and most everyone in the palace will be preparing to watch the games. The practice rooms will most likely be empty." Isa's day in bed had given her ample time to indulge in self-pity, but now she needed to *think*.

"Just return in time to dress for the contest, since you're determined not to leave this gown on." Cerise shook her yellow curls indulgently as she picked the stiff blue gown up from the bed where Isa had tossed it. "And Isa," Cerise called out as Isa knocked for Norbert. "Please be careful. Something about this place makes me nervous."

Isa gave her friend a smile, trying to look confident. She used the same smile to assure Norbert that there was no need for him to accompany her. She was only going to the training room downstairs. As soon as she was on her way, however, the smile melted away. Cerise was right. Something felt very off and had since the moment they'd set foot in the palace. If only Ever would tell her *what*.

Following a servant's instructions, Isa climbed down several flights of stairs to the ground floor. After turning down a few hallways, which Isa hoped she could remember on the way back, she came to a large square room with twelve bright windows lining the southern wall. And to Isa's satisfaction, it was empty.

She unsheathed her sword and walked to the center of the large room. As she prepared herself to practice the form, Isa noted with appreciation how smooth the floors were in here too. The Fortress's practice rooms were rough and uneven, but Ever refused to have them smoothed down. The ground was never smooth in battle, he would always say. And while Isa knew he was right, the level, red stone floors would make her practice a bit easier.

Closing her eyes, Isa pictured the form in her head. Ever had taught her a number of combat forms, specific movements, blocks, and thrusts that followed one another in rapid order. Isa had struggled with them at first, until she realized they resembled a dance. Thinking of the movements as such had made memorizing them much easier. With her eyes still closed, Isa began.

Though she would never tell him, sometimes it was easier to practice without Ever present. She could move at whatever speed she wished, and it gave her time to ponder. This morning, she needed to understand what exactly had happened at the ball. The slow, steady rhythm of the steps would help her do that.

Ever's behavior at the ball had hurt Isa more than she wanted to admit. When he had returned to the room, however, she'd felt more comforted, more loved than she had in a long time. The idea of Lady Jadzia being chosen by Ever, cradled in his arms, dancing with him, practicing swordplay with him, although the latter image was rather unlikely, provoked Isa beyond reason. True, her powers were failing, but Isa had been the one to face the curse with Ever. Isa had fallen in love, not with the daydream of a king, but with a broken, twisted, and hollow man. Isa had been forced to watch him die, and then had to be willing to live on without him. And it had been Isa whom the Fortress had returned him to. No, Lady Jadzia could daydream and plot all she wanted, but the Fortress had chosen *Isa*, and Ever would be *hers* until the day she died.

A shock rippled through her as a wave of blue fire slid from her hand down her sword. How long had it been since she'd felt such pure power? Isa knew there was only one definite way to search for more.

Isa carefully placed her sword at the edge of the practice floor, near one of the windowed walls, then returned to the middle of the room. With a renewed vigor, Isa threw herself into a different kind of motion. Dancing, though far less practical than swordplay, was her surest way to find her power. Unfortunately, Isa had been kept so busy at home, that there hadn't been time for dancing in months. But she was here now, and no one was watching. Faster and faster she went. Her body was fluid, flowing like water into steps, leaps, and turns.

The power wasn't strong, but she could feel it as it churned its way through her. Like water to a parched desert, she drank in the presence of her beloved Fortress, despite being in another kingdom. In this state of joy, she could feel it, even from afar.

If only she could stay in this moment forever.

In the middle of one of her hops, however, the toe of her shoe caught, and she found herself stumbling. But instead of tripping forward as she ought to have, Isa began to fall to the right, directly into one of the windows. She placed her hand on the glass in an effort to steady herself, but when she tried to pull away, it stuck. Something was keeping her there, and despite her attempts to pull herself away from the glass, it held her fast. Her fingers might as well have been melded to the pane, and the oddest trickle began to move through her. Fear seized Isa as frigid air blew on her face. Gathering all of her strength, she pushed herself away so hard that she fell to the ground.

Her breath was ragged as she stared at the window. Nothing looked out of the ordinary from where she'd fallen. Through the window she had just been held captive to, she could still see the tall trees rising into the autumn sky with birds flying past them. The window itself looked absolutely commonplace. In wonder, Isa held up her right hand. It also looked as it should. It was as though nothing had been amiss. But she had most assuredly felt a new kind of power, and one that differed vastly from hers or Ever's.

"Would you like some assistance, Your Majesty?" A servant hurried toward her, but stopped just a few feet away. He seemed torn between approaching her and waiting for her approval, one arm outstretched, the other still hanging at his side.

Isa tried to stand, but was forced back down onto the floor when a dull pain shot through her leg. She tried to smile as she nodded. "Thank you. I seem to have twisted my ankle."

As he got closer, she studied his thick mop of tight, silver curls and his cheery face. He wasn't tall. In fact, he seemed a good deal shorter than Isa. As he helped her stand, however, she could tell that he was physically more than capable of helping her return to her rooms.

Gingerly, she tested her ankle, but could make it no farther than a few steps before she was obligated to ask for his help again. "I don't know what the matter with me is," she said ruefully as they began the tedious climb up the first set of stairs. "I never stumble when I dance."

"I don't mind a bit," he said in a singsong voice, which Isa thought to be quite pleasant. "My name is Brokk. Or at least, that's what my mother called me. And I must confess," he paused and gave her a shy smile, "I have actually been hoping to meet you, ever since I found out you were going to be staying in the palace."

"You have?" Isa felt a flutter in her stomach, though she couldn't say what for.

"Your Highness, there is such news of what you have done for the people of Destin, for your husband! It has traveled far, and your power has inspired many!"

"I wish I could accept such praise with a clear conscience." Heat gathered in her neck as Isa considered his words with shame. They walked in silence for a few moments before the servant spoke again.

"I hope I am not being too forward, Your Highness, but are you referring to the little stumble you had? Or rather, was that incident perhaps related to a greater problem?" When Isa couldn't bring herself to answer, he nodded slowly. "And what does your husband think of your struggle?"

"He's not sure." She sighed. "My power is different from

his." As the words left her mouth, Isa found herself very grateful for the kindness of this unusually forward servant. But even as she thought it, Ever's warning at the ball about speaking too freely of her strength suddenly echoed in her mind. She hadn't meant to say so much to the servant. In her exasperation, it had just slipped.

"Yes, I heard about that. What is it that you possess differently? Strength of the mind, was it?"

"Of the heart," Isa whispered.

"Ah yes, now I remember. Well, here we are." They had stopped in front of Isa's door. Isa nearly asked how he knew where she was staying, but then remembered that at her own Fortress, Garin made it the business of all the servants to know who all their guests were and where they were staying. Thanking him once again, she held out her arm for Norbert to help her into the room. The older guard gave her a look that threatened violence to whomever had injured her until she assured him twice over that she had only tripped. As much as she loved Norbert, she decided not to tell him of the strange power that had briefly held her in its grasp. It was too confusing.

Once Norbert had left her inside, Isa lowered herself onto the bed, misery overtaking her once more. She had fled her room that morning in order to escape the thoughts she'd awakened to when she realized Ever had already dressed and gone. The way he'd kissed her brow softly and had fallen asleep holding her to his chest for not one but the last two nights, had been the sweetest moments she'd shared with her husband in a long time. Still, she should have known better than to hope for him to continue his attentions in the morning. If nothing else, Ever was dutiful, and whatever had him on edge now had called him away again.

If only he trusted her enough to tell her, she nearly moaned. So much for finding a distraction.

CHAPTER 13
GAME OF GLASS

I was hoping that was you," Cerise said, walking in from the small room that was attached to Isa's chambers. "It's time you began to dress for the games." Isa did her best to smile as Cerise pulled the cranberry dress from the wardrobe. This one had sleeves at least. Sleeves so sheer they were nearly invisible.

"Did Gigi have to order every dress to show my shoulders?" Isa grimaced. "For eternity's sake, it's almost winter!"

"I'm sure your husband won't complain." Cerise raised an eyebrow and smirked. "The last time you wore this he noticed." When Isa raised her own eyebrows, Cerise just laughed. "I may be a servant, but to miss that man's stare, one would have to be blind."

Doubts still lingered, but Isa did feel a little better. They continued in silence, which gave Isa time to think, although she did get a quick scolding about her ankle. Rather than give thought to her worries, however, Isa decided to think about how grateful she was that Ever didn't insist on her wearing tightened stays in her dress, as was high fashion. Not that she would have worn them even if he had.

The first grand gathering they'd hosted after the curse was broken had been an attempt to reestablish Destin's place with a few of their neighbors. There had been no ball held with the gathering, so most of the guests had been men, foreign ambassadors and princes.

As her tutor's female assistant had prepared her for the evening, hammering names and etiquette into her head, one of the servants had brought out a long piece of stiff fabric with dozens of thin metal rods running up and down its entire length. Without a word, the servant had begun to fasten it about her waist and chest. After tying it in place, she took the strings that dangled down Isa's backside and with a great heave, began to pull. Isa had nearly passed out as her chest seemed to collapse and her waist had nearly disappeared.

"Stop!" she had gasped, desperate to draw in air. "Please! I can't breathe!"

"You will learn, as all the ladies of the court do," her tutor's assistant had said with a shrug. "It will not be so bad when you become used to it." She had nodded at the servant to begin pulling once again, but Isa had quickly yanked the strings away.

"I am not wearing this! I don't care what the ladies of fashion do!"

What she hadn't expected was for her tutor to report Isa's obstinance to Ever. Sometimes it seemed no one could remember that she had just as much right to the throne as her husband did. His response, however, had been so enjoyable that it hadn't mattered.

"But all the ladies of the court are wearing it, Your Highness," Master Claude, her head tutor, had complained. "It will be expected!"

Ever had only rubbed his eyes. "Pray tell, what exactly are stays, Master Claude?" And so the tutor had brought forth the disagreeable contraption and had explained precisely how a fashionably tiny waist was gained. Ever's response, however, was not what the etiquette master had seemed to expect. The horror on Ever's face still made Isa smile when she remembered it. That anyone could be so daft as to restrain one's ability to breathe, much less run or duel, was beyond Ever, and Master Claude was instructed never to bring the matter up again. Gigi had taken over Isa's wardrobe soon after that, and to Isa's relief, the awful stays had never resurfaced. And yet, Isa thought with annoyance, the older woman's obsession with the see-through sleeves had brought her just one more way to stand out tonight.

"Are you nearly ready? They're beginning soon." Ever's voice came from the doorway.

"Almost," Isa called back, and for the hundredth time that day, resented the simplicity of men's fashions that allowed Ever to dress so quickly without assistance. Her vexation was slightly dulled, however, when she turned to catch him staring fixedly at her figure.

"First I need you to heal my ankle, then I need to talk to you." That broke his trance. A dark look came over his face as he went to her and bent to examine her ankle.

"Come sit." He drew up a chair.

"I stumbled in the practice room," Isa said carefully, doing as he'd directed and measuring his reaction. He didn't look up from her ankle, which he had laid in his lap. She waited for a moment as he twisted it gently in different directions, freezing when she winced.

"It's not broken," he said in a low voice. "How did it happen?"

"I'm not sure," she admitted. He raised his eyebrows skeptically, so she rushed to explain, hoping to avoid the overreaction she knew was highly likely. "I'd been practicing alone . . . and dancing some, when I stumbled and fell into a window pane." She glanced up at him again to see the blue fire blazing dangerously in his eyes, his lips mashed tightly together. "When I touched the glass, something touched me, as though it were trying to pull me into the window itself. It was a power somewhat like our own, yet different."

"Did it hurt you?" he asked in a flat voice.

"No, I only twisted my ankle when I stumbled. But it was strong. Perhaps . . ." she paused, knowing that what she said next could put her husband into one of his famous brooding moods, "stronger than Nevina's power."

A daring thought flitted across her mind. It was a subject she had long wished he would broach, but not a word had been said about her fledgling powers since they had begun to wane. It didn't seem to make a difference how many times she seemed to fail. Maybe, since they were in the right context now, she could finally draw out of Ever what he truly thought of her struggles. And even more, *why* he thought the fire was beginning to fade from her eyes.

"I can't help thinking," she whispered before her courage fled, "that I might not have fallen had my powers been stronger. What do you think?" She placed one trembling hand on his to stop him as he continued to test her ankle, and used the other hand to raise his face to hers. When their eyes finally met, she stared into his, praying he would see what she meant. That he would assure her everything would work itself out. Or even that he too was concerned, but they would overcome it. When he did speak, however, she found only disappointment crashing inside of her as her hopes were dashed to pieces.

"I think that we will be late if we do not hurry." Without another word, he placed his hands around her ankle. Blue fire briefly danced around it until he let go. Taking her hand and then placing it in his arm a little more firmly than necessary, he strode out the door, dragging Isa along with him.

He still hadn't spoken by the time they'd reached the stands, but Isa knew all she needed to know. He had seen her failure to grow, to thrive in her new position as queen, and the disappointment on his angular features was written as clearly as with parchment and ink. He also knew the fire in her eyes was fading. If he was disappointed in these things, how could she ever get him to share what was bothering him so with King Rafael? How could she prove she was worthy to know?

CHAPTER 14
ONE AND THE SAME

Disappointed with Ever's disappointment in her, Isa sighed and studied the stands around her. The stands themselves formed three quarters of a full grand arena, with the fourth side missing completely. The palace guests had already filled the majority of the stands by the time Ever and Isa were seated. The men elbowed one another and pointed at the gathered competitors at the bottom of the arena, while the ladies made faces at the biting wind that blew in from the northeast and mussed their hair.

For once, Isa was thankful to have been singled out as a guest of honor, for that meant being sheltered in a tent-like covered box in the center stands with the royal family. She slipped the princess a small smile, and to her delight, the girl sent her one back.

Princess Olivia had also changed since the tea, and was now dressed in a sunset orange gown that matched her mother's. Isa nearly smirked to herself. The princess put up a good show of being timid and submissive, but after watching her up close, Isa knew that whatever her fate, Princess Olivia was unlikely to go quietly.

The queen was busy chatting in low tones with one of her ladies-in-waiting, and the king was nowhere to be seen. Which reminded Isa, neither was her brother.

"Where is Launce?" Her question seemed to briefly pull Ever from his dark musing, enough for slight misgivings to flick across his face.

"He's with the other competitors."

Isa stared at her husband blankly for a moment before his words sank in.

"Wait, he is truly competing in the games?" Panic and anger filled her as she stared at Ever in disbelief. "He can barely lift a sword properly! You said so yourself! What in the blazes is he doing in the games?"

It was Ever's turn to look startled as the salty language fell from her lips, but at the moment, Isa didn't care. "Isa, others can hear you. Please keep your voice down. You heard the king invite him last night—"

"And I didn't think you would be foolish enough to allow it!" She wouldn't have cared if the whole kingdom heard her, except that she knew her words could affect Launce. "And I know this wasn't his idea!" she hissed. "Everard, if he gets himself killed out there for the sake of your curiosity—"

"The games are not designed to kill!" Ever raised his own whisper slightly in defense, and Isa sent him her most withering glare in response. Ever ran his hand through his hair, a sure sign that he felt guilty. "I'm sorry, Isa. But . . ." he paused and closed his eyes, as though admitting something against his will. Still, his words were slow, as though he were choosing them with great care. "Something is wrong, but I do not yet know what. I needed eyes in the stables. He's already gathered useful information. As soon as we know what Rafael is up to, I will pull him out." He finally looked at her directly, his gray eyes probing her for any sympathy she might harbor. "I promise."

Though the look he gave her threatened to soften her heart,

Isa couldn't quite voice forgiveness yet, or her blessing. If he would just tell her what was wrong, they might have avoided all of this. But for all the repentance in his eyes, Ever was clearly not ready to share all of his worries with her yet. Isa finally turned sharply to stare down at the competitors on their horses, searching for her brother. She couldn't find the Fortress's colors, and from a side glance at her husband, she knew he was thinking the same thing.

"So, Everard, are you ready to watch the Maker choose the heir to my throne?" the king's voice boomed and made Isa jump. Ever's only response was a grunt, but Rafael didn't seem to notice. Instead, he walked to the edge of the large wooden platform they sat in and made a flicking motion with his hand. In response, trumpets blared, and the chattering in the stands died.

"It's not every day that we get to see the Maker in action!" Rafael called out, his voice echoing through the arena. "But today we have one of the Maker's very own holy men to guide us through the journey of choosing my next heir, the future husband of this kingdom's precious flower, my daughter." He turned and threw Princess Olivia an adoring glance before turning back to the people.

"The contestants will be competing in three events. A joust, a melee, and the final contest, which will be announced at the end. The general regulations will take precedent in combat. May the Maker's man win."

The crowds roared as a herald announced the first contestants, and the king sat down with a thump in his chair between Queen Monica and Ever, a satisfied smile on his face.

"It seems you couldn't care less for the first two events," Isa heard Ever murmur to the king. "Usually you can't wait for the combat."

"And miss the fun of the holy man's challenge?" Rafael shook his head and clapped Ever on the shoulder. "Oh no, the first two events are merely children's play. The third event will truly tell me who the Maker has chosen."

"So my brother is fighting for no true purpose?" Isa blurted out, unable to conceal her disgust any longer. The king looked at Ever, his wide smile wavering on his face.

"Of course, it is important for me to see the combat skills of the future king as well."

Ever snorted at Rafael's mention of combat skills, and Isa took a deep breath to prevent herself from saying anything she might regret. The insincerity in the king's voice was thick, and Isa tried to satisfy herself with ignoring him and studying the competitors below.

Isa had never seen a tournament before. The Fortress never held them, not that she would have been important enough to watch one until recently. Still, she'd heard of the violence they often showcased. In Soudain, she'd had neighbors who traveled and witnessed them in other lands. The town boys would run through the streets reenacting scenes of bloody carnage as they pretended to run each other through with long sticks. As the first contest began, however, Isa realized with some relief that the boys had indeed been exaggerating.

"This is a joust," Ever leaned in to explain as the first round was begun. "There will be two men, one on each side of the divider. They will ride toward one another and each will attempt to knock his opponent from his hose. When a man falls from his seat, he is disqualified."

"This is ridiculous. I've never heard of anything so barbaric and pointless in all my life." Isa crossed her arms.

"They were once meant to help knights practice their battle skills, but I agree. To make them public makes light of war, which is why we don't host them at home. You need not worry though. They are not allowed any further combat besides the initial attempt."

"That doesn't guarantee someone couldn't make a killing blow."

"Their lances have been checked by the games keeper beforehand. Nothing sharp is allowed upon the field. This is simply a test of skill, to see who would be the victor in an actual battle." As Ever spoke, Isa grudgingly found herself slightly relieved that there were such rules. Still, the horses rode fast and hard, and even with the rules, the palace healer was called out onto the field often. Isa was thankful to see that Launce was not among the contestants during the first match. Not that it would make a difference when he fought. She didn't want him fighting at all.

Holding her breath, Isa suffered through joust after joust for Launce to ride out onto the field for his turn.

"Where is he?" Ever muttered. Just then, the herald paused as he read the names, looking confused.

"The next contestants are Josepha, Earl of Faunton of Giova, and . . ." He squinted at the parchment. "Armand."

Whispers moved through the stands. It was unheard of for a rider to list only one name. This contestant not only listed just a single name, but also claimed no place of origin, nor a family name. Just Armand.

Which happened to be Launce's second name.

Of the two men that rode out onto the field, neither wore the Fortress's colors. The first wore Giova's red and gold, but the other was dressed in the most peculiar armor Isa had ever seen. From Ever's expression, he thought it no less bizarre. The knight's armor, from head to toe, was made of a polished bronze, so bright it hurt to look at in the afternoon sun, and his horse was the largest and fiercest she had ever laid eyes on. Despite her anger, Isa was sure her eyes were failing her completely, so she leaned over and whispered to her husband, "Could that be—" Before she finished speaking, however, the knight in question fumbled his weapon so badly it fell into the mud.

"It is," Ever said, rubbing his temples in wide circles.

The copper knight now had the attention of King Rafael, who had until then been talking with the queen and ignoring the tournament in general.

"Who is this?" he asked Ever, his mouth falling open as he peered closer.

"He wears no kingdom's colors," Ever said, glancing at Isa. If the king had been paying attention, he might have realized that Launce was the only contestant who had not yet been announced, but from the way Ever had looked at her, it appeared that keeping this knowledge from Rafael would work best to Launce's advantage.

Isa's breath sped and anxiety made her stomach flutter as she watched the copper knight make his way to the end of his lane. Their mother would faint if she could see Launce right now. There was a reason her family had never apprenticed him out to the blade smith who had requested him as a boy.

As the signal was given, and the two opponents positioned themselves, Isa found herself fervently whispering prayers of Launce's preservation.

The signal was given. Launce's opponent sped forward, poised, sleek as a fish through the water as the two men approached one another. Launce sat straight up, and it was easy to see that he struggled to hold his weapon properly. As they raced forward, Isa fought the need to close her eyes.

The two met in the middle. Launce's opponent's weapon landed with a solid thud directly into Launce's chest. Isa cringed as his opponent's weapon splintered upon impact. Launce fell from his horse, landing on his shoulder at an awkward angle. He lay there for a long moment, but when he stood unevenly and limped off the field, Isa finally let out a sigh of relief and sat back in her chair, suddenly exhausted. She could hear the chatter around her begin about the unfortunate, unusual knight, as the king declared the winner, but she couldn't care less. He was alive, and that was all that mattered.

The next sport was ground combat with the sword, but instead of a duel between two men at a time, all of the contestants would participate at the same time, according to Ever. It was easy to pick Launce's bright copper suit out as the contestants tumbled around the ring. Isa sent up a prayer of thanks as Launce stayed near the outside of the ring, and the other competitors seemed to leave him alone. She wondered if they'd figured out early on just how helpless he truly was with a sword.

"If he would have just allowed me to train him, this might have turned out differently," Ever mumbled.

"My guess is that he had no desire to even be a part of this," Isa replied, pausing for Ever to challenge her assumption. But he did not. "So it should not matter whether he wins or loses."

"It doesn't," Ever said, "but he might have been a little less humiliated in the process."

To Isa's great relief, the king announced a winner soon after, and declared that it was time for the third and most important event. Guards herded the contestants out of the clearing, and the king raised his hands once again. Isa noticed a gleam in his eye as he spoke, one that seemed just a bit too bright.

"This will be the final and greatest challenge of them all! Three days, the contestants will have, to lay claim to my daughter's hand and to my throne. Three days and three of these!" He held up what three apples that appeared to be made of solid gold. "Whomever shall present me with all three of these apples, given by my daughter's hand, shall be my heir, chosen by the Maker.

"Before your eyes, you will see His hand working through the holy man as has not been done in thousands of years." Isa felt Ever stiffen beside her. His jaw was set like stone, and the gray in his eyes was nearly eclipsed by the blue flame that leapt inside them.

"Daughter?" Rafael held the three apples out to the princess. She paled a bit, but took them and gave a small curtsy before making her way down to the center of the clearing. It might have been Isa's heightened sense of suspicion, but the look of fear on the princess's face seemed no longer a mask. Princess Olivia looked terrified.

When she reached the center of the clearing, the princess just stopped and stood there. A tense, uncomfortable silence blanketed the stands for a long moment. Then, the ground began to quake. Women shrieked, and the men's hands went to their swords. The ground stretched, and with a sickening crack, a bump in the land began to develop. Isa watched the princess, wondering what insanity her father had bought into that would have him send his daughter into the center of this chaos. Still, the girl stood dutifully as the ground beneath her began to tear and swell.

Before she could whisper to him, to ask what was happening, a strange cold sensation crept through her. Quickly, she recognized the same feeling as the one she'd felt that morning when she'd touched the pane of glass.

The ground that should have separated with such violent shaking began to twist and turn, growing up, pushing the princess higher and higher with it. At first it was only a little mound, but within seconds, the mound was growing. As it moved upward and began to widen, the center began to darken into a deep blue. The higher the hill rose, the wider the blue spread, until nearly the entire mound was one solid heap. The grinding and cracking continued until it came to rest, nearly as high as the Fortress watch towers back at home. The mound had become a solid hill.

The newly born hill was so wide around that it nearly touched the lowest level of the stands. And at the top, the princess now sat, clutching her three golden apples to her chest.

"Is that . . . glass?" Isa whispered. Ever didn't answer. For the first time since she'd met her husband, he seemed just as confused as she was.

Rafael slapped Ever on the back and the gleam returned to his eye.

"You see, Everard. The Maker blesses *others* with wonders and signs too." He walked to the edge of the box once more and called out, hushing the fearful whispering of the spectators. "This is our sign that whomever can make it up to the top of the hill thrice will be our answer from the Maker, a sure promise to bless their union."

As he finished speaking, a flurry of sparkling light fluttered down upon the stands. The crowd exclaimed in delight as it floated down like little jewels in the sky. Isa felt Ever put up a shield around the two of them as the glitter came to rest on every surface, even the inside of their covered platform.

"You missed some," she told him wryly, brushing a few pieces out of his hair, only to realize she'd gotten some in her own eyes. From the way he was blinking, it appeared that Ever had done the same. Isa held her hand up when her eyes were clear, and examined it in awe. The sparkles looked like glass as well, but lacked the sharpness that Isa would have assumed them to have.

Instead of brushing the sparkling dust off like everyone else, the king was holding his arms out as he raised his face toward the sun. A smile spread upon his lips as he seemed to be whispering the words *thank you, thank you* to the sky.

Once the excitement over the glitter dust had settled, the contest was begun. The contestants were lined up outside of the arena, far enough away that their horses could gather speed for their attempts to ride up the hill toward the princess.

First up was a duke. He wore six feathers atop his helm, and when Isa asked Ever about their meaning, he scoffed.

"That's Duke Tareq. He's young, and after winning a few rounds of jousting in his own kingdom, has become convinced he's the Maker's gift to the world. He reeks of ale though, and would hardly give the princess a second look. He's usually too busy with the women from the back of the alehouse."

The duke's ride was dramatic, his feathers adding to the flare of his pose. For all the show he put into his speed, however, his horse only made it up the hill a few paces before sliding back down. It served him right though for all that pomp and show.

As the contestants continued to try their hands at winning the princess, it soon became evident that the first duke's fate would be the norm. One after another, they raced forward like dogs to prey, only to fall back down after a few steps. At least, Isa thought, Launce wouldn't be alone in his struggles here. He was a fair horseman. This time he might blend in with the other competitors in skill.

The sun was close to setting by the time Launce's turn arrived. Isa wondered if his placement was because he had come in last in everything else, or if he was simply too nice to shove his way to the top. Or because he was a commoner. Whatever the reason, Isa was glad it was nearly over. Her backside smarted from sitting for so long, and her stomach rumbled. She'd been too nervous to eat much when the midday meal had been brought out on platters.

The copper-clad rider sat astride his horse with nearly a pose of confidence. Beside her, Ever leaned forward in his chair as the signal was given, and just like the others, Launce raced toward the hill. The crowd had long ago also grown weary of watching riders. As the mysterious copper knight approached the princess, however, a hush fell upon the people.

As soon as the gigantic horse set a hoof on the hill, a slight ringing hit Isa's ears. The feeling of foreign power hit her once again.

To everyone's surprise, far beyond the initial steps of the other competitors, Launce didn't stop at the foot of the hill. Isa felt her mouth fall open as he ascended. Only when he was two thirds of the way up did the copper rider pause. Somehow, the princess had just enough time to snatch an apple from her lap and toss down it to him. Launce caught the golden apple and began his descent.

Instead of stopping at the bottom and returning to claim his first victory, however, the copper knight continued to race away from the hill, past the stables, and into the forest at top speed. Knowing Launce's aversion to crowds and attention, Isa might have considered his strange behavior understandable if it weren't for the one thing that was bothering her more by the second.

"Ever?"

"Yes?"

"Did you feel that?"

"Yes." He turned to look her in the eye. "Why?"

"Because that's the same power I felt this morning when I touched the window."

As soon as the words left her mouth, Ever stood. His jaw flexed and his right hand twitched. "Are you sure? It is exactly the same?"

"Absolutely." She paused, glancing around as the people surrounding them gossiped and tried to surmise who the mystery rider might be. "What do you think it means?"

"I don't know, but I shall certainly find out."

CHAPTER 15
LIKE MY FATHER

After the contest, Isa and Ever returned to their chambers to prepare for that night's banquet. Isa was strangely quiet as they readied, hardly even talking to Cerise. That was never a good sign.

To make matters worse, once they arrived, still without speaking a word to one another, Rafael's banquet lasted much longer than Ever had hoped. The king was clearly enjoying the talk brought on by the glass hill, and was basking in the attention, answering the same questions over and over again with vague, cryptic cackles that made Ever want to strike the man unconscious.

Isa was looking lovely, but miserable. Of course, that didn't stop him from noticing her. The dress she wore draped around her tall, slim frame like red wine spilling down a steep, tightly curved staircase, and the gossamer sleeves displayed her bare, lean muscled shoulders enticingly. On much more than one occasion throughout the party he caught highborn men staring unabashedly like unpolished village boys. One glare from him though was enough to send most of them scattering.

Isa seemed to notice little of it though. She'd spent the

whole evening at his side staring vacantly out at the other guests as they laughed and gossiped and drank. She plastered a smile on her face every time Ever introduced her to someone new, but none of it was real. Even her dancing was wooden.

"Isa," he finally leaned over to whisper. "Are you feeling well?"

"I'm fine," she answered too quickly. When he cocked his head, giving her a wry, knowing smile, she caved. "I'm concerned about Launce."

"Would you like to return to our room?"

Before she could reply, he could see the eager answer in her eyes, so he quietly excused them and escorted her back to their chambers, where he called her lady-in-waiting to attend to her before he returned. Given her distant mood all evening, she surprised him, however, with a request just as he was ready to leave.

"Can't you stay?" The misery in her plea was pitiful. Chagrin washing through him, he leaned down and stroked her hair once before shaking his head. As he stared into her eyes, simply retiring for the evening and spending it quietly with Isa suddenly sounded enticing, and he had to fight his own longing to do as she asked.

"I need to see what else I can learn about whatever strange power it is that's using your brother." He tried to soften his words so she wouldn't think he actually wanted to leave her.

"I thought we could do that together." Isa frowned. "That was actually what I had been hoping . . ." She let her words trail off though as she studied him, long and hard, and he wondered uneasily what conclusions her study drew her to. "Well, if you must," she finally finished, and with that she slipped into the bed. His hopes at being forgiven were neatly dashed when she curled into a ball on the far side of the bed. He did his best to noiselessly step out, but not before her near silent sniffles reached his ears.

Hot shame started along his back and arms and worked its way up his neck and face as he walked back toward the raucous party. For all of his power and riches, he couldn't grant this one simple request. *Or you won't grant it*, some part of his mind nagged at him.

Ever could count on one hand the number of times Isa had requested something of him since they'd gotten married. And her last request had been granted grudgingly at that, he thought with guilt, recalling how nervous she'd seemed as she'd suggested bringing Launce along. A far cry from the way he'd vowed to himself that he would keep her happy the day they were wed. To make matters worse, he got absolutely nothing accomplished, as Launce had returned to the stables before they had time to talk, and Rafael was too drunk to talk at all. The whole night was a waste.

If Ever hoped for anything different that night after he'd finally gone to bed, he did a fantastic job of dashing those hopes the next morning.

"Where are you going this early?" Isa stretched and yawned. It was hard not to see the dark circles beneath her eyes, despite the early hour at which he'd dropped her off the night before.

"I have some business to attend to." He paused, wondering whether if he told her any more, she would let him go without too many more questions. He decided it was worth a try. "I'm meeting with an ally who might have some insight into Launce's position."

"You mean you're going to meet with *her*, aren't you?" The way Isa's eyes narrowed for a moment, raking him up and down as though she could see through to his soul, was slightly frightening. She surprised him, however, by then hopping off the bed and moving to dress herself without even ringing for her lady-in-waiting. "I'm coming with you then," she announced as she began to pin up her runaway locks.

Despite his rush, Ever had to appreciate that Isa's status as queen hadn't ever gone to her head. Like him, she preferred escaping her servants and dressing herself as often as she could. Unfortunately, today was a day he couldn't afford the delay. Or the distraction.

"I want to hear what she thinks about this whole spectacle," Isa continued as she went over to the corner of the room and opened her wardrobe, staring at its contents, tipping her head to the side as she did. At first she chose a yellow dress, then a more practical brown one, perfect for riding. Ever inwardly berated himself for what he had to do next, particularly amid the stream of sweet and happy chatter she was somehow conjuring.

"I'm sorry, Isa." He took the dress from her hands gently and hung it back up in the wardrobe. Her expression immediately changed from amiable contentment to suspicion. "I need you to stay here where it's safe."

"You're just going to leave me here?" Out of the corner of his eye, Ever noticed her knuckles whitening as she held on to the mahogany wardrobe door. "No. No, I thought about it last night, and I decided that I need to help you with this. The Fortress didn't make me queen to sit idly in my room all day. Besides," the blue flames that had risen up in her eyes for just a moment lessened as she said in a more pleading voice, "I'll be with you. You can keep me safe."

"We'll be outside palace grounds, away from nosy ears. It would be more dangerous for you out there, even *with* me. I need you to stay here." And with that, he turned and began to walk toward the door.

"And who says I have to listen to you?" Isa shouted.

When Ever turned back to look at her in surprise, tears were streaming down her face, making the dark circles beneath her eyes stand out even more. For a moment, he was stunned. It didn't take long for anger and frustration to well up within him though as he stomped back over to where she stood with her fists clenched and trembling at her sides.

"What if I choose not to be treated like a commoner?" She held her chin high, and her eyes held his, defiant and provoking.

"I think you will listen to me because you know I am trying to protect you," he growled, glaring down at her willful expression. "And if it behooves me, I shall tie you to a chair if I must to keep you safe."

Shock slowly registered in her features, and she fell a step back. "You really don't think I can help you then?" Her voice shook so hard that it cracked, and so did his anger. Ever took a deep breath and closed his eyes.

"Kartek has been gifted from birth. I need her—"

"More than you need me. I understand."

"Now, Isa, that's not fair, and you know it!"

"You've made your point, Everard. Get on with it then and leave me alone." Isa slammed the wardrobe door so loudly it made the windows rattle. The red streaks in her hair stood out more prominently than usual as she threw herself down on the bed and crossed her arms.

Ever took in a deep breath before making his mind up about what to say. A million words of apology and regret coursed through his mind, the greatest of them being the truth. He hadn't expected such a reaction from Isa, not even in the slightest, and from the glower she was giving the ceiling, it was evident he had wounded her deeply. But the truth would hurt even more, he reasoned, and there would be no respite from it until he had things figured out.

"I'll make sure you get your meals," he said softly as he paused on the threshold. But he received no answer. She just lay there in her blue nightdress, her glare never once wavering from the ceiling. Sighing, he turned to go before stopping and adding one caution more. "Just don't touch the windowpanes."

"Someone is toying with my family." Ever glowered straight ahead as they walked. The red of the leaves waved to him, signaling like a ship in distress. There was no time though to bask in the unusually warm autumn sun or to enjoy the colors of nature that surrounded Rafael's palace. Ever could feel Kartek sending him a wary glance every few paces, but he ignored her concern. If Isa had been present, she would have teased him and called it his beastly brooding. A stab of guilt slashed at him, dangerously close to breaking his concentration. Isa would not be teasing him for a while if the words they'd just exchanged were any indication.

"Speaking of your family, where is your wife?" Kartek's low voice was smooth like oil, and the familiar cadence of it usually comforted him when she spoke. This time, however, it only worsened the guilt.

"In our chambers."

Kartek stopped walking and fixed him with a look of knowing disapproval.

"And did you leave her there by her choice?"

"I left her there for her protection," Ever huffed, exasperated with his friend, avoiding her gaze by staring over her head at the distant waves that crashed on the white beach.

"Everard—" she began in a chiding tone.

"You would have done the same for Unsu!"

"No, I would not have locked him in his room and left him there like a little boy. He is a man, and it would hardly be respectful of my husband for me to treat him as anything but a man." She raised her eyebrows as though inviting him to challenge her.

"You don't understand." Ever, still staring at the beach, suddenly felt very small. It was a moment before he could bring himself to say the next words, and they came out almost as a whisper. "Her powers are floundering." He paused, not wanting to utter any more. Saying them aloud suddenly made the truth seem more real. But aside from Garin, if anyone could help him, it would be Kartek. "The fire in her eyes burns a little less every day." He turned to her, hating the way his voice caught in his throat and made it warble. "You know what happens when our fires go out."

Kartek stared back at him for a long time. She no longer looked reproachful, just thoughtful.

"I cannot fully empathize with you, as Unsu's power is quite different from your wife's." Her lips curved up into the smallest of smiles. "With the exception of his love. Like Isa, Unsu is *good*. My husband has the heart of a thousand men. Still," she took a deep breath and resumed a grave expression, "have you spoken to her of your concerns?"

"Of course not!"

"And why is that?"

"She doubts herself enough already!" Ever ran his hand down his face, fatigue suddenly seeming to overwhelm him. He hadn't slept well in over a week. "She questions everything she does, from her posture to the way she speaks to the way she chews. I've tried helping her, teaching her to use weapons, something to build her confidence, but her strength just continues to stall." He let out a gusty breath. "On top of all that, the Fortress gossip is ripe with talk. I try to intercede when I can, but you know women's tongues . . ." He stopped himself when he remembered with whom he was speaking. To his surprise and relief, Kartek let out one of her deep, saucy laughs.

"I know a little of that." She continued to chuckle after she was done laughing. "It took me seven months after my marriage to conceive our first child. The women of our palace just knew I was barren." She patted her belly and raised her chin high. "Five children later, and the old toads have not gossiped in a long time! So yes, I know how terrible court gossips can be. Surely you at least warned her when you were on your honeymoon."

Ever shifted uncomfortably again. Time with his old friend was rare and precious, but like an older sister, from what he gathered of closely knit families, she knew just how to make him squirm like a punished puppy.

"In truth . . ." he gathered up his courage for the look she was sure to give him, "we never had one." When he finally dared to peek at her, the look Kartek was sending him wasn't quite as reproachful as he'd anticipated. It was worse.

"You did what?"

"We were going to go!" he hurried to assure her, but it didn't dull her cutting glare of disappointment.

"Let me guess. A war broke out. A famine struck the land. Some poor city was flooded. Everard, after seventeen years of marriage to a king, I can guarantee you this: something will always come. But you still cannot put everything above your queen!"

"I'm trying! The world just suddenly seems ripe with distractions."

"The distractions were always there. They always will be. The difference between then and now is that your father took care of them while he lived."

"He always knew what to do." Ever sank onto a fallen log on the side of the path, rubbing his temples and closing his eyes. "I just wish I knew how he did it all."

"It is quite simple. He left you and your mother behind. She was never allowed to share his burdens or know his heartache. And look at how that turned out."

Ever shook his head, staring morosely at the sand beneath his boots. "Isa worries about so much. I just wanted to let her be. I don't want to burden her with more than she's already struggling with." His jaw hardened as he remembered what she had told him the day before on the way to the events. "To make matters worse, she was attacked by the same source of power that created that spectacle yesterday.”

“The same?” Kartek quirked an eyebrow at him.

“In a pane of glass in the practice room.”

At his words, the southern queen fell silent, a dark look overshadowing her usually serene face. She stared out at the ocean, and it was a long time before she spoke again.

“I do not like this, Everard. I do not like it at all. It is too . . . familiar.” Ever nodded, hoping his friend would not continue to judge his actions too sharply now that she knew the foundation of his fears. “But it cannot be.” Her voice was a whisper. “It has been nearly three thousand years! Surely they could not have survived!” She shook her head again. “Rafael should know better, either way. Whatever this power is, it is no good. I can feel it. And its attack on your wife yesterday just confirms that.”

“I told you, someone is toying with my family. My wife is attacked inside our host’s home, and my graceless brother-in-law wins the first day’s competition with a horse and armor that aren’t his.” He paused before adding, “And all of it comes back to glass.”

“And you think keeping your wife locked up while you talk with me is the answer?” The sharpness of Kartek’s question took Ever by surprise. He stood and looked down into her deep honey eyes as they stared coldly up at him. “You are a fool, Everard, if you think walking and talking with me is going to save your wife while you hide her away. And if Unsu could have come on this journey with me, you know he would say the same!”

“I didn’t know who else to turn to!” Ever objected, hoping she couldn’t see just how badly she had wounded him. As she always did, however, Kartek seemed to sense just that. Her glare softened and she patted his arm as she gathered her thin, golden skirts and turned to make the walk back to the palace.

“I will consider this puzzle of glass you have presented me, but you are not a lost little boy anymore." She smiled at him affectionately. "And it is not my job any longer to find you someone to sit with at the banquet. I think your wife, however, will prove to be a great dinner partner. But first, you have to allow her to sit with you."

CHAPTER 16
THE WRONG COLOR

I'm not supposed to be here, you know." Launce's voice was sour. "The stable master forbade any of us from leaving the stables without permission once the events began."

"I am well aware of that." Ever kept his voice cool as he glanced at his brother-in-law. The young man was back in his village clothes, despite the perfectly good raiment Ever had sent down to him on the eve of the first contest. The dark circles beneath Launce's eyes mirrored those of his sister's from earlier that morning.

"I think you know just why I wanted to meet you though," he continued, before Launce could interrupt him again.

"She doesn't like that color."

"What?"

"Whatever you've done, Isa doesn't like orange. You're not going to win any affection back with that necklace."

The smug smile on Launce's face annoyed Ever more than words could express, but he took a deep breath and handed the piece of jewelry back to the stall owner. It pained him to admit that there were many things about his wife that he still didn't know, but it wouldn't do to make the situation worse.

"If I may be of assistance, Your Highness," the stall owner mumbled, a nervous, short man that reminded Ever of a hedgehog, "what color does she like? I have many stones of all different shades . . ."

Ever opened his mouth to answer, but stopped. Embarrassment flooded him as he struggled to answer. How in the heavens did he not know his wife's favorite color?

"She likes light purple."

Ever was both relieved and livid when Launce finally answered the merchant for him. The smile in the young man's voice was about more than he could bear at that very moment. Thankfully, the merchant held up a silver bracelet that was inlaid with lavender-colored roses that had been carved out of tiny purple garnets. When Ever grudgingly looked at Launce, Launce just shrugged and gave a half nod. At least Isa wouldn't hate it.

If there was one thing the merchants in Cobren excelled at over the ones in Destin, it was curating foreign wares. Though he had never been one for collecting baubles himself, Ever had never been able to stay away from the markets when he visited Cobren. When he was very young, he would beg his father to let him find gifts for his mother. As he grew older, and realized his chosen gifts were not to his mother's personal taste, after finding them all hidden away in a dusty box, he began instead to bring gifts to Gigi. Her reactions to his presents had been much more satisfying than Queen Louise's tepid acceptances.

Perhaps, he wondered now as he scanned the rows and rows of tents and stalls, he would bring Ansel the next time he came. Isa's father would have loved this. The bright colors of the foreign tents, the shine and sparkles of the wares, and the savory smells of the unfamiliar dishes being cooked up right in the square could easily overwhelm someone who tried to take it in all at once. Cobren was known far and wide for its exotic markets. King or not, Ever felt the burning desire to please his new in-laws. Perhaps it was because his own parents were gone, or maybe it was because they were the kind of parents Ever had always wished to have.

He paused at another stall. "What would your mother think of this?" He held up a thin copper ring, centered with a delicate green stone. Launce studied it for a moment before shrugging again and turning away, and Ever had to remind himself not to smile. He had finally succeeded in making Launce uncomfortable. Now he could begin his real work. "Speaking of shiny copper things," Ever began as he paid for the ring, "you certainly found yourself quite the new prizes."

"So you know about that." When he spoke this time, Launce stared at the ground, all bravado gone.

"And I find myself enormously curious as to what you have gotten yourself wrapped up in." They stopped at another stall. The owner held out a plate of small pieces of meat, no doubt anxious to test the generosity of one of the many kings present in the city. The bits of meat were nearly yellow, sprinkled with red spices and smelling strongly of bay leaves. Ever wasn't hungry, but he allowed Launce time to sample it and consider his response. After Launce had decided to buy himself a full leg of the bird, they continued their stroll, and the young man finally spoke between bites.

"How did you know?"

"Aside from the herald announcing a mysterious man with your second given name? There aren't enough contestants for you to lose yourself that easily." Ever tapped his temple. "And you forget that we're more acquainted now. It's easier for me to sense your presence. And your sister is even more attuned to you."

Launce's face crumpled, as though his turkey had turned sour.

"But that doesn't answer my question. What happened?"

"I don't see why it's so important!" Launce said. "Is it that shocking that I might actually be good at something?"

That was it. Ever was done with this foolishness. He took hold of the young man's forearm and dragged him past the lines of bright tents and a little ways into the forest the market bordered. Launce looked for a moment as though he might protest, but when Ever threw him his most dangerous look, daring him to make a scene, Launce complied, however unhappily. Once they were a ways into the woods, Ever left Launce standing at the center of a small clearing, where mottled sunlight filtered down through the trees. Ever stalked around the little circle, listening for curious busybodies that might be in the immediate vicinity, before returning to Launce and pressing in until they were at an uncomfortable proximity.

"Stop acting like a spoiled oaf! You are far too old to be playing these games! Isa was attacked yesterday, just before the competition!"

At these words, the rebellion drained from Launce's face.

"Was she harmed?"

"She only twisted her ankle. But a strange power is at work here, and your mysterious garb and horse last night aren't making it any easier for me to understand." Ever ran his hand down his face for what felt like the hundredth time that day. What he wouldn't give for a nap. He pulled in a deep breath, asking the Maker for some self-control, if nothing else. The world suddenly seemed much weightier than he had ever lifted, and the thread of patience that he struggled to hold on to on any given day was about to snap.

Launce was silent for a long moment, staring first at the blanket of moss beneath his muddy boots and then up at the sky that peeked through the thick foliage above. When he finally did speak, his words came out in uneven bursts, and his tone was at least appropriately disconcerted.

"After I talked to you yesterday, I did as you instructed, looking for anything that felt like power. It took me a while. For hours, I had nothing. Then I realized the entire stables were covered in a shiny dusting. So I decided to spend the evening on the stable roof where it was clear, so I could see what was happening."

"You didn't fall asleep?" Ever asked.

Launce shook his head. "I nearly did, I think because I must have still had the dust on me from inside the stable. But I guess I managed to shake enough off." He paused. "It was a good thing I had, because the earthquake was much stronger on the roof than it had been in the stable. I nearly lost my balance and rolled off, but managed to cling to the roof tiles, pulling myself just to the edge.

"When I looked down to see the guard, however, I realized the shaking wasn't an earthquake at all, but a horse, larger than any I had ever seen, charging up the path from the thin forest that surrounds the palace. The closer it got, the harder its hooves pounded the ground. Every jolt moved the stable like a wave crashing upon the side of a ship. It was all I could do to hold on to the roof tiles.

"The horse came to a stop before the new guard. The guard seemed nearly frightened out of his mind, and kept waving his sword at the horse. Stupid fellow thought he might stand a chance against the beast." Launce paused and looked up at Ever, for once, without resentment in his face. "King Rafael doesn't spend much time training his men with horses, does he?"

Ever nearly smiled. "No, but it's something I've advised him to do a number of times." How many times had the two men had that conversation? But no matter how much Ever chided, Rafael would remind him that wrestling was their national pride. A lot of good that would do them against enemies with swords and bows. But Ever hadn't come out to think about Rafael's wrestling army. "Go on," he told Launce.

"The horse kept rearing, slicing the air with his hooves, each movement bringing them closer to the guard's face. I was trying to think of a way to save him, but before I could come up with one, a particularly hard slam of the hooves sent me sprawling off the roof, right next to the guard.

"He screamed at me to run, holding his sword as high as he could between himself and the horse. I told him to lower his sword, but I couldn't help, as the horse kept pounding the ground too hard for me to get up. He told me that I was insane, but when the next hoof barely missed his head, he finally listened." Launce gave a distant half smile.

"'If I die, my blood will be on your head!' he told me as he put it down." Launce looked at Ever, just a glimmer of resentment in his eye his time. "I may know little of swords, but horses . . . I know horses." Ever was aware of this. It was the reason he'd never added horses to the practices during the few days Launce had agreed to train with him. But for the first time, Ever wondered if perhaps it might have been better for Launce to have had the chance to perform well in at least one arena.

"When the horse quit bucking quite so hard, I held a hand out low and began to whistle a soothing tune that my horse at home enjoys. Slowly, I crept toward the animal. It took me forever, but he finally let me touch him just between his shoulder and neck. When I did, the horse shuddered a bit, but let me continue to rub him. I rubbed until I thought my arm might fall off. When I'd made my way down his back though, I realized his saddlebags were full." Launce frowned at this and paused, as though what he was about to say troubled him.

"And?" Ever prodded, trying not to sound too impatient. He had to go soon to meet with Rafael's soldiers, but Launce suddenly seemed lost in his own world. At Ever's prodding, he gave himself a little shake, but when he spoke, his words were still slow.

"A note fell out of the saddlebags. It said, 'Job well done. This horse is now yours. Treat him well, and he will carry you to your first victory.' When I looked in the saddlebags they were full of the armor."

"And let me guess," Ever said. "The same thing happened again last night." A look of surprise and then annoyance flashed across Launce's face.

"Silver this time," was all he said.

Ever studied him for a moment, trying to quell the maelstrom of questions that swirled in his head. Something was still missing. There was a piece of this puzzle that had been lost, or stolen, rather, but Ever wasn't sure who held it. To be sure, Rafael was teeming with secrets. But had Launce told Ever all that he knew? Did he really grasp the danger of the situation? Ever doubted it.

"How did you keep the other competitors from knowing your identity in the copper suit?"

"They couldn't care less about me, for the most part," Launce said. "I didn't show anyone the armor. Only the guard knew of the horse, and I swore him to secrecy with a few coins. I dawdled until everyone else was lined up and ready, and went into the woods where I'd tied the horse." His dark eyes tightened. "You don't want me to compete tonight, do you?"

"Actually," Ever chose his words carefully, "I think you should. It can't be an accident that your sister was attacked, and you were gifted a monstrous horse all on the same day. We need to know more about this entity. But," he leveled his sternest look at his brother-in-law, "you must take care."

"So you worry about me then?" Launce's eyes glinted mischievously in the yellow sun that slipped through the trees.

"I worry about myself," Ever responded dryly. "Your sister will have my hide if something happens to you. I would like to make it home in one piece." Ever had begun to make his way back to the edge of the woods toward the noise and bustle of the market, when Launce called out one more time.

"Everard?"

"Yes?" He paused, looking over his shoulder. Launce had begun to follow him, but stopped several paces back, all signs of mirth gone from his thin face.

"I don't know if it makes a difference, but the undersides of both saddles, as well as the bottoms of the horse shoes, are made of glass."

Ever had to use every ounce of his self-control to keep himself from sprinting to the palace. He and Rafael needed to talk.

CHAPTER 17
WISDOM OF KINGS

So who is this famous holy man that has such a talent for glass architecture?" Ever nocked an arrow as he awaited Rafael's response. He worked hard to appear casual after finding out about the glass in Launce's mysterious gifts.

"So that's why you dragged me out here." Rafael shook his head as he nocked his own arrow. "I knew it couldn't be simply for old time's sake."

"You know me too well for that."

"I suppose I do," Rafael sighed as they nudged their mounts into the shadowy greens of the woods.

The horses obeyed, but moved along at a leisurely pace, not suitable at all for hunting. This was fine with Ever, as he had no intention of actually hunting with the king. He simply needed to get Rafael alone. Hunting was merely the invitation that was sure to draw the king from his courtiers.

"You never had fun much as a youth either. You spent enough time in my courts disconcerting the men and driving the girls mad by refusing to look at them."

Ever snorted. "It's not practical to woo women when a rebel is lurking in every corner, waiting to kill you."

"'Tis true, but you have a way of unnerving people, Everard. And you know it. In fact, you're doing a wonderful job of it now. Have you forgotten completely how to smile? Half of my servants are terrified of you, and I'll wager at least half of the guests."

At this, Ever allowed himself a small grin. That had been his plan precisely. "Your court needs a bit of fear driven into it. Everyone is too complacent, including you."

"And you blame all of this on my holy man?" Rafael pulled his horse to a halt and looked directly at Ever. The breeze moved through the trees in quick darts and whirls, trying to find a way through Ever's cloak to warn him that winter was fast approaching.

"I simply do not see how you can trust him so implicitly after such a short period of time. The message you sent before last seemed as though all was proceeding as usual. Why the sudden change in allegiances?"

"There is no change in allegiance, Everard." Rafael shook his head and nudged his horse forward again at a slow pace. "And the holy man has been here for quite a while. I have gotten to know him well. Besides . . ." Rafael looked at him again, but this time, a strange gleam came to his eye, the same maddening look he'd worn since they'd first arrived. "He has shown me many signs. Too many to ignore."

"I could show you signs, and I'm no holy man. Even such," Ever said, fixing the king with his most intense stare, "don't his signs remind you of a certain dangerous character?"

"Rubbish!" Rafael waved him off, but refused to meet Ever's eyes. "He's been dead for three thousand years. Just because one enchanter used glass doesn't mean no one else can ever touch it. Now, are we going to hunt or not? We haven't even left the path yet, and my wife is expecting me back for the midday meal."

Frustrated, but knowing he would get no further at that

moment, Ever nodded, and they turned their horses off the trail.

Ever heard the arrow before he could see it. With a sharp crack, it hit the tree behind them, missing Rafael's neck by inches. Rafael's horse reared, but Ever's had been seasoned with more battles than he could count. Another arrow missed Rafael as he tried to get his steed under control, this time it came from further to the left. While Rafael continued to wrestle with his horse, distant hoof beats told Ever all he needed to know. With just a touch to his horse's sides, he and his beast were off in pursuit.

Ever laid low so the trees wouldn't hit him as they sped through the woods. It wasn't long before Ever's horse snorted. Ever gave him the lead, knowing he would follow the scent much faster than Ever could track by sight. Soon, the rear hooves of their prey's ride came into view. It was a gray steed, and blended in well with the surrounding forest.

They moved up and down hills, and even forded a small creek before Ever was able to come up alongside the attacker. Anger coursed through him as he caught sight of the man's saddlebags. Seeing the familiar red crest was like being thrust back into his youth, when he had chased hundreds of the separatists from the Cobrien borders with his father.

Yanking his sword out, Ever pointed it at the horse, hoping not to spook the animal too badly, just to bring him to a halt. It was the rider he was interested in. Blue fire gathered around his forearm, swirling about it briefly before shooting down the tip of his sword and into the beast itself. It let out a whinny of pain as the blue fire engulfed it. The encounter was brief, lasting only long enough for the horse to stop so quickly its rider fell off. Once it was free, the beast trotted off, completely unscathed. Ever couldn't say the same would happen for its rider. Without pause, he was off his horse as well, crouching over the man and pressing his sword into the man's neck.

"Who sent you?"

"I act alone!"

"You're lying."

The man started to protest again, but stopped when the blue flame returned to Ever's hand, the one that held him down. The man's eyes grew wide as it flowed and swayed in place. Ever leaned down to whisper in his ear, "As you can see, my fire doesn't burn unless I tell it to. It can, however, leave a dastardly stinging sensation."

The man's cry was loud, and long enough that Ever hoped it would change his mind about his next answer. "Now, who sent you?"

"I... I was paid!"

"By whom?"

"You saw my crest! Who else?"

Just then, Rafael rode up, flanked by a dozen of his guards. "I see you haven't lost your touch."

"And I see you have." Ever sheathed his sword as the guards gathered up the unfortunate young man to take him away. "You've gotten fat, Rafael. And slow."

"We can't all be you or your father, Everard," Rafael sighed.

"Does this happen often?"

Rafael shrugged and made an impatient gesture with his hands. "The rebel attacks resumed not long after you and your father returned to Destin."

"Why didn't you say anything?"

Rafael shrugged. "They were very few for a while. But they've been steadily increasing in number."

Ever stayed quiet as he swung back onto his horse, and they began their trek back to the palace. Rafael spoke again, and for the first time his voice was tired, void of the jovial sound he'd kept since Ever had first arrived. His large frame sagged, and the wrinkles at his eyes seemed to double.

"Do you see now why I need someone here though? I appreciate your help. I always have. But you cannot be here all the time to rescue me." Rafael pulled at his beard as he stared out ahead. "I need someone here who can do more than I. I might be fair at trade, but we both know I was never that strong."

Ever didn't answer at first. What Rafael said was true. In fact, it was probably the first sincere admittance Ever had heard since arriving. Still, a needy king only made the situation direr, riper for an intrusion, and Ever had yet to find out who exactly had come to the king's aid, claiming to be a holy man with signs, no less. "Have my years of friendship at least equaled a sign in merit to you?"

Rafael turned and gave him a weary smile. "What is it you want, Everard?"

"Let me meet him. At least let me get to see him face to face."

"Very well. Tomorrow, after the games are done. Meet me at the naval dock."

As Rafael said the words, a huge weight was lifted from Ever's shoulders. He finally had an end in sight. The sooner he could see this mystery solved, the better. They could go home, and he could care for Isa the way she deserved.

The two kings rode in silence for a few moments, the only sound the crunching of dead leaves under their horse's hooves.

"Perhaps," Rafael finally said in a soft voice, "you will allow me more grace when you have a child of your own, one whose future depends solely on your strength and wisdom. Then, maybe, you will not judge me so harshly."

CHAPTER 18

BOY INSIDE THE MAN

The rap on the door startled Isa so much that she jumped, not enough to fall over, but enough for the unruly fire she'd been attempting to wield to shoot off into a ceramic vase on one of the bedside tables. The crash felt loud enough to wake the entire palace.

"Your Majesty?" Norbert called through the thick wooden door. "Are you well?" It was a moment though before Isa could gather her dignity enough to answer.

"Well enough. What do you need?"

"Queen Kartek of—"

"Send her in." Isa knew she was being more than rude, but she'd had about all she could take of the southern queen. Isa had been grateful for her rescue on the night of the first ball and the queen's kindness at the tea, but Ever's constant talk of his old acquaintance was grinding on her nerves. Then the pointed looks he and Kartek had sent one another over supper the night before, and finally, his abandonment of Isa for their meeting had been too much. She was on the verge of telling her husband that if he was so impressed with the queen, he should volunteer to be one of her servants.

As she bent down to pick up the larger shards of the vase, Norbert opened the door and the southern queen glided in.

Even without looking at Kartek, jealousy filled every cranny of Isa's being. The woman was everything she was not. The natural ease with which she kept her posture, the confidence in her stride, and the calm intelligence of her dark eyes as she took in everything around her, including the unseemly mess Isa was attempting to pick up, were flawless. It was this kind of perfection that Ever and the rest of the Fortress staff kept pushing her toward. And she was failing at every turn.

"Pardon me," Isa managed to mumble as she shuffled the broken shards on the floor, anything to keep her from having to make pleasant conversation. If this wasn't the most uncomely way to welcome another regent, Isa couldn't imagine what was. To her surprise, however, she felt the queen kneel beside her and silently begin to gather the shards as well. The clinking of the white-blue pieces quickly grew too loud for Isa to bear though. She had to say something.

"My maidservant wanted to visit the market, so I let her go."

"And you chose to pass the time trying to escape."

When Isa looked at the queen, Kartek wore a knowing look, and Isa felt her face redden. She finally sighed, not yet able to enjoy her guest's company, but tired of being contrary. She already had enough annoyance stored up for Ever to last the rest of the trip and longer.

"He sealed the lock so that only Norbert's key or he himself can open the door. I was trying—ouch!" Bright red blood ran down Isa's thumb, thanks to a particularly sharp piece of porcelain. She reached down to her skirt to pinch the throbbing cut, but Kartek was quicker. She grabbed Isa's hand and gently but firmly held her own index finger over the wound. To Isa's amazement, a soft pink glow emanated from between their hands where they touched, and even though Isa knew the cut had been deep, the pain lessened until it was gone. Kartek examined Isa's thumb before releasing her.

"Everard probably told you, but my gift is healing."

"No," Isa said, her voice suddenly tight. "He didn't tell me."

Without word, the queen gently took Isa by the shoulders and led her to sit on the bed. "Your power is being tainted by your frustration."

"You can sense that?"

Kartek smiled wryly.

"I may have a different kind of power, but I can sense yours. And your power is troubled."

Isa shrugged helplessly. "I am at my wit's end. I don't know how to wield this power. I don't know how to be the queen Destin needs. I can't ask Ever for help because he's never around. I mean, he trains with me, and I know he can see it as well as I can, and yet he says nothing. He refuses to talk about it even when I bring it up." Isa stopped, unsure of how much she should share with this woman she barely knew. Although, she reasoned, she'd already allowed her into their chambers, and Ever followed the woman around like a drooling puppy. If something happened, she could blame him. Besides, she really did want to talk to someone about what was happening to her.

"I thought the power was supposed to be mine. I thought that as the queen, it was my right. But it stagnates, and I cannot master it." Isa paused. "Still, I could live with that, if it weren't for my eyes."

"Your eyes?"

She looked her guest directly this time so Kartek could see the proof. "I think I'm dying, Kartek. My eyes haven't burned brightly in months. And if I am dying, I have to wonder if it's my fault, if I'm neglecting some part of my duty that just can't be neglected any longer."

Minutes of silence passed after she spoke. Kartek's face was somber, her golden eyes distant as she stared at the window. Isa stood restlessly and walked the full length of their chambers, wondering why Ever couldn't have locked her somewhere else, like in a garden. The space was decently sized for guest chambers. Not as large as the Fortress's, perhaps, but long enough to fit two rooms, the one they slept in with the bed, bedside tables, a desk, its tall, blocky wardrobe, and a small, round table with two spindly chairs. The other room was where Cerise slept on her pallet. Isa had left that room unexplored, as she knew from childhood that Cerise liked her privacy.

"I wish I could help you," Kartek finally spoke in a husky voice.

"Have you ever had problems with your power?" Isa blurted out.

A small smile formed on the queen's cinnamon lips. "I did. They were different from yours, but . . ." She chuckled a bit. "They had everyone in my palace wondering what kind of joke the Maker was playing on them. I was sixteen when I became queen. My parents were killed in a carriage accident, and I was their only heir." Kartek looked down at the intricate blanket she sat upon and absently fingered the deep red silk that had been embroidered into it. The pattern wove in and out of itself to form desert roses, the kind that filled every corner of the city streets beneath them.

"My healing power had manifested when I was twelve, which is late by my family's standard. Most queens' power shows by the time they are ten."

"How did your family receive the power?"

"Our gift is not as old as that of your Fortress, but it is old enough. My ancestor was a wealthy woman. Jal was her name. She lived in a lovely home beside an oasis in the middle of a wide desert. It was a grand house, one her parents had paid to have built, purchasing the materials from many distant lands. Great columns made up the face of the home, which was all white plaster, and windows upon windows filled every wall. Jal could look out upon the duned desert that surrounded her, and the oasis which lay before her home. Dates grew wild, and her garden prospered, despite the harsh, sandy winds that threatened to tear the produce from the ground. People would come from far and wide to visit her oasis, as water was scarce for miles around. Over time, people began to stay and make their homes near hers, and she became the caretaker of the little village that grew.

"On the seventh year after the village was planted, famine struck, and even the oasis became dry. Jal had to let her servants go, though it pained her to lose them. They were as family to her. She also encouraged people to leave the town to find water elsewhere for their families. Some refused to go, or rather, they could not go. Too old and frail to make the journey to the next oasis, or too young and delicate. In order to keep them fed, Jal began to sell her lavish possessions to passing caravans in order to purchase food and water for the stragglers, but soon even all the possessions of her many-roomed home were gone. All except for her most prized possession.

"Jal's mother had given her a family heirloom, a jewel that had been passed down through the families that lived in the long, white-walled mansion in the desert." At this, Isa realized Kartek was fingering the jewel at her own neck. A deep pink, the jewel was round, nearly the size of a grape, embedded in a disk of gold that had the thickness of Isa's thumb. Kartek nodded.

"She had managed to get all of the families to leave with the exception of one, but the last family could not go. A young widow had just given birth to a daughter, and without her late husband, she was not healed enough to make the journey. Jal was torn. She did not want to leave her family home, but she could not watch the young woman and her child die. So with great sorrow, she told the first merchant who came their way that she would give him her jewel if he would take the three of them as far as the next city. The man agreed, and at the end of the four-day trek, true to her word, Jal handed over the jewel.

"When she did, however, the man smiled and said, 'You have given everything to care for those who had nothing. The Maker has seen fit to test you, to see whether you are ready to lead many, many more than you have yet. And you have passed His test. By this time tomorrow, you will have back all you lost and more.'

"True to the caravan driver's word, she went to sleep in a poor house that night with the young woman and her child, and awoke the next morning back in her palace home by the oasis. But instead of the small, empty village she had once over-seen, an entire city was stretched out before her door, and the oasis was once again filled with life. The young widow's husband had been returned to life, and all of Jal's beloved servants were home once more. Even the jewel was returned. It has been passed down through every daughter in the line since."

"How did she find out she could heal?" Isa asked.

"The young widow had experienced great pain during her birth, and it did not go away after they left the oasis. In fact, she grew worse, nearly delirious. Before they went to sleep in the poor house that night, Jal helped the young woman lay down on her pallet. As soon as she touched her, the young woman was healed. And so it has been ever since for the women in my family."

"Is every firstborn child a girl in your line?" Isa couldn't help asking. Kartek nodded.

"Just as the Fortress kings always sire boys first, my line gives birth to girls. It is only the women in our family who have the healing powers, never the men."

"I wish . . ." Isa began, but did not finish the thought, just let the words hang in the air like the last leaves of autumn. What she wished would never be accomplished by wishing.

"Isabelle," Kartek's voice grew stern, "there is something you need to know about your husband."

Isa felt her throat tighten. For some reason, it felt shameful to have another woman telling her things about her own husband that she should have already known.

"I am sure you know what Ever's relationship with his parents was?" Kartek raised a dark eyebrow. Isa nodded, so the queen continued. "Good. Then you should also know that his father's determination to raise him as superior to his royal peers meant he was alone much of the time, even on the few occasions that he was surrounded by other children. His unusual strength only made their differences that much greater. I tell you this so you will know just how desperate he is to protect everything he has been given.

"Your husband, for all his faults, is one of the Maker's most loyal creatures, and he loves you with a potency that even he cannot understand. He is terrified to lose you, and if he does not gain control of his fear, I am afraid he might do something dangerous and irreversible in the wake of his determination. Everard is a good man, but a dangerous one as well. You cannot allow him to think he will solve this quandary alone, because he will do so by any means necessary. He needs you to balance him, to temper him."

But Isa was already shaking her head. "He won't let me in. I've tried! He refuses to even tell me what has him on edge here in Cobren."

"Then that, my queen, is the puzzle you must solve. There is a reason the Fortress did not leave him alone. Unbridled, he will destroy himself in his attempts to right the wrongs of the world. Your duty as queen is to be the partner he needs. You must find a way to save him from himself."

"But my power is failing," Isa protested. "How do I stop him?"

"That is your duty to find out. The Fortress queens have not always been weak as Ever's mother was. They had their own difficult choices to make. You are no different." With that, Kartek stood, her colorful wrapped skirts swishing lightly around her legs in the process. Just as she raised her hand to rap on the door to let the guard know she was finished, Isa had to ask her the question that had been burning inside of her for months.

"I know you spoke with Ever this morning. Does he think that I can do this? Master my power and fulfill my role as queen?"

"That is something you will have to ask him," Kartek said slowly. As she left the room, her footsteps echoing down the stone hall, a chill moved through Isa.

That was exactly what she was afraid of.

CHAPTER 19

A MIDDAY MEAL

Isa was still mulling over what Kartek had told her when another knock sounded at the door.

"Midday meal for the queen!" a lilting voice sang out. Despite the many, varied accents Isa had heard at the palace during the last few days, Isa knew this one immediately. Sure enough, Norbert opened the door to let in Brokk, who was carrying a covered silver platter.

"Your husband notified the kitchen that the queen was in need of some food."

"Thank you, Brokk. That is very kind of you." Isa wasn't particularly hungry, nor was she really in the mood to entertain more company, but the servant's presence lit up the place like a chandelier. As he placed the platter on the table, he glanced about the room.

"Are you not getting a bit bored in here?"

Isa let out a burst of laughter. "Yes, but ..." She paused, not knowing how much to say about Ever's orders. As much as she resented them, it felt risky to make the world privy to their personal disagreements. Brokk seemed to understand, and to her surprise, looked remorseful.

144

"I fear I am not a very good servant. I tend to put myself up on a pedestal where I do not belong, with the palace guests as equals. But may I let you in on a little secret?"

Amused, Isa nodded. While Brokk certainly didn't act the part of a typical servant, she rather preferred his little quirks. It was nice to have a friend somewhere in this new, unfriendly world.

"I have only been serving here for a little while," Brokk said with an unreadable expression. "And I don't plan on continuing for very long, either."

"You sound as though you're on a quest." Isa smiled. A sad half grin crept up on one side of the older man's mouth, and suddenly, his typical joviality was all gone.

"I guess I am."

"What for?" Isa leaned forward, all thoughts of the meal nearly gone.

Brokk hesitated, throwing a slightly nervous glance at the door.

"Please," Isa pressed, suddenly in great need of a distraction from the tumult of her thoughts. "If they say anything, I will explain that you were assisting me."

His eyes crinkled kindly at the corners and he nodded. "Very well. But please sit and eat at least."

Sighing, Isa did as he asked. As soon as she was comfortable, and her steaming platter of chicken, seasoned corn, and rice was served, Brokk settled himself across from her as she ate.

"I was even a bit younger than you when my path to this end was set, and I met the girl of my dreams. Her name was Agatha." His voice was low, and the expression on his face affectionate, as though he saw her even now before him. "I was much younger back then, but I sometimes still awaken in the night, and it feels as though she could still be beside me." He stood mostly straight, but bent just enough to lightly twist the hem of his green uniform, and the troubled creases that filled his face made him look suddenly much older.

"Agatha was from another province. But she was so lovely, with skin nearly the color of milk, and eyes almost as dark as the night." He paused before adding, "It wasn't long before I'd begged her to marry me."

"What happened?"

"It's rather uncomplicated. A sickness swept the land. Thousands died." He sighed. "She succumbed after weeks of fighting, much longer than most other victims had to suffer. But she was determined ..." He suddenly had to clear his throat.

"I'm sorry," Isa breathed. She looked down at her picked-at plate, wishing she could help. It felt so wrong to see Brokk's sunny face so full of sorrow. Before she had time to say anything else, however, the door swung open, and Ever strode in, carrying a full plate of food.

"I brought you lunch—" Ever stopped, unhappy surprise registering on his face when he saw Brokk.

In that moment, Isa realized that someone had lied. Ever hadn't sent Brokk with her meal. Someone else must have sent him. But who would lie about her lunch?

"Thank you, Brokk." Isa hurried to put the cover back on the platter, and shoved it all back into Brokk's hands. The servant took the hint, and after bowing to both of them, quickly excused himself from the room. As much as Isa wanted to know about Brokk's quest, she knew the look in Ever's eye only too well. Ever didn't say a word, just watched every move the servant made.

As Brokk left, Isa closed her eyes and inhaled deeply in order to calm herself. This was not a good way to start the conversation they needed to have.

After he was gone, Ever thrust the plate he held onto the little round table.

"You could have been a little nicer to him," Isa huffed. "He was only trying to help."

"The second competition will start soon," he muttered, ignoring her objection. "Where's Cerise? You need to be ready."

"I let her have a day in the town," Isa said. She went over to the wardrobe and began to go through her clothes for lack of something better to do as she tried to find the words she needed to say.

She had been so angry that morning when he'd locked her in her room. She'd contemplated every possible way to communicate her fury, everything from shouting to ignoring him completely. But when Kartek had come and shared his story, a bit of compassion had seeped into her. *Forgive him*, a voice in her head whispered. *He's just trying to protect you.* Unfortunately for that voice, however, every brusque word he uttered, and every abrupt move he made, made forgiveness just that much more difficult. Nevertheless, Isa took a breath and searched for words.

"Thank you for bringing me something to eat."

"What? Oh, you're welcome." He was still glaring at the door as she pulled on a more practical dress for the outdoors. When he ran his hand down his jaw as he spoke, Isa knew immediately that it had been the wrong thing to say. He turned to glare at her. "Isa, what were you thinking?"

"What do you mean?"

"Inviting someone in when I specifically wanted you to stay here alone? What good is it being hidden if you invite the world in?"

"He was told that I needed a midday meal!" Isa felt the anger stir within her once more. "How was I supposed to know you were going to bring me something? I assumed you were the one to send him!"

"I certainly did not send him! Why would I send strange

men into our room after you were attacked?" Ever stopped, his eyebrows going up. "Who sent him?" he asked in a deadly tone.

"He didn't say! And I'm not a child, Everard! You can't dictate my every word and move!" Isa's resolution to forgive him dissolved as she held his furious glare, which grew only more intense when she used his full name.

"I will do whatever I have to—" he stopped, and cocked his head. It only annoyed Isa more when she realized he was hearing something she couldn't, something she *would* have heard had her powers been working properly. "We need to go," he said finally. "It's almost time."

Isa fumed as she struggled to pull on her dress. Despite it being less complicated than most of the gowns Gigi had sent her, she still needed Cerise to close the back. But Cerise wasn't there.

"Then I need you to help me with this," she spat out. With a huff, Ever stomped over to help her, but she could feel the tension rolling off of him as he did. "We will finish this conversation later," she added icily, spinning around to glower up at him when he was done. Ever said nothing, just turned and walked to the door. Isa followed, swearing to herself that he wouldn't get off that easily. They *would* talk about this.

Ever paused at the door and fixed a withering look at Norbert. "I will have a word with you later."

Isa tried to throw the guard a look of pity as she scurried after her husband. It wasn't Norbert's fault she'd let the servant in.

As they walked down the halls, she realized she was still quite curious as to what he had been up to all day. His visit with Kartek had obviously not lasted the whole time that he was gone. Isa found herself nearly skipping to keep up with Ever as he stormed towards the outdoor arena. She would have to be quick, before other ears were near enough to hear them.

"What did you find out?" She pitched her voice as low as

she could. If she caught him off-guard, maybe he might let her in and tell her the big secret he was consumed by?

He waited so long to respond that it didn't seem as though he would answer at first, but just as she was adding this to her list of grievances, he said, "I got Rafael to agree to introduce me to the holy man tomorrow after the final contest." And for the first time that afternoon, Ever turned to look at her with something not akin to anger or frustration. Instead, he seemed to be measuring her response. "And I wouldn't be shocked if your brother ends up next in line for the Cobrien throne."

CHAPTER 20

SILVER

Launce tried to relax his taut muscles as he waited, imagining each one a piece of leather that was strong and supple. Though the humongous beast he sat astride seemed to obey well enough, every horse could feel fear, and that was the last thing he wanted as they prepared to climb the hill, which somehow looked twice as tall today as it had the first day.

The decision to ride under his second name had been, if he was honest, made on a whim. It wasn't as though he was doing anything wrong, he'd told himself as he'd written his second name on the herald's parchment. If through some fluke, he won, everyone would all know who it was in the end. But just this once, just for a few days, Launce would be riding as his own man. Not the Destinian queen's pathetic little brother, and not The Commoner. The moment Launce had seen the beautiful red of the copper suit shining up at him in the moonlight, he had known it was meant for him and him alone. For just a short time, he would be the mysterious copper-clad knight.

Blanchette might regret her choice if she could see him now. Not to say that keeping the secret had been easy. In order to ensure himself the most privacy, he'd slipped the herald a few coins so that his name would be last for each contest. As soon as each event had finished, he had raced into the edge of the forest, where he'd first hidden his new steed and suit of armor, and waited for his next turn. No one had thought to follow him, and it had given him time to marvel over the beauty of the gifts he'd been given.

The armor was surprisingly light, and to his relief, Launce was actually able to put it on himself. He would have needed help from a servant with the armor Everard had given him. The strange horse *had* made him a bit nervous. Launce was certainly good with horses but, he reminded himself, this was the beast who had very possibly brutally trampled seven guards to death.

After sending up a prayer to the Maker, Launce watched from the edge of the wood until it was his turn. His new beast had stamped around, impatient to let go and run, but Launce delayed each time until the very last minute. For the third event, he waited even longer, until the herald was looking confused. One touch to the animal's sides sent him shooting out of the forest, straight for the hill.

Launce still couldn't believe he had actually made it even partially up the hill. During his preparations, he had noticed that the horse's shoes were not metal, but glass, just like the lacy underpart of the saddle that he rode upon. *Have I lost my senses?* he'd asked himself as he barreled towards the great blue hill that stretched up as high as the Fortress's watchtower at home. And yet, somehow, the glass shoes had held, and as he climbed, he realized that the princess was sitting on top of the hill, looking as confounded as he was, and in her hands she held a single golden apple.

As soon as he saw the apple, his nerves had taken him, and the animal slowed its ascent. Launce had cursed himself as the animal began to turn on its own accord, but just before he shot back down, the princess had managed to toss him the apple. In his fright, he'd nearly dropped it. Somehow, however, it stayed in his hands, and he raced out of the arena just as quickly as he'd come. Back to the forest they went, and by the time the rest of the riders had returned to the stable, he was back as well, brushing Everard's horse and wearing an expression that was as cowardly as he could muster.

Only Randolph, the short, muscled knight who had intervened on his behalf two days before, had given him an inquisitive look. Launce hoped the foreign knight wouldn't dwell on his questions, whatever they were.

While Launce had told himself that he was just being careful because of the strange power he was dealing with, the more honest part of him had to admit that part of his secrecy was purely due to vanity, and relishing the looks that would be on his competitors' faces when he brought down the rest of the golden apples.

Well, he had to get the rest of the golden apples first. After the events of last night, however, he was almost sure he would win.

After the first contest, as everyone in the stables had prepared for bed, Launce had noticed another film of glassy dust all over the stables. The dust looked different this time though. It was most decidedly silver in tint. This had piqued his interest enough to lead him to spend another night on the roof, and as a reward, he had received another horse, gray this time, and a new set of armor. Only this armor was silver, and the second horse was somehow even larger and fiercer than the first. Other than that, everything had happened just as it had with the first horse. Including the glass on the horse's hooves and the edging of the silver saddle.

Launce's musings were interrupted by the herald as he announced Launce's singular second name. He kicked the horse, for no gentle nudging would budge the beast, and they shot forward, like an arrow loosed from a bow. As they sped towards the stands, into the arena, Launce felt his heart drop into his stomach. He had been right. The hill was twice as tall as it had been the night before.

In his surprise, he jumped, and the horse immediately began to slow. Panic filled him as he tried to fix his mistake, kicking the horse once more and attempting to turn his heading back to the center of the hill. His quick actions seemed to work, for the horse's glass shod hooves hit the steep incline with a jarring crack, one that left a great web of white lines shooting up the glass. He didn't have time to see how bad the glass had been broken, for they were already farther up the hill. Launce's body felt strange as they raced upwards, like he was leaving his insides behind while his skin and bones continued to lift off the ground at an alarming speed.

The speed still wasn't great enough, for as they neared the top, coming even closer to the princess than he had the day before, the silver beast began to slow. They weren't going to make it. Again.

Anger and shame filled his breast as the horse began to turn, despite his urgings, but before he could berate himself for his mistake too much, an apple landed in his lap. If the suit of armor would have allowed such movement, he would have turned to look back at the princess, whose ability to toss apples at moving targets was unmatched in any woman he knew. And yet, it didn't matter, he smiled to himself beneath the helmet.

The second apple was his.

CHAPTER 21
GAMES WE PLAY

"Since our secret rider is too shy to sup with us tonight," Rafael's voice boomed down the length of the ridiculously long dining hall, "I will simply have to give someone else the honor of dining with my daughter. You." He waved at an older gentleman two table lengths down from the head of the table, where Launce sat with Everard and Isa, near the king. "How far up the hill did you get?"

The poor man balked as all eyes turned on him. "My horse refused to attempt it, Sire."

The king harrumphed and pointed at another competitor. This one was younger than the first, but still looked to be a good fifteen years older than the princess, at least. It was a man Launce already knew far too well for his taste.

"Absalom, how far did you get?"

"Two paces, Your Highness."

"Fine, fine then. Come. You shall sit with my daughter tonight."

Launce wanted to make a face. Now he would be forced to watch the horrid man sit across from him for the entire length of the meal, which was only just being served. Of course, he had little to complain about, when compared with the truly unfortunate victim.

At least he wasn't the one Absalom would be attempting to woo.

Launce snuck a quick glance at the princess, curious as to what she would think of the king's choice for her. Thus far, she'd seemed perfectly obedient, compliant down to the letter of her father's seemingly haphazard laws. But as she waited to be greeted by her dinner partner, she seemed to have paled. He couldn't tell for sure, for her head was suddenly tilted down as she studied her plate with the ferocity of a scholar. Perhaps even her obedience had its limits. Launce almost smiled as he watched her stab her dinner violently.

It wasn't polite to stare, he tried repeatedly to remind himself. And yet, he couldn't keep himself from it. It wasn't as though he could distract himself by listening to Isa and Everard talk. Despite Launce's dislike for his brother-in-law, even he had to admit that their disagreement, whatever it concerned, was making life most uncomfortable for everyone around them. Normally, Launce enjoyed baiting Isa to agree with him, trying to get her to acknowledge her husband's faults. But something was different this time. The silence between them was tangible, so thick it was nearly suffocating. Everard had stomped about all evening like a storm cloud trying its best to make thunder, and Isa ... Isa was far too quiet. The look on her face was almost empty, and too close to the surrender he had watched her sink into after her first fiancé had left her on their wedding night.

Memories of that depression, the deep hole she'd fallen into for months, kindled a fire in Launce. It was a dangerous fire, for when lit it didn't take into account how strong Everard was, nor how he was the greatest soldier known to the northern kingdoms. It simply knew that somehow, Everard had caused his sister pain, and if Launce wasn't careful, he would act very foolishly upon that anger. No, it was far less dangerous to watch the foreign knight torment the princess. At least that situation he could have a bit of fun with.

The princess was stabbing at the final pieces of roasted fowl on her plate as Absalom talked incessantly. He was actually daring to whisper in her ear. Launce gawked, first at the odd couple, then at the king, then back at the odd couple. The princess was clearly uncomfortable, cringing when certain words were too loud, and particularly when he made the *s* sound. But the king was too busy to notice his daughter's discomfort, too busy boasting about the holy man's great plan to Everard, who wasn't even pretending to listen. Launce suddenly had a wicked idea. He hoped the princess would catch on.

"You know, Sir Absalom ..." Launce spoke loudly. The princess and the knight both looked at him, her expression grateful, and his vexed. "The way to a girl's hand is through her mother's heart."

"Really? And pray tell, young man, how did you come upon such enlightening wisdom?" Absalom's voice was practiced and smooth, but it had an edge to it.

Launce widened his eyes innocently. "My brother-in-law." He gestured to Everard two seats over. "He always brings my mother a new baking spice when he travels to other lands. Perhaps, if this mystery rider chooses not to reveal himself, you might have a chance at wooing her mother." As he spoke, Launce kept an eye on the princess, and to his relief, she was already struggling to smother a smile. The knight, however, was staring at him. Launce could see him weighing his options, and in the end, it seemed that suspicion would win, until Absalom turned and looked at the princess.

Launce nearly pitied the man. It would be difficult for any male staring into those warm, chocolate eyes to deny her sincerity. And with a start, Launce wondered if the princess might not be a more practiced opponent than her father in a battle of schemes and wits.

"It's true," she told the knight with large eyes. "However," she turned to glance at her parents, "my father is the one who would most need to be impressed." She gave an adorable giggle before leaning in to say in a voice Launce could barely make out, "If you truly want to impress my father …" She continued speaking, but Launce could no longer hear her. As soon as she was done, Absalom pulled back in surprise, his thick eyebrows knitting together as he looked back and forth from princess to the king.

Launce was dying to know what she had told him. As he couldn't ask from across the table, he had to content himself with watching the knight stare vacantly at his food for the remainder of the meal, occasionally glancing up at the princess now and then. Whenever he did, she would catch his eye and send him the sweetest smile Launce had ever seen. If it hadn't been for the amused, fiery looks she would flick his way every now and then, he might actually have been convinced that she was taken with the imbecile.

Supper was finally finished, which to Launce's great relief meant he was closer to escaping the silent battle being waged beside him. But first, they had to live through the same introductory dances he'd watched the first night they'd arrived at the palace. The king and the princess, followed by Rafael with Queen Monica, and Isa and Everard. Rafael and Monica were perfectly decent dancers, but Isa and Ever put them to shame. They moved as one, as though the music itself came from them instead of the musicians.

But they were too perfect. Isa's smile was overly brilliant, her eyes too bright, and Ever's powerful frame moved like a great animal's, savage and agile. The cheers at the end of the dance were wild and real. They had been flawless, but to Launce's surprise, an unexpected sadness filled him. As little as he approved of his sister's husband, it hurt Launce to see her like this. At their wedding, he had seen the blue fire that flitted upwards from their feet and swirled about them as they moved. It was wrong that the others, particularly the catty women present, couldn't see what his sister was truly capable of. What she had become. But then, not even she could see that.

Much to Launce's relief, other couples began to fill the dance floor, which meant he was free to move about the throne room. His first inclination was to hide behind the hors d'oeuvres tables again, but a flash of red caught his eye. The princess was spinning, to his dismay, in the arms of Sir Absalom.

"What are you waiting for?" Everard's harsh whisper made Launce jump. He turned to look at his brother-in-law with disdain. Did the man ever stop watching him? It wasn't as if he was without his own problems to solve. Everard inclined his head towards the princess. "You won't get anywhere with the girl by gawking at her."

Launce scowled at him outright. "I have enough problems with royals as it is. I don't need another one complicating my life."

"Cowards never—" But before Everard could finish his thought, Launce stormed off to stand somewhere else. Of course, that didn't mean he was done watching the princess. But he was merely interested in protecting her from the likes of the horrid knight, he assured himself. She seemed as miserable as he was at this event. Surely it was only natural to feel a certain camaraderie in such a situation.

When Absalom claimed his third dance, Launce's resolve to stay hidden dissolved. The princess's panicked look was more than he could stand, and the knight continued to move closer and closer with each turn. Launce just hoped his action wouldn't be interpreted as pursuance. As he walked out amidst the twirling couples, he knew his saving grace would be his status. She couldn't expect a commoner to aspire to kingship.

"May I cut in?" Launce tapped Absalom's fine silk-covered shoulder, interrupting the couple mid-twirl. Absalom glared at him, but stepped aside as etiquette required, and for once, Launce was thankful for the stiff formalities Everard had hammered into him during their preparations at the Fortress.

Launce took the princess's arms, but once they began dancing on their own, was shocked to find her frowning at him.

"Did I do something wrong?" He glanced back at the knight's retreating coat.

"I nearly had him," Princess Olivia sniffed.

"I'm confused. If you want me to go—"

"No, you ninny. I just meant that he's getting desperate to impress my father. I almost had him ready to try. Besides," she arched one of her perfect eyebrows, "what took you so long?"

"I was under the impression you were enjoying the sweet little nothings he was whispering so tenderly in your ear. Ow!" Launce's foot throbbed as the princess continued to move lithely through the crowd of dancers with an ease that made Launce wonder how often she had practiced stepping on her partners' feet.

"That's for taking so long." She smirked. Launce limped to keep up as she twirled away again.

"You certainly play both sides," he said, wondering how he had mistaken her for a pitiful, helpless damsel just the day before. Everything about her was spirited and lively. The ruffled dress she wore snapped back and forth as though it were stepping forth for a challenge with each sharp move she made. Her dark, shiny hair had just enough curl to fly upwards even when she was still. The flush of her cheeks and the red of her lips contrasted beautifully with her olive skin.

Actually, Launce realized, she was quite beautiful. He had to focus on keeping his eyes on her face while they danced, for her figure was graceful in its generous curves as she moved, and her dress had been cut to pronounce those curves quite expertly. As this revelation dawned on him, he also realized she still hadn't answered. A dark shadow had come over her face instead.

"What's wrong?" he asked, his voice soft enough to keep most busybodies unaware of their conversation.

"I wasn't always like this," she whispered, then let out a shaky chuckle. "Well, I mean, I've always enjoyed pranks, but ..." She took another deep breath. "It's my father. He's changed over the last few years. Ever since the holy man came—" With a start, she stopped dancing, clapping her hand over her mouth. Launce glanced around furtively, as he took her hand from her face and continued dancing. Hopefully no one had seen her slip. Well, Everard had, he noted, as his brother-in-law continued to watch them with eagle eyes. But when was Everard not watching?

"That's what my sister's husband tells me," he whispered in her ear. A small, smug part of him rejoiced when she didn't cringe at his words the way she had for Sir Absalom's. Instead, she stared up at him, dark eyes wide on her smooth face as she spoke.

"He never ordered me around so before. He was considerate, and always asked me what I thought. But now ..." She shook her head and lifted her chin a bit, defiance gleaming in her eyes. "He's obstinate, pompous, and doesn't listen to anyone but the holy man."

Launce opened his mouth to ask, but was interrupted by Rafael's shout.

"Sir Absalom, put your trousers back on this instant!"

Launce turned to see Absalom standing at the top of the main staircase. The foreign knight swayed a bit, but that wasn't what caused the gasps from the ladies or the shrieks of laughter from some of the children present.

"Your Highness!" Absalom shouted in a warbling voice. "I am bold! I am brave! And I am not afraid to stake my claim to your daughter! With or without trousers!" He hiccupped the last word.

"You *will* pull up your trousers, and you will *not* make any such claim! Now get back to the stables before I return you myself!" The laughs and titters that ensued from the crowd created a slight roar as two guards appeared at the knight's sides to guide him.

"Father is going to be upset the rest of the evening now."

Launce turned incredulously to look at the princess as she stifled more giggles and stared at the king.

"That was what you told him? To take off his pants?"

"I merely told him my father appreciates men who are brazenly bold. I just didn't expect so much wine to be involved." She chuckled. After a moment, she added more seriously, "I suppose your sister had an easier time finding her husband without interference from a father who was slowly losing his mind, as mine seems to be."

Launce laughed without humor, and it tasted bitter. "You really haven't heard how they met?"

"Rumors float." The princess shrugged. "I choose not to believe them until I find a source of truth though." She didn't ask the question aloud, but Launce knew what she wanted to know.

"Not here," he said. "Too many ears."

"Well then," the princess said. "I expect an answer when we're a bit more secluded. And," she sighed, "apparently that will have to be tomorrow or later. My father is calling for me."

Launce stepped back and bowed. "Until next time, Princess."

"One more thing. Call me Olivia." Then, with a nod and a twist, she was gone, and Launce allowed himself one small smile, although he couldn't tell whether it was more because he'd spent most of the evening dancing with the princess, or because she wanted to see him again.

Seeing no reason to torture himself any longer than necessary, he excused himself from the festivities and returned to the stables, hoping to get a little bit of sleep before curfew was called. With the final race the next morning, Launce had the feeling he would be up on the roof for one more night.

As he laid down and tried to ignore the straw that poked him through the rough mattress, he smiled to himself. It had been more than slightly brazen for him to imply that there *would* be another chance to discuss Isa's marriage. But the princess had not objected. *Cowardly* was a word Everard could never use to describe him again.

CHAPTER 22
DOUBTS

Isa took Ever's arm when he offered it, but he could feel her stiffness beneath the lace that draped so delicately around her wrist. When he dared to peek at her face, her expression was tense, almost fearful, and the sinking feeling that had lived at the pit of his gut all night grew even stronger. Whatever she wanted to talk about must be a difficult topic for her to broach for her to appear so nervous.

And if it was difficult for her, it would be next to impossible for him.

Unfortunately for Ever, Rafael was still babbling on about his plans for the kingdom, how the holy man would make all the difference in putting a final stop to the rebels. Ever was trying to nod and comment in all the right places, but his growing dislike for his father's old friend was becoming nearly too great for him to stand. Still, he'd reminded himself all evening, it would get him nowhere to treat the ungrateful king as he truly deserved. It would be better to play along and see which webs Rafael had ensnared himself in. As a result, the entire banquet had been spent watching Launce unknowingly flirt with the princess, trying to guess at Isa's source of unhappiness, and putting up with Rafael.

All he wanted to do was go to bed.

Before he could finish fantasizing about sleep, however, the sound of a staff knocking on the floor brought him to his senses, and he realized Rafael had risen from his throne, and was standing behind the herald.

"His Royal Highness, King Rafael, wishes to make an announcement!" When the ballroom was finally quiet, the herald turned and bowed to the king before slipping off the dais so the king could step forward.

"My friends," Rafael said, a patient, rather irksome smile upon his face. "I have told you little by little of how the holy one, our builder of the glass hill, has plans for this kingdom. Now I can tell you that he not only has plans for Cobren, but for the good of *all* the northern kingdoms!"

Ever tensed. What did he mean all of the kingdoms? But the king continued.

"I know these new signs from the Maker can seem a bit overwhelming after being silent for so long, so as a symbol of promise to promote peace between all lands, the holy man has asked me to give you these gifts as a token of his good will towards you all."

As he spoke, he gave a little wave with his right hand, and simultaneously, a servant came to stand before each visitor or party of visitors, and removed the covers from the silver platters. When the servant standing before Ever and Isa lifted the cover from the platter he held, Ever felt his heart stop as Isa gasped in delight.

One delicate glass flower, the Isabelle rose, and a miniature glass fortress, exactly like the one he called home, rested on the tray, neither piece longer than the span of his hand. The rose was a light shade of pink, and the glass fortress was blue. They weren't cloudy, the way most glass objects in the markets were, but sparkled as clear as water and as detailed as their originals themselves. Ever looked up from the tray and searched the room until he found Kartek, and her look of horror mirrored the one he knew he must be wearing now.

"Each of these gifts has been made specifically for you," Rafael continued after the crowd's elated murmurs died down, "so that you will know the Maker knows exactly who you are and what you need. Through these, and the future actions of the holy man, you are to know that He is watching over you, always."

The servant held the tray up closer, and panic filled Ever as Isa reached for the rose. Before she could touch it, he snatched both the rose and the miniature fortress and ground them to pieces in his hand. As the pink and blue dust fell to the floor, Isa's face went from glowing to crushed, and he suddenly hoped desperately that she wouldn't make a scene. Remorse filled him as she stared at the ground where her rose pieces lay. When he'd touched the glass, he hadn't felt any power emanating from it as he'd feared he would. But he'd been so filled with fear in that instant, that the overriding need to protect her had pushed away all other thoughts.

Thoughts such as: was the glass truly unsafe, or was it simply something pretty?

"We need to talk." Isa's whisper was low and dangerous, and though she didn't raise her head to look at him, he knew the pained expression was long gone from her face. Without waiting for him to respond, Isa began to walk away from the king's dais, where they had been standing, and towards the hall that led to their chambers. Without a word, Ever followed her. Since they'd been married, she had never spoken to him that way before. Her silver cloak billowed out behind her as she walked. She held her chin up heroically, but he didn't miss the tremble of her jaw.

Before Isa, Ever had never struggled with being direct. His

father, King Rodrigue, had been insistent about speaking the truth as plainly and candidly as possible. It disallowed confusion, he always said, making communication efficient and useful. Ever had learned to speak the same way with his generals and soldiers, and they with him. But since Isa had come into his life, Ever had struggled with words in a way he never had before. It wasn't that he wanted to hide the truth from her. He simply didn't know how to share it in a way that didn't sound callous or brash. She wasn't one of his military officers, nor was she a servant to be ordered about. She was good and kind and ethereal in a way he'd never known anyone to be before. Speaking boldly and directly with her felt as though it might break her, as though *she* were made of glass. It was the reason he had not been able to speak of her struggle with her power yet. It was why he couldn't bring himself to tell her how great a threat the enchanter was to them all.

Isa approached their door and stood silently as Norbert opened it for them, and the surprise in the old guard's eyes told Ever that the difference in Isa's countenance was not imagined on his part. As soon as the door was shut behind them, Isa turned to face him. Her eyes reflected the light of the single lit candle in the room, making them look like those of a large cat.

"Why would you do that?" Her voice was still pitched low and menacing, but the slightest quiver gave her away.

"It was dangerous."

"Was it really?"

Ever stared at her, carefully weighing his next words. He wasn't sure where she was going, but he knew he was in perilous waters. Even in the dark, her midnight eyes flashed, and her breathing was deep and unsteady. She stared back at him, the expression on her face pained and ancient.

"If you want another rose, I'll get it for—"

"It is not about the rose, Ever!" Isa's shout exploded from her like thunder from unseen lightning.

"Then what is it about?" Now he was shouting too.

"You never ask!" she cried. "You just carry on as though you have no queen, and I have no ability to make choices! You assume I am weak! Locking me in my room?"

"I am trying to protect you!"

"I am not a child!" Isa snatched the jeweled tiara off of her head and thrust it out at him. "In case you forgot, there is a reason I have this."

"If you were able to fulfill the duties that came with that crown, I wouldn't have to treat you this way."

"Perhaps, if you ever spent a moment away from the kingdom to actually see me, we would know why I'm failing. Sometimes ..." Isa shook her head and held her hands up helplessly, "I feel like marrying me was simply the easiest way for you to get everything back."

"What other choice did I have?"

As soon as the words left his mouth, Ever knew they were wrong. The silence that filled the room was stifling, and he wished with everything in him that he could take them back. But as he watched her drink them in, watched her face strain not to show the tears, he knew it was too late.

"None, Ever. You had no choice whatsoever."

The air was suddenly too thick, and Ever turned before he choked on an apology that would only make things worse, stomping out the door before Norbert could keep it from slamming. He could hear the echoes of the merriment down the hall, but in no mood for a party of any sort, Ever escaped through one of the servants' exits.

THE NIGHT WAS cool in a cutting way, hinting at a difficult winter to come. Ever drew his cloak more tightly around himself, unwilling to even consider returning to his chambers for his warmer coverings. That would mean seeing Isa's tear-streaked cheeks, and facing the depths to which he had cut her. What had possessed him to use such cruel words? He hadn't meant to say them. They had simply tumbled from his tongue, as though some menacing imp had discovered all his meanness and awful secret thoughts that he worked so hard to rid himself of, and dumped them out of his mind and into his mouth.

Of course he'd wanted it all back. Namely, he had wanted *her* back. *She* had become his world. She and the Fortress were all he had ever wanted. Marrying her hadn't been an option, but a necessity. It was like being asked if one wanted air to breathe.

Why the blazes hadn't he said that instead?

Ever paused as he reached the path split. The red pebbled path he was on now continued down to the stables. The thin dirt path on the right, however, led down to the beach. Though he was tempted to check in on Launce, as he was sure the young man had left the festivities early as well, the roar of the ocean called to him, offering to wash away the stain of his wrongs.

"What am I supposed to do?" he groaned. The Fortress didn't answer, but he felt the stirrings within his heart that told him he knew the answer. "I'm just trying to protect her," he argued back. "And the kingdom. I don't know how else to do this." When no audible answer came, he began his trudge down to the beach.

The Maker had seen it fit to bequeath the Fortress's powers on Isa in the beginning. Ever had seen the bright blue flames burning in her eyes as he'd vowed to love and cherish her on their wedding day. How marvelous those eyes had been as they'd sparkled with hope and joy. And they had continued to flame with vigor until about a month after the wedding. Twenty-seven days, to be exact.

Spring had ended early that year, and the hot season had

jumped right in to take its place. The day was particularly sticky when he'd first noticed the difference in Isa.

As usual, Ever had awakened before the sun. Nothing had seemed amiss then as he'd leaned over and kissed his wife good morning. She had given him the same sleepy smile that she always did, not quite able to open her eyes, but doing her best anyways. The smile she'd shared with him upon waking, however, was the last true smile he would see that day.

When she had joined him to break fast later that morning, her steps were uncommonly slow, and she kept her eyes distant, focused only on the ground or the walls or the food which she pushed around on her plate. No amount of small talk could bring her from her reverie, and though Ever wasn't one for idle chatter, Isa's lack of words blared like trumpets at the table. The servants glanced at her nervously throughout the meal, and even the stuffy nobles who were visiting them at the time gave her wary looks.

Ever had wanted to ask then and there what the matter was, but they had two diplomatic meetings to attend, and a training session with some of his newer soldiers. It would be hours before they were free to talk alone. By the time the first meeting was over with, Ever had suggested that Isa looked tired, and maybe she should rest rather than attend the next session. Isa had glumly nodded and left without a word. As soon as she was gone, he'd summoned Garin.

"Do you know what's wrong with her?" he'd asked the steward.

Garin had nodded slowly, but to Ever's surprise and annoyance, had said in a soft voice, "This is a matter that would better be discussed between a husband and wife alone."

Ever had stared at him, incredulous. He knew Garin well enough, however, not to ask where he had gotten such delicate information. He had a feeling though that Gigi had much to do with that.

It wasn't until later that afternoon that he was miraculously free to check in on Isa, who he found still in their bedroom, staring at the ceiling from their massive four poster bed.

"Find anything new up there?"

Isa didn't laugh at the joke or even crack a smile. She just continued to lay there.

"Are you unwell?" He gently laid his hand on her forehead. She shook it off, and sat up with a frown, but a slight grimace gave her away as she moved. "If you're feeling sickly," he said, "I can—"

"There is nothing unusual about the way I feel," she had snapped. "I feel exactly the way I do this time every month."

Ever suddenly felt confused, watching her cautiously as she stood up and threw the pillow she'd been hugging back down on the bed with an excessive amount of force. He stayed still as she paced the room silently for a few minutes before placing her head on her hands and leaning against one of the pearl bedposts. Ever had felt as though he should go to her, but the strange temper she was in kept him seated. He had no idea as to what he was supposed to do.

Finally, she sighed. "I'm sorry, Ever. I shouldn't be angry with you. This isn't your fault. I just ... I thought things would be different. I was assured they would be." When she had finally looked at him, the confusion and pain in her eyes was piteous, and she suddenly looked very vulnerable. Slowly, he'd stood and walked over to her. He didn't embrace her, still unsure of what she wanted him to do, but he could at least better study her, so he stood beside the bedpost opposite of hers. For the thousandth time that day, he wished his father had spent less time training him in the art of war and a little more time teaching him about women. Not that his father knew much about them either.

When the silence finally became too much to bear, he began, "I'm sorry, Isa, but I still don't understand."

"I'm not pregnant, Ever."

Ever had blinked. Where had that come from? "Were ... you supposed to be?"

"Master Claude said I would be by now."

"What in the heavens does Master Claude know of women or pregnancy?" Ever had never liked that man.

"He says every Fortress queen has conceived within a month of her coronation."

Ever had started to protest, but stopped. In truth, he had no knowledge on the subject. Women of the court would titter about such a subject, but never within direct earshot of the men. He had only ever picked up snippets of conversation now and then. He wanted to contradict Isa's snide tutor, but then he remembered the sadness in Garin's face that morning, and he knew immediately that Claude must have been right.

Understanding and fear had washed through him as he stood there looking at his wife. Was something truly wrong? Why would Isa be any different from the others? Apparently, even his mother had followed suit, and she'd never had the Fortress fire to begin with.

With no words to comfort either himself or Isa, he'd simply taken her and drawn her close, holding her to his chest as tightly as he could without hurting her. She had wept into him then, and he had to fight the desire to run down to the practice room and break something. Actually, he had realized, distraction wasn't a poor idea.

"I'll talk to Garin later and see what he knows about the old queens." He'd lifted her chin and forced her midnight eyes to meet his. "But for now, how would you like to go down to the practice room with me? You were getting rather good at the sword form I taught you yesterday." Isa thought about that for a moment before nodding, much to his relief. As he began to walk to the door, she caught his hand and drew him back to her, and without a word, took his face in her hands and pulled him down into a warm, soft kiss. His heart had thundered as she kissed him, and his breath was as fast as if he'd just sprinted across a battlefield. In that moment, he'd known they were exactly where they were supposed to be. Together.

A while later, as they began to practice, however, he'd noticed that while her form was neat, the power she usually wove into her thrusts and parries was rather weak. The blue flame that had always moved down her sword and whirled about her as she twisted in and out was lazy and thin. And since that day, it had only grown worse. Along with her diminishing power, the fire in Isa's eyes had begun to dim as well.

Ever had relived that day over and over again in his mind, raking over every detail, trying desperately to find some significance that might unlock the mystery of her failing power. Garin was solemn whenever they discussed it, but he always cautioned Ever to be patient, trusting the Fortress to know what it was doing with its daughter. Ever trusted Garin, and he knew more than anything that he should trust the Fortress, but time was running out. He couldn't bear to see her fire extinguished the way his father's had been.

In order to distract them both, to keep them from mulling over the problem day after day, Ever had thrown them both into their duties with more vigor than ever. Hardly a second was free for either one of them, always spent in study, work, or exercise. This would keep her from worrying, he'd convinced himself. But if he was honest, he had to wonder sometimes if the distractions were more for her or for him.

Now, in the cold of night, as he threw rocks into the waves, Ever wished that Garin were there. Garin would know what to do. Garin always knew what to do, even when there was nothing to be done. But he took a deep breath; as Garin was not there, Ever would have to make do with what he had. And at the moment, since he couldn't imagine what Garin would suggest, a piece of advice his father had given him long ago was all he had.

"Make a plan and stay the course," King Rodrigue had always said. "If you don't, you will wander about uselessly, solving problems for no one."

That, Ever decided, was what he would do. The greatest threat now was the enchanter. Ever might not know how to help Isa, or how to fix the cruel words he'd hurt her with, but he knew he could best this enchanter, and once it was done, Ever would focus only on his wife. He would take her away and dote on her until she hadn't a piece of her left that could question his need, his devotion to her. They would find a way to heal her, and she would never be able to doubt his love again.

CHAPTER 23

DUTY

Isa didn't even realize she had fallen asleep until she awakened the next morning to see early purple filling the sky. It had been the longest night she could ever recall, the kind that trapped her in sleepless dreams, images and words that made no sense, but were frightening all the same. Over and over again, she'd had to relive the moment when Ever had walked out and slammed the door. The worst part of it was that even after she woke up, Ever had never returned, despite her tears and prayers. Shouting, Isa reasoned, would have been better than contemplating the meaning of his absence alone.

It was so early that Isa decided not to ring for Cerise. She loved her friend, but was in no mood to explain the dark circles beneath her eyes or where Ever was. Instead, she washed her face in the porcelain basin and opened the window. Ever had told her not to touch it, but she was suffocating. After staring at the walls for two days, she needed to get out.

The street below, despite the early hour, was bustling with the sounds of poultry clucking, horses' hooves, and merchants gabbing as they walked to the market to set up their booths. The breeze had the chill of early winter, but Isa welcomed it, leaning even farther out the window. The frozen bite made her feel alive.

But it wasn't enough. Isa needed to do more than simply lean out of a window again to breathe. She needed to escape. The cold water and crisp morning air had given her courage, and suddenly, Kartek's words came back to her.

She was the queen of the Fortress, and she would not sit idly by as she wasted away and Ever destroyed himself.

Excitement thrumming through her bones, Isa quickly dressed in a yellow long-sleeved dress, another training outfit that hid a pair of trousers beneath it. Gigi had ordered it in exasperation when she'd found out that Ever was determined to train his wife in the ways of war not once in a while, but every day. Isa hoped there would be no fight today, but she wanted to be prepared. If Ever wasn't going to tell her what was going on, she would find out on her own.

And now for the hard part. Isa needed to escape her well-intentioned guards, but as they had sworn to Ever to protect her, there would be no talking her way past them. She would have to use her powers. Whispering a silent plea to the Fortress, Isa gingerly placed her hand against the rough wood of the door. She inhaled, then gently pressed.

Nothing.

Again, she took a deep breath and pushed. This time, her hand began to disappear, beginning with her fingers, then traveling up her arm and down the rest of her body. When she looked down, much to her satisfaction, she was completely invisible. It was one of the first tricks she'd learned at the Fortress.

Once more, she pressed into the wood, and just as she'd hoped, began to melt through it. Pushing through the door felt strange, like moving through a rough, wool blanket. Just as she was halfway through, however, far enough to see the other side, Norbert's head jerked up. Though he didn't seem to see her, the distraction had done its damage, and Isa was now stuck within the door. Panic seized her as she pulled and pulled, but it was no use.

Calm, she struggled to focus, *I must be calm.* More slowly this time, Isa tried pulling her right leg from the door without bumping into him. The older man had seen enough of the Fortress's power to guess what she was up to if she tipped him off. As though freeing herself from quicksand, Isa had to be ridiculously patient. Finally, she was free from the door. Thankful to be done with it, she ran silently down the hall, glad to stretch her legs again. It was empowering to walk through the halls alone. Isa felt strong and confident, though she hadn't the slightest idea as to how she would discover whatever her husband was hiding from her.

Then it came to her. Launce. Launce was grudgingly obeying Ever, but she was sure it wouldn't take much convincing to get him to share what he knew with her. Isa felt a bit guilty about sneaking around her husband, but Kartek was right. Whatever scheme Ever was so obsessed with would drive him to distraction if he was left alone to it.

Besides, his words from the night before still stung more than she wanted to admit, and his absence even more. She would go to Launce's final competition, then she would explore on her own.

The final ceremony was one of excitement and chatter, not to mention much earlier than the first two contests. The roar of many voices reached her before Isa even arrived at the arena. She was both relieved and saddened when she saw that Ever sat in his usual post beside King Rafael. She would have to find a new place from which to watch the contest. Others couldn't see her, but Ever would sense her presence if she was nearby. Invisibility was one of the few skills Isa had ever had a decent handle on with her powers, but if she became too upset or flustered, it would fail her too.

"Presenting his Royal Highness, King Rafael!" The trumpets blared and the crowd hushed as the king walked to the front of his box.

"My friends, it is the time at last for us to see who the holy man, the architect of this feat, has selected to marry my daughter and be the next king of Cobren. Whosoever shall present the three apples to me today shall be our next king!" Isa wondered if Launce would have a third suit today. It still irked her that Ever had allowed Launce to continue in the competition when he discovered that the holy man was using him. But Launce had gone along with it, particularly after the first horse and suit had shown up, and between the two men, there was no stopping it. She only hoped her little brother wouldn't get hurt.

Isa found a spot just beneath the raised benches, on the far right side of the arena. From there, she could see the distant line of riders awaiting their signals to ride. She tried to pick out Launce by the gleam of his armor, but then she realized he might well have a new suit of armor today, if he had fared as well as he'd done the two days before.

Once the final game was begun, as usual, the other nobles, knights, kings, and princes attempted the great hill. It was apparent, however, that their numbers were dwindling. There were far fewer competing today than there had been the day before. It didn't seem to make a difference to the people, however, as the whole arena seemed to be waiting for Launce. No one even took notice when the hill lowered itself for the princess to walk upon its summit, then raised itself up again with a grinding creak to a height even greater than the day before.

"Do you think the knight will ride again today?" someone sitting above Isa asked.

"Of course, why would he compete in two and not the third?" someone else snorted.

"I told you, it's not one rider, but two from the same kingdom. I'll bet they are here to make a fool of Rafael by showing him up and giving three different people an apple so he'll have to choose."

"But wouldn't it make sense for the riders to each compete? Wouldn't they rather be kings than servants?"

"Unlike *some* people, not everyone's allegiance can be bought."

Heavy hoof beats could be heard fast approaching from outside the arena. Like the streak of a shooting star, a golden blur of horse and man burst past Isa and into the stadium. This horse seemed the largest of any he'd ridden thus far. Isa couldn't imagine how the monstrous creature could get three feet off the ground, let alone climb the sleek hill, which was now at least three times the height of the Fortress's Tower of Annals.

Gasps went up as the horse charged up the hill without hesitation from horse or rider. Yesterday, Launce had slowed, but tonight he rode as though demons chased him. Somehow, he moved closer and closer to the princess as though the hill were flat. Fear made Isa nearly sick as her brother neared the summit. The crystalline blue beneath him let out a sharp cracking sound. White veins splintered beneath the hooves, extending with each successive touch. Isa gripped the edge of the platform above her until her fingers hurt, praying desperately that she or Ever would be able to save him if something happened.

Just when it seemed the entire hill might shatter to pieces, Launce reached the top. Time seemed to stand still as he held out his hand to the princess, who placed the final golden apple in his hand, a look of amazement on her young face. Then, he was down the hill as if he'd never reached the top at all.

"Halt!" the king shouted.

It didn't seem as though Launce would be able to hear him,

but the giant horse somehow slowed just before reaching the edge of the arena, and Launce turned him to face the king.

"Come here," Rafael ordered.

Launce paused for a moment, the gold of his magnificent suit nearly blinding in the light of the early morning sun. Isa wondered what he would do. What would Rafael do?

The horse began to slowly make its way back to the king. Isa's heart pounded as Launce neared the royal box. Surely when the king saw who it was, he wouldn't announce Launce as his successor. Ever had said Rafael was a man of honor, but that was before this strange holy man had filled his head with vain dreams and grand schemes. Launce had never actually expected to *win*, something he'd told Isa himself.

"Show me how many apples you possess," Rafael said when Launce's horse stood below the royal family's platform. "I have decreed that only the rider who possesses all three apples shall have my daughter's hand and inherit the kingdom."

Launce paused for a long moment before slowly reaching into the horse's golden saddlebags. A gasp went up from the crowd when he produced all three apples.

"I *told* you the rider was only one person," Isa heard someone whisper behind her.

The king walked down the steps and into the arena, where he held his hand out for the apples. "What is your name? I cannot pledge my kingdom to a man whose identity I do not know."

When Launce removed the golden helmet, the shock was palpable. Isa thought she heard a snicker from Ever as Launce stared warily at the king, and the king gaped back with his mouth open, clearly not pleased.

Surely, Isa thought, he would postpone his announcement. There must be some way to keep the most unwilling and unlikely candidate from being forced to take his throne. But to her surprise, the king swallowed hard and grasped Launce's arm before raising it high.

"I announce to you the chosen one of the holy man, Launce Marchand, brother to Queen Isabelle of Destin, future king of Cobren!"

Launce looked around wildly, and Isa guessed he was searching for her, his mouth open in horror as she felt him silently pleading for her to do something. But what could she do? None of this was supposed to happen. And yet, there they stood as Launce was declared inheritor of a kingdom he'd never wanted.

The holy man wanted something with her little brother, and Isa realized that if she didn't find out what, and very soon, that man just might get it.

CHAPTER 24

SLIPPING THROUGH THE CRACKS

Isa felt terrible for leaving Launce alone as he was ushered away with the king. He would hate all of the court's attention, but he would survive. It was now or never, and Isa didn't know when she would get another chance to slip away. Launce would be free of it all if she could discover whatever this strange holy man had in store for him.

Isa hovered at the bottom of the arena while the people began to pour out. The king had announced that they would all have a break before their celebration luncheon began. With chagrin and relief, she watched Ever join Rafael and Launce as they made their way back to the palace. How she longed to be with him. With both of them. But since Ever wouldn't let her help him, she would just have to do it on her own.

Isa waited to leave her hiding spot until the arena was finally clear of all but a few servants left behind to tidy up. If she could only know that her invisibility would remain effective, it wouldn't have mattered when she ventured out, for no one would be able to see her anyway. Since her powers had been so unpredictable as of late, however, she preferred not to take the risk.

As Isa made her way to the glass hill, it began to look much steeper and slicker than she'd originally thought. Launce was a good horseman to be sure, but nothing aside from a special power could have moved a man and beast up such an incline for such a distance on a surface of glass.

When she touched it, the hill felt exactly as she'd imagined, like placing one's fingertips on the surface of a clear, frozen pond. The longer she left her hand against the glass, however, the more she felt a secondary sensation. Though the glass sat perfectly still, it hummed with life, and not just a little. Harder and harder it pulsed, until it stung like water that was too hot.

Isa yanked her hand off and rubbed it as she walked slowly around the hill's great base. It was at least as wide as the ballroom. A strange fear crept into her heart. She was used to being surrounded by power. Even when the Fortress's power wasn't residing in her the way it did in Ever, she could feel a wave every time her husband drew near. Even Garin had his own odd sensation that entered and left a room when he did. But this power felt . . . old. There was no other word for it. And in its age, it carried a weight too heavy for her to touch for very long.

A movement caught Isa's eye through the glass. About a quarter of the way around, a servant stood, staring up at the hill as she did. The glass warped the man's face a bit, but after a moment of study, Isa realized she was looking at Brokk. He didn't see her, of course, as she was still invisible, but Isa suddenly wished she could share one of his warm smiles. She could use one today.

She stopped walking and watched him as he studied the glass. He had been raking the dirt to level the arena, as some of the other servants were doing, but now his rake leaned against the hill. Placing his hand against the glass, just as Isa had done, he gave a small smile. She realized he was touching one of the cracks that had moved down the hill during Launce's final ride.

After looking to his left and then his right, a violet flare leaped from his palm into the glass. A sharp icicle of dread formed in Isa's belly as she watched the strange flame jump from crack to crack, sealing them up as though they'd never been there.

Then, as if he'd heard a sound, though she'd been completely silent, Brokk looked away from the crack and directly into her eyes. The look of surprise on his face told her that he could see her just as plainly as she could see him.

Dropping her invisibility, for it didn't matter anymore, Isa turned and began to sprint as fast her legs would carry her. She didn't stop to see whether he was following her. He didn't have to. The power she'd felt in the glass was far beyond the need to chase someone. Someone with that power could have stood perfectly still and caught her without a second thought.

Still, she pressed her feet onward until she had climbed to the top of the arena and down its exit, heading straight for the palace. As she ran, she was struck with the realization that she should have brought her sword. Her power wasn't great enough to use it the way Ever had been trying to teach her, but simply having the weapon would have made her feel a little safer.

In the sharp cool of the late autumn morning, her breath quickly grew ragged, and her chest ached, but Isa pressed herself on. Only when she was within the palace walls did she grab the first servant she could find.

"Find King Everard!" she gasped. "Tell him his wife needs him. It is of the utmost importance! Tell him to meet me in our chambers."

The young woman looked slightly frightened when Isa finally let her go, but Isa was too upset to care. The walk back to their rooms was frightening on its own accord. Each time she turned a corner, each time she spotted a servant or courtier, Isa nearly fainted with fright. Where was Brokk? Was he looking for her?

Isa berated herself for being so naive. Ever had been right to be angry when she had allowed Brokk into their room. It was careless, and, she thought guiltily, she had told him far more than she ever should have shared with anyone outside their trusted circle. It would serve her right if he did find her then and there. Not that he had to look. He already knew of all the places she could be.

"Norbert!" Isa nearly ran to him in her relief when she turned the last corner. The old guard looked immediately disconcerted, then fierce.

"You should not have left, Your Majesty!" he scolded her, his silver and black peppered eyebrows raised. "It is not safe—"

"I know!" Isa grasped his rough hand and took a shaky breath to steady herself. "The enchanter Ever has been whispering to you about is here," she said, not at all sorry she'd been eavesdropping. "He is the servant that brought me the midday yesterday. I saw him fixing the cracks in the glass hill! He will be looking for me, I'm sure of it."

Norbert's thin, weathered face turned to stone as she spoke. "We must summon your husband!"

"I've already sent a messenger to find him. But while we wait, I'll need you . . ." her voice trailed off as it dawned on her that she had just put one of her favorite guards in great danger as well. The older man wouldn't think twice about sacrificing himself to keep the enchanter from reaching her.

Norbert must have sensed her fear, however, because his harsh look softened just a bit. "No one will cross this threshold," he said gently, squeezing her hand. "I swear it."

Isa gave him the most grateful smile she could muster as he unlocked the door and ushered her in.

Once she was inside, she paced. Cerise had laid a scone and some fruit out on her little table, but Isa wasn't even slightly hungry. How had this happened? How could she have been so blind? It seemed impossible to have been so close to Brokk twice, and yet to have missed his incredible power completely.

Ever had disliked him from the moment they'd met. This annoyed Isa more than she could say. He had been right. Again. Her power, even her ability to sense power, must be failing faster than ever. It was the only conclusion she could reach for such an oversight. Isa ran to the mirror to study her eyes. How thin the blue rings of fire seemed! They had been so bright, so illustrious when she was first crowned.

"Are you truly leaving me? Am I that unworthy already?" she whispered. But the Fortress didn't answer. The silence that filled the room though was just as loud as a shout would have been. In spite of all the more important events taking place at that moment, Isa felt her heart break. Ever had grown tired and angry with her foolishness. The people of Destin were confused and rightfully asking what was wrong with their new queen. And now, it seemed, even the Fortress had grown tired of her ineptness.

Where was Ever?

Isa paced even faster as she wondered how it could be taking so long for the servant to locate her husband. At the Fortress, the servants were the ones who knew all of the comings and goings of the great citadel. It couldn't be that different here.

As Isa passed the rose-colored mirror in her pacing, something made her stop. Looking back at its glass, Isa realized it no longer reflected the room. Instead, it was just slightly beginning to glow.

CHAPTER 25

MISSING

This is your fault," Launce glared at Ever as he paced.
Ever simply crossed his arms and stepped back so the young man had more space to walk off his frustration. The dock was long, jutting out into the sea far enough to fit a dozen boats on each side, or even two of the larger war vessels if they were fitted tightly enough, stern to bow. It was strangely empty today, however. Not even a fisherman was nearby. Ever wondered if Rafael had ordered everyone to a different port so he could keep his holy man's identity a secret.

"True, it was my idea, but I wasn't the one who won the contest. You could have thrown the results and no one would have been the wiser," Ever answer coolly. "Admit it, you liked winning. That's why you kept your second name. You wanted to take everyone by surprise."

"I didn't think Rafael would actually grant me the victory when he saw who I was! Who chooses a successor based on a game?"

"It was never about the game. This self-proclaimed holy man, whoever he is, has decided that you were the one he wanted to be king. There is something he wants from you that he thinks none of the others can give."

Launce stopped walking, and for the first time Ever saw understanding sink in, and the disgust on Launce's face turned to true distress. Before they could say anything else, steps sounded on the dock.

Finally, he thought as he turned to greet Rafael. But it was not Rafael who approached him, only a servant girl.

"Your Highness," she curtsied hastily, "I have a message from Queen Isabelle for you."

Ever couldn't keep the surprise from his face. He'd been certain he would have to be the first one to make amends. Which, he had to admit, was only fair.

"The queen says that she needs you, and that it is of the utmost importance."

"Was she hurt?" Ever demanded, but the girl shook her head.

"No, Sire. But she did say to meet her in your chambers. That was all." Ever expected the girl to go, but instead of leaving, however, she just stood there, twisting her fingers and biting her upper lip.

"What is it?" Ever had to remind himself to keep his voice calm and kind. "Is there something else?"

"Nothing she wanted me to say, Your Majesty. It's only . . ." she drew a deep breath. "She appeared to be quite frightened." Her voice trailed off, and she just stood there for a moment, staring at the ground, before she seemed to remember that she needed to be somewhere. Bobbing another curtsy, she skittered back down the dock toward the palace.

"Aren't you going to go see what she needs?" Launce asked.

Ever just looked at him, unsure of how to answer. His body was completely still, but inside he was at war.

If she were truly in danger, he would be there in an instant, but given the timing, she most likely had simply heard of

Launce's victory, and was worried about it. Or perhaps she wanted to discuss the night before. If he left now, something told him he wouldn't get another chance at meeting Rafael's holy man alone again.

"Well?" Launce pressed.

Slowly, Ever shook his head. "If this man is who I think he is, Isa will be in greater danger than ever if I allow him to escape, given his sudden interest in our family. I need to know for sure who he is and what he is about. Norbert will keep her safe until we return." And if Ever was right, and the holy man was the enchanter he suspected, Ever would strike him down on the spot. Judging by Launce's expression, he wasn't at all happy with Ever's response, but before they could argue, two more sets of steps sounded on the dock.

"Rafael," Ever growled, "you're late." And, to make things worse, it was only a servant with a tray of goblets that accompanied the king. Fury burned in Ever's gut. The king had gone back on his word.

"You know how these things go," Rafael snapped. "I was busy."

"Your Highness." The servant bowed and held the tray of silver goblets out to Ever then Launce. After Ever and Launce were served, Ever gave the servant a curt, not-so-subtle nod that his presence was no longer needed. What he was about to say to Rafael wasn't appropriate for the palace gossips.

"So," he took a swig before giving the king his most displeased look, "I thought we had an agreement."

"I still do not see why you insist on getting to know him." Rafael stuck out his lip in a ludicrous pout. "It is not your kingdom that he's assisting with."

"But the man he has chosen is my subject," Ever said, ignoring the disgusted look Launce gave him at the term subject. "I want to know who I'm sending him off to before I let him go. Besides, my wife would have my head if something happened to her brother." When he finished speaking, the servant was still standing there. Annoyed, Ever finished off his drink as quickly as he could and then placed the goblet back on the tray. Perhaps he was simply waiting to take the empty vessels back to the kitchen. "Well, do I get to meet him?"

"Be my guest!" Rafael waved a meaty hand before stomping back down the dock toward the palace. Ever watched him go in confusion.

"Brokk." Launce nodded at the servant.

The servant smiled back, the crinkles in his eyes deepening with pleasure as though he'd just seen his own grandson. "Young Master Launce, I hope you are well?" The older man's eyes gleamed with satisfaction as he affectionately shoved Launce's arm. "How does it feel to win?"

Ever studied the servant more closely. Then it dawned on him that this was the very same servant he'd found in their room the day before, serving Isa her midday meal uninvited.

As if he'd heard his thoughts, the servant, Brokk, turned and looked at Ever directly. "How was the drink, Your Highness?" As he uttered the words, a blast of power punched Ever so hard he nearly stumbled backward. Strength, so ancient that his mouth immediately tasted of dust, emanated from the man, and Ever could only stare in horror. How had he missed this? Either the man had accidentally let down his guard, or he no longer feared being found out. From the appraising look in the small man's eye, Ever was assured that it was the latter.

Launce, however, seemed unaware of the wriggling streams of power that flowed from the man. "It was wonderful, Brokk. I don't think I've ever tasted anything quite so sweet."

"I'm glad you enjoyed it." Brokk didn't move his eyes from Ever.

A ripple moved down Ever's body.

"There's an intriguing history behind this drink. It's a

nectar, you see. One found only in the deep forests of the north."

Ever's feet were still planted on the wooden planks of the dock, but his head began to spin. Brokk continued to speak, but Ever couldn't make out the words. Blinking rapidly, he tried to fight the fog that was rolling into his eyes as he squinted at the remnants of the thick, red liquid in his goblet.

Bleary-eyed, Ever dipped his finger into the chalice and pulled out a few drops. The bright sunlight, which had been so cheerful only a few moments before, nearly blinded him, but he was barely able to make out the tiniest pieces of a crushed herb, though he couldn't tell which one. Dread and anger coursed through his veins like fire. He had been right.

Isa.

She must have known. And now she was by herself. Ever turned to grab Launce so they could run to her, but when he tried to pivot, the world tilted, and the force which should have held him to the dock failed him. Down Ever went, flailing his arms like a newborn, thrashing uselessly as the sea swallowed him. Through the murky water, he sensed another body sinking beside him. It sank, still as a stone. Spots began to fill Ever's eyes over the fog, and he stupidly sucked in a mouthful of salt water.

Even as he fought the water, Isa was the only thought on his mind. She had called for him, waited for him, and if he couldn't escape soon, the enchanter would have her first. *Not this!* he called out to the Fortress. *For her sake, please don't let me fail! Not like this! Not without helping her first!*

As he cried out to the Fortress, some of his sense returned, and Ever was finally able to find the surface. His pleas were answered, to his great relief, as his eyes began to regain their clarity, and he coughed up bile and salt. As he clung to the side of the dock, he could barely make out the retreating figure in a servant's uniform. His first impulse was to pull himself out of the water and hunt the bastard down. But the memory of the sinking figure came to mind. *No*, he thought, shaking his head. *I need to reach Isa.*

Pulling himself from the water, however, he knew he couldn't leave Launce behind. With a cry of anger, he dove back into the depths, putting the remainder of his strength into aiding his eyes. Every part of him screamed to leave the water and run to his wife. But Isa's voice, the one that seemed to now reside constantly in his head, wouldn't allow it.

As he searched, it seemed that Launce had simply disappeared. The deeper he swam, the more leaden his limbs felt. Unnaturally thick and opaque, the water seemed to fight him. His searching was in vain, for he found nothing. But just when he was about to give up, a dull shine caught his eye. Ever's lungs burned as he swam closer to find the buckle of a boot. When he grabbed hold of it, Ever praised the Maker that it was attached to a leg. Once again, he turned and swam upwards, trying to ignore the feeling of knives slashing at his lungs as they demanded air.

It took every ounce of strength for Ever to heave himself back onto the dock and then to drag Launce up behind him. For a long moment, try as he might, Ever could not move a muscle. The effects of the drink were still lingering within him. The Fortress had removed much of them, but he wasn't quite free yet. A yelp of pain slipped from him as he thrust one hand palm down against the wooden planks, and then the other. Gritting his teeth, he pushed himself onto his knees.

Please, he asked the Fortress. *Don't punish her for my mistake!* A familiar heat, which started in his heart, began to warm his shivering limbs, and slowly, ever so slowly, he was able to stand. Launce, however, lay still, his chest moving so slightly it was difficult to see at all. Again, Ever wanted nothing more than to leave him there in the pathetic pile he'd collapsed in. But was that what the enchanter wanted? For him to leave Launce behind, unguarded?

Ever sucked in a deep breath and placed one hand on each side of the young man's head. His arms trembled with the effort, but finally a thin blue flame moved between each palm. As it did, Launce coughed up a lungful of seawater, and his eyes flew open.

"Isa!" Ever wheezed. But he didn't have to say more. The look in Launce's eyes told Ever that he understood. Launce, too, struggled to stand, and then they were off. At first, Ever's steps were nearly as clumsy as his brother-in-law's, but as he left the dock behind and crashed through the royal gardens toward the palace, a new determination filled him. The clean, crisp air of autumn cleared his mind, and soon, Ever had left Launce far behind.

"Move!" he bellowed as he sprinted down the halls, willing to trample whoever got in his way. His heart beat as though it might burst, but it wasn't from the exertion of running. Fear drove him on like a madman. Against his will, images of all the things the enchanter might do to his wife invaded his imagination. Still, it didn't matter how fast he ran, because to him, it would never be fast enough.

Relief threatened to wash through him as he rounded the final corner and saw Norbert still standing guard, looking as fierce as ever.

"Norbert, move!" he ordered. The old guard barely managed to step to the side before Ever gathered his wavering strength and moved right through the thick wooden door. Stumbling to a halt, he watched in horror.

The room was filled with a sickening, violet glow, swirling about at ever-increasing speeds. Thin streaks of lightning flashed within the thin cloud that hung over the rose mirror in the center of the floor. Inside the mirror was Isa.

"Ever!" She banged against the inside of the mirror,

shrieking his name in a way that tore his heart. Placing his hands on the mirror, Ever closed his eyes and hunched his shoulders, drawing every bit of power within him. His hands grew hot and began to scald as he kept them against the glass. Willing it to break, he breathed in and out in deep, even breaths.

When he felt the resistance begin to lessen, he opened his eyes, only to see Isa still trapped. It wasn't the mirror's power that was giving out. Rather, it was Isa that was receding and being pulled right along with it.

He didn't know how to save her.

Tears begin to slide down his face as he placed his hands against hers on the glass. He could no longer hear her, but the pain and fear on her face was only too visible in the purple glow that lit the room. The midnight blue of her wide eyes burned into his as he struggled to hold on. Slowly, she began to fade.

"No!" he shouted, banging on the glass. When he did, a great *boom* sounded, and he was thrown back against the bed. The mirror shattered, and his heart leapt with hope. Upon opening his eyes, he could see that the glass was indeed broken.

But Ever was alone.

CHAPTER 26

TAKEN

Isa called out his name until her voice grew hoarse, but it made no difference. The glass she was trying to cling to became rough like frost, and Ever was gone. She pounded her fists against the mirror, and when it didn't break, she reached for her sword, only to realize she had once again forgotten to put it on back in her chambers in Cobren. When she looked at where her sword belt should have been, Isa gasped.

The floor was made of light blue glass. And not just the floor, but the walls, the ceiling, even the door across the room. Where was she?

The room she stood in was high, three times the height of that which she'd just left behind. There were no candles or torches lit, but there really was no need. Everything held the same strange blue glow, as though a great light lay beyond the walls and illuminated it from the other side. A single round window sat above the bed across the room from the door. The window was also made of glass, but the clear familiar kind, not the rough, frosty surface that made up the rest of the room. The bed was small and simple, neatly made as though it were expecting company. The only other piece of furniture was an old wooden wardrobe that stood to the left of the door. The wardrobe was open, and Isa could see that inside of it were stacked and folded blankets, a few gowns, and a large fur coat, the kind the northern trappers often wore when they traveled to Soudain to trade their goods. Only this coat was far more elaborate, with intricate stitching on the body and along the sleeves. It had clearly been made for a woman.

Only as Isa noted the coat did she realize that she was cold. Isa walked over to the window, which faced east; she nearly fainted when she looked out. Whatever structure she stood in was balanced precariously on the precipice of a great cliff. Razor-edged mountains that rose up into the lake-blue sky like daggers encircled her. The sun was up, and though she couldn't see it directly, its light wasn't the friendly autumn light they had been enjoying in Cobren. It was the light of a winter sun, tired and old, and hinting of sunset. The mountains themselves were covered in snow and ice, and Isa sensed they hadn't been thawed in many, many years, if ever.

She turned back to the room, to the wall that she'd come through, and wondered what had happened. She remembered pacing in her Cobrien chambers. She had been waiting for Ever when a strange violet light had begun to pulse from inside her rose mirror. Knowing better than to touch it, Isa had only stepped forward a little to get a better look, but it must have been too close. Before she knew what was happening, she'd felt herself being sucked into the mirror. Piece by piece, she had begun to melt away from her room in Cobren, but even as each piece of her had begun to fit back together in this strange room, she had held on. She had tried to pull the power from her aching arms to fight. It must not have been enough though. By the time Ever had returned, it was too late, and she couldn't hold on any longer.

Still, she had hoped. She was gone, but not completely. Ever could save her! The Fortress might not have left her with enough power to escape, but his was strong. If only he could find her.

A knock at the door made her jump, then freeze as Brokk's voice called out, echoing as though in a great cavern.

"Your Highness, I have some food. I thought you might be hungry." He sounded meeker than ever, but Isa didn't care. He had lied to her, gotten her to trust him. Whatever power he used was deep, and she would have nothing to do with it.

"Please, Your Highness. I know you're angry with me. I would be too. But if you only give me a few moments, I promise there is the best reason for this. I would never take a woman away from her husband and family against her wishes if it were not for the direst of needs. Please, just listen."

Still, Isa said nothing. There was nothing he could say that would move her heart from the place it was in now. Instead, Isa walked over to the window, made a fist, and tried with all her might to push the blue fire forth from her soul to open the window. But it was no use. Her insides felt dry, as though all of her blood had dissipated into the air.

And, she realized, she was very, very tired, the kind of tired that no amount of sleep could ever cure. Months of feeling her power, and then Ever, slipping away from her had been almost too much. Now, alone and terrified, it seemed there was nothing left in the world that she had to give.

"I'm sorry I lied," Brokk called quietly from behind the door. "I needed your help, but it would have been impossible to speak with you alone at the betrothal celebration. Your husband is a good man, but I knew he would never, ever allow me to speak candidly with you under his watch. I just need a few moments. I promise."

Still Isa stayed silent.

"I didn't lie when I told you that Agatha died."

Before Isa could respond, the wall she faced suddenly lost its frosted blue color, and instead became a scene, like one from the stories her father used to tell her. Despite her anger, she was in awe. Lovelier than any painting she had ever seen, this picture was flawless. Lush fields of corn and barley covered a countryside, which rolled with hills that glowed green and yellow in the dying day's sun. A young woman wearing a style of dress Isa had never seen before walked along the road, carrying a bucket in each hand. To Isa's surprise, the picture began to move. It felt as though she were there with the girl.

"She's lovely, isn't she?" Isa wasn't sure how he was doing it, making the scene move and change, but she felt the ancient power flowing again around her.

The young woman in the scene was indeed fair, but it was the openness of her face that was most breathtaking. A kindness lay there, like a refreshing crystal pool just waiting for a thirsty soul.

"She is lovely," Isa heard herself whisper, in spite of her promise to ignore the wretched man completely.

"I met Agatha while on a journey doing business for my mother," he said as the scene on the wall began to change. "In fact, we first saw one another in a tavern, where my companions and I had stopped to stay for the night. She was easy to spot, in spite of the crowded room, for girls of her manner and dress were never found milling about places like that."

Mesmerized, Isa watched as an older man yelled something unintelligible, and Agatha nodded and darted over to the tavern keep. The old keep nodded and poured her three mugs of what looked like ale, which Agatha immediately brought back to the table, keeping her eyes on the floor the whole time. After she'd handed the loud man the drinks, he gave a raucous laugh before issuing another order. Again, the girl simply nodded and half ran out of the ill-lit room.

"I followed her out to see if she was in need of assistance." Brokk spoke again. "When I found her outside, tending to her father's horse, however, it was she who helped me." He gave a strangled laugh. "Instead of answering my question, she placed her hand on my head and informed me I had a fever. And she was right. Within an hour, I was so sick I was delirious. Days later, by the time I was coherent enough to tell my companions my name, I was informed that it had been she who had kept me alive, as my companions knew absolutely nothing of nursing a dying man back to health." The wall began to move again, quickly this time. Summer turned to autumn, which turned to winter.

"I sent word to my mother saying I had found a matter of the utmost importance, and that I needed to remain gone for a time. Being the good woman she was, I was given full allowance to remain for as long as I needed. While I was there, I did odd jobs for whomever needed them, chopping firewood, bringing in the harvest, even helping the village holy man care for the chapel. Agatha and I spent every moment together that we could find." Brokk gave a sigh, and Isa knew he must be approaching his unhappy ending. Again, the scene on the wall began to move.

"Her father demanded payment for her hand. The amount was much higher than was expected for young women of the region, but he had long discovered I came from a high place, and he was adamant that he get his fair share. Of course, I had no qualm meeting his payments, using my . . . gift to bring in more than he had even demanded. With the rest of the money, I had planned to hire a coach to bring us back to my home in comfort as soon as the winter was over. I could travel without trouble in any weather, but she was made of more delicate stuff."

Suddenly, the wall stopped moving, and the scenes of happiness and contentment disappeared. The young woman with laughing eyes and light brown hair was gone, as was the younger version of Brokk. Once again, there was just a wall of glass. Isa sank slowly onto the bed, too distracted to notice whether it was clean or not.

"My mother sent word, however, that I must return at once. There was a matter of urgency that threatened all the regions, including that of my wife. Because she had taken to sickliness that winter, I left her with friends, promising to return for her as soon as possible."

Isa waited for him to continue, but instead he stopped. Silently, for the young woman's sake, Isa mourned the loss that she knew was coming. Whatever had happened hadn't been her fault.

"What happened?" Isa finally whispered after a long pause, unable to bear the unspoken any longer.

"A plague had begun to ravage the lands," he said in a hollow voice. "Not just one or two regions, but nearly all of the northern lands had been touched. My mother needed my assistance in deciding what to do."

"What to do?"

"My mother's power was also a gift of the Maker's, as yours is. Her gift was glass too, but it was much stronger and more potent than mine." He paused. "I can show you better in person later if you like. For now, I will simply say that we could have rid the lands of the plague easily. All of them. But curing the people would have required each land's regent to allow us to briefly take control of his lands. Some of the regents agreed readily. But there were some who would not."

"Why would the kings not allow it?"

"I'm sorry," Brokk said politely. "I forget you are not as old as I am. You see, we didn't have kings, or even separate king-doms in our day. Regents stewarded different regions, but they all paid respect to my mother."

"Who was your mother?" Uneasiness returned to Isa's stomach as she fingered the thick, brown coverlet of the bed.

"My mother was the most powerful enchantress who ever lived. Her name was Sigridur, but the people knew her as the Glass Queen."

CHAPTER 27
LEGENDS

It took Isa a moment to find her voice.

"So the legends are true?"

"If you come out, I will show you."

Her common sense screamed for Isa to stay put. This man, this lying enchanter, had taken her from everything and everyone she held dear, and was keeping her captive in a strange glass prison. It felt rather familiar, she thought bitterly. Must she go through this again?

Still, she hadn't broken the Fortress's curse by sitting in her room and moping, and it didn't appear as though the glass wall was going to open again for her to step back through. If he was so desperate for her to see something that he thought he needed to abduct her, then she might as well see it. And a small, childish part of her did want to see if the legends were true. So without a word, she went to the door and cautiously opened it, ready to slam it shut if she needed to.

Brokk stood in the hall. "It's a bit cold here." He gave her a hesitant, almost bashful smile, and gestured back to the wardrobe in the room. "I think you will be more comfortable if you're warm."

Seeing no reason to argue, Isa pulled on the fur coat from the wardrobe, and after a deep breath, left the room.

From the moment she stepped out the door, Isa knew she would be forever changed, if by nothing else, by the place itself. She had never dreamed such an edifice could exist. And yet, the longer she turned in circles, staring up at the vaulted blue arches and the ethereal light that seemed to be part of the glass itself, she immediately couldn't imagine a world without it.

They were standing in a hallway nearly wide enough across to fit three large beds. Her room stood at the far end of the hallway. The other end of the hallway was so distant it was impossible to make out, and the ceiling above them was high enough that its details were fuzzy. Even so, she could make out that every single wall, beam, and corner was made of the same frosty blue glass as she had found in the bedroom. Even though she stood on a dark purple velvet, silver edged rug that looked to run the length the entire hall, she could feel the hard glass beneath it.

"Where are we?" she breathed.

"This is my home." He raised his hands, palms up, in a simple, happy shrug. "Its true name is Galdur Gler, but like my mother's true name, it was never used. It was simply called the Glass Castle."

"How did such a place become forgotten?" Isa stopped turning in circles to stare at him.

"That depends on what you've heard." The slightest shadow of unease crossed his face.

But Isa shook her head. "I really don't know many stories, to tell the truth. Mostly . . ." She paused and tried to remember the nights when traveling bards would come to Soudain, and tell frightening stories to the children in the firelight. "Everyone claims that there was an old queen once who lived in a glass palace, but that she died unexpectedly. Some said she had contracted the plague, while others said she died of a broken heart when her husband passed." Isa shook her head. "The other children and I mostly made up adventures about the palace and the queen's knights."

At this, Brokk's shoulders relaxed, and his welcome smile returned. He began to walk down the hall, motioning for Isa to join him. She did so, but they didn't speak, and for a few moments, all she could hear were the swishing sounds of their long fur coats and the sounds of their boots' muffled taps on the rug. Isa tried to memorize all of the details around her. Still, neither all the intricate curves in the glass molding, nor all of the fine lines in the ornately carved walls, could distract her from the one question she needed answered most. She stopped walking and stood as straight as she could.

"Why did you bring me here?" How she wished she could sound as calm and collected as Ever always did! "And why did you use your power on me in the practice room?"

"For that," Brokk sighed, not meeting her eyes, "I'm sorry. Honestly, if there had been any other way, I would have taken it instead." Isa steeled herself, determined not to allow his sorrow to sway her good judgment. He drew a breath before speaking again. "I needed your help."

"That doesn't answer my question about the practice room."

"I hope I didn't frighten you too much there. I merely meant to test your sensitivity to my power. I never meant for you to fall."

"You could have just asked!" Isa knew she was taking a chance with such sharp words, as he was an enchanter of sorts and, it seemed, a very powerful one. But the annoyance of being taken against her will for the second time in one year was too much. Walking, against her will, down great, silent halls of an enchanted citadel was too fresh, too familiar for her to feel comfortable. And she was *not* going to fall in love with her captor *this* time.

"Please forgive me for being frank, my dear, but your husband is a bit . . . overprotective. He never would have allowed me to discuss my problem with you." Brokk finally met her eyes and held her gaze. "You know that."

Isa just turned and continued walking down the hall faster than he had been going. To her annoyance, however, he kept up unusually well for an old man.

"Please, listen first, then make your judgment!" His words, louder than any she'd heard him speak before, echoed up and down the hall. He stopped. "I have been searching for someone like you for two hundred years."

Isa came to a halt. "What for?"

He didn't answer at first, just studied her. As he did, Isa realized, he looked much different than the servant she'd first met in the practice room at Rafael's palace. He stood straight, his bearing very much as regal as Ever's. Though his hair was still silver, it seemed less unruly than before, and his eyes suddenly flashed with a determination.

"I told you that my mother called me back here from the cottage I shared with my wife. When I arrived, my mother brought me in to her meeting room immediately. That was when the regents of each region turned to my mother to ask what they should do about the sickness. As soon as I arrived, my mother and I worked day and night until we found a way to heal those who suffered."

Curiosity overtook her once again. "What did you find?"

To Isa's surprise, he put his hand in the pocket of his robe and drew out a small goblet. He held it out, so Isa took it, carefully turning it over in her hands. The entire goblet was made of a purple frosted glass, much like berries caught in an unexpected freeze.

"All they had to do was drink from the goblet. They could drink anything from it to be healed."

"What went wrong?"

"My mother and I were given much power, but there were limits to even our abilities. For our goblet to work, my mother asked that the regents of the different lands allow us to visit their lands personally, to serve the cure ourselves. Since there were no kings, only regents, it should have been simple. And yet," he sighed, "she gave them the choice anyway."

As he said this, he motioned for her to follow him again. They came to the end of the hallway, where the walls opened up into the largest room Isa had ever seen. Their path had become a bridge that hung suspended above the center of the room. Curved railings, much like glass branches of ivy, bordered each side of the walkway. One staircase spiraled down from the right, and one from the left, each on the opposite side of the path. In this room, the ceilings continued to vault up into soaring arches, but between the thick glass beams which lifted the lofty ceiling, giant, colorful windows painted the distant floors below. The windows themselves had to be at least the height of the throne room in the Fortress. Each one depicted a scene, though the scenes were too complicated for Isa to comprehend at just a glance. She would have needed hours of study to see what they truly meant.

To her right side, two doors that were taller than the Fortress's highest tower stood gleaming in the rainbow sunlight let in by the windows. They were simple rectangles without design or color, but their sheer size held Isa awestruck. On the left side of the glass bridge was a dais as wide as her parents' cottage, with two glass thrones whose backs nearly matched the height of the doors. Rather than blue glass, however, these thrones had also been given color, and looked as though someone had shredded a rainbow and thrown the pieces wherever they chose. The chaos was surprising in what otherwise appeared to be such a meticulous design, but the longer Isa looked at them, the more she realized they were possibly the loveliest objects she'd ever seen.

She was so caught up in wandering back and forth to gaze down upon each side of the bridge that she jumped when Brokk spoke again, breaking the brittle stillness that surrounded them.

"My mother built this palace when she was just a young woman, even before she married my father. Her power was so great that the size of this place helped her bear the weight of her strength. And yet, to heal the people, she was willing to leave and carry the burden on her own." It took Isa a moment to remember what they had been discussing before entering the throne room.

"The regents said no?" Isa turned to him incredulously.

"Some said yes, but others were too afraid. For one person to bring so much power to their lands, they said, was too much a risk. She might try to overthrow the peoples she visited. If she couldn't promise them a cure from her own home, she had no right being in theirs." The older man paused and looked away from Isa, but she didn't miss the sudden glistening in the corners of his eyes. When he spoke again, his voice was husky.

"The regent of my wife's land was such a man. When I heard it, I planned to go in and get her out myself, ill or not. The regent's order was sent to his fighting men though, and they watched the border day and night for me. By the time I was able to bribe someone into letting me in, it was too late," he said. "I arrived to find that both my wife and unborn child had taken ill and died the day before."

Isa closed her eyes. She tried to imagine what it might be like to lose Ever in such a way, but couldn't. And a child? Her mind shivered away from that train of thought before it could even get close to imagining such devastation. She'd lost him once. Unlike her, however, Brokk had never gotten his beloved back. He had never even met his child.

"You don't know what it's like." A quiet sob escaped him. "To be one of the most powerful creatures in the world, but still stand there helplessly as you hold the lifeless bodies of those you should have saved first." Another sob, louder this time, racked his own body, and his hands shook as they covered his eyes. "I didn't even know she was with child when I left! I never would have allowed her to stay!"

Isa stood a few feet away from him, unsure of what to do. Her first instinct was to reach out and touch his shoulder, to try and comfort him in some way. And yet, she stayed still. Something, possibly a stray breeze from the Fortress, the kind it often loosed inside its own walls, whispered in her ear to be wary. Such sorrow could only produce powerful reactions. And these reactions, she sensed, had been building for a long, long time.

"I'm sorry," she finally whispered. "But I still don't see what all of this has to do with me, or why you've been searching for so long."

"I apologize." He sniffed, and gave her a sad smile. "I haven't spoken of this to anyone since it happened. I still miss her . . ." He gazed longingly out one of the colossal windows before shaking his head and heading toward one of the spiraling staircases. "A man came to the palace when my mother had finished visiting the lands who had allowed her to come. His wife had also died in the plague, and when he realized that she could have been saved, he went mad. He burst in, roaring about how things could have been different.

"My mother had lived over a thousand years before I was even born. She had seen much death in her time, but this was more than she could live with. In her sorrow, she placed a sleeping curse upon herself. She must not have realized, however, that it would take the entire palace with her. As soon as the servants realized what was happening, they packed as quickly as they could and left. I couldn't leave her though."

They came to the bottom of the staircase and turned left out of the throne room and down another hall. This one wasn't quite as tall as the first.

"So you fell under the curse too?" Isa asked. As they walked past countless more glass doors, she was suddenly glad for the coat. It was growing colder as the sun began to fade.

"I did."

"Why did you wake up then, if she is still asleep?"

He turned and looked at her, surprise in his wide, leathery face.

"My dear, my good mother is dead. Even sleep gives way to death eventually."

"I'm sorry," she murmured again, but he shook his head.

"It could only have been expected. As to why I awakened, I'm really not sure, to be quite honest. I can only believe the Maker has greater plans for me."

They reached a door near the end of that particular hall, and Brokk pushed it open. This room was more decently sized, and was filled to the brim with glass objects of every shape and size imaginable. Isa had to remind herself not to touch anything as she walked past little dolls, plates, baskets, even a pair of dancing slippers that were all made of delicate, colored glass.

"Which brings me to the reason I need you," he said, walking over to a small fireplace in the corner where a pot of stew was bubbling. As the smell of its contents wafted over to Isa, she realized she was famished.

To her relief, he ladled out two bowls of the stew and handed one to her, along with a pink frosted glass spoon.

"Use this spoon, and no meal which you use it to eat will run dry until each member of the household has eaten. Then clean it, put it away, and use it again for the next meal." Isa took the spoon and examined it, a bit afraid to put his honor to the test. Would there be a reason for him to use it against her?

He must have sensed her suspicion, however, for he gently took the spoon back from her, poured most of his soup back into the black pot over the fire, and began to eat from the tiny puddle that remained in the bottom of his bowl. Isa nearly gaped when she realized his soup refused to run dry. Without a word, he held his right hand over her bowl. Snapping his fingers over her soup, he caught something invisible in his palm. He brought it back to his face and whispered into his closed fist. When he held out his hand to her again, a new glass spoon lay there. Hesitantly, Isa took it and, unable to resist the mouthwatering aroma of spices and beef for any longer, began to eat.

"Unlike your gift, my power, which I inherited from my mother, lies mostly within the gifting of objects. The objects are given the ability to help the recipient in a way specific to them. People from all over the lands used to line up in the throne room to see my mother. For hours, she would sit, or sometimes stand, and listen to their worries. If their hearts seemed sincere and their needs true, she would give them something to help." Brokk gave her a distant half-grin. "She loved people like that."

He moved over to the work desk and picked up an item Isa hadn't noticed before. It was a small mirror, barely larger than the palm of her hand. It was made up of two layers of glass. The outer layer, which served as a frame, was opaque, and had miniature trees and stars carved into it. The reflective part of the mirror was flawless, like an undisturbed lake that had just frozen over.

"I am now older than my mother ever was," he said as he studied the little mirror. "I have seen more heartache and sorrow in the world than I will ever be able to describe. After waking up and recalling what had happened, I traveled as a poor journeyman. I went in search of a way to heal the world that has become so far gone since my mother and I fell asleep." He took the mirror back and stared at it. "I was young when my mother placed the sleep on us, barely two hundred. We slept for two millennia and seven centuries. Since then, I have been searching for more than two hundred years. And yet, for all my searching, I was in despair, until I heard about you."

Isa paused, her heart suddenly hammering within her as she locked eyes with him. Without warning, gone was the meek, gentle face she had thought she'd known, and instead, she sensed that she sat in the presence of a powerful, passionate enchanter.

"What about me?" she stammered.

"You were given a magnificent gift, Isabelle. The Maker gave you a purpose. You can do what no one has been able to accomplish in nearly three thousand years. With your power of the heart, you can help me bring peace to the northern kingdoms."

"How?"

He glanced up, and when he did, she noticed that the angelic light that had seemed to light the entire castle earlier was fading. The sun must be setting

"It is getting late. Tomorrow, I will tell you. For now," he paused, his hand on the door and a strange smile on his face, "simply know that no plague or pestilence or war or famine or disaster of any other manner will hurt the northern kingdoms again as long as you and I and your husband, should he choose to join us, learn from my mother's mistake."

Isa was still terribly confused as he led her back to her room, but something within her, that small breeze from before, silently screamed that the choice he offered her seemed to be really no choice at all.

CHAPTER 28
BEFORE YOU GO

Launce watched in a stupor as Everard knelt before the broken rose-colored mirror in Isa's chambers. Despite their long run, water still dripped from his clothing, and his head felt as though it were stuffed with goose down. He still couldn't quite remember how he had fallen into the sea to begin with, only that Everard had dragged him out of the water and tossed him up on the pier like a fish. Their sprint had something to do with Isa, that much he knew. But for the life of him, that was all he could recall.

Even now he wasn't wholly conscious. A strange sensation still clung to him as the water rolled off his body, as though another skin had been laid over his own. This invisible second layer, however, squeezed his mind and dulled his senses, and even though he knew Everard was shouting, nothing his brother-in-law said made sense.

"Rafael!"

Everard's bellow made Launce's already aching head throb even harder. By the time Launce had caught up to him, Everard was still kneeling on the floor, his hands, bleeding, pressed against the remnants of the mirror. The thought of glass made something inside of Launce squirm, but for the life of him, he couldn't get his head clear enough to know what was wrong, and why glass had anything to do with his brother-in-law's distress. A familiar voice behind him broke through the cacophony in his head, sounding quite put out.

"Will you stop terrifying my guests and tell me what you're going on about?" In two giant steps, Everard was off the floor, and had the portly man by the shoulders, azure fire encircling his fists. At first shock, then anger and fear mingled upon the big man's face as Everard shook him so hard his head snapped back.

"He took her! Your blasted enchanter took her!"

"Who? Who did he take?" It seemed the man, whoever he was, was wise enough not to try and fight Everard, considering the state he was in. Something inside Launce niggled him again, suggesting he should try to save the man's life, but a distant memory of the familiar blue flame kept him firmly in place.

"Isa! He took my wife! Now where is he?"

The mention of his sister's name burned a hole through the thick fog between his ears, and with sudden clarity, Launce began to recall everything. Being on the pier with Everard, the warm, sweet drink Brokk had given him. And falling. Falling into the depths of the green, murky sea as a foreign drowsiness consumed him. But none of that mattered as Everard's words finally sank in.

Isa was gone.

Launce suddenly had the urge to join Everard in beating the answer from Rafael, but he held back, more from his fear of Everard's uninhibited power than from a desire to see the older king safe and well.

"I do not know!" Rafael's face was the color of tomatoes, and his breathing was raspy as he struggled against the strength in Ever's hands. "But if you let me call my servants, I will have them search!" For a moment, the feral light that had filled Everard's eyes only burned stronger, and Launce fleetingly wondered if Everard just might kill the king then and there. Slowly, however, his hands began to loosen, and as soon as they were gone, Rafael stumbled out of the room, only looking back once he was on the other side of the door frame. Yanking his clothes straight, he stood as tall as possible, and raised his chin defiantly.

"Meet me in the throne room in ten minutes. I will let you know what I find out then. But I must warn you, I expect you to keep control of yourself in my palace, Everard. I will not allow such blatant disregard for order in my kingdom."

"You will do as you promised," Everard growled, "or I will kill you myself."

Launce let out a small sigh of relief as the older king paled and disappeared, if for no other reason than that the princess would keep her father for another night.

"What was his name?"

Launce looked up to find Everard's glare in his direction. Launce stared back stupidly. "Whose name?"

"The servant!" Everard shouted. "The one who nearly killed us just moments ago! You were friends with him! What was his name?"

"Brokk," Launce stuttered. Everard's gray eyes hardened into granite, and the blue flames nearly engulfed them.

"Bronkendol," he whispered. Without another word, he turned and stormed back out the door, and it was all Launce could do to keep up. Norbert stood outside, but looked more distraught than Launce could have imagined the old soldier capable of. "Prepare my horses!" Everard called behind him as they walked. "I want you to bring the servants back to the Fortress as quickly as they can move, but Launce and I will be gone as soon as the horses are ready."

Still shaking off the effects of the sweet drink, Launce was breathing hard by the time they made it to the throne room. He felt clumsy and dull as he stood before the king, Queen Monica, Princess Olivia, and a number of Rafael's advisers. Still, he didn't miss the way the princess's shrewd eyes continued to flick toward him throughout the hearing.

"I'm glad to see you've regained control of yourself, Everard," Rafael began.

Launce blanched as the words left the king's mouth. Even Queen Monica looked at her husband in shock. Was he really going to provoke the king of Destin after his wife had been stolen? Still, Rafael continued on, suddenly a very different man than the one Launce had seen shaking in his boots just ten minutes before.

"Where is he?" Ever's voice was cold and smooth, like a polished slab of stone.

"My servants do not know where he has gone at this present time. He is not a dog on a leash."

"Do you know exactly who you have been housing?" Everard asked. "And if you reply that he is just a holy man, I will cut your tongue from your mouth." Rafael looked as though he wanted to snap, but the queen leaned forward and spoke first.

"Who is he, Everard?" Her voice trembled just a bit, and Launce was suddenly impressed by the queen's self-control.

"The same day your invitation reached the Fortress," Everard said, "I also received a message from the Lingean king that ten holy men had been murdered in a field."

The queen went pale, and Olivia's eyes grew wide, but Everard continued to speak.

"I received word this morning from my own healers that the holy men had been cut with glass shards . . . from the inside."

"Just what are you implying, Everard?" Rafael crossed his arms as though he were talking to an impertinent courtier.

"I imply nothing! I am telling you that in your pride, your

greedy desire for power and strength, you have opened your doors for none other than Bronkendol himself."

Gasps and whispers erupted from those surrounding them, but Everard ignored them, keeping his eyes bored into Rafael's.

"Nonsense! He's been dead for nearly three thousand years."

But Queen Monica's hand flew up to her mouth. Slowly, she stood, as though in a daze.

"Everard, how do you know?"

"Could you not see the signs?" Everard's words weren't as sharp for the queen, but he was still just as frank. "A glass hill? Gifts of glass?" He paused, his shouts finally over. "No one truly ever saw him die."

Rafael continued to glower, but everyone else stood frozen in silence. Finally it was the queen who first roused herself from the fear that seemed to paralyze them all. Launce was dying to know what Everard was talking about. He'd never heard the name before, and it obviously meant something significant, but he would feel much better if they were already on their way to search for Isa.

"What will you do? What should we do?" the queen asked.

"I am going to search for her," Everard said. "We will be riding fast, but if I were you, I would gather my horses and the court as quickly as possible, anyone who wants to come, whether it be peasant or noble. Take shelter in my kingdom while I hunt him down. The Fortress will protect you there."

"We will do no such thing!" Rafael slammed his palm down on the arm of his ebony throne with a smack. "You come into my home and threaten me, then blaspheme a man sent by the Maker to help us! I am warning you, Everard—"

But Everard had already turned to go. A strange sense of division filled Launce as he began to follow Everard. He wanted to go find his sister. And yet, he had the sudden desire to talk to the princess before they departed, although he didn't know what possessed him to think she would want to bid him farewell. The game was off, and he was no longer competing for the hand of the princess. He was still just a merchant's son, and would likely never return to her country again.

With regret churning in the pit of his stomach, Launce finally tore his gaze away from Olivia, and began walking toward the hall. Before he reached it, however, he heard the sound of padded footsteps following him. A cool hand grasped his arm and whirled him around. Olivia stood there, a determined look on her face as she ignored her father's shouts to come back that instant. Without hesitating for even a second, she took hold of his sleeves in both hands and drew his face to hers.

Her smooth lips pressed into his, and the tenacity in her kiss surprised him. He could have remained there for much longer, but all too soon she was pushing him away.

"Our betrothal might have been designed by a monster, but I like you anyway," she whispered, a coy smile upon her face. "Please attempt to stay alive." And with that, she turned and walked back to her father, her chin held high as he protested her audacity.

Somehow, Launce remembered where he was supposed to be, but as he ran to the stables, he couldn't help the grin he felt spread upon his face. He liked her too.

CHAPTER 29

MINE FIRST

What in the name of Gahfferon—" Launce woke with a start. "Get this off of me!"

But Ever continued to ride. Launce was more than capable of untying himself. "You were about to fall off of your horse. I simply made sure you wouldn't be trampled to death while you slept." Ever ignored the sneer that Launce sent him, keeping his focus on steadying their horses as they raced up the mountain bend. To his relief, Launce decided not to pick an argument. But then again, for once, Launce and Ever were in pursuit of exactly the same thing.

"Will we be there soon?" Lance asked, ducking low as they passed under a thick patch of trees that reached across the mountain path.

"We are almost to the pinnacle. Once we make it over the top, the Fortress will only be a little way down."

"I still don't see why we couldn't just head straight for Brokk's home," Lance said. "If you already know that it's in the north—"

"That is not his name, and you would do well not to use it," Ever snapped. "As for his home, I do know that it is to the north, however the castle itself has been hidden for almost three millennia. It would be foolish to run in blind only to get ourselves caught in a blizzard or something worse of his own making. Garin is our best hope in planning our next moves. Garin and the Tower of Annals. We will consult and make our decision there."

Launce seemed at least somewhat placated by Ever's answer, but Ever himself wasn't sure he was correct in his assumptions. Garin was old, but from what Ever had gathered over the years, even he hadn't lived long enough to see the days of the glass castle.

The journey that had taken them two full days to make the first time took only one day and one night in return. Ever had used every bit of his strength to push the horses on so that they ran harder while needing less rest and water. He had used so much of his strength in aiding their furious pace, however, that he had little left for himself or the young man beside him.

To Launce's credit, the young man hadn't complained. But his ability to remain awake had finally waned, and after nearly twenty hours of riding, Launce had been unable to go farther. Ever had allowed them one hour of rest during the night before, but not a minute more. When Launce had begun to doze off again as they rode on, Ever hadn't had the power to keep him upright. Thankfully, there was enough rope in his pack to secure Launce to his horse without waking him. Had they been in any other situation, he would have thought it great fun to tie up the young man, passive revenge for the stubbornness Launce had shown him since the day they'd met.

It had occurred to Ever more than once that he would have moved much faster without the young man. It would have been easier to leave him in Rafael's court, where at least he had a warm bed and a decent number of eyes to watch him. And yet, just as Ever could almost hear Isa begging him to save her little brother's life as he sank into the sea, he could now imagine her begging him to keep Launce safe with him. These imagined pleas were constantly at war with the need he felt to dash off alone and find her himself.

Dark thoughts of what the enchanter might want with his wife endlessly swirled about his mind. Intrusive images of what she could be suffering bombarded him with every breath that passed through his lungs. Up and down the hills, through the canyon, and up the mountain, Ever had prayed that the Fortress would strengthen her, that her power might be returned for even just this time.

And with those prayers surged the desire to leave his clumsy young charge behind. But if he knew anything about Isa, it was that she loved her brother, and that if Ever sacrificed Launce in his attempt to save her, Isa would never forgive him.

It was afternoon by the time they reached the mountain's summit and began down the other side. Ever had never used so much of his power so fast for so long, and everything in him ached. But he ignored it and pushed the horses on until nausea almost got the better of him. Eventually, however, they did make it through the servants' gate, taking a number of the servants by surprise by racing right up to the stables. Even before they arrived, Ever could see Garin waiting outside the stables, elbows out and his hands behind his back in his usual position.

"Norbert's message arrived last night." Garin's voice was as steady as ever, but there was an undercurrent to it. "He wrote only that you were returning home today, but nothing more. I assumed he feared the bird might be intercepted?"

"Isa has been taken." Ever swung down from his horse easily, but his muscles screamed in protest when he landed. Garin's eyes flashed and his jaw tightened as he waited for him to say more, but Ever didn't want to incite panic. He leaned forward and whispered, "Bronkendol." Ever watched his steward's face carefully.

The comprehension took a moment, but it was clear when Garin truly understood. His face turned to stone and ash, and his eyes widened in a way that made Ever more than uncomfortable. Immediately, the steward turned and began to head toward the Fortress. Ever followed without a word, dragging Launce along behind him.

The trek from the stables to the Fortress's highest tower had never seemed to take so long as it did this time.

"If you value your life," Ever called softly back to Launce, "you will do well not to touch anything. This is sacred ground. Only Garin, the kings, queens, and a handful of servants have ever stepped inside of this room." Well, Ever thought with chagrin, those select few, as well as a dozen dead Tumenian soldiers and their dead princess, Nevina.

"Perhaps," Launce puffed as they climbed the winding tower stairs, "it would be best if I just waited outside."

"No. You're a part of this now, whether we like it or not. Just mind yourself."

By the time Ever and Launce had crossed the threshold, Garin was already clearing a large mahogany table at the center of the room and covering it in maps. Before joining the steward, Ever made sure Launce was standing in a place where, if he fell from exhaustion, he wouldn't break anything too old. Then Ever threw himself into a deep search of the great tomes he knew so well, grabbing as many as he could from the old, wooden shelves.

"How was she taken?"

"Through the mirror in our chambers." Ever wanted to gut himself for forgetting about the blasted mirror in their guest quarters, the one he'd used every day they'd spent at Cobren.

"You are certain it's him?"

Ever looked up from a dusty page he was skimming and nodded.

"But nearly three thousand years?" Garin slumped against the table in disbelief.

Ever struggled to keep his demeanor calm as he watched Garin waver. In all his life, only a few things had ever rattled Garin, and all of them had happened while Ever was under the Fortress's curse, which had been brought on by his own foolish mistakes. Nothing outside of his actions or his personal mistakes had ever seemed to even bother the steward. Until now. Now Garin's face was taut, and his suntanned, slightly lined face seemed suddenly much closer to the age it should be, whatever that was.

"I don't understand," Launce called from the other side of the room, where he was now sitting against a wall. "What kind of man lives for three thousand years?"

"Bronkendol is the only child of the Glass Queen," Ever said as he grabbed the first book from his pile and began to skim it. "And he has lived for nearly four thousand years. We've only assumed him dead for three thousand."

"Wait, the Glass Queen was real?"

"More than real," Garin snorted, recovering himself a bit. "The Glass Queen is the reason our kingdoms exist the way they do."

"No one knows where she came from," Ever added as he continued to skim the dusty pages, "but we do know that the Glass Queen was gifted from the Maker, much in the way the Fortress monarchs are. Her gift was incredibly potent though, even when compared with many in my line."

"She could conjure glass objects," Garin said, "that would fill specific needs. There were no actual kingdoms in the land of what we now call the northern kingdoms. There were simply regions with low-ranking overseers. If disagreements between regions arose, they took them to the Glass Queen. She either mediated, or, if she was able, created an object from glass that would help both parties."

Ever finished the first book with annoyance. Nothing. He had read nearly every book in the Annals, but suddenly nothing seemed to have the information he needed. Tossing it aside, he moved on to the next.

"Like the gifts we were given at the banquet?" Launce's voice was hushed, nervous. Still skimming the book before him, Ever nodded.

"When a plague began to spread throughout the lands, the regents asked Bronkendol and his mother to find a cure. Bronkendol had inherited many of his mother's abilities, and together, it didn't take them long to create a cure. In order to administer the cure, however, a great deal of power would need to be poured out upon each land, and not all of the lands wanted that power."

"Why wouldn't they accept it?" Launce had moved closer, and was frowning deeply.

"Power gifted by the Maker can be terrifying to those unfamiliar with it." Garin, who had been poring over various maps, looked at Launce with half-lidded eyes. "If the Glass Queen had attempted to invade the opposing lands, she would have faced local armies. Too much blood had been shed already, she said. She did not want blood on her hands."

"Bronkendol's young wife took ill and died," Ever spoke again. "Bronkendol blamed his mother because she had not forced the cure upon that particular region after they had refused her help. In his anger, he attempted take control of the Glass Castle himself. He planned to murder his mother and seize dominion over all the regions on his own. The queen found out just before he succeeded, and she knew she would have to stop him. She couldn't bring herself to end her own son's life, however, so she told the servants to leave, and in her sorrow, placed a sleeping curse upon every living thing left, which at that point, was only her son, herself, and the castle."

"How do we know all this?"

"Servants escaped the glass castle carrying their belongings, as well as words from the queen," Garin said.

"In truth," said Ever, "it's Bronkendol and his mother that we can thank for our kingdoms being shaped the way they are. Once the queen, who was mediator between the regions, was gone, the lands eventually solidified into their own kingdoms, which led to Destin's eventual rise." Ever closed another book and joined Garin in looking at the maps. "Now, Launce, when you spoke with him, did he ever mention any of his plans?"

At this, Garin turned his gaze to Launce as well.

"No," Launce said slowly, then his face lit up. "But he did say he was from the far, far, north! When I asked him what made him leave, he said something about some decisions being made for us."

"I don't understand it." Ever glared at the maps spread out before him. "The entire continent north of us is inhabited. We know the Glass Castle was here somewhere..." He traced the northern Lingean border, his voice trailing off as frustration filled him. Every moment they wasted, Isa was alone, but their efforts felt fruitless. The lands north of them, Lingea and all of its neighbors, were too populated for anyone to have missed an entire castle.

"What about the murdered priests in Lingea?" Garin asked.

"They were found in a meadow not far from here." Ever pointed to a mountainous region that was surrounded by small villages and many farms. During the winter, the land was treacherous. Only the hardiest farmers could grow crops there. But that still didn't explain how an entire castle could go unseen.

"How do we even know he brought her to his castle? What if the castle is gone, and only he survived?" Launce asked.

"The power he uses was tied to that castle the way my power is tied to the Fortress," Ever said. "He would need a safe place to plan whatever he has been scheming, as well as the source of power. No, his castle is still standing. If only we could find it."

"Ever," Garin said, staring out the window. "I might have an explanation."

Ever turned to Garin, curious, but with trepidation as well. The steward only used that tone of voice when his knowledge of deeper power was called upon. By practice, Garin never spoke of such subjects unless he had to, and the hesitancy with which he recalled it had always kept Ever from enquiring any further than necessary. Ever trusted Garin more implicitly than anyone else in the world. Garin had practically raised him. But when he spoke of old power, a dangerous glint touched Garin's eyes, and Ever knew better than to prod.

"There was once a race, long extinct now, that could cut paths between realms. They could create bridges between their world and ours, somewhat akin to the way you use your power to speed your horse between locations."

"Different realms?" Launce balked. And for once, Ever was as confused as the young man.

"It is difficult to explain if you haven't been there to see it," Garin frowned.

Did that mean Garin had seen such things?

"The Maker created our world as one of many," Garin continued. "Sometimes, those worlds touch, overlap, even. In fact, that is how individuals like you, Ever, and the Glass Queen and Kartek can foster power at all. The Maker has allowed just a little of His world to touch and spill over into ours.

"These beings from long ago had the innate ability to build roads directly between the worlds, rather than spend the years it would take to reach the distant lands by foot, sea, and air. But first, they had to possess an item from that world before they could trace it back to its place of origin. Sometimes the Maker would allow them to come across items from other worlds through trade or miracle. I wonder," Garin stopped and looked at Ever, "if Bronkendol might have created such a road of his own."

"But his world was once part of ours," Ever said. "We know the castle and its queen occupied a particular place and time." He gestured at the books before him, as though that might change things, but Garin was already shaking his head.

"We don't know what was in the spell that the queen cast. I would wager that she not only put a sleeping curse on the castle itself, but sealed it off into a world of its own. She couldn't kill her son, but she could not risk this world's safety. As long as he was breathing, even in his sleep state, he was dangerous."

"But how did he get back to us then?" Ever asked.

"Bronkendol has engaged in deep planning." Garin began to gather the books and pile them on the edge of the table, away from the maps. "And he is his mother's son. Obviously, her sleeping spell didn't hold him. If he was able to awaken after all these years, it only makes sense that he found a way to tear the veil between worlds as well. He would only have needed a single item in his palace that had been made in the old world."

"But I still don't understand why he would want Isa," Launce, interrupted.

"Your sister," Garin said in a grave voice, "was granted more power than any other queen I have ever seen. She simply doesn't know it yet." He paused. "It would only make sense for Bronkendol to want to harness her power."

Ever said nothing, wishing with all his might that Garin was right about her power, because if he was, Isa might stand a chance of saving herself from this ancient foe. But the dying flames that had barely lit her eyes haunted him. Even if he found a way to reach her, would he be too late?

"So," Garin looked at Ever, as though reading his thoughts, "what are we going to do?"

"We're going to study these maps more. I will also be

sending out messenger birds to Lingea to ask more about their priests that were attacked. Launce will return to Cobren—"

"I'm going nowhere except with you." Launce crossed his arms and straightened his shoulders.

"You will do as I say, return to the Cobrien court, and send messenger birds to Garin about what Rafael and Bronkendol are up to."

"You are not my owner!" Launce exploded. "And I am not your dog to do your bidding! My sister is gone! Who gives a husk about the Cobrien court?"

"I am your king, and you will do as I say!" Ever thundered back, slamming his fist down on the table. When he felt the wood crack, he knew he needed to calm down before someone else got hurt, particularly the obstinate young man before him. Taking a deep breath, Ever lowered his voice, closing his eyes so he wouldn't have to see the insolence on Launce's face.

"Rafael is the enchanter's puppet. I need to know what the enchanter wants with him. Saving Isa would do no good if there were no home to bring her back to. Besides," he said more gently, "I believe there is one member of the court that you would like not to see harmed. Watch over her while you're there. She needs someone she can turn to."

Launce snorted. "As if I could save her."

"Why do you think I spent so many hours trying to teach you?" Ever felt exasperated. For once, would the young man ever simply do as he asked? "Did you think I was practicing with you just to make you angry?" The look Launce gave him was answer enough, and Ever had to take a deep breath again. They were past the time of pointless arguments.

"Life with the Fortress is one of possibility and danger," Ever said. "Now, I have another reason I'm sending you back if you'll listen to me. Look closely at my eye." Ever leaned close to the young man, ignoring Launce's look of disgust. "Do you see this?"

Launce glanced down and up as quickly as he could before shaking his head.

"Look closer," Ever demanded. "There's a rough spot, right in the corner."

This time, Launce sighed, but did as he was told. When his eyes grew bigger, Ever knew he had seen it.

"Are those . . . splinters?"

"Slivers of glass," Ever said. "Everyone who was in the stands that first day at the arena has them."

"I don't," Launce said.

"You weren't *in* the arena when the opening ceremonies began, as you took it upon yourself to hide in the woods. But you were the only one. The other competitors have them. All of my personal guards who were there with us have the slivers also. Isa does too, although I don't think she's aware of it. When the enchanter rained down his bright show of glittering glass that first day, they became lodged in everyone's eyes." Ever looked at Garin, regret coloring his voice. "I tried to shield us, but I was too late."

"And you can't purge it?" Garin's voice was calm, but the look he gave Ever was too sharp to be genuine.

Ever shook his head. "I've tried, repeatedly. But this power . . ." he faltered, not sure how to tell his mentor and oldest friend how lost he really felt. "It's like nothing I've felt before."

Turning back to Launce, Ever said, "I don't know what the enchanter is plotting, but since you are not under his control, you are safer than any of us in that court. Now please," he said, wishing his request didn't sound so much like begging. "Go, so I can focus on saving your sister."

Launce stared at him for a long time. Ever held his gaze, wondering what the young man saw. Like Launce, Ever's chin and upper lip were covered in tough stubble, but it suddenly occurred to Ever that Launce looked older than he had only a week before. Finally, Launce simply nodded and left.

EVER DIDN'T REMEMBER LEAVING the tower, but somehow he woke up in his own bed while the morning was still dark. A knock sounded at the door, and Ever realized that must have been what had awakened him in the first place.

"Yes?" he mumbled, rubbing his eyes. He still felt so tired he could hardly get his bearings. "What is it?"

"Master Garin says to tell you that your brother-in-law is ready to leave soon. He thought you would like to see the young man off."

"Thank you," Ever said. "Tell him I will be there." He couldn't stop the groan that escaped him as he pulled himself into a sitting position, and out of habit, was careful not to disturb the other side of the bed.

Just because his strength allowed him to push himself harder than most others, it didn't mean he never felt the pain. Very quickly, he was realizing that riding as hard and as fast as they had could bring some serious pain. Still, he pulled on the clothes someone had laid out for him, and headed to the stables.

When he arrived, Launce was already seated upon his horse. Ever wondered what kind of trick Garin had used to get the young man looking so well so quickly after Ever had pushed him so hard the two days before. Full saddlebags hung from the horse's sides, and for the first time, Launce was actually wearing the official colors of the Fortress.

"Would you walk me to the gate?" Launce asked him quietly.

Suddenly curious, Ever nodded.

As they left the stables, Ever wished he'd worn a thicker cloak. Autumn was leaving more hastily than usual, and winter was definitely in the air. A mischievous breeze moved in and out around their legs and arms, squeezing into every cranny that wasn't completely covered. Aside from the breeze, everything else was still as they walked quietly across the browning lawns behind the Fortress to the servants' gate. For official business, Ever always used the main entrance, but the servants' gate was farther up the mountain, and made the ride to the main path much faster.

Unsure of what Launce wanted with him, Ever waited. Sometimes, he knew from experience, more could be learned from silence than from unwanted questions. Sure enough, just a few minutes into their walk, Launce finally spoke.

"If you could see the enchanter right now, speak with him face-to-face, what would you do?"

"I would kill him before he could speak a word."

"Then would it be safe to say that you hate him?" Launce turned and looked directly into his face, and in the light of the full moon, Ever could feel the intensity of his gaze.

"Garin has taught me that hate never accomplishes anything, hate for others, at least. We can hate circumstances, and we can hate tragedy, but hating others brings us close to a place of danger within ourselves," Ever answered evenly. "But that said, yes. I hate him with every bone in my body."

"Then you finally understand."

"Understand what?"

"How I feel about you."

Something violent stirred within Ever. He felt heat pulse from his hands, and the desire to taste blood surged within him. And yet, as he stared up at the lanky young man who rode his horse with such infuriating serenity, Ever realized his fury wasn't for Launce. It was for himself.

"She is your wife now," Launce continued in a calm, resigned tone, "but she was mine to protect first. After you hurt her the first time, I was the one to help pick up the pieces. I was the one to talk her out of daring attempts on her horse. While you were off fighting your glorious battles, Isa was my responsibility. On the night you gave orders to kill her, I carried her to the cart so we could flee the city before your bloodbath ensued. And as if that weren't enough," Launce's voice grew hard, and he glared openly at Ever this time, "you demanded her, like chattel. You took her from us. My parents had planned to escape, but they didn't know her like I do. I knew that just as she had given up her horse for me, she would give up her life for the rest of us. I even caught her just before she reached your gate."

Ever felt sick as he listened. There had been a time when he thought his heart had been beaten to its very core, but that was nothing compared to hearing what Launce had to say now. Because he knew, deep down, that the young man spoke the truth.

"It was only for Megane's sake that I let her go," Launce said. "And until we received news that you had died, and that Isa would be crowned queen, I had to look at that Fortress on the mountain every day, and imagine what you were doing to her there, all alone. And I knew that it was all because I had failed to keep her safe."

They had reached the gate, and Launce pulled his horse to a stop, turning it so he could look at Ever head-on.

"The only reason I didn't go mad on the day you married my sister was because I could see that she truly believed in you. And I thought to myself, if anyone can save my sister from her own brave, foolhardy schemes, it would be you." And with that, he turned his horse and gave it a kick.

CHAPTER 30

CRYSTAL TRUTH

After walking her back to the room she'd first arrived in through the mirror, Brokk gave Isa a few candles to see by as the darkness continued to fall.

"The mountains surround us on every side, so the wind becomes trapped within them, and grows cold and strong. Use as many blankets from the wardrobe as you need. I have also added a few of my mother's old gowns for you if you wish to change. She was nearly your size."

Once he was gone, Isa looked doubtfully at the bed. It looked old, but when she sniffed it, it somehow smelled clean and free of dust. Grudgingly, she laid down. Sleeping was the last thing she wanted to do. Still, she wouldn't be able to go far if she found the chance to escape, but was too tired to do so.

As she gingerly tucked herself under the blankets, Isa looked up at the strange shadows the candles cast upon the glass walls. Ever would know what to do, she thought to herself.

But Ever wasn't there.

Suddenly, Isa didn't care if she was mad at him or not. Just having his warmth beside her would have done wonders to soothe her frightened soul. And he would come, she promised herself. If anyone could find her, it would be him.

Isa would have given anything to have him with her at that moment. It stung to think about the last words they had shared. The yellow firelight on the white-blue ceiling danced eerily as though it could feel the gales of wind that rushed and roared around the castle. The shadows seemed to leer at her.

What if he doesn't come? they whispered. Isa rolled over, as if ignoring the flames could quiet the fears that whirled around inside her head. *Perhaps*, she prayed to the Maker, *you could at least send me dreams of him rushing to my side. Just let me escape in my dreams for the night.*

WAKING up was difficult the next morning. The Maker had answered her prayers, and sweet dreams had taken her during the night. Images of Ever, and the sensation of his touch had brought her to a deeper sleep than she'd had in months.

And yet, their disappearance made waking up all the more difficult. Instead, shock and fear rippled through her as Isa struggled to remember where she had fallen asleep. At least it wasn't dark anymore, she tried to comfort herself. The glass castle's opaque walls were bright with gray sunlight once again, but there was not a sound to be heard, aside from the constant wind. Isa lay in bed, shivering for over an hour before she was decently sure Brokk wasn't listening outside her door again.

Finally, she slipped out of bed, only to be greeted by the coldest air she had ever felt. She hadn't intended to touch the Glass Queen's gowns, but as soon as she saw how warm they really were, made of thin, soft leather, and lined with white fur, Isa changed her mind, and quickly changed into a warmer dress and covered it with the thick robe. Then she waited one more time with her ear to the door before cautiously peeking out into the hall.

"Brokk?" she called. There was no answer. Twice more she yelled out his name before concluding he wasn't nearby. She suddenly wondered if he had gone back to Cobren. If he had brought her here through a mirror, he must have been able to return through one as well.

Her suspicions were all but confirmed when she made her way to his workshop and found one steaming glass bowl of porridge set out on the table. As she ate, Isa hoped he would be gone for a while. Since the moment she had discovered where she really was, Isa had longed to explore the ancient castle on her own. Legends of the Glass Queen had been some of her favorites when she was a child. Even more importantly, however, she hoped to find some hint as to what the enchanter was truly planning. Then, when Ever came for her, she would at least have something to tell him.

Her boots made sharp clicking sounds against the frosted glass floor that echoed down the halls as she walked back to the throne room. As she went, she dragged her hand along one of the walls. Though her ability to produce the Fortress's fire seemed to be all but gone, Isa wondered if she would at least be able to feel the power of one room if it was more important than the others.

Just as she entered the throne room, Isa stopped. It felt as though someone had poured something thick, icy, and hot into her blood. Her heart began to race, and the sudden urge to sprint up one of the spiraling staircase nearly overwhelmed her. Her chest grew so tight she could hardly breathe, but as soon as Isa removed her hand from the rough glass of the wall, every-thing stopped. Her breathing returned to normal, and it was as if nothing had happened. Mystified, Isa tentatively placed her fingers along the wall again. Immediately, the draw to go upstairs consumed her once more.

Could this be one of Brokk's tricks? Might he be watching, waiting for her to follow? As she continued to hold onto the wall, Isa realized the power was different even from that which she'd felt in the glass hill. As ancient as Brokk's power was, this felt impossibly older.

When she reached the throne room, the urge to go forward grew even more urgent. Sucking in a deep breath, Isa let go of the wall and walked to the closest staircase, and decided to let the strange pull, whatever it was, take her. The urge to run overtook Isa, and as she flew up the shiny steps, a thrill moved through her. Suddenly, she felt as though she were a bird climbing higher into the clear blue sky.

Eventually, she had to reach the bridge she had walked upon the day before, and the exhilarating flight was over. Whatever had first yanked her along, however, did not allow her to linger. Instead, it kept her hand upon the rail, then the wall, before pulling her down the hall opposite that of her room, the side of the castle she hadn't explored the day before.

As she went, the walls began to change. Instead of ivy, the walls here were carved with stars and moons. The impulse to continue walking grew stronger until she reached the last door at the end of the great hall. Isa placed her ear to it and listened, but she heard nothing. With curiosity now nearly as strong as the force which compelled her forward, Isa began to slowly push on the door only to realize it was locked.

"You would think a castle this old would at least have loose locks," she muttered to herself. But no matter how hard she pushed, it wouldn't budge. Stepping back, Isa stared at the glass handle. If Ever had been there, a lock wouldn't have posed a problem at all.

Ever wasn't there, however, and her need to see what was behind the door grew more incessant by the minute. Isa huffed impatiently, knowing what Ever would tell her to do even if he were there.

Placing the palm of her hand against the door, Isa exhaled, trying with all her might. She imagined the little bit of fire left within her gathering in her hands. Groaning with the strain, Isa pressed her hands into the door until they hurt. The faintest blue aura lit up the glass around her hands, but only for a second. Then, nothing.

The pain in her hands was nothing compared to that within her heart. If the Fortress's fire continued to leave her at this rate, she would be dead in a week. It wouldn't even matter what the enchanter had schemed up for her. Isa sighed and leaned heavily against the door. The glass was cool, but warmed quickly under her touch, and that nagging sensation continued to dance throughout her body, biting her as she stood still. If only she could do something to quell it.

As if someone were watching her struggle, the door clicked open on its own. Without hesitating to wonder why the door had opened by itself, Isa darted through, hoping that wherever Brokk was, he couldn't see or hear her. Something, perhaps the strange urgency in the glass, told her that she was not meant to see whatever was behind that door.

As soon as she was through, Isa came to another flight of stairs. These stairs led up to a tower that was tall and isolated, much like the Tower of Annals at home. This staircase, however, was much, much steeper, and the glass walls were no longer opaque, but perfectly clear. So clear, in fact, that Isa nearly screamed.

For the first time, she could see the castle in its entirety. The whole structure was indeed made of glass, and it was balanced atop a single island in the center of a mountain range that encircled them entirely. Between the castle and each monstrous mountain was a gorge so deep that the bottom was completely hidden from sight. The only way to reach the mountains on the other side of the gorge was to cross a thin glass bridge that spanned the chasm. It must have been nearly as long as the castle was wide. The bridge might have been quite sturdy itself, but over the deep, black chasm, it looked brittle, as though the wind might smash it to pieces at any moment.

When Isa looked up instead of down, she found herself staring at the jagged, snowcapped peaks. Their height made her dizzy, and the brightness of the snow in the sun made her nearly blind. It all made Isa want to suddenly lie on the floor, clinging to it with all her might, never to move again. Only the incessant sting of the glass gave her the ability to begin slowly climbing the steps that were as transparent as air itself.

Finally, after what seemed like an eternal death march, Isa came to a door in the sky. One more room sat upon the tallest tower. Like her own room, this one had frosted walls, but they were a rich blue. Cautiously, Isa gently pushed the door. This one, to her relief, opened immediately.

Suddenly feeling exposed as she stood between the nearly invisible stairs and the room's dark, tapestried walls, Isa practically dove into the room, thankful for the privacy of its walls. Only when the door was shut and locked behind her did Isa turn around and truly look at what lay before her.

A beautiful woman was stretched out upon the widest bed Isa had ever seen. Her hands were folded upon her chest, as though she might be taking an afternoon nap. Hair so yellow it was nearly white lay strewn out around her head, glorious in its brilliance. Bone-pale skin covered a thin face with high cheekbones and bloodless lips. Her exotic gown, lined with fur the way Isa's borrowed gown was, shimmered sky blue with purple jewels scattered about it.

She was the most beautiful woman Isa had ever seen. As Isa began to look around to study the rest of the room, however, a movement caught her eye. When Isa looked at the woman once more, her heart nearly stopped.

Isa was not the only one in the room who was breathing.

CHAPTER 31
GIFT OF THE HEART

Isa tried to imagine who the woman might be, but the urgent sensation that had brought her here prickled her skin, even though she was no longer touching any glass with her hands. Instead, the air was thick with it, archaic power, heavy and hard to breathe.

And Isa suddenly had the overwhelming urge to touch her.

With a will that wasn't her own, Isa stretched out her hand and rested it lightly upon the woman's ashen cheek. When she did, the tapestried walls around her began to fade into oblivion, and instead she was standing upon the dais of the throne room below. Courtiers dressed in an exotic fashion similar to that which hung in Isa's new wardrobe stood loosely clustered about the throne. Her gaze rested on the scant assembly of what looked to be wealthy nobles and several dozen commoners. Brokk, though much younger, knelt before her.

"Come, Son," Isa said, realizing immediately that though she said it, the voice wasn't her own. "We will not speak of this here." She glanced up at the people milling about her. There was a sadness in the air, an urgency that Isa couldn't understand.

The two of them left the throne room and walked at a quick pace to a smaller room down a side hall behind the throne. Isa nearly screamed when six giants encircled her, two in front, one on each side, and two more behind her, until she realized they must be her guards. She tried to study them without looking too obvious.

They almost resembled the ice sculptures some of the artisans in Destin would create in the town square every winter. Their movements were surprisingly fluid, and their steps as light as one of Ever's personally trained foot soldiers. Each one stood a full head taller than Launce though, and they wore no human clothes, but garments that seemed carved into their glass bodies. Their opaque, pupil-less eyes seemed to see everything and nothing at the same time, and each carried a long, sharp glass scythe, as though it were merely an extension of its hands. The gleam of the weapons made Isa shudder, and suddenly wonder if they had disappeared with the spell as well, or if they still lurked in the shadows unseen.

After walking in silence for a few minutes, Brokk at her side, chewing his lip and looking very much as though he might burst, they turned and entered a sunny room made only of glass windows. Though it shared the southern wall with the rest of the building, the other three walls and its ceiling were unfrosted and clear. The walls weren't smooth either, but made of many six-sided small panes. Together, they played with the room's reflections, some parts of the wall concave while others were convex. The non-uniformity was strange and beautiful.

The room itself was nearly the size of Isa and Ever's sleeping chamber at home, but it was stuffed so full of plants and tables and growing tools that one could scarcely move without knocking something over. And it smelled of soil. Isa immediately felt at home in that room of green paned glass. In the great citadel of glass perfection, this room felt homey and lived in.

Isa's host body knelt near a little lemon tree, which stood in a pot wider than Isa's shoulders, and lifted one of the tools. She began to prune it methodically. "You know why I called you," Isa heard herself say in that low, melodic voice. Brokk paused in his pacing briefly, the long, deep purple cloak swishing around his feet, gathering dirt as it scraped the floor. His eyes were wild, and deep bags hung below them. He glanced at her, but remained silent, so she spoke again. "This is not the way the Maker intended us to use our gift." Her voice was kind, but authoritative.

"Then He meant for us to rest while we watched thousands die before us, simply to placate the vain concerns of mere men?"

"We are not gods, Bronkendol. You are a man, and I am just a woman, the same as them. Possessing the ability to help does not mean we are to possess dominion over all other peoples."

"You have not seen what I have!" Young Brokk exploded, suddenly so close that Isa could feel his breath. "You sit in this sparkling citadel and see them one at a time, withdrawing for the day when you tire. But I have walked among them. This sickness is only the beginning of their struggles! They fight amongst themselves constantly, killing one other for gain! The poor eat scraps, while the rich flaunt their overabundance. Mothers cannot feed their children, because fathers abandon them . . ." His voice trailed off as he held his head in his hands. The body Isa occupied rose gracefully to wrap her arms around him, but he shook her off.

"It wasn't your fault," she said softly, putting down the tool and standing.

"No, it was yours."

Isa's borrowed body drew back as though he'd slapped her, and a sharp pang filled her heart. "You don't think I mourn the loss of a daughter I never met, and even more, my grandchild?" She shook her head. "Had there been time, I would have brought her here myself. But sometimes the Maker brings them home to Him for reasons we cannot explain, the way He took your father. We are strong, but we cannot prevent death."

"Because you never tried!" He backed away, glaring at her, his eyes too bright in the reflection of the dancing firelight.

"Bronkendol," she warned, "you think I saw nothing in the thousand years before you were born? You think I know not suffering? I have seen more anguish than you can ever conceive of! This gift of strength and long life has its blessings, but it also brings trials. Witnessing the hardships of man is part of our lot in life. They suffer, and thus, so do we." Isa felt the woman tremble. "I told you, the Maker never gave me dominion over the people. He simply told me to help them."

Young Brokk began to walk away, but stopped when she spoke again.

"I know what you have been doing." As she said the words, memories that were not her own crowded Isa's mind. Unfamiliar faces began to appear, begging her to remove something so small Isa had to squint to make them out. Tiny shards of glass, grains the size of sand rested in the corners of their eyes, nearly too small to see. Embedded in the skin, they looked like tiny crystals waiting to catch the light.

Isa gasped, and though she couldn't see her own body, her hands flew to her eyes. To her horror, she could feel them there in her face as well. Before she could dwell on the horrible discovery, her host spoke again.

"These people are not your puppets! I have seen the glass you have begun to inflict upon the servants. They came to me, begging me to remove them while you were gone! I love you more than anything in the world, my son, but I cannot allow you to finish this."

"I have inflicted nothing! By doing this, I will save them from themselves!"

"By controlling them, you will take away what makes them most human!" Isa heard herself shout back. They stood there for an immeasurable time, and as they stood, mother and son, Isa felt an unnamable pain fill her body, so intense it was nearly crippling, as though lightning had streaked across her muscles and lit everything on fire. It was a moment before she realized that sorrow was what plagued her, a sadness unfamiliar because it was one she hadn't yet experienced. Isa suddenly understood that the woman whose eyes through which she now looked was feeling the pain of losing her son. Though he stood before her, they both knew what he was about to do, and that she would be forced to stop him.

"Brokk," she pleaded, caressing his face with her hand the way she had every day when he was a babe. "I beg you, give yourself time to heal." As she held his cheek, a raw, vulnerable expression crossed his face, making him look very much like the little boy she loved so much. "Promise me you won't do this."

"Father always said that I should be a man of my word," he finally said.

"Yes," she whispered. "He did."

And without a word, he leaned forward to kiss her on the cheek before walking out the door. Tears rushed down her face as she watched him go, and the crippling pain that had begun in her heart moved outward until she was forced to kneel on the dirty ground. She stayed that way for a long time, unable to move.

"Vidar," she finally called out, her voice so raspy it was nearly inaudible.

An older manservant appeared. "Yes, my lady?"

"Tell the servants to leave. They shall not pack their belong-ings, nor shall they prepare for a journey. There isn't time."

"But my lady." The man's cornflower blue eyes were wide with fear. "What about you?"

"I cannot leave my son. But I can stop him."

As soon as her servant had hastened to obey, the Glass Queen had closed her eyes and raised her hands before her. The power the Maker had given her so long ago still rushed strong through her blood, and though Bronkendol's power had never equaled hers, he was strong enough that her last spell would require all that she had. Not that it mattered. She would never be able to live in a world without him anyway.

The Glass Queen pulled in a deep, even breath before she began her work. Her hands moved in slow, steady circles. The light they created was nearly invisible at first, but began to glow more and more brightly as she continued. Streaks of violet, like webs, began to fill the air, hanging brilliantly as she wove them together. As she worked, she hummed a haunting melody. It sounded to Isa like a dangerous lullaby.

"Sleep well, my son," she murmured, as though telling a child goodnight. Then she paused for only a moment before clapping her hands together so hard that it hurt. The web-like streaks collapsed, and when she opened her hands again, a glowing, purple orb rose and floated toward the door. The woman stood and followed it, pausing once before leaving the room to stroke her favorite cherry tree fondly. She would miss this place of sun and life.

As she re-entered the castle and began walking toward her destination, fewer and fewer servants filled the grand halls, and by the time she neared her son's room, she could feel in her heart that the magnificent glass palace was finally empty. But the only person that mattered, she tried to reassure herself, was still there.

She finally came to a door that was partly ajar. How many happy hours had she spent rocking and singing to him here? After his father had died, how many times had they wept together upon the hearth? She paused at the entrance, running her fingers over the glass carvings of elk and does, the first carvings he had ever attempted, and she smiled as she remembered how proud he was of the does with their stick legs and the elk with their disproportionate antlers.

Inside, the violet orb glowed softly and steadily above the young man. Bronkendol was stretched out upon his bed, his hands peacefully at his sides, the forced sleep making breaths slow and even. She sat on the edge of his bed and gently pushed a copper curl from his face. Then just as she had done countless times all those centuries ago, she sat upon the floor, crossed her arms over the edge his bed, and nestled her head upon them.

"Sweet dreams, my son," she whispered. "I will be here, just as I have always been."

Heavy steps interrupted the bitter serenity of the moment, and Isa startled. The cool air made her realize that tears had been running down her face, but the vision wouldn't allow her to leave just yet.

"Isabelle? You must leave that room immediately!" Brokk called.

But still, she could only see the son through the eyes of the mother. The Glass Queen uttered a few words in a tongue Isa didn't recognize, and she, too, began to drift away. It occurred to Isa that the mother had fallen asleep at the bedside of her son, rather than in this dark, cloaked room.

"Isabelle!" Brokk shouted this time, losing the patience he had always kept before. "You cannot be in there! You don't know what you are seeing!"

Just before the vision faded completely, Isa heard the Glass Queen's voice once more.

"You must stop him, young one. Even if it means you must finish what I could not bring myself to do. I love him too much to let him commit such evil."

The Glass Queen had kept just enough strength to summon Isa. And now, with a final breath, she was gone.

As the vision left Isa, and she began to use her own eyes again, the large door flew open. Brokk, along with two of the glass giants Isa had seen in her vision, burst through the door.

Before she could run, one easily managed to pin her arms behind her back.

"What did she show you?" Brokk shouted. When Isa didn't answer, he grabbed her by the shoulders and yanked her forward, making her cry out when the guard didn't let go. "What did you see?"

Though it hurt, Isa somehow managed to keep silent. One of the first lessons Ever had taught her after their wedding was that knowledge is power. So when she still didn't answer, Brokk grew even more agitated. "Take her to my work chamber," he barked at the guards. "Apparently, I have run out of time."

Panic filled Isa as the guards carried her down the glass steps, and suddenly the feeling of falling through the glass tower didn't bother her at all. "My husband will find me!" she shouted at him, struggling with all her might. It was no use, however, for the glass guards were as solid as the castle itself.

In desperation, Isa begged the Fortress, pleaded with it to give her just enough power to flee. But helpless she remained for the rest of the way down the tower, and then back down to the workshop where she had eaten.

Instead of dropping her at the table or in one of the chairs near the door, they moved to the back of the room, an area Isa had not seen before. The two guards sat her down in a heavy, metal chair that faced a large furnace as wide as she was tall. Heat blasted her as one guard turned to feed the flames, while the other shackled her wrists and ankles to the chair.

Isa wept as she struggled in vain against the chains, praying that Ever would find her. He had promised he would protect her.

He had promised.

CHAPTER 32

I PROMISE

I know what you want to do!" Isa warned the enchanter as the glass guards retreated to the door. "And I swear to you, I will not be a part of it!"

"My dear," Bronkendol said in a patient voice, as he studied a set of thin poles that leaned against the furnace. "You cannot even control the power that is within you. I advise caution when making oaths so easily." He glanced back at her. "Your struggle with the Fortress's legendary fire is not the secret you think it is."

"He *will* find me," she said, ignoring his jab. But the tremor of her voice was far less convincing than she had hoped, even to her. "Besides." She licked her lips, which had grown dry from the furnace's heat. "If my fire is dying, I cannot see how you plan to use me."

"You need not worry about such trifles." He finally chose the pole in the center. When he lifted it, she could see that it was hollow, a long tube made of steel. It looked unlike any weapon Isa had ever seen. There were no points or sharp edges on any part of it. "When I speak to the hearts of the people, there will be no more war. When they have sickness, I will come. Where there is hurt, I will heal."

He began to turn the pole over and over again in his right hand, while rubbing it against the palm of his left as it turned. As he did so, a thin layer of what looked like wet glass began to appear, thickening as he continued to turn the pole around his hand.

"You cannot touch everyone," she warned. "You have only seen a very few in Rafael's court. The monarchs may follow him, but the armies will never listen. They will fight you. Hundreds will die."

"Thousands," he said, continuing to spin the pole, the lump of molten glass nearly as thick as his thumb. "But in the end, mankind will survive." He glanced up at her for a brief moment, his eyes burning with intensity. "And from the way men plunder and kill now, nothing is guaranteed our children. At least I can save some." The glob of thick, gooey glass was now nearly the diameter of Isa's fist. He removed his hand, but continued to hold it inches away from the still-spinning pole. Then he leaned forward, his eyes suddenly kinder, bright as though he were sharing a delightful secret.

"You have the chance to give life to this world, Isabelle! Just imagine it!" His voice dropped to a whisper. "No one else's child must pointlessly die."

The words of his mother came back to Isa from the vision, and they were on her tongue before she could consider their wisdom.

"We're not gods, Bronkendol."

His ancient name felt strange as it left her tongue, and Isa suddenly wished she could take it back. If she had wanted to delay him, those were surely not the words to do it with. Where was Ever?

Bronkendol had frozen in place, and Isa couldn't tell whether his expression was one of fury or fear. She hurried to distract him, searching for something else to say. Sweat poured down her back and neck as the flames of the furnace continued to grow. Even the liquid glass was giving off heat.

"Just as well," she stammered. "I could not give it to you even if I wanted to." A stupid thing to say, but it was all she could think of.

In one last attempt at conjuring her strength, Isa's fingers dug into the sharp edges of the chair's arms until they burned. The air had grown disgustingly thick as the heat continued to build, and Isa pressed even harder into the chair. But her fingers wrought nothing

"The Maker has not abandoned you, child."

Bronkendol's words took her by surprise, and for a moment, Isa stopped struggling. He nodded at her shackled wrists. "I see your fear. You think the Maker and your Fortress have deserted you, withdrawing the power you should have commanded by now."

Tears stung her eyes as she stared at him, fighting back his words. The Fortress abandoned no one, Garin had assured her. The problem was with her. She had not fulfilled her duties. Somehow, she had overlooked something she was supposed to do. She shook her head so hard her vision swam, clumps of her hair sticking to her sweaty face.

"No, I do not believe that!"

"But you do," he said. "I can see it in your eyes. You wonder why you cannot control the fire, why Ever is not here now." He paused. "Why you are not yet with child."

Against her will, the tears began to flow freely, and with them, the pain she had been holding back. Anger, fear, longing, and confusion swept through her, and with them the memories of all she had dreamed for, and how all those dreams had died.

She was not a mother. Her husband had not come to save her. And worst of all, the Fortress, the home she had grown to love more than life, had somehow relinquished the life-giving fire that should have burned hot in her soul. And now she was weak, captive, and very, very alone. Not even the Fortress's little breeze had accompanied her into this sweltering room.

"I promise." He gently lifted her chin and stared into her face, a tear running down his own cheek. "Your purpose is not gone. He was only preparing you. Your purpose is here. Your gift will be to the entire world, not only to your husband or even to Destin. The power of your heart will be for everyone."

"How?" she whispered. She wouldn't be able to delay him much longer, and suddenly, Isa realized, she didn't have the will to do so either.

"With my help," he said. "Now, I'm so sorry, but this will hurt quite a bit." Without waiting for Isa to reply, he lifted the pole and placed the molten glass against her chest, just above her heart.

Isa's vision exploded as excruciating pain wracked her body. Blistering white heat made her blood pulse as tendrils of white lightning lit every muscle within her. Her fingers, wrists, elbows, ankles, and knees felt as though they had been smashed to pieces with mallets. *Please*, she begged silently as she wept, *give me strength one more time. Let me know I am not alone! You said you would never leave me!*

But there was no answer. The agony only dragged on. Anger flooded her enough that she was able to force her eyes open, and to her shock, the thin ball of glass that was pressed against her chest did not burn her skin. Instead, it was alight with streaks of violet that stretched out in every direction. As she watched it, willing herself not to pass out from the pain, the glass turned the color of blood. Then, to her amazement and horror, all of her anger was gone. Every last bit of it.

Instead, the glass began to change to gold, the color of the sun.

"No!" Isa cried as she realized joy was beginning to slip as well. Despite the terror of the last few days, it was still there, hiding beneath her sorrow and frustration. Sensations of pleasure took her as she felt the joy rise like cream to the top. The way Ever's lips had lingered upon her own at their wedding, the love in her mother's embrace, the way her brother watched over her, even from a distance. The hunger in her husband's eyes when he had seen her in Gigi's ridiculous ball gowns. The feeling of belonging when the Fortress had welcomed her home. The hope she had felt when Master Claude had told her she should soon expect a baby of her own.

An even greater despair took her as she watched the golden joy slide from her heart into the liquid glass. As soon as the gold had been devoured, more colors followed. Moss green for jealousy, Jadzia's attempted conquests coming to mind. Guilt the tint of mulberry, frustration the shade of rust, and even the cobalt of sorrow were painstakingly torn from her chest and devoured by the pulsing, molten glass. Finally, only one emotion remained.

"You can't . . . you can't have that one," she gasped. "Please . . . just let me keep it."

"I'm sorry," he said sympathetically, "but it won't be complete without them all. Besides, this is the one that gives you more strength than all of the others combined."

"No." She shook her head pathetically. "I will not let you take it!"

"Just let it go," he crooned. "Without it, no one will ever be able to hurt you again."

Isa considered that. It was true. Without it, she would never again have the cobalt blue of sorrow, the mulberry purple of guilt, or the blood red of anger born of pain. But then, she knew, she would never be able to give Ever the life she had vowed to share at their wedding; she would never again bask in the peace of the Fortress's glistening marble walls. Without it, she would never again be whole.

"He hasn't come for you," the enchanter said softly.

Something inside of Isa broke. At first it felt like the smallest of cracks, the kind that allowed trickles of water to drip through the walls, but nothing more. But the crack did not remain small, and before she knew it, the crack had widened into a chasm within her. As the glass continued to turn in his hands, the other colors that mingled within the burning glass disappeared, washed out by the flood the color of a dusty rose.

It was done.

Isa watched stupidly as a sad smile came over the enchanter's face. Carefully he lifted the glob of burning glass from her chest, and Isa exhaled deeply as the pressure released her. She felt him cup her jaw in his hand the way her father used to do, and he softly kissed her hair. Without lifting his face, he said, "I am so sorry. But it will be better this way. I promise."

Then he righted himself and walked over to the only work table that was completely clear of all clutter, and began to roll the glowing ball of soft glass against its metal surface. As he continued to roll it back and forth with his left hand, he grabbed another long metal tool, flat this time, about the width of three fingers, and pressed it against the glob of glass.

Hours passed as he shaped it, but Isa found that she didn't care. She watched him until the daylight of the glass walls faded, and the orange of the giant furnace began to light the room instead.

Finally, he held up his workmanship. It was a little glass mirror, just like the one he had shown her the day before. There was no handle, just the circle of glass and its frame. Waving his hand over it, then whispering a few words, the enchanter watched with a fervor Isa couldn't understand. He sucked in a quick breath as it showed not a reflection, but another scene entirely. Ever stood before Garin in the Tower of Annals. Isa knew she should feel an overwhelming relief to know her husband was safe and back at home, but when she searched herself, she realized she felt nothing. The enchanter waved his hand over the mirror once more, and this time she saw Launce standing in Rafael's court.

"Oh my!" Bronkendol startled as though he'd forgotten she was there. "I apologize, my dear. You need to rest." With that, he placed the mirror in his belt, and helped her up to her room. Every bone in Isa's body screamed, but she found that she had no desire to tell him. As soon as she was tucked into her bed, still in her clothes from earlier that day, he left and returned with a steaming bowl of broth.

"It will be all better from here," he promised as he lifted the spoon to her mouth. Without thinking, Isa parted her lips and swallowed, the soup scalding her throat as it went down. "One day you will see that it was worth the sacrifice."

But Isa didn't care about seeing that it was for the best. All she wanted to do was sleep. Soon enough, he left her alone, and within moments, and for the first time since she could remember, Isa fell asleep without wishing for anything more than the very bed she laid in.

Isa awoke the next morning long after the sun had risen, but didn't bother to stir. She wasn't sure why it was so hard to rouse herself, but she didn't have long to wonder. The enchanter was back again, this time with a bowl of warm biscuits and fruit.

"Now that you're finished eating," he said as he rose and went to the wardrobe, where he pulled out the thick fur coat he had given her the first day and wrapped it around her, "we must get you warm. You have a long journey ahead of you."

Isa allowed him to lead her to a long set of stables that were directly attached to the castle.

"Up you go," he said, getting down on his knee so she could

climb up. Isa's limbs still ached as though someone had beaten her with a bludgeon, but she said nothing, simply grimacing once as she mounted. As soon as she was firmly on, he took her horse's reins and led her to the main stable door.

"You are going home now," he said. "The horse knows the way. I've placed rations in the saddlebags, so you shouldn't go hungry." When she didn't answer him, he took her hand. It shook just slightly as he patted it and then held on. "I have been thinking, and I've decided that the fate of the others should not be your own. You have given far too much for that."

As he spoke the strange words, a wave of warmth moved from the hand he held to her face, and Isa felt a sharp pain that stretched from her already aching heart to her eyes. Eyes open wide in pain, she watched as two pieces of glass fell into his other outstretched hand, along with a few drops of blood.

"I promise," he patted her leg, "you will make it home. And I never break my promises."

CHAPTER 33

MERCHANT'S SON

It crossed Launce's mind more than once that he could vomit on the foot of one of the guards as they dragged him through the palace. Inwardly, he cursed Ever for sending his horse back at the same speed they'd left Cobren the first time. It wasn't natural for a man to speed along, racing the wind for hours on end.

"Sire," one of the guards bowed while the other held him tightly, "we found him in the border woods."

Launce braced himself for another round of the nausea that was sure to hit as he lifted his head. He was in Rafael's throne room once again, just before the dais. Rafael stood, but Olivia and Queen Monica stayed seated. Launce wanted to search the princess's face to see what she was thinking, but had to drop his head once more so he wouldn't be sick.

"Do you not recognize who this is?" Rafael's voice was indignant. "This is King Everard's brother-in-law, and my daughter's intended. Unhand him at once!"

Launce could feel the guards hesitate, but finally they let go. And though the drop was rough, laying on the cool tiles helped him get his bearings. As he rubbed his aching head, Launce wondered if he had heard correctly. Was he still supposedly the king's successor? Rafael had been livid with Everard the last time they'd parted. Why the sudden change of heart? And where was Bronkendol? Then Launce spotted him, standing placidly behind the throne.

"King Everard," Launce paused, wincing as he stood, "tasked me with acting as his regent while he is otherwise occupied." There, he'd said it. Everard had made him practice for hours the day before.

"Of course!" Rafael walked down the steps as he spoke, motioning to someone behind Launce. "Davin, I want you to accompany young Master Launce to his old chambers. Bring him something to eat, and make sure you're available to him for anything he might need."

As Davin nodded and turned to lead him to his new chambers, Launce threw one last look at the enchanter, and then at Olivia. Olivia's eyes were wide, although he couldn't read her expression clearly. Brokk . . . or rather, Bronkendol, looked unnerved. His hair stuck out in different directions, and his expression, for once, wasn't utterly calm and collected. Actually, Launce decided, the enchanter looked exhausted.

Once he was in the room by himself, Launce realized that Everard's plan for him to send the messenger birds wasn't going to work. Launce was fully aware that Davin was only there to spy on him. He'd even heard the door lock after Davin had stepped out. Surely Everard must have expected some sort of precautions to be taken against him. What did his brother-in-law really expect him to accomplish by being here?

His spirits lifted a bit when a plate of rolls, fruit, and pastries was delivered. As he devoured them, Launce tried to imagine who he might turn to for help. With Davin following him wherever he went, learning more about the enchanter's plans would be impossible. But with a partner, he might stand a chance, even if it was only enough time to send a single messenger bird to the Fortress to tell Garin that the enchanter was back.

Who could he trust though? If Everard was right about the shards of glass affecting everyone, even Norbert would have been touched. Not that they knew exactly what the shards were for, but, Launce decided, he would prefer not to take the chance.

That's when it hit him. The hill. Everard had said that those in the stands had been showered with the glass, but there was one person who had not been in the stands because *she* had been on the hill.

He would have to find a way to get her alone, away from listening ears. That in itself would be a monumental task.

Although Isa was grown and married, she was hardly ever left alone at the Fortress. Between her lady-in-waiting, curious courtiers, Garin, the ever-present kitchen mistress, who was rarely actually in the kitchen, and Everard himself, Launce realized he'd hardly seen his sister unaccompanied since the wedding. And she was a grown, married woman. As a young, unmarried princess, Olivia would be the last person in the palace they would ever allow him to be alone with. Launce smiled to himself, for if anyone knew how to lose her escorts, it would be her.

Launce walked back to the door and knocked. Sure enough, Davin was right there to answer immediately.

"I have a message for the princess," Launce said. From the look on Davin's face, it seemed that he was just as pleased with the princess's pending betrothal to Launce as her father had originally been.

"Very well. What would you to relay?"

"I would like to meet her in the garden. I have an important matter we need to discuss." After making sure the message was given to a runner, Launce allowed Davin to shut the door again. He needed to think anyway.

Launce knew he was taking quite a risk. But he couldn't think of any other way to get the princess alone. It had only been one week since they had met, and they'd only really had one full conversation. He suspected she would pick up on his hints, he hoped she would at least. But there was no way of knowing until he tried.

The queasy feeling returned to his stomach. He didn't have long to wait at least. Within minutes, the runner returned to report that the princess would meet him down in the courtyard garden. Launce walked as quickly as he could, which seemed to annoy Davin even more. Launce didn't care what the stuffy servant thought though. With every moment wasted, Isa could be enduring hunger, torture, or worse. Later, he promised himself, he could explain everything to Olivia . . . if she gave him the chance. For now, he just needed her to fall for his cruel trick.

As Launce reached the courtyard garden, his stomach leapt into his throat. Could he keep a straight face while he hurt her? Self-loathing briefly heated his cheeks as he wondered how many more decisions he would have to make that were similar to Everard's. It galled him to think that there was a reason his brother-in-law was so callous. Launce didn't have time to mull on it, however, because the princess was approaching him with her entourage.

"Your Highness," he said as he bowed. When he looked up, however, he nearly forgot what he had come to do. Her dark, shiny hair was swept to one side, where an orange-red desert rose had been pinned expertly beside her chin. In the weak late autumn sun, her skin was the color of wild honey, the kind that could be found in the untamed forest that lay north of Soudain. The sunset yellow of her dress made her round face glow like a warm summer day, and Launce found himself imagining her cheeks feeling like sunbeams to the touch. Blinking to regain his focus, he tried to settle on an expression that matched what he was about to say. He hoped, prayed that she would take the bait.

"Launce," she said, her eyes wide. "I'm glad to see that you've returned so soon. Did you find your sister? I have been sending up prayers for her since you left."

Launce nodded, not quite sure how to proceed. He offered his arm, and she took it as they turned and set about for a stroll through the garden.

"Well?" she prodded when he remained silent.

Launce took a deep breath. "Everard thinks he has a way to track her, but that isn't what I came out here to discuss." He paused, wishing she weren't so distractingly beautiful. "I . . . I've been thinking. And . . . I'm not convinced this life," he gestured at the finery of the garden around them, "is suitable for me." As soon as the words left his mouth, he wanted to kick himself.

A brief look of bitter disappointment flashed across her face before she recovered her poise. As he waited for her reply, he decided that he wanted to kick Everard as well. If it hadn't been for all the time spent around his dogged brother-in-law, he would never have dreamt up such a plan on his own. Even without being present, Everard was still in his head.

"I see." The princess was quick to move from pain to anger. Her hazelnut eyes flashed as she turned to look directly at him. Out of the corner of his eye, Launce saw the princess's escort and their accompanying guard share a small smile. Apparently, many people here liked him about as well as he liked them. "And why would that be?"

Launce shrugged, trying to keep up the act. "I was born a merchant's son. The mercantile has been in my family for three generations. It would hurt my father to die one day, knowing he had no one to pass it down to."

"And you did not consider this before you asked to compete for my hand?" Her words were ice. Launce opened his mouth to answer, but glanced back at their escorts first. She followed his eyes. "You will remain here," she snapped at them. "We will walk alone."

"Your Highness," her escort protested, fingering the ribbons of her bodice nervously. "It is uncustomary for a young woman such as yourself to be unescorted."

"The garden begins and ends here. Where on earth would I go?"

"I apologize, Princess." The guard stepped forward. "But I cannot allow you to go unattended. I am under strict orders from your father."

Launce felt his stomach, still weak from his midnight ride, do a flop. If the princess couldn't lose her guard, his whole plan might accomplish nothing aside from angering her.

"Then at least give me the dignity of walking where I cannot see you!"

Launce felt both hope and shame when he saw the resignation in the guard's mouth and the hints of angry tears in the princess's eyes. She and the guard continued to stare one another down for another long moment before the guard finally rolled his eyes. "If that is what you wish, then you will not see me."

Without waiting for Launce to offer his arm again, the princess grabbed his right sleeve and began to walk as quickly down the path as she could, dragging him behind her.

"Olivia," he whispered, "I'm sorry for deceiving you, but there is something I must tell you."

"You should be sorry," she said, not slowing for a second.

Launce glanced up at the three white palace walls surrounding the courtyard. The palace wasn't very tall, only three stories, but the hedges were short enough to allow busybodies to see them from the third story, had they wished to. Launce hoped no one was watching them from above now. He didn't have long to wonder, however, because without hesitating, the princess lifted her skirts in her free hand, and deftly stepped through an invisible break in the hedge, pulling him along with her.

As soon as they were through, Launce realized that they had not only left the maze-like courtyard, but that they had left the palace proper entirely, and were standing at the edge of the forest that filled the land behind it.

"Keep walking," Olivia said. "And while we do, I expect you to explain your dishonesty to the fullest."

"They'll think I've taken you," Launce said, frowning at the backside of the hedge.

"If you cannot give me a satisfactory explanation as to why you've deceived me, then yes, they will. If you can at least pacify me, then I might know a way to get you back unnoticed."

Clearly, she had done this before. Launce stared, dumbfounded, into her eyes, wishing more than ever to know what she was thinking. She was truly one of the most confusing people he had ever met. Perhaps his plan had worked too well. Gathering his thoughts, he shook his head and determined to explain himself, even if it meant he would have to clamp her mouth shut.

"We're not safe in the palace," he blurted out. "I was trying to find a way so that we could have a moment alone to speak. I need your help." As he spoke, her face lost some of its anger. Encouraged by her silence, he continued. "We think the enchanter, or the holy man, as your father calls him, is going to use her for her power somehow."

"How do you know?"

"Our Fortress Steward says she's more powerful than even she knows. But he isn't just using her. Everard thinks the enchanter plans to use everyone here too." As Launce went on to explain the slivers, he was sure she would deem him a fool. It sounded ridiculous as he spoke it.

To his surprise, however, she was slowly nodding as she

stared at the ground. Before she could answer, low voices could be heard. Launce could just make out the low tenor of the guard's voice and the mouse-like squeak of Olivia's escort. Olivia grabbed his hand once more and began to drag him toward the west wing of the palace.

"It makes sense," she said in a low voice as they walked.

"It does?"

"Some of the servants have been complaining about their eyes hurting. Then my mother said the same thing. When I looked at my eyes, however, nothing was there. But how does he plan to use them?"

"Not even Everard knows, nor does he know how to remove them." Launce shook his head. "All *I* know is that we need to get Isa back. And that's why I needed you to get us alone."

"Wait." She stopped walking. "You said all of that because you knew I would find a way to get us alone?"

Launce dared a tight smile. "You're good at getting what you want."

They held one another's gaze for an immeasurable moment. Birds late to fly south chirped here and there, and the quiet chatter of the forest filled the silence left by their voices.

"Yes," she finally said in a small voice. "I am. I've had to be since the holy man came. Here, come this way." She held up a low branch so Launce could see a clearer path as they skirted the northern edge of the palace. Launce marveled at how lightly she stepped, and how she miraculously kept her skirts from tearing on the dry winter brambles that littered the forest floor.

"My father wasn't always the puppet he is now," she called back in a low voice. "You would never know it now from the way he flaunts the holy man's gift, but when the man first arrived after the rebellion was quelled, my father was cautious, suspicious even. This foreign man promised my father great power and stability for his kingdom. He would make his line even greater than the Fortiers of the Fortress, he promised. My father was hesitant. He was fond of King Rodrigue and his son.

"It was the continuance of small pockets of the rebels that eventually drove him to accept the holy man's help." Olivia shook her head, causing a tendril of silky hair to fall into her face. "When the holy man assured my father that he, of course, wouldn't harm the Fortier family, simply make my father's line their equal, my father finally accepted." She sighed. "It is little-known, but my father's health has been rapidly declining since the war. I'm afraid to think that all of this might be his attempt at providing for me."

Olivia paused and looked up into the gray of the afternoon light before looking directly back at Launce, her deep eyes searching his own. "I'm frightened, Launce. This man has changed my father into someone I do not recognize, and I fear that by the time my father's soul leaves this world, there will be nothing familiar left in the man or this kingdom." Still holding his gaze, she moved closer to him. The worry on her face stirred up a burning desire in Launce that he could not understand. Never had he wanted so desperately to protect someone that wasn't one of his own. Not even Blanchette had ever brought forth such a need. And yet, all he could do was stare back.

"I don't know why the holy man chose you," she said in a quiet voice. "Still, I can honestly say that for the first time since he arrived, I'm glad he did." She stepped so close that he could have leaned down and kissed her. "But I need to know whether you truly mean to take up the mantle of the Cobrien monarchy, or whether your words back in the courtyard were true. Because if they were truly a ruse, and you mean to stay, then I want no one else at my side. You are different from the others, and I admire that. However," her eyes darkened as she spoke, "if you *did* mean that you have no intention of marrying me and being king, then as soon as we return, I want you to pack your things and leave, and I never want to see you again as long as I live."

Launce stared at her, his mouth open, but no words could come. *They were a ruse*, he wanted to assure her. *I simply needed to speak with you alone!* But the truth weighed heavily upon his heart. For no matter how much he wanted to help her, Launce was still only a merchant's son. He had never wanted to be a courtier in Destin's own court, much less a king in someone else's. And even if he desired a crown of his own, what did he know of being a king? How could a commoner rule a country he hardly knew?

The longer Launce warred within himself, the more understanding dawned in the princess's eyes.

"I see," she said. Swallowing hard, she opened her mouth once more, and Launce dreaded hearing the words he knew would come.

Before she could speak, however, a distant moan sounded from somewhere deeper in the brush behind them. Without hesitation, Olivia took off toward the sound, and Launce followed as quickly as he could. Their chase took them over three small, wooded hills and a thin stream before they reached the source of the sound.

"Queen Kartek!" Olivia shrieked as she rushed down into the ravine. Launce followed, but more slowly. As soon as he saw where the southern queen lay, at the bottom of another small hill, it occurred to him how easy one could be ambushed at the bottom.

As he drew nearer, he could see that the queen was covered in blood. Her olive-green skirt and light cotton tunic were soaked with a dark red, and Launce's stomach lurched when he realized the spots of red were still growing on the queen's right side just above her hip.

"What happened?" Olivia cradled the older queen's head while Launce watched stupidly, too stunned to know what to do.

"My . . . my necklace," the queen gasped. She pointed a

shaking hand at Launce's feet, and when he looked down, he realized he was standing just above a round pink jewel, inlaid in gold. Slowly, he bent to pick it up out of the dirt and twigs, but Olivia was faster. She snatched it up and placed it in the queen's shaking hands. The longer the queen held the jewel, the less she trembled. Launce felt himself let out a sigh of relief as a bit of color began to return to the queen's face, and the red stopped seeping into her clothes.

"I was searching to see if Everard was right," she whispered. "To see if Bronkendol truly was the one who stole your sister."

Launce only then realized that she was talking directly to him.

"He . . . he must have realized what I was doing, for when I returned to my chambers, a maid was there, holding a dagger of glass. She came upon me with it, and I was not fast enough to escape!" She paused to pant, and Launce was again aware of how easy it would be for someone to attack them in the low ravine.

"We need to get you to safety," he said. "Do you think you can walk soon?"

The queen flashed him the shadow of a patient smile before groaning once again as she held the necklace to her side.

"My powers are strong, boy, but not that strong. It will be days before I am ready to walk." She coughed. "If it were not for the sound of your steps, the girl would have killed me here. You frightened her away."

"I will call the guards!" Olivia began to stand, but Launce grabbed her wrist.

"Don't you find it odd that no one noticed her being chased through the palace with a knife? Something is wrong here." Launce recalled the strange slivers of glass Ever had told him about. It was quite possible the enchanter was already at work. He turned to the queen.

"Do you by chance have any pieces of glass—"

"In my eyes?" She cut him off and nodded. "I did, but after Everard sent me a message telling me about it, I was able to pull them out." Olivia looked at him as though he were mad, but Launce knelt in the dirt beside the queen.

"How?"

"With more pain than I ever care to suffer again. It was only because of my gift that I was able to heal enough to pull them out in the first place." It was only when he had drawn closer that Launce noticed the queen's eyes had just a bit of dried blood about their edges. He inwardly grimaced at the thought of what she must have done to get the glass out. It was better to focus on the problems at hand instead.

"Do you have any guards or servants you trust that could escort you home?"

"Yes. Call for Apu, my eunuch. Do not tell the servants what you need him for. Only bring him to me here."

Launce looked up at Olivia. For the first time, he saw real fear in her eyes. The confidence was gone, and she suddenly looked very young as she bit her lip.

"Olivia, I need you to go for help. Find Apu and bring him back."

"But I want to stay with Queen Kartek." Her words were as bold as ever, but there was uncertainty in her voice.

He shook his head. "It's not safe for you to remain here. I need you to go back where you'll be safer." She opened her mouth to protest again, but he stopped her. "I promise, I will explain later. But now I need you to go."

She studied him hard for a moment longer before grabbing one of his hands and squeezing it. "I cannot understand why you fear taking the crown so much. You are the bravest man I know," she whispered before darting back up the hill.

CHAPTER 34

KING

Launce heard the voices before he could see them, but there was no time to try and conceal either himself or the queen.

" . . .Still don't understand why you couldn't just tell us where he was from the beginning," Rafael said as he and about a dozen others crested the hill. Olivia sent Launce an apologetic look as she answered her father.

"I thought you would be busy with the banquet preparations."

"When you and Launce didn't emerge from the walkway, Alejandro came to get me." Rafael frowned at his daughter, then at Launce. Launce felt himself blush under the scrutiny of the king, but Kartek spoke for the first time. Her voice was still weak, but she looked much more confident than Launce felt.

"They came to help me, Sire. They heard me calling for help." As she spoke, a tall man emerged from the crowd, pushing his way through. He had darker skin than anyone Launce had ever seen, and he looked nearly as muscled as Everard. If his physique didn't intimidate, however, the glower he wore certainly would. As he drew nearer, Launce also noticed the dried blood at the corners of his eyes as well. Apparently, Kartek hadn't only removed her glass. Immediately, the big man knelt down and gently scooped the queen up in his arms.

"Who did this to you?"

"I was walking, and I tripped and fell upon a sharp piece of wood."

Launce exchanged a glance with Olivia. Surely the others wouldn't buy such a blatant lie, but it was obvious the queen didn't want to discuss what had happened in front of everyone. He wondered why until he spotted another familiar face in the crowd.

Bronkendol now wore an ice-blue robe lined with a thick fur trimming along the arms, neck, and bottom edging. He seemed to feel Launce's eyes, and turned to smile at him as though nothing was wrong, as though he were actually delighted to see him.

"I think it best if we return home, my queen," Apu said.

Kartek looked from Apu's face directly into Launce's, and he knew what she was telling him. Once she was gone, he would be alone. Everyone else, even Norbert, Cerise, and the other guards could not be trusted now that the enchanter was back and everyone had the slivers. Well, Launce thought to himself, all but one. He would not be alone after all.

"Now that we know the queen will be seen to," the king turned to his servant, "I would like you to escort my daughter and young Launce to the throne room. I have an announcement to make."

Everyone began to walk back toward the palace, including Olivia, who was now too surrounded for any more real conversation to take place. Launce, however, held back. He noticed the enchanter pausing as well. Bronkendol's eyes never left his face, and it more than unnerved him. Launce leaned over and whispered as fast as he could before the enchanter could make his way down into the ravine with them.

"Don't go home."

"And why not?" Apu demanded.

"I don't think they mean for you to leave the continent alive. Our guards and servants should have departed yesterday. If you follow them, you should make it safely to Destin's borders. The Fortress should protect you there while you heal." Knowing her guard wouldn't listen, Launce pleaded directly with the queen. "I know our steward will want your counsel to help find my sister."

Kartek looked at Apu for a long moment. Launce wished they would hurry. The enchanter was still watching them intently, and Launce knew they didn't have much longer.

"He is right," Kartek finally said. The look of resentment never left Apu's eyes, but when she spoke, he simply inclined his head once toward his queen. The queen looked back at Launce again, her eyes probing. "I have not known you as well as I should have liked," she said, "but I can tell you now that this enchanter is more powerful than anything you have ever seen or sensed. He is playing a game with you that I do not understand. Take care."

"Master Launce," Bronkendol called out from halfway down the ravine. "I was hoping we could converse on our way back to the palace."

Launce gave the queen a short nod and bow before standing and heading reluctantly back up the hill. Bronkendol opened his mouth, but Launce cut him off.

"I know exactly who you are, and I have nothing to say to you." Launce stalked by him.

"I am truly sorry about the wine incident," Bronkendol called as he began to follow him. Launce swung around to face the enchanter. In that moment, he didn't care how powerful the man supposedly was.

"You abduct my sister, and you think I care about being put to sleep?"

"I swear, you will have your sister back. I was only trying to help—"

"Trying to help?" Launce shook his head in disgust. "By stealing her from her husband and family?"

"Your sister is dying, Launce."

Launce stopped short. A sudden dizziness filled him, but he forced his hands to stay steady.

"You're lying," he said. The conviction wasn't there though.

Bronkendol shook his head, a small, sad smile on his face. "I wish I were. Your sister is a . . . a magnificent creature. She is more like my mother was than anyone I've met. But the light in your sister's eyes has been dying, and you know it."

Launce wanted to shout, to strike out at someone. His sister wasn't dying. But he caught the enchanter's gray eyes, and as he glared into them, he knew he couldn't deny the possibility at least. As much as it killed him to admit it, Launce had known it for a long time. Perhaps, he thought, it was the reason he had accepted such a ludicrous offer when she had begged him to come with them. Her eyes had dulled too much, and he wanted to see her just that much more. Of course, that didn't mean he trusted Bronkendol any more now than before.

"And what do you plan to do about it?" Launce asked, hoping the enchanter wouldn't mistake his question for enthusiasm.

Bronkendol opened a side door of the palace. They entered one of the winding, back hallways. He suspected Bronkendol had chosen this door on purpose to extend their time alone.

"It is already done. I cannot be sure that it will work. To be honest, it has never been done before. But if does," he looked into Launce's eyes, "I promise, she will be returned to your family soon."

"And Everard?" Launce wondered if the enchanter knew of his brother-in-law's scheme to attack the enchanter's own home. Probably. It wasn't as though anyone expected Everard to sit and wait for Isa at home.

To his surprise, however, Bronkendol only swallowed and said in a low voice, "I fear we will not have need to worry about that."

A cold feeling settled over Launce. "Why?"

"The king will make everything clear once we arrive."

They didn't speak again until they were in the throne room. Now that he wasn't feeling so ill from the ride, Launce noticed that all signs of the week's festivities had been taken down. Instead, the room looked now as Launce assumed it always did. Orange banners hung from the ceiling with the Cobrien royal crest upon them in gold. Under the largest banner, the king and his family stood upon the dais. Launce and the enchanter found places to stand at the dais's foot, against the wall that backed the thrones. Launce tried to see Olivia better, but she was facing the crowd.

The number of people in the room took Launce by surprise. As he studied them, he realized that they weren't just Cobrien citizens, but all of the guests from the betrothal celebration were still there as well. It was odd, considering the contest had been won two days earlier. But it seemed that most foreign dignitaries had simply stayed put. Some new faces had even appeared.

Rafael stood, and the noise of the people died down immediately. Compared to the pomp of the week before, everything felt suddenly very informal to Launce, and he realized it made him somewhat uncomfortable, though he couldn't say why. "I apologize for the strange turn of events. I had desired to see my daughter and her suitor ceremonially betrothed by now." Launce stiffened. It would have been nice for Everard to tell him the betrothal would be so soon, considering he wasn't supposed to have been betrothed in the first place. The king continued. "But put your fears to rest. Everything will be explained now.

"First, however, I have some tragic news." Rafael turned to look directly at Launce. "You may have heard the rumor that Queen Isabelle of Destin disappeared two days ago." How anyone could have missed the scene Everard had caused was beyond Launce. Many must have been unaware, however, for a murmur of unease rose up from the crowd. Rafael shook his head and held out his hands in what looked like an attempt to calm the people. "I have now confirmed that Queen Isabelle is indeed ill, but she is not missing. She is simply in the care of our holy man." With that, he gestured at the enchanter. Looking solemn, Bronkendol walked slowly up to the dais, where he joined the king.

"It is true. I have the queen in my care, but if it is the Maker's will, she will fully recover."

"I fear, though," Rafael spoke again, "that I do not have such good news of her husband."

The room went deathly still. So did Launce. How could the king have news about him already? Launce had only left early that morning. The silence began to stretch, and frustration welled up within him. He wanted to run up the dais and shake the king until the news spilled out. Why did Rafael look so pale and shaken? Why was he suddenly so still? Everard couldn't be dead. Launce wouldn't accept that.

"King Everard was a dear friend of mine," Rafael said hoarsely. Launce could feel the blood drain from his face as a tear rolled down the king's wide, weathered face. "I am sorry to say that in his fear, he set out to find his wife early this morning, before the holy man could tell him what he was about. I have just received word that the young king was found dead after riding into a blizzard in the upper pass of Destin's northern mountains."

Launce felt as though someone had punched him in the gut. He had not realized until that moment how much he had come to rely on his insufferable brother-in-law. Despite his awful sense of superiority and unrelenting fierceness of character, Launce had come to see that Everard undeniably loved his sister. The wild panic on Everard's face after Isa had disappeared had been proof of that. Launce had never seen such ferocity and fear mixed together in one. Surely there had to be a mistake. Garin would never use a bird messenger to announce such a thing, would he? And yet, a bird was the only way anyone would have received the news so quickly.

Launce's head was spinning. Unfortunately, before he had time to gather himself, he realized that Rafael and Bronkendol were both looking at him again.

"I have one more announcement to make," Rafael said softly. The crowd quieted again, but it took longer this time. When they were finally silent, the king gestured for Launce to join them. Launce didn't remember telling his feet to move, but somehow he found himself standing at the top of the dais just beside the king. Rafael placed a heavy hand upon Launce's left shoulder.

"Although Queen Isabelle should indeed heal, our holy man says that she will not be strong enough to handle the duties of a ruler for a long time, perhaps never again. It is with great sorrow and yet, with hope as well, that I wish you to meet the next two rulers of great Fortress of Destin."

Launce gaped at the king. Was he insane?

The king ignored Launce's look and instead, pushed Launce and Olivia to the front of the dais. "I present to you the future King Launce Marchand of Soudain, and my daughter, future Queen Olivia Edite Raquel Rocha of Cintilante Areia, Cobren.

May their union be blessed with much prosperity and many children."

Strained conversation broke out amongst the people. Some bowed or curtsied, while others simply looked angry or afraid. Launce could only look over at Olivia, and for the first time, he knew exactly what she was thinking. Her wide brown eyes and strange pallor told him that she was just as terrified as he.

CHAPTER 35

PRISON OF PRIVILEGE

After Rafael's bold announcement about crowning Launce and Olivia king and queen of the Fortress, the enchanter made an even more brazen statement to the crowd.

"As of now, if you would please be so kind as to return to your chambers and prepare to leave immediately. We all shall soon make the journey to the Fortress together in order to witness this momentous occasion of two countries joining blood."

The crowd erupted with protests, questions, and all other sorts of cacophony. Launce stood, still too stunned to move as he watched the chaos unfold.

"My men and women have journeyed far enough to come here! We will not be continuing on any further," one king called out.

A queen from one of the eastern regions also called loudly, "I have duties to attend to at home! This nonsense has gone on for long enough."

"My liege only allowed me time to come for the tournament. I am not at liberty to extend it!" When the third protester spoke, Launce realized it was Sir Randolph, the foreign knight who had saved him from Sir Absalom in the stables.

Neither the king nor the enchanter responded to their protests, only watched as though measuring the people's reactions. Sir Absalom also looked around them, and when he caught Launce's gaze, Launce knew exactly what the knight was thinking. Would more blood be shed here today? Launce wanted to speak with him, but it would have been impossible to leave the dais without Rafael or Bronkendol noticing.

As the crowd continued to protest, Bronkendol pulled something small from his robe. He brought it to his mouth and began to whisper into it. Launce couldn't hear what the enchanter said, but he could see the thin bursts of blue and violet light begin to glimmer in the eyes of those around him. Everyone but him and Olivia.

Launce watched in amazement as the people fell silent and looked at Bronkendol with trusting eyes. Light glimmered from the corner of each eye with an eerie glow, but that wasn't what Launce found so strange. Instead, he was hit with a strong sense of familiarity. As he looked around him, he couldn't find its source. Olivia wasn't far off, but this sensation went far beyond what he knew of the princess. In fact, it wasn't coming from a single person at all. It was coming from the blue light that shone from the people's eyes.

It was Isa's power. Everard had said the enchanter's power influenced glass, but Launce would have known the feeling of his sister's power anywhere. It was the power of the heart, Everard had said. Somehow, the enchanter was using Isa's gift.

A new understanding of the enchanter's true strength dawned on Launce. How did one steal the power of another? Isa wouldn't have given it to him willingly, of that Launce was sure. What did this man want? And why wasn't the Fortress stopping him? And if the Fortress wasn't, why did Launce think he even stood a chance?

As if there hadn't been enough confusion already, the room filled with black and orange coats as Rafael's soldiers dispersed into the crowd. Not a single party was without a uniformed body nearby.

"I have assigned an escort for each party." Rafael spoke again, his eyes also glimmering violet and blue. "Your escort will accompany you to your chambers and then guide you to our designated meeting place so we can begin our journey soon. We will take our leave on the morrow."

Before Launce could consider what this meant, a heavy guard stepped up onto the dais and addressed him. "Master Launce." He bowed, but the gesture was shallow, and his words were stiff. "I will escort you to your chambers now. We will be leaving shortly." Light glimmered in the guard's eyes as well.

Back in his chambers, Launce threw his last pair of trousers into his pathetic sack with as much force as he could. As he thought of his sister, a shiver ran up his spine. If the enchanter was back, where was Isa? What had happened to her? While Bronkendol had been right about the fire in her eyes dulling, Launce didn't for a second trust the man to keep her safe, nor did he believe that Everard had died in a storm. There had been too many half-truths already.

Launce was herded out to the clearing that surrounded the stables, just like everyone else. It was disconcerting to see so many kings, queens, diplomats, and even knights being ordered about. The majority of the western kingdoms were ruled by the people who surrounded him. Many stood outside their fancy carriages, though a few, such as the knights, stood beside their horses. Most of the servants looked as though they would walk.

Launce found his horse, and was directed by the guard to lead it to the front of the throng. Despite the chaos erupting around him, he was glad to have this horse beside him. The monstrous animals that had been gifted to him during the contest had seemed wondrous when they'd first appeared. But now that he knew their origins, he was glad to have a familiar piece of home, even if it was one of Everard's horses.

He could see Olivia and her mother being escorted to a fine carriage not far away. When the guard held out his hand to help her up the carriage steps after her mother, however, Olivia shook her head vehemently and pointed to a group of people on horseback. Launce wished he could hear what they were saying. After a moment of arguing, it seemed Olivia had won. She wore a triumphant look and crossed her arms as she watched the guard stomp off toward the stables. A few minutes later, the defeated guard emerged with a cream-colored horse.

In spite of himself, Launce nearly laughed at the scathing look Olivia sent her father. She didn't move though until she was sure Rafael had seen her. Then, her chin lifted high, she stepped up onto the carriage step and lifted one leg to mount the horse in the most unladylike fashion Launce had ever seen, fine silk dress and all. King Rafael looked as though he might say something, but only closed his mouth and shook his head before turning back to the servant he'd been speaking with.

"Let us begin," Launce heard the enchanter tell Rafael.

"Wait!" Olivia cried out. "I want to ride beside Launce!"

"Whatever pleases you, my dear," Rafael said, sounding dazed and tired. Launce looked at Bronkendol, but to his surprise, the old man was watching them, looking pleased, as though it had been his idea.

Why, Launce wondered, was Bronkendol so eager to get them together? As much as he admired the princess, and as much as his heart told him he was already falling for her, it made him nervous to think that their relationship was part of some plan that also plotted Everard's death and the exploitation of Isa's power. Why were they the only ones without glass? Why did Bronkendol so desperately want them to fall in love?

The questions continued swirling about in Launce's head. Even so, a part of him relaxed when Olivia pulled her horse up next to his. Her hand slipped inside of his own, and he gave it a squeeze. They said nothing to break the dreadful silence that hung over the strange company of travelers, but Launce gave her a meaningful look as wheels, hooves, and the sounds of many feet began to move forward. The warmth of her palm against his matched that of the sun as it hung low in the western sky behind them, and the tiniest seed of hope sprouted inside of him. The outlook seemed dire now, but it couldn't always remain that way. They were going home, to the Fortress itself. The Fortress would keep this invader out, and the Maker would surely have pity on them. And when He did, Launce would make sure the enchanter's hopes would never see the light of day.

CHAPTER 36
BRING HER HOME

I still cannot fathom how we never managed to receive a single relic from the Glass Castle!" Ever slammed another book shut in disgust.

"It's been twenty-seven hundred years since the castle was sealed with the curse, Everard," Garin said, picking up the book and moving it before Ever could abuse it more. Not that Ever was in the mood to care.

"Wait!" The steward looked up. "What about Launce's armor? Didn't you say it was coated on the bottom with glass?"

But Ever was already shaking his head. "The armor and horses disappeared after Launce was declared the winner. Either someone stole them all or they simply vanished." Ever rubbed his eyes and moaned. "If I hadn't been so stupid and broken Bronkendol's glass gifts, we may even have had a chance with that." Ever picked up another book, unsure whether he wanted to read it again, or hurl it through a window.

"There is something you haven't told me yet, isn't there?" Garin said. Ever just looked at him miserably, and Garin nodded. "I could tell from the moment you arrived. What is it?" When Ever still didn't answer, he added in a soft voice, "You know you can tell me anything. You knew that as a boy, and you should know right now."

"She sent a message, begging me to come to her." Ever looked at his hands, dry and cracking from arranging and rearranging the maps. "It was something urgent. I could tell from the way the servant relayed the message!" He shook his head. "But I was so dead set on carrying out my plans, that I missed what was right in front of me. If I had only listened, she might not have been . . ."

Ever paused and let out a gusty breath, placing his hands over the edge of the table and leaning on it heavily. He felt as though his body had been clapped in irons, and he was dragging his chains behind him. No matter how hard he tried, finding her simply seemed impossible.

They had been back at the Fortress for three whole days, and Ever was nearly beside himself. He had sent out messenger birds to all of the western kingdoms. Many of his peers were still away in Cobren, so many respondents had been stewards and ambassadors, who knew nothing of the Glass Queen's reign at all, and the few kings who had responded had nothing to help him either.

Even Garin was running Ever's patience thin. Ever had never doubted the steward's attachment to Isa. Once the spell had been broken, Garin had spent his every free moment ensuring that she was comfortable in one way or another. But for someone so devoted to the girl, he seemed to be dragging his feet more and more in sending Ever off.

"There is a reason you haven't found an answer," Garin said. "Trust the Fortress, and wait to see what happens. If you cannot find her, there is a purpose in your inability to go."

"And do what? Sit on my haunches? Or should I just wait for her to drop out of the sky?" As the sarcastic words dripped from his mouth, a small voice inside of Ever wondered what he was doing. Garin's voice was the one that Ever trusted most, after the Fortress. He had never let Ever down before. But his words of caution were just too much for Ever to bear at the moment.

Instead of waiting for Garin's response, Ever stomped outside for some fresh air. They were getting nowhere. Without thinking about where he was going, Ever found himself in a part of the fortress grounds he had not visited in what felt like a very long time.

Although their season of bloom was long past, the cherry trees somehow still displayed a surreal beauty. Their bark had grayed, but the shapes of the branches still resembled dancers reaching for the sky. Or at least, that's what Isa said. The grove wasn't large, but was deep enough to hide a weary soul who did not wish to be found by the outside world. Dead leaves crunched beneath Ever's feet as he closed his eyes and walked slowly to the grove's center. To his relief, the only sounds here were the chirping of a few winter birds, and the scampering of chipmunks as they hurried to finish their winter nests.

Falling to his knees, Ever kept his eyes shut as he leaned his head backward and waited for the presence he knew would be listening. "I don't understand," he said. "How do I continue to lose all that You give me? Even when I realize the error of my ways, why is it that I am unable to make it right?"

There were no words that responded, but then again, Ever knew there wouldn't be. Instead, he simply stayed upon the ground and listened to the rushing of the wind through the trees, knowing he was not alone. "Please," he said softly, "not for my sake, but for hers. I do not deserve her, but she deserves to be safe. I just wish I knew what You were doing." He didn't realize he had been weeping quietly until the breeze brushed his face, and he felt for the first time that his cheeks were wet.

"So it's true." A hollow voice came from just a few feet away. Ever's eyes opened as he drew his sword. As soon as he saw who it was however, the grief that he was sure could not grow heavier doubled. Isa and Launce's father, Ansel, stood there watching him, his own face a reflection of the despair Ever felt inside.

"Garin said that you were busy, but you have been home for three days, and I had to know . . ." He let his words trail off, the fear in his eyes saying more than Ever needed or wanted to know.

"Your family has all the right in the world to despise me," he said, sheathing his sword. "I have done nothing but bring you pain." Ansel didn't answer, just stood there staring at the leaf-littered ground, opening and closing his hands as though they searched for something to do. And yet another wave of failure washed over Ever.

They had come so far since his first meeting with the merchant, when, to his shame, he had demanded the man's eldest daughter in desperation, hoping she could be the one to save the kingdom from the curse he had brought upon it. By the time Isa had helped him break the curse that had held the Fortress in darkness, Ever had been changed, his soul cut and healed in a way that would never go back to what *he* had been, an insecure, self-reliant beast. His complete transformation, along with Isa's winning spirit, had coaxed her family, all but Launce, of course, into a sort of uneasy trust, one that had been deepening slowly with time.

As he faced Ansel now, however, Ever despaired of ever having any sort of relationship worth keeping with his father-in-law. Not that he deserved one in the first place.

For a long time, they stayed still, Ansel leaning against a tree, and Ever standing before him. Ever begged the Fortress once more. *If not for me, for him. For them. Show me where to go! Do not let them suffer this way for my mistakes!*

"I would die in a moment if it would bring her home," Ansel finally said. "But as much as it kills me to say, the fact of the matter is that she chose this life."

"I didn't give her much choice."

"You were dead for a week, son. Isa hated it, but she accepted who she was and what she had been chosen to do. She wanted . . . she needed this life. She would have met this foe with or without you." The older man let out a deep sigh and rubbed his eyes. "You are not a father yet. I pray to the Maker that one day you will be. But as of now, you cannot know the pain of having your child ripped from you again and again."

Ever flinched, but Ansel continued. "I have seen too much in the last year to know anything but that the Maker has used the Fortress to call my daughter to a higher purpose. I do not know what it is, but I do know that whatever it is, the purpose is hers. Nothing you do or don't do will break her of that purpose. Now, you can choose whether or not to help her bring that purpose to fruition, but I can assure you one thing." Walking up to Ever, he placed his hand on Ever's face and lifted his chin, as only a father could do. "I have not lost hope. And neither should you."

As though confirming Ansel's words, a sudden tug at his heart alerted Ever of the familiar presence before the shouts of a servant did, and without a thought, he found himself running as though a demon chased him toward the Fortress. His heart felt like it might leap from his chest. *Is it . . .?* He asked the Fortress, too afraid of the answer to finish the question. Up the field and across the gardens, he tore. His head pounded and he was nearly lightheaded from the delirium that drove him on. *How?*

His sensitive intuition had not failed him. As soon as he crested the mountain meadow upon which the Fortress sat, he could see the multitude of servants that was gathered round a single horse at the front Fortress steps.

"Be gentle!" he could hear Gigi order. "Watch her head! She can't hold it up!"

Despite his speed, his approach seemed painstakingly slow. "Hold back, all of you!" Garin ordered from somewhere above the din.

"Move!" Ever shouted. So loud was his call that the startled servants scrambled to clear a way for him. Finally he reached the crowd. Everyone watched solemnly as he slowed, gasping for air.

There she was. Draped upon the horse as though there was no life in her, Isa clung to the horse's mane with fingers that looked like they might break. Her auburn hair had fallen from its place, and spilled in tangled bunches down the horse's side.

"Isa."

She did not raise her head to look at him when he called her name. With unsteady hands, he reached up and pulled her limp body from the horse. As she fell into his arms, her eyelids didn't open, and her lips barely moved as her shallow breath went in and out. Cradling her to his chest, Ever began the long walk up to their chambers.

By the time they arrived, Garin already had an army of servants preparing the room. Blankets were pulled back from the bed, and curtains were drawn shut. A healer had a tray of potent poultices and herbs prepared beside the bed, and he was arguing in a low voice with Garin over their necessity, but Ever shook his head at all of them.

"Out!"

No one objected, and soon the room was clear of all but Garin, who paused to squeeze Ever's shoulder before leaving and closing the doors behind him. With more care than he had ever taken in his life, Ever laid his wife in the center of their bed.

Her cheeks were red and dry with the early stages of frostbite, and her fingers were even worse. No warmth emanated from her skin as he felt her head and then her neck. The only sign that there was still life in her was the ever-shallow rise and fall of her chest, and the sense of purpose that the Fortress now poured inside of him. He knew what he needed to do.

Before he began, he laid his lips on hers and lingered there. To think he might never have kissed those lips again.

"I'll make this better," he whispered. "I promise." Then, with all that was within him, he gathered his power and let it go. An ocean of blue light filled the room and lit the walls. He wondered how long it might take before she was healed enough to open her eyes, but then decided it didn't matter.

She was home.

CHAPTER 37

NOTHING

Even in the dark of the early morning, Ever couldn't take his eyes from her. The soft glow of the moon peaked in around the curtains, lighting her face in a dreamlike glow. Isa's eyes were no longer sunken in, and all sign of frostbite was gone. The Fortress's power had healed her body in every way. But, Ever wondered, what state would she be in once she awakened? She had not so much as stirred since he'd first laid her in the bed.

"I will never have the power to express how truly sorry I am," he whispered into the silence. "But I promise you that never will I fail you in such a way again. I do not know why I ever doubted you. You were the one who broke the curse, and you were the one who taught me to be alive once again." He tenderly brushed wayward strands of hair away from her face. It was easier to practice his apology when she couldn't hear him.

"I hope," he breathed, "that in spite of all my blind foolishness, you've never had reason to doubt my need for you." He leaned down placed his lips on her brow. "Or that place which you hold in my heart." He smiled into the darkness as the words which he should have said months ago now flowed with abandon.

"I cannot wait to begin the rest of our life after all of this is finished. You will make the most intelligent and wise queen the Fortress and Destin have ever seen. And," he leaned forward, as though telling her a secret, "when the Fortress so chooses, the most wonderful mother our children could ever ask for. Whether it is sooner or later, I will be overjoyed."

As he spoke to her, Ever wondered how he would ever be able to let her out of his sight again. To think he had nearly lost her was unbearable. And yet, an unease wriggled within him. Unless she had escaped on her own, there was a reason the enchanter had allowed her to return. Her body had been pushed to the brink of exhaustion, and she had to been without water and food for a few days, but for Ever, those wounds were simple enough to heal. And the enchanter would have known that.

What Ever feared was not the injury done to Isa's body, but that which had been done to her mind and spirit. If only he could know what else had been hurt, he might be able to help her more. But such was impossible, as he was unaware of what had happened during her abduction. Without thinking, for the thousandth time that night, he leaned down and softly kissed her lips once more. What was he going to do?

"Ever?"

"Isa?"

Joy and fear and trepidation rushed through him as he lifted and cradled her to him, tears running down his face. Relief flooded him so entirely that it felt as though he might drown. But Ever couldn't have cared less.

"Isa," he whispered over and over again. "You're home. You're safe." He could feel her swallow hard, and loosened his grip so she might breathe more easily. He was nearly giddy as he felt her lean back into the crook of his arm.

"Where . . .?" She stopped and cleared her throat. "Where am I?"

"You're home," he said. "Do you not remember your journey here?"

Isa paused. "Not much, I suppose."

"What do you remember?"

"The . . . the enchanter . . . he took my power. He took my power, and placed it in a mirror."

"What?" Ever had never heard of such a thing. Alarm raced through him, but he knew that for her sake, he needed to remain calm. She was in no condition to handle more stress. "This is not something we should worry about now," he said. "We will talk to Garin in the morning. For now I simply want to be with you." He leaned down once more to kiss her, but instead of leaning in like she always had, Isa turned her head away instead.

Pain hit him, along with confusion. She had never turned away from his kiss before. Worse than her refusal though, was the realization that for her to move the way she just had, she must have opened her eyes. If she had opened her eyes, why weren't their blue flames piercing the darkness?

"I'm tired," she said. "And hungry. Is there something to eat?"

Ever shook his head and scrambled to bring her the tray that had been waiting in the room, just as she had asked. But as he did, panic threatened to overwhelm him. Isa's fire was gone.

"She never even asked about her brother," Ever muttered as he paced the floor in front of Garin, who sat more patiently in one of the great chairs pulled up before the fire in the king's study. "All she wanted was to be left alone."

"Patience, Ever," Garin said mildly. "We do not yet know

how deeply she was injured. Perhaps quiet and solitude is what she most needs to heal."

But Ever was already shaking his head. "When she awoke the second time, she told me she wanted to go outside. I tried to warn her of the cold, but she insisted." He sighed and scratched his head. "I'm supposed to be getting our horses prepared as we speak."

"Well then, you can tell me more as we do just that." Garin stood and pulled one of the bell chimes upon the wall beside the grand fireplace. Moments later, a knock sounded at the door. "Prepare the king and queen's riding horses," Garin told the servant boy, and with a quick bow, the boy was gone.

Ever could see that his mentor was curious as to what had riled him so, but it was difficult to explain. He didn't yet have words to describe the disappointment that had filled him when she'd awakened the second time that morning.

"Garin, her fire is gone."

This time, there was no soothing calm in Garin's face. He put down the parchment he had been examining and stood straight.

"What?"

"It's just that. She has no fire left. The flames are gone!"

Ever had convinced himself he was wrong after she had first awakened. He'd been so relieved to simply hear her voice and see her move that he'd hoped that perhaps he had been wrong, distracted. The second time she'd awakened, however, had been different. She'd allowed him to kiss her quickly that time, but there was no warmth, no return. She had merely seemed to tolerate it, turning away from him as soon as he was done.

It was then, as he searched her face for some hint of affection that he realized her eyes were indeed as hard and cold in their blue depths as glaciers. The Fortress's fire was completely extinguished. And yet, she was still alive. Ever had never heard of such a thing in all his years of studying the Fortress's history.

How was there breath still in her when the Fortress's life-giving fire was gone?

"What do you feel?" Garin's voice was strained. "What do you sense when you're near her?"

"Nothing." Ever hated the words even as he said them. "I feel nothing."

Garin's eyebrows rose, and Ever knew the steward was beginning to understand his state of panic.

"She shows no sign of joy at being home, no anger toward me for failing her, not even sorrow at what the enchanter did to her." He shrugged. "And whenever I ask her about what he did to her, all she does is repeat herself, saying he stole the power from her heart."

"My lord." A young voice came from the other side of the thick wooden doors. "The king and queen's horses are prepared." The two men left the study to fetch Isa for their ride, but Garin looked far from done with the conversation.

"Go with her," Garin ordered him outside the chamber door, his voice suddenly fierce. The fine lines at the corners of his eyes and on his forehead were more pronounced with worry than Ever had seen them before. "Do not let her out of your sight. I don't like this. I will see her myself later."

Ever gathered his courage as he knocked on the door. Garin gave him a curt nod and stalked off.

"Our horses are ready," Ever called through the doors. It felt foolish to ask permission to enter his own chambers, but for all Isa had suffered at his hand, he was willing to play the part of any fool if it would help her heal.

Isa appeared in her riding gear, but remained silent as they walked down to the stables. Her eyes stayed trained on the end of the hall. Not a word was spoken as they mounted their horses and left the servants behind. Only the early winter wind whipped around them, as though agitated with everyone and everything, threatening to send them back home. Dead leaves hit their faces, and the gray of the sky did nothing to cheer the somber mood. Ever had hoped that being outside would help him find the words he was looking for, but he didn't gain the courage to speak again until they were far from everyone and everything, way out on the far end of the back field.

"Isa," he finally said, clearing his throat twice before he could continue. "I wish you would tell me what's wrong. I want to help you, but I can't unless I know how."

"Nothing," she answered. "Nothing is wrong."

"Something is most definitely wrong." He pulled his horse in front of hers, forcing her to stop. "Have you tried using your power?"

Isa stared at him as though he were dim. As he waited, Ever decided he disliked the way she had told the servants to fix her hair. It was too tight, too severe for her young face.

"There is nothing left to use. I told you, he took everything."

"Well, at least tell me how you feel about it." He was grasping for smoke, desperate for some answers. "Surely you must feel something for me, if not for him. Anger? Sorrow? Hatred?" He took a deep breath, steeling himself for the answer he knew he deserved to receive. "Do you hate me, Isa?" For a moment, he was sure she would say yes. A brief flash of recognition lit her eyes, but then she only resumed the bored, impatient expression she'd worn all day.

"What part of *everything* do you not understand? My power came from my heart, little as it was." She sniffed. "He took what was left, and with it everything else in my heart as well. So when I say I feel nothing, I truly feel nothing. Not for you, not for my brother, not for my family, not even for Bronkendol himself. Now, if you'll excuse me, I'll go before I say something that will assuredly injure you more." And with that, she kicked her horse into a gallop.

What had he done?

CHAPTER 38
AN ENCHANTER'S BLOOD

Remembering Garin's words of caution about leaving Isa alone, Ever pushed his horse to follow hers. To his relief, she simply returned to the stables and dismounted. Once he knew she was back inside the Fortress, Ever called one of his messengers.

"Go to Soudain and find Ansel and Deline Marchand. He's a prominent merchant with a shop in the main square. Bring them to me immediately."

Ever decided to go find Garin while he waited for the Marchands' arrival. As he climbed the curving stone staircase of the tower, he prayed that Garin might have found the answer. Never had Ever heard of anyone being able to steal a monarch's power. He wondered if Isa had truly understood what the enchanter had done. But then, he conceded, he had never heard of a strength like Isa's before he had witnessed it himself.

The Fortress monarchs had always possessed one form of strength or another. Most had exceeded the physical abilities of the average man. Others had the ability to discern lies from the truth. Still others could heal, and there had been one or two on record who could converse with the animals. Ever's own powers were unusual for even a Fortress king, according to Garin, in that he had most of the powers combined, animal communication excluded. But none were like Isa's power of the heart, and that made her current struggle all the more puzzling.

"Anything of interest?" he asked as he finally reached the tower. As Ever had expected, Garin was deep in thought, his head bent over a number of old books spread out upon the table.

"Nothing that will help us now," Garin sighed. "If this truly is Bronkendol, then his power is much older than I am, much older than our most ancient texts. The first kings gathered a few scrolls and such here and there, but even those were written after the kingdoms formed." He looked up at Ever. "Did she tell you anything new?"

"Only that it is Bronkendol." He paused. "And she says that when he stole her power, he stole everything."

"What do you mean everything?"

Ever shrugged. "Her feelings, her emotions. She says her heart is empty."

"Your Highness, the Marchands are waiting in your study, just as you requested," a servant called out. The look Garin gave him was not a hopeful one, but Ever only shook his head.

"It was all I could think to do. It can't hurt anything." At this, Garin inclined his head once and went back to searching his books. Ever began the long descent down the steps with a hope he feared was in vain. But if anyone could reach Isa, it would be them. If they could not find her, Ever worried that no one would. He put such dark thoughts from his mind and smoothed his face, however, as he entered his study. He would not give them false hope, but they still deserved their best chance, too. Despite his intentions, however, Deline didn't give him a chance to even begin explaining. She ran straight up to him, her dark eyes hopeful.

"Where is she?"

"Resting in her room." Ever took a deep breath. "Before I bring you to see her though, there is something you must know." Deline exchanged a worried look with her husband, but let Ever speak. "Since she has returned," Ever began, "Isa has seemed . . . different." He stopped and bit his lip, trying to think of how to explain in a way that would not be too painful, but would prepare them for the daughter they would soon meet.

"Just tell us what the matter is," Ansel said softly. "She is our daughter. You know we will do anything and more that she needs. Now, what does she need?"

"That's just it. I wish I knew. Since she's returned, Isa has said she feels empty. She does not wish to be doted on, nor does she wish to speak of those she loves. She has not even asked of Launce's welfare since she's arrived." Ever felt his careful façade fall as he spoke. "She won't even allow me to touch her." The weight of what he was saying suddenly drained him, and Ever rubbed his eyes and allowed himself to sink into one of the chairs.

Ansel was a merchant, nothing like the father Ever had known, but there were times like this when he wanted so much to think that his father-in-law might see him as a son in some way or another. Part of the family, at the very least. "I need you to help her remember," he said, looking up at them wearily. "That is all I know and that is all I can ask."

"Then that is what we shall try to do." Ansel looked at his wife and with a comforting smile, gently took her by the waist and led her from the room. Before they left, Ansel placed a hand on Ever's arm. The gesture was kind and for a moment, Ever felt a little less alone. There were others who shared his grief, others who loved her nearly as much as he did.

When they were gone long enough to ensure that they wouldn't see him, Ever followed their footsteps down the hall to his own chambers. He stood outside the door where he could just hear the conversation inside.

"I thought he might send you." The slight tremor of uncertainty in Isa's voice was the closest thing to feeling that Ever had heard since she'd arrived home. His heart leapt with a dangerous, uneven sense of hope.

"Ever says you're having a difficult time since you arrived home." Deline's words were as sweet and welcoming as an embrace.

"I am perfectly fine, and I cannot understand what all the fuss is about."

"Have you heard from your brother?" Ansel's voice was also kind, but more reserved than his wife's had been. He was testing her, Ever realized. *He wants to see what she does when I am not around.* A part of him both dreaded and hoped to find that Isa's strange behavior was simply born from resentment for him, but the longer Ever listened to the family speak, the less he dared to dream.

"Launce is a man now," Isa retorted. "I wish everyone would simply leave him be."

"Ever says your brother is alone in another country under the thumb of a king who despises him." Ansel's voice grew agitated. "And you don't wish to know of his well-being?"

"We are done here." Isa's footsteps quickly approached the door. Before Ever could move, Isa had opened the door and fixed him with a cold stare. "You may see them out." And with that, she whirled and began marching toward the hallway that led to the Tower of Annals.

"Everard." Deline was looking up at him, beseeching him with her eyes. Commanding him. "You must help her." She stepped forward and clutched his sleeve. "She would not be in this mess if you had protected her. Now help her!"

"If you don't help her," Ansel's voice was not so accusatory, but the sadness in his eyes was somehow worse than the anger in his wife's, "I don't know that anything or anyone can. Please." He held Ever's gaze for a long moment before turning and guiding his weeping wife out. Ever could only watch in misery.

"IT'S BEEN THREE DAYS," Ever growled. "I don't know how much longer I can stand this." He gestured at the lone form sitting in a chair on the south side of the Tower of Annals. Though Garin and Ever were on horseback at the edge of the field that bordered the mountain road, it was easy to see her small figure through the glass walls of the round tower room.

"Have patience," Garin cautioned him. It annoyed Ever to no end that his mentor seemed to know Ever's actions before he did. "Isa needs to find peace with the Fortress before she can find peace with anyone else. There is nothing you can do to make that happen faster than it will."

Ever shook his head. "We don't have time. I need to know what he did to her and what he plans to do with her power. This foolish mess is all intertwined somehow. I need to reach the heart of the matter. But I cannot do that without her help."

"Don't do anything rash. I know you want to help, but she is the Fortress's daughter. It is watching her just as it has been all of her life. It's best not to interfere." He eyed Ever suspiciously. "You might learn a thing or two as well by watching." They sat for a few moments longer, watching her in silence. But Ever knew, and he knew Garin knew as well, that there would not be much more waiting for him.

Once more, Ever promised himself and his mentor silently. *Once more, I will try, and even if it kills me, I won't hold back.* Urging his horse forward, he let his mount carry him with the wind, back to the cold, beautiful eyes he could feel watching him from above.

By the time he reached the Annals, Isa was nowhere to be seen. So intent had he been on his mission that the thought of speaking with her anywhere else made his heart sink within him. He let out a gusty breath before walking over and letting himself fall into the chair Isa had been sitting in when he'd seen her from the fields below.

The Tower of Annals was one of the few places the monarchs could escape to for true solitude. Since the Maker had so uniquely blessed the Fortress with a life of its own a thousand years before, the tower had been created as a place of sacred rest.

Constructed of only windows for walls, the entire room was one large circle, allowing a view of nearly the entire kingdom. Each of the floor-to-ceiling windows could open to the balcony that ran around the entire tower. A single large fireplace stood in the center of the room, surrounded by tall bookshelves and various pieces of sitting furniture. The air smelled of musty pages and sweet cedar from the logs they burned in the fire. As soon as one stepped from the stairs into the tower, a veil of solemnity and age hung in the air, making it just heavy enough to notice when one breathed.

It was in this room that Ever and Isa had nearly died, and in which they had been brought back from certain death to life. It was here he had hoped to speak not to the silent, mysterious stranger, but to the heart of the companion he missed so much.

"What happened?" he muttered, closing his eyes and leaning back, allowing the warmth of the sun to cover him like a blanket. "How did we end up here?"

"You failed."

Ever nearly fell out of his chair when Isa spoke. She must have known he would come. She stood behind him now, several paces back. The silk lavender gown she wore was simple, but it fit her frame well. The purple made the copper streaks in her hair more vibrant than usual. Everything in him yearned to close the distance between them and will her back to him. But he stayed still, and so did she. The expression on her face was neither hateful nor angry, but there wasn't a trace of warmth in it either.

"You asked what happened," she said when he didn't speak, "and the answer is that you failed. While you were traipsing off with Kartek, trying to find the answers all on your own, you failed. When you ignored my warning, he took me, and you failed." She shrugged. "It's as simple as that."

Ever knew everything she told him was true, but hearing her say it was so much worse. "No amount of victories in the battlefield can redeem me from the way I've neglected you." His throat sounded gravelly, too tight. "Everything you say is true."

Ever didn't realize he'd fallen to his knees until he looked up at her once more. The pain inside him felt as though he might split in two, but somehow her face was unmoved. Even in the few months they'd been married, he had come to rely unquestionably on Isa's forgiving nature, the grace she extended with a tired smile when he was back late from a journey, or when he had time and time again cancelled plans for picnics and special suppers up on the tower balcony. The softness of her sweet touch and the adoration of her eyes had always brought him through, even in the short time they had been together.

But this woman made of stone, this cold, unfeeling heart in the body of his beloved was more than he could stand. Anger, screaming, tears, anything would be better than this silence. "Can you forgive me?" he pleaded, his voice almost too quiet to hear. "I just wanted to protect you."

"Whether I forgive you or not makes no difference. You let him steal everything from me, and no words of mine or yours will bring it back." With that, she uncrossed her arms and began walking toward the door.

A feeling of wild angst overtook Ever, and in that moment, something told him that if he allowed her to walk out that door, the Isa he loved would never return. *I beg you*, he cried out to the Fortress, *let this work!* He was on his feet in an instant. In three long strides, he'd overtaken her. A feverish hope consumed him as he grabbed her by her waist and pulled her back into him.

How many times had he taken this embrace for granted? Ever reached up and gently but firmly guided her jaw up to his. All the pain and loneliness and worry and passion that he had been harboring poured into his kiss like oil into a flame. Never had he loved her more.

For one brief, glorious moment, his lips melted into hers.

But only for a moment. All too quickly she pushed herself from his arms. The shake of her head was nearly imperceptible, but it was still there. The all-too-familiar cool solidity quickly chased away the fleeting look of uncertainty that her eyes had held for that short second.

"I told you. I have nothing left to give." With that, she was gone. A hollow ache filled him as he watched her begin the winding descent down the tower steps. It was not long, however, before he became aware of the anger that had been simmering within him since Isa had returned. Common sense had cautioned him against allowing his desires to control him, but the loss of his wife was simply too much.

"Garin!" he shouted as he took off quickly behind her. Only a few steps down, and he had passed her on the stairs, but Ever didn't stop. "Gather my things!"

As always, despite the distance, Garin somehow heard him, and was waiting at the foot of the tower steps. He didn't work to conceal his disappointment, his mouth turning down on one side as it always did when he was displeased. He followed Ever, as Ever burst into his chambers and began to gather his belongings in a violent storm of purpose.

"And where might you be going?"

"I'm going to find that enchanter."

"How?"

In response, Ever held up the robe he'd taken from Isa when she'd first arrived home.

"All I have to do is follow this. It's from Bronkendol's castle. It should lead me between the realms."

"And then what do you expect to do?" Garin continued to trail Ever as he stormed down to the armory to gather his favorite weapons. "You still have the slivers of glass in your eyes. You don't know what he plans to do with those."

Ever paused on the threshold.

"It doesn't matter. I will find him. And then I will kill him."

CHAPTER 39
BLINDSIDED

Isa watched as Ever's horse carried him down the mountain road. Only once did he slow to look back. Though she couldn't see his eyes, she knew they were searching for her. She thought about waving, but what would the purpose be in that? It would only encourage him in this foolhardy end he was racing toward.

It was so strange not to feel. Tears should have stung her eyes, and apprehension should have seized her chest, nearly suffocating her. As strong as her husband was, Isa knew now that Ever was no match for Bronkendol. He hadn't even been able to remove the glass slivers from his own eyes, let alone come rescue her. The Fortress's strength was old, but it was infantile in comparison to that which ran through the enchanter's blood.

Morbidly curious, Isa continued to dig down deep inside of herself. She had once felt as though words could never come close to expressing the connection she felt with Ever. But now it all seemed in vain, for her heart felt as hollow as the animal skin drums the soldiers used to signal battle.

"What was it?"

"What was what?" Isa kept her eyes on the distant figure below as she felt Garin move behind her.

"You kept something from him."

"I didn't lie, if that's what you mean." She swerved to face him.

"Omitting a fact of importance can be just as dangerous as a blatant lie, if not more so."

"He never asked for every detail of my time there, so I didn't give it. Is that such a crime?"

Garin scowled. "Your husband could hardly think clearly enough to eat once you were home. Now he's riding off into the jaws of the enemy for you, and you have the brazenness to sit here and play semantics?"

"I don't know what is so difficult for you all to understand." Isa looked him straight in the eye. "I have told you time and time again that the enchanter emptied my heart. I have tried, believe me!" Isa realized her voice was growing louder as she spoke. It was the closest she'd come to feeling since she'd been in Bronkendol's chair, and the feeling she drew near to now was exasperation. "I can't understand why he went at all. He cannot challenge the Glass Prince. No one can. I thought I'd made it perfectly clear that he would simply be wise to allow things to pass as they will. His decision to ride off for my sake was foolish and rash, and I had no part in it."

"Your husband will die if you do not do something! Look deep inside yourself, Isabelle! Do you truly wish him dead?"

Despite her lack of feeling, Isa had to fight the urge to cower. It was the first time she'd ever heard Garin shout in such a way. Worry lined his face, and the slight lines of gray in his dark hair stood out. And though the Fortress steward did not have the blue rings of fire in his eyes that the monarchs kept, Isa thought she saw a hint of the same blue emanating from around his entire being. Her heart thumped once in a strange, uneven way.

"I do not wish him dead! I wish to know why my fire is gone. I wish to know why I'm still breathing even though my fire has died! I wish to know why I was allowed to go through such pain and suffering if I truly am a daughter of the Fortress!" She was shouting now, although she wasn't sure why.

Garin watched her, his arms crossed and his eyes still flashing, but he didn't interrupt as she continued her tirade.

"I have tried to feel! But when Bronkendol emptied my heart, then placed me on the back of a horse with little water and even less food, and sent me through terrain which no one should survive, every bit of feeling I'd tried to hold onto was blown away into nothingness. I have nothing left!"

Garin simply stared at her. His eyes were not cruel, but they were determined, and his silence was suddenly worse than if he had shouted hateful words at her. A familiar yet foreign feeling attempted to enter her. She couldn't tell though whether it was anger or sorrow or worry or foolish, foolish joy. Instead, she took a deep breath and steadied herself on the corner of the solid cedar table that was littered with every kind of book and scroll imaginable.

"My husband did not listen to me, and he failed to keep me safe. The Fortress has failed me too. I simply don't see the point in trying to fight for or against this heinous fate any longer—"

"Now stop right there." Garin was suddenly so close to her that he had to tilt his head down to look into her eyes. It was a challenge she didn't flinch from. "Do you think you're the first Fortress queen to suffer? Have none before you ever felt pain, too?"

"The Fortress abandoned me! It let that monster steal all that was left of my power!"

"And?"

Isa stared at him in shock. What did he mean *and*? Isa had put all of her trust in the Fortress, and thus in Ever, and neither of them had kept her from the pain that had ultimately broken her.

Garin walked over to a bookshelf four shelves down and pulled an ancient leather book. "Queen Adeline." He flipped open the pages with a puff of dust that made Isa cough. "Lived four hundred years ago. Was stabbed in the chest by one of her handmaidens who had been paid off by an enemy. She was journeying to investigate the welfare of Destinian merchants who were disappearing." He slammed the book shut before laying it down and pulling another book from the shelf.

"Queen Dione, who lived seven hundred years ago, was abducted and tortured by a sorcerer who demanded to be shown into the Tower of Annals. When she told him she would not desecrate that which was sacred, he beat her for days on end until her husband arrived. By then, she was blind in both eyes." Placing this book on top of the other one, he folded his arms and began to rattle off more names.

"Princess Martine never married because her father and brother were killed by her betrothed the eve before their wedding. Queen Odile lost five of her sons in the War of Boars. Queen Mother Radelle was forced to take the throne again when her eldest son, King Aubin, was killed before her very eyes, and she did not have time to properly mourn until her youngest son was of age to be crowned, thirteen years later. Need I go on?"

Isa wanted to retort that none of those women had watched their hearts being ripped from their chests, but her throat was too tight. All she could do was blink rapidly while her eyes developed a strange sort of sting at the corners. Garin placed his head in his right hand and inhaled deeply. He stayed like that for a long time, as though the memories or stories, Isa did not know which, had overwhelmed him.

When he did speak again, his voice was kinder, and his eyes held something closer to the affection she was used to seeing.

"You are not the only one who has been taken advantage of. As shrewd as he is, even Ever's power has been taken advantage of. Those who do not wish to solve their own problems call out in distress, and your husband, dutiful as always, rushes in to help."

Garin looked down at her left hand. Isa followed his gaze to the blue, crystal ring that hadn't glowed in quite a long time. "And yet," he said, "Ever's strength does not run dry. It cannot, for it is not his to run out of. The power comes from the Fortress itself, which is gifted to the Fortress from the Maker. So truthfully, the power was stolen from the Maker, not from you."

Isa swallowed, her throat suddenly dry.

"I still don't understand why the Fortress would allow me to be used in such a way, why it would allow my power to all but disappear, and then to have the rest, along with all my feelings and emotions, stolen away." As she spoke, a small smile suddenly flickered across Garin's face.

"I don't believe that Bronkendol stole all of your power or your heart. You say your heart is empty, but I think it's merely boarded up. You feel things deeply, Isa. It's part of who you are. But you make the mistake of allowing your feelings to be too tied up in your willingness to do what is necessary."

"I told you, I—"

But Garin held a hand up. "If you are truly without feeling, then why are you glaring at me with such disdain?" Again, that small, irritating smile crossed his face, and Isa swallowed what she had been about to say. As much as she hated to admit it, he had a point.

"I know you don't feel like helping your husband," Garin said in a soft voice. "But love isn't doing things when we *feel* led to. Love is doing what someone needs when they need it. Hang feelings, Isa! Good wine will bring feelings, but when the night is over, none of those feelings bear witness to the truth! Feelings can come and go any time. When the Fortress wants you to do something, it will give you the power to do it. And it will expect it of you, whether you feel like it or not."

Isa sighed and turned to walk out upon the balcony. The world below her looked still. Specks of animals grazed in distant fields, and patches of wood dotted the land from the mountain on down to what she knew was eventually the distant sea. Garin's words spun circles in her mind. What she wouldn't give for a way to put her thoughts in place, to know what she was truly thinking, for in that moment, she did not know.

"I'm not blind to the way Ever has treated you since the wedding." Garin placed a calloused hand on top of hers and squeezed gently. "He tries, but the boy still has much to learn. Sometimes anger manifests itself in strange ways."

"You think I'm angry with him." It was all Isa could do to keep her voice steady.

"If I'm wrong, then why are you so opposed to helping him?"

Something inside of Isa burst. Like a dam bursting from the surge of spring rains, what felt like scales flew violently from her heart. With a cry, Isa clutched at her chest and fell to her knees.

Loneliness from Ever's constant absence.

Pain from his doubt.

Fear, now that her fire was completely gone.

Sorrow for all she had done and seen flooded her and poured from her eyes in unending streams. Immediately, Garin was there, holding her shoulders as she wept.

"The fire is gone, Garin! I woke up here, and it was gone! And now Ever is gone, and Launce is gone, and I don't even know who I am anymore." She continued to weep as Garin pulled her gently to her feet and began to wipe the tears from her cheeks.

"That's the wondrous thing about the Fortress. Just because

you have temporarily lost sight of who you are, that doesn't make you any less the Fortress's daughter than it would separate you from your blood father if you disowned him."

At the word *disown*, Isa began to sob even harder. She truly had disowned the Fortress. If Ever had been unfaithful to her in his attentions, she had been unfaithful in the Fortress a thousand times more with her words and careless actions. But Garin lifted her chin so she was forced to look him in the eyes.

"And whether you feel like it or not, the Fortress chose you. You are its daughter. And you are Ever's wife. Never, in all my time here, has the Fortress ever taken that lightly."

"I still don't understand though. How is it that when I look in the mirror, I see nothing? My fire is gone."

"So your eyes can see all, can they?" Garin gave an amused snort. "You can see the birds in the treetops of the orange grove, from here? What your mother is doing at her hearth in this instant? Or the—"

"Ever can't see it either."

Garin chuckled. "Dear, your husband is gifted, but hardly infallible. Just because neither you nor your husband cannot see it doesn't mean it's not there."

Isa studied Garin for a moment more before looking down at her hands. Could he be right? Deep down, she knew he was. But fear of failure made her shiver, and her hands shook as she closed her eyes and reluctantly tried to conjure the blue fire that always came to Ever so easily.

There was not even a tingle in her fingertips. She started to protest again, but Garin shushed her.

"Do what you know is right," he said. "Feelings will eventually follow."

"Will my power ever return?" she asked, unable to keep the sadness from her voice.

"If the Fortress believes you need it, then the power will be yours when the time comes. Until then, trust that the Fortress will not leave you alone, ever. Even when you *feel* alone."

Isa looked out once more to the northern mountains. She had barely survived the journey through them. Was she really ready to risk another brush with death so soon, and without her power at that? Her heart told her that no, she wasn't.

"Ready my horse."

Garin grinned.

"It's already been done."

"And my sword? I think I left it in..." She let her words trail off as his smile grew even wider.

"After a few centuries, you learn a thing or two."

In no time at all, she was dressed in her warmest combat clothing and on her horse. Gigi hovered and fussed, as usual, but Garin was as calm and collected as always.

"It will take time," she admitted in a low voice. "I still don't feel the way I used to."

"Remember, do what is right. Feelings will follow. Now," he patted her knee, "go."

Before she knew it, Isa was thundering down the same road that Ever had taken less than an hour before. She shook at the thought of returning to the terrifying, white, blinding beauty she'd left behind.

Well, she thought to herself wryly, fear had returned, at least. And if fear was there, the other feelings were lurking somewhere as well. If only she could locate her courage before she faced the enchanter once more.

CHAPTER 40
SACRED GROUND

If Launce never traveled the road between Cobren's capitol and the Fortress again, he would be more than pleased. For the second time that week, Launce was on his way back to the Fortress, but this time, rather than racing along at Ever's pace, the royal company crawled. It had taken the multitude of royals and nobles and their entourages all afternoon and evening to leave the hill country behind, which should have taken only a few hours. Carriages, horses and riders, and caravans filled the road behind him so that Launce couldn't even see where the multitude ended.

Red sandstone pillars stood ahead of them, the same gorge Launce had stood in to argue with Isa not so long before. His heart ached as he thought of the unkind words he'd used to cause both Isa and her husband pain. Everard had been right. Launce did often act like a spoiled child when life didn't go his way. He would sacrifice much to go back to that day now.

"He doesn't look happy." Olivia interrupted his thoughts. Launce looked ahead to where she was pointing, to see the enchanter staring into the distance with a deep frown upon his face.

"He's probably upset about how long it's taking us," Launce said. "At a decent trot, we would have reached the Fortress by tomorrow night. At this rate though, we won't be there for *at least* another five days. Serves him right for bringing a bunch of royals along." As soon as he'd said it, Launce bit his tongue. Olivia didn't have time to answer him, for Rafael had stopped, and was gesturing for everyone to do the same. Even halting was painstakingly slow.

"We'll camp here tonight" Rafael called to the captain of his guard. "Tomorrow, we will resume our journey at a faster pace." Immediately, people began to dismount their horses. Servants scurried to piece together their masters' tents and prepare the cooking fires.

"Hello there." Launce hopped off of his horse and called to a passing boy. "Aren't you Sir Randolph's squire?" The boy nodded eagerly.

"Yes, sir!"

"Tell me, when was your master supposed to return home?"

The boy blinked a few times, as though trying to recall. Finally, he said, "I suppose we were to return once the betrothal ball was done."

"Well, why didn't you?"

"We just don't want to anymore. It's important we stay with the holy man." The boy shrugged. "Now, if you'll excuse me, I need to go." With that, he scampered off in his master's direction. Launce looked up at Olivia, who still sat upon her horse.

"They don't *want* to anymore?" she echoed, one eyebrow quirked.

"Your Highness." A servant came up and bowed to them both. "Master Launce, both of your tents are prepared. Princess, you are staying with your mother. Master Launce will have his own tent."

Of course, when the servant pointed, Launce saw immediately that they had placed him near the king's tent. Rafael wanted to keep an eye on him, no doubt put up to it by Bronkendol. But Launce knew better than to argue. He led his horse beside Olivia's as the servant brought them first to her tent, then to his. At her mother's tent, Olivia pursed her lips and simply gave him a weak shrug before going inside.

His own tent was surprisingly lavish and tall enough for him to walk inside without ducking. Thick, vibrant rugs of blue and orange covered the dirt floor, and silk pillows were piled up against the corners. A silver tray of artfully arranged dried beef, cheese, and herb bread was already laid near the biggest pile of pillows. Launce shook his head. How many pillows did they think he needed? Back at home, Launce had been famous for his ability to fall asleep anywhere since he was a small boy. But an excess of pillows wasn't his main concern right now. After gobbling down his supper as quickly as possible, he marched off in the direction of the king's tent. He was going to get some answers.

Before he reached Rafael, however, a gloved hand rested heavily upon his shoulder. "I'm afraid you won't be getting many answers out of him tonight." Launce turned to see Bronkendol himself. A rainbow of emotions colored his vision. Anger, frustration, and to his annoyance, fear. The fact that he was two heads taller than the old man steeled him a bit though as he turned to face the enchanter.

"Then where do you suggest I go?"

"I actually was hoping you would come speak with me in my tent." Launce was tempted to use words his mother didn't approve of, but instead he swallowed them and simply followed the enchanter inside.

Bronkendol's tent didn't look any different from Launce's, with the exception of a full-length standing mirror and a tray of tea. Bronkendol sank slowly onto one of the cushions and poured himself a drink.

"Tea?" He held up the second empty cup, but Launce shook his head. "Before you become too angry with me," Bronkendol continued in a soft voice, "I need for you to understand my purpose."

"Then you should know as well that I am aware of your little trick," Launce replied, his voice acidic.

The enchanter stared at him blankly.

"Isa's power?"

"Ah. Yes, that is an astute observation. Before I can explain that, however, I must tell you *why*."

"I'm waiting."

The enchanter took a long sip of his tea. "When I was placed under the sleeping curse, I slept for a long time." He sighed. "Twenty-seven centuries is a hateful amount of time to be gone, young man. Imagine now, waking up to find your home empty, your mother eternally still, and all of your friends and servants gone. Even the road which we used to reach and leave my castle by was gone. Wind and rain had carved my valley home into a place of isolation with deathly drops on each side. Every sign that I or my loved ones had ever existed had disappeared, with the exception of the castle and its contents.

"My shock was even greater when I emerged back into the word of civilized man to find kingdoms and boundaries, which borderless lands had once stretched on forever." Bronkendol shook his head. "I wandered like an addled vagabond. Indeed, that's what I was. I hadn't a penny to my name, nor in my state of loss did I think to bring anything with me but the clothes on my back.

"For years I wandered. Kindly folks here and there would take me in, and sometimes I would find solace in the corner of a church where I could lay my head at night. As I moved from place to place though, I began to relearn how to be a man. The local tongues became easier to speak and understand, and customs were no longer completely foreign. But the part of this new life that I could not grow accustomed to was the suffering." His eyes were wet when he raised them to look at Launce again.

"There is so much war here. So much selfishness, so much suffering! You must understand that when my mother was the mediator between men, this kind of evil did not happen. So many die, and so few care! I couldn't allow it to continue while I had strength in my hands. Then I heard of the Fortiers." He took another sip of tea.

"Launce, I have been watching your sister's new family for the last three hundred years. I even journeyed to the Fortress a few times myself in hopes of gaining audiences with the different kings."

"Did you?" In spite of his anger, Launce found himself curious.

"A few times. But more often than not, they were off on some war campaign. When I finally did have the chance to speak with them, I found they were not what I expected at all. The first time I'd heard of them, I had been overjoyed. Though much younger, their power was similar to my own, a gift passed down from the Maker through the generations, as my mother's had been passed down to me. But where my mother had kept the peace through gifts and wise words, the Fortiers did so through blood and battle."

"Perhaps they tried words first, and the others refused to listen." Was Launce *really* defending Everard's clan?

"Perhaps. But with time, I recognized the mistake that kept this land of kingdoms constantly at odds, despite the Fortiers' constant interference."

"And that was?"

"They would subdue the uprisings and evil when it came, but they would go no further. The strength I felt when I was in the Fortiers' presence was more than enough for them to have united these miserable kingdoms to bring them to a permanent peace."

Launce gave a start. "You mean overthrow the other kingdoms?"

"Don't you see, my boy? By not conquering the evil where they found it, they merely beat it down as a temporary solution. The same evil was able to return again in the future, even stronger! And it did, time and time again. After three hundred years of watching, I decided that I had only one choice. I needed to rectify this constant bickering between the peoples for their own sakes. In fact, I had already begun to prepare Cobren for this, but then I received word of your sister."

Launce had been gazing out the entrance of the tent at the people as they milled about, but at the mention of Isa, he looked back at the enchanter. Bronkendol's face was careful, and Launce knew he was measuring Launce's reaction. Taking a deep breath, he steadied his own expression so that it was unreadable. At least, he hoped it was.

"Just as I had predicted, the Fortiers' constant obsession with war had brought down a curse upon their own heads, and one ultimately from the Fortress at that. But when I heard of the work your sister had done, breaking the curse with her heart's strength, I knew she would be the one the Maker had chosen to save the western kingdoms."

Launce crossed his arms. "So you lied to King Rafael about being anointed directly by the Maker."

"No, not at all!" Bronkendol was on his feet, suddenly alive with energy. "How else could you interpret this power?" He held up his hands. "And the fact that I awakened from a curse of over two thousand years? The Maker might not have spoken to me aloud, but I knew what I must do. Your sister had the power to change others' hearts. What better way to keep people at peace?"

"So where do Olivia and I come in? And what about Everard?"

The enchanter blew out a breath and ran his hand through

his curly silver hair. "I *am* sorry about your brother-in-law, truly. I hadn't expected him to go like that..."

"To be frank, I don't believe that he's dead. But even if he wasn't, you would still be scheming about his death somehow," Launce spat.

"If he was willing to be a part of this, then by all means, I wanted him to remain! But when it became clear that he was dead set on keeping her away from me—"

"So you do aim to kill him."

For the first time, Bronkendol's face darkened, and a flicker of purple flashed in his eyes.

"Before you go any further, do remember what happened the last time your brother-in-law lost someone that was dear to him."

It pained Launce, but he had nothing to reply with. It was true. Ever had been the one to plunge the Fortress into darkness after he'd lost his father.

The enchanter spoke again, but this time his voice was more sympathetic. "I wasn't expecting your sister to be so sick when I first met her. I have tried to help her in the best way I know how."

"I still don't see what Olivia and I have to do with all of this. We have no powers, and I'm the last person anyone would want as king, including myself."

"But that is what's so perfect about you. There are too many old bloods in the royal lines. I have searched far and wide throughout the lands, but when you spoke to me that first day in the stables, I knew I had to have you. You will make a good king because you are kind, and you have more common sense than the rest of these prigs put together."

He waved his hand at the rest of the camp that lay behind them. "The princess is young, and has a fire in her spirit." He paused. "I assume you've noticed that neither of you have the glass slivers."

Launce hadn't planned on discussing what he knew of the glass, but he reluctantly agreed. The enchanter put his tea on the tray and leaned toward him.

"As much as I know, and as well as I can advise you, I am still aware that it would be unwise to keep *everyone* under my influence." So he was intending to put the glass in even more people.

"You are of a kind heart and sound mind," Bronkendol continued. "I want you to be free."

"And if I don't accept?"

The enchanter's face grew hard.

"Then I suppose one of you shall not remain free after all."

It was all Launce could do not to shout every vile word he knew at the man before him. Before he could say anything, however, the ground began to shake. Launce was knocked off balance, and landed hard on his right side, while Bronkendol dove to catch the mirror. Screams rose from the camp, along with the sounds of objects crashing to the ground. And just as he had known the feeling of Isa's power when he felt it, Launce now recognized none other than the power of the Fortress itself.

The earth continued to tremble as Launce watched Bronkendol cradle the mirror, and suddenly he knew what to do. Getting on all fours, Launce crawled as best he could over to the enchanter. Bronkendol protested as Launce pried the wooden frame from his hands. With all his might, he threw the mirror to the ground. The shatter was satisfying, as was the look of injured betrayal on the enchanter's face. Launce wanted to skip with joy, but the earth still quaked so hard that he couldn't get off the ground.

Finally, the shaking stopped. Launce stood unevenly, but the enchanter remained on the ground, holding shattered pieces in his hands, looking stunned.

"Why would you do that?"

"We crossed over into Destin's lands just before we set up camp. That was the Fortress, telling you that are not welcome here. Nor are your schemes." With that, Launce turned sharply and marched out of the tent.

"Launce!" Bronkendol called out behind him. "Remember what I said about the glass. Do not force my hand!" But Launce didn't answer.

CHAPTER 41

HONESTLY

aunce." Launce looked up from the rock he was sitting on to see Olivia approaching. As usual, her guard followed close behind, but this time he also carried her supper tray as well. "May I join you?" Launce scrambled to his feet to fetch a cushion for her. When they were both seated again in front of the tent, she spoke, but her voice was so low he could barely hear it.

"I saw what you did with the mirror."

"I think he's been using it to travel."

"He does. I saw him once, shortly after he came to our kingdom." She set her spoon down and squeezed his knee. "You have to be more careful! He fixed the mirror, but my father is furious. He says you might have derailed the Maker's plans. There are dozens of young men still vying for your place, and the moment this strange enchantment ends, they're going to be at your throat." She went back to eating. "Thankfully, the holy man likes you for some reason."

Launce rolled his eyes. "Bronkendol is no holy man. And he's deluded himself into thinking I actually *want* to be his puppet king."

"Am I so grim a future to be stuck with?" In the dying light of the red sun, tears suddenly glistened in her eyes. "So you were telling the truth back in the courtyard." Before he could explain, she handed her tray to her guard and stood to go.

As he watched her, Launce decided that he was possibly the dullest suitor ever to walk the face of the earth.

"Wait!" He bounded after her. She scowled at him, but allowed Launce to take her hand and drag her to the edge of the camp. Her two guards followed closely behind. Launce didn't stop until they had reached the edge of the first sandstone rise that stood as a sentry outside the red gorge.

Launce had the urge to climb up the little foothill and never come down. He could imagine seeing the entire country for miles. On one side lay the gently winding hills that led to the sea. They were covered in the yellow remnants of aged grass. On the other side stood the gorge. The sandstone was easy to climb. It felt nearly sticky to the touch, and yet wonderfully dry. But the red stone only went up so high, because right behind it was the mountain that held the Fortress.

Olivia instructed the guards to wait on the ground while she and Launce went up just a bit higher. The two men exchanged nervous glances, but she huffed, "You will be able to see us the entire time. I simply don't wish for you to be right on top of me."

Once they had gone high enough to sit above all the tents in the valley, they stopped. Olivia plopped down and arranged her skirts while Launce hovered awkwardly, unsure of how close she really wanted him. This was not a conversation he was ready for yet, but the only way to stop the prolonged pain, he decided, would be by getting it all over with at once.

"I'm going to be honest with you," Launce said.

"That would be nice." She glowered up at him.

Launce took a big breath. "I hadn't planned on even entering the contest until we arrived at your home. Once we were there, Everard could sense that something was wrong. So he convinced me to join the competition, simply so I could tell him what was going on in the stables. I never expected to win." He sat down a few feet from her and let his head drop between his knees.

"No one forced you to win." Launce could hear the resentment still in her voice. "What do you want, Launce? You don't seem to want me or my way of life, and yet you continue to seek me out. It's quite vexing. Actually," she said, "I'm not quite sure that *you* know what you want."

"I couldn't agree more," Launce scoffed, then paused. "My old sweetheart's father made it clear that he wanted her to have nothing to do with me after Isa and Everard married. I'm not common enough for the commoners anymore, but I have no place in courtly matters either." Launce prayed for her to understand. "I'm a man of two worlds now, and neither I nor the world knows to which one I belong."

The anger melted from Olivia's face just a bit, but Launce hated that she still looked sad. He hadn't wanted to bring up his former girl, but if they were being honest, she needed to know everything. "I swear," he scooted just a bit closer, "I never expected to love you."

"*Love* me?" Olivia's voice quivered.

Launce faltered. He hadn't meant to use that word. It had simply come out. And yet, as his father always said, if it escaped the mouth, it had to have been hiding inside of him somewhere. Launce spoke slowly this time, trying to choose his words with more care. "I'm not sure," he admitted. "I've only known you for a few days. But . . ." He caught her hand and held it, even when she tried to pull it away, silently begging her to look at him again. "If not yet, I will be soon if you keep dragging me around like this."

Olivia almost smiled, her lovely skin the color of brown sugar in the fading light of dusk.

"Do you love me?" he pressed. "Because a girl of your sensibility seems far too intelligent for that."

This time, Olivia laughed outright. "I suppose I don't know yet either." Then she sighed, all traces of laughter gone as she looked out at the multitude of campfires dotting the valley below. "All my life, I've been trained in what to say and told how to dress. And when my father told me we were choosing my husband through a contest, I was expected to go willingly." She shuddered delicately. "Until I saw who was competing for my hand. Many of them were older than my father, and most of those that weren't were vulgar, dim-witted, or desirous only of my father's lands.

"But you," she said, finally meeting his gaze again, "you saw me." Then she frowned. "If you entered the contest, how could you expect not to win?"

Launce snorted. "Were you paying heed to any of the games? I couldn't win a duel if my opponent begged me to run him through." Launce stood again and walked a few steps higher. He knew he was making their guards jumpy, but he didn't care.

"I was only able to speak with your sister once," Olivia said softly, "but I liked her right away. She seems kind."

"That she is," Lance said. "So now you know the truth. All of this began because I wanted to take care of her. But there's more now, whether I'm ready for it or not." He looked down at the girl. "I want to take care of you too. I may be a commoner, but I know a good woman when I see one."

"No one has ever called me that before . . . a woman."

Launce wasn't sure, but he thought he could hear a smile in her voice. A foolish sense of joy wriggled through him as he listened, but all too soon it was chased away by the sense of danger he had felt before.

"Your Highness," one of the guards called up. "It is growing dark. Your mother wishes for you to return to your tent soon."

"There is something that you must know, regardless of whether you decide to love me or not." He crouched before her and took her hands in his. "That earthquake earlier today? That was no accident. I have been in and around the Fortress enough to know its power when I feel it. And that earthquake was a warning. If we accept the thrones once we arrive at the Fortress itself, I have no doubt that we will die."

"And how do you know that?" Her voice was suddenly small.

"Only the Fortress chooses its heirs, and to assume we know better than the Maker who placed it there is nothing less than treason." He gripped her hands even more tightly. "At all costs, we must prevent them from placing *anyone* on those thrones."

"How do we do that? How do we stop an entire army that's under Bronkendol's command?"

Launce grinned in the dark. Never had he liked the Fortress steward more.

"That's what Garin is for."

CHAPTER 42

VENGEANCE

It was tempting to push his horse even faster through the icy pass. But deep down, Ever knew that would be unwise. Using the stolen robe he had followed Isa's original trail to reach what he thought felt like a different realm, although there was no way to tell for sure. Isa's original passage from the Glass Castle to the Fortress was thin, but still present. Like the scent of another man's house, the string of power was similar to that of the Fortress, but was just different enough to stand out against the cold winds that burned his nose.

Ever had traveled the continent with his father numerous times even as a boy, but he'd never even considered that there could be other realms aside from his own. And yet, occupying the same lands that should have been Lingea, Destin's northern neighbor, the familiar territory was nowhere to be found. Instead of the fields of lavender, Ever and his horse were now braving beautiful, dangerous, jagged mountains that stretched for miles and miles, packed with snow that looked as though it had never melted.

Ever hadn't seen another human soul since he'd left the Fortress. Judging from how long Isa had been gone, he knew he should be approaching the castle anytime. Hunger gnawed at him, but he pressed on. The length of time it was taking made him uneasy, and he hoped the strange bridge between realms hadn't closed already.

Ever's horse came to a violent halt, and he was nearly thrown from his seat. "Well, boy, keeping me on my toes, are you?" He rubbed the nervous animal's neck and whispered soothing words in his ear as he dismounted. The horse had come to a stop just at the edge of a new mountain range that stretched from east to west as far as Ever could see.

Knowing the horse would not take him farther, Ever took the reins and began to lead the animal himself. The sense of power was much stronger here, and though his horse, Hugon, was familiar with Ever's own strength, it seemed he did not like the new power one bit. Ever somehow knew that the narrow pass through the towering heights was where he needed to go, so there was no sense in pushing his faithful friend past his limit.

Ever found a protected cave at the base of the mountain to his right, where he fed and watered the beast. "You know what to do," he crooned as he brushed his animal down.

On the day Ever had been presented with his first horse, his father had insisted he train the horse himself, and one of the first major lessons he was instructed to practice was setting the horse free in case of disaster. The practice had taught him to use his unique strength in an entirely new way, and now, as he spoke to his horse for perhaps the last time, he was grateful.

"One day," he told his old friend. "If I'm not back in one day, you need to go home as fast as you can." The horse tossed his midnight mane and nudged Ever's hand for sugar. With a heavy heart, Ever gave him another lump from his pack before checking his weapons once more, and then setting off on foot.

Ever drew his sword as he walked between the towering peaks. The road was notably easy to follow for one that had been used so little in the past three thousand years. The powdery snow crunching beneath his boots, and the warning moans of the wind as it bounced off the mountain sides were the only sounds he could hear. The farther he walked, the more the gusts pushed back at him as well, as though he weren't taking their warnings seriously enough to leave.

"I'm not afraid of death," Ever muttered to the worrisome wind. And it was true. Perhaps he'd feared it once, before he had known what it felt like to witness Isa dying. But this brush with eternity was different. He would give his last breath and more if he could be sure that it would return Isa to herself. No, he did not fear death.

But failure was another consideration entirely.

After a ten-minute walk, he came to the crest of the small hill between the mountains. And what he saw brought him to a halt. As angry as he was, nothing, neither stories nor dreams had prepared him for the beauty that lay ahead. On both sides of the little path he stood upon, a black chasm separated the towering, pointed, snow-encrusted cliffs from the island that they encircled. Only a narrow bridge connected the island of land to the world outside. It wasn't the island that took his breath away though. It was the castle.

Stories of the Glass Queen had been passed down for so many generations that few knew what was truth and what was myth. As a boy, Ever had searched the scrolls and books for anything and everything that even hinted at the mythical citadel.

"Why don't others believe?" he'd once asked Garin as the steward had tucked him in. Garin had patted his head and smiled indulgently.

"Others don't know the Maker's power the way you do. It takes a lot of faith to believe in something you can't see or feel."

"But I don't see or feel the Glass Castle," Ever had argued, "and I still know it's there." Then he'd leaned forward eagerly. "Do you think I will ever see the castle one day?"

"No one has seen that castle in three thousand years. But who knows? Perhaps you shall."

Ever had passed many hours of his early childhood dreaming of meeting the Glass Queen. Surely she would understand him, he'd thought. She would know what it was like to be powerful, to be different. And now, here he was, ready to visit the Glass Castle at last. But instead of meeting the Glass Queen, he had come to kill her son.

Drawing his cloak around him against the chill of the air, Ever steeled himself for what was to come as he began the treacherous journey over the chasm. The further out he went, the icier the path became. It narrowed as well, until it was too thin for more than two men to walk at a time.

The trip across the bridge covered in snow and ice took him much longer than he had expected, but finally Ever arrived at the base of the castle. Glistening blue and purple glass plates with frosted swirls like ivy and wind were etched into the solid gates. Again, despite his hatred for the enchanter himself, Ever had to wonder at the beauty of it all, and his soul ached just a bit. Why couldn't the son have died, and the queen have survived instead? There were so many things he longed to ask her. What was it like to have so much power? Had she always felt slightly deserted, the way he had growing up?

Was there a way to return Isa's power to her?

But he hadn't come to gawk. Ever removed one of his leather gloves and placed his palm against the right gate. Closing his eyes, he pressed firmly, and blue flame leaped from his hand. With a creak, the gate began to open. He stepped through, relieved. He hadn't been sure until then that the ancient castle would respond to the Fortress's power.

Four blue, sleek steps stretched across the entire entrance and led up to the castle itself. Two more great doors towered above Ever, and again, they opened for his power. A small flicker of hope warmed his heart. Perhaps he did stand a chance of surviving this encounter. After all, it was all the Maker's power, and his cause was the righteous one.

Vengeance isn't generally considered a noble cause, a blunt voice inside of him whispered, making him pause before passing through the gigantic door.

But he wasn't doing this for vengeance. The man needed to be stopped.

True as that may be, you know you wouldn't be satisfied if he simply fell over and died of old age after all he's done to Isa. You want to make him suffer.

And it was true. Never had Everard longed so much to shed one man's blood.

Just as he began to enter, something made him stop once again. It was faint, but it sounded like someone was whistling, an eerie noise in the empty halls. He followed the unfamiliar tune through the longest and highest throne room he'd ever imagined. The entire Fortress could have fit into this room alone. The whistling took him down a smaller hallway, out of the throne room and to the left. Ever's heart sped up to an alarming rate as he got closer. This was it.

When he pushed the door open, however, there was no one, only a large furnace in the far corner of a cluttered room filled with worktables and glass odds and ends scattered everywhere. He stepped in and listened harder. The sound was still getting closer. By the time he realized that the whistling was coming from behind him, however, it was too late.

"Ah, there you are. I've been expecting you."

CHAPTER 43

READY OR NOT

Ever whirled around to find the short, curly-haired servant from Rafael's palace holding a steaming tray of tea and biscuits. Ever lifted his sword, but the small man only waved his hand as he walked on by. "You won't be needing that. I'll tell you whatever you want to know, so long as you allow me my nightly cup of tea. It helps me sleep."

If the little man had meant to make Ever more comfortable, he had done exactly the opposite. Knowing his enemy would tell him everything meant he had only one purpose for Ever. Death, or some fate even worse, where he wouldn't be able to utter a word of it to anyone. Still, as Ever warily watched the man pour, stir, and sip his own tea, the idea of discovering what the enchanter had planned was tantalizing. Ever didn't sheath his sword, but he did lower it enough to stand directly before the enchanter as the small man served himself a biscuit.

"You'll tell me anything?"

"Ask away." Bronkendol smiled and leaned back in his chair as though he were merely having a friend over to gossip. Ever wasn't sure where the question came from, but it was the first one on his tongue that didn't tempt him even more to kill the enchanter then and there.

"Why Launce?"

"He recently asked me the same question," the enchanter chuckled. "I like that boy. You see, I knew I needed someone new, unsullied by the world, hence the contest. I had hoped that of the many contestants, I might find someone that I could at least tolerate. And then you thrust him right into my hands."

"Launce hates the court."

"But he's also young and impressionable. And also desperate for some approval."

Was he? Ever tried to remember if he'd ever noticed that about the young man, but his mind was too cluttered to remember.

"I know what you're not asking though." Bronkendol placed his tea on a table's edge and stood up, all signs of joviality gone. "And I can assure you that I will never be able to express to her how sorry I am for what had to be done."

Ever tightened his grip on the sword.

"I know it must be difficult for you to understand now, but in time you will."

"You sent her back a shell of who she was before!" Ever exploded. "Her fire is gone, and she can no longer laugh! Why did any of that have to be done?"

"I saved her life." He crossed his arms and studied Ever. "Your wife was losing her fire already. Before it left her on its own accord, I took it from her so that she would continue to live at least in body." His voice grew softer. "I didn't want her to die the way your father did when his fire was extinguished."

Cold fear trickled into every part of Ever's body. What had this man done to her that was so bad that he still refused to tell him? As if the enchanter knew what he was thinking, he pulled a small mirror from his pocket and held it out to Ever.

"It would be easiest if I simply showed you instead."

Ever glared at him for a long moment before looking into the mirror.

He could see Isa bound to the chair that faced the furnace in the corner of the very room he was standing in. The fear on her face broke Ever's heart. Isa wasn't a warrior, nor had Ever trained her to withstand torture. She shouldn't have needed *that* training.

The enchanter's light hit Isa's heart with such a force that her chair slammed backward, straining against the chains that bound it to the floor. Her face went specter white as the glass which he held to her chest began to suck the life from her body. Tears of rage welled in Ever's eyes as he watched her suffer. The worst part was hearing her cry out his name over and over again. No wonder she believed he'd failed her. She had pleaded with him to come. And he hadn't.

Ever thought the scene would end soon. It must. But instead, it dragged on as Isa fought for every bit of her heart as it was wrenched from her. Despite knowing the outcome, panic slipped through Ever as he realized she was giving in. Her fight, valiant as it had been, had come to an end, and as her head rolled forward, Ever saw for himself what she had truly lost.

"That kind of pain should have killed her!" Ever's voice was not his own. It sounded strangled.

"I shared some of my own strength with her so she would last," Bronkendol said as the mirror went dark. "I promise, I made it as short and simple as possible. But it will be for the best."

"For the best?" Ever slammed his fist into the enchanter's temple. Bronkendol went flying backward, and Ever hated him all the more for surviving the attack. That kind of hit would have killed an average man. "You killed your mother for power, and now you've taken every sliver of happiness from my wife!" This time, Ever kicked him so hard he heard the satisfying crack of a rib. "Was it worth it?" he shouted.

The enchanter slumped against the floor, shaking with the effort, but at last, he raised his head to speak.

"The power to influence hearts and bring peace to the people? Yes." Bronkendol's eyes darkened. "It was worth it."

Ever raised his sword, but it didn't come down as it was supposed to. It felt like it had caught on something. Looking back, Ever realized that it had.

A glass man, taller than any human, had caught his sword with one hand. With a shout, Ever sent a bolt of blue flame up his weapon, and the glass giant shattered to pieces. Before Ever could turn back to Bronkendol, however, another glass man emerged from the far wall. This one had his own scythe, a piece of glass twisted to reveal hundreds of razor edges along its blade.

Each time a new guard came at him, it was no match for Ever's sword and flame. But his glass opponents began to come faster and faster, and Ever soon realized the enchanter was nowhere to be seen. The glass guards were coming too fast for him to go searching, as he had to take care to actually dismantle the warriors entirely. Cutting off an arm only made it a new weapon, a limb of broken glass that swung wildly about, sharp enough to shred his skin to pieces if he allowed it to touch him. He was getting nowhere.

With a loud cry, Ever exhaled and pressed every bit of fire within him out into a ring of blue flames. It was exhausting, but the ring rippled out, and this time no glass warriors emerged again. There was only Bronkendol, huddled in his corner, holding his precious mirror up in front of his mouth. Like a frightened babe talking to its doll, he whispered to it.

Ever moved toward him like a storm, but just before he was there, a thick red filled Ever's sight. Clouds of crimson smoke burned and made it impossible to see. But if the enchanter had wanted to stop him, he would have to try harder than that.

Ever had wanted to learn all of the enchanter's plans, but he would never have the patience for that game now. A crash sounded from behind him, and when Ever turned, much to his dismay, he saw the small form that had been huddled against the wall just seconds before had somehow made it to the door, and was watching him stupidly as though in a daze.

Ever launched himself at the figure. This time, he would hit him so hard that Bronkendol would never again open his eyes to see anyone or anything. The dance of war carried him to his foe, the taste of blood already on his tongue.

Isa shivered as the shining blue walls came into view. She didn't recall much of her journey from Bronkendol's castle to the Fortress. Her pain had been too great, and her mind too muddled. All she could really remember was wishing to fall asleep and never awaken again. Sometime during the first day, the bag of food and water the enchanter had strapped to her horse had been blown off by a strong gust of wind. It had been all Isa could do to stay astride the horse herself.

This time, pain and hunger weren't her sources of discomfort, but rather the ache in her chest. Yes, the feelings were there once more, but she still felt raw inside, as though the return of her emotions had chafed her heart until it was ready to bleed. Isa was going because she knew she should save her husband. But like the stark gray and white of the land that surrounded her, the sunbeam delight she'd possessed on her wedding day was nowhere to be found. She kept her heart blank, choosing not to remember all the ways Ever had hurt her . . . and all the ways she had hurt him. And like her joy, her strength was still gone too.

Now that the glass citadel was in view once more, Isa knew she would need to focus not on the aches inside, but rather the impossible undertaking ahead of her. Garin had told her how to follow Ever's path between realms, using the Glass Queen's dress that Isa had worn home, but she hadn't plotted out a course of action for what she might do once she arrived. For while she rode into the wilderness, that moment had felt like it would never come, and she nearly didn't want it to.

A whinny caught her by surprise. Shielding her eyes from the bright snow and strong gusts of wind, she found a large cave to her left. Inside, shielded from the elements, was Ever's horse, Hugon.

"You should stay here too," Isa said to her own horse, dismounting and rubbing his neck. It hadn't been hard to fall in love with her horse again at least. A few nuzzles and she was all his. If only Ever were so easy.

After leaving her mount alongside Hugon, Isa took only her sword and started toward the castle alone. When she got to the pass that cut between the two mountains, her stomach flopped at the sight of the icy bridge she would have to cross.

To distract herself as she crossed the bottomless chasm, she thought back to her conversation with Garin. Was he right, about gaining her feelings back in time? It wasn't that Isa didn't feel now, rather she didn't feel the way she once had. It was too easy to recall every instance when Ever had left her for some other business, particularly when it was to go see Kartek. She recalled every time he spoke with another woman who had once been one of his admirers; each time, she'd wondered if deep down he had wished for someone who was able to fulfill her duties to the Fortress and the kingdom. Someone to give him an heir and command the Fortress fire.

To be fair, he had been most attentive upon her return to the Fortress. His words and touches had seemed earnest. But had he truly missed her? Or was he simply feeling guilty?

By the time Isa reached the other side of the bridge, she had nearly convinced herself it would indeed be easier never to feel again. Still, she had a job to do. It wouldn't do to let her nonexistent emotions hinder her from protecting him. Isa drew her sword as she crept up the glass steps into the castle. The fact that the gate and the doors were still open was at least a small comfort. It was unlikely they would have opened if Ever had died below the bridge before reaching them.

The throne room was empty, but Isa could just make out the sounds of voices. Anxiety squeezed her insides as she came to the end of the throne room and realized where they were coming from. She would have to go into that horrid room again. Every part of her cried out to go back. Isa paused halfway down the hall from the hateful door, which was ajar. Voices no longer spoke. Instead, collisions sounded as metal clanged and glass shattered.

The glass giants, Isa realized. Readying her sword, she crept to the door, wondering how she could help without her power. Perhaps she should just watch and see what had happened. When she peeked around the open door, there were no glass giants waiting for her.

Only her husband, with his sword raised and his body ready to strike. And his fiery eyes of steel were trained right on her.

CHAPTER 44
BLADE'S EDGE

Isa stared in shock as Ever charged toward her, his sword blazing with blue flame. By the time she thought to run, it was too late. Their weapons met with a violent clang that jarred Isa's bones. Her movements were flimsy and weak against his. Still, even if they weren't empowered in the way Ever's were, the hours of practice had stamped at least the rudimentary skills of swordplay into her head. To escape their locked weapons, a contest she was sure to lose, Isa twisted and rolled. As soon as she was on her feet again, she took off running as fast as she could back toward the throne room.

Dismay hummed in her mind to the rhythm of her heartbeat. Why was he trying to kill her? No matter how confused her feelings were about her husband, Isa knew *this* was not what she wanted.

Halfway down the hall, Isa dared a glance over her shoulder. Ever was pursuing, but not at his usual speed. Pushing herself faster, she wondered what she was going to do when she got to the hall's end. There would be more room to run in the throne room, for sure, but there was no place to hide. The entire room was empty, with the exception of the two thrones.

No, she decided, she needed to go somewhere where she could hide and catch her breath as she figured out her next plan of action.

When she reached the throne room, Isa was already out of breath, and she could hear Ever quickly coming up behind her. Without thinking, Isa darted up the closest set of spiral stairs that led to the bridge that overlooked the entire room. She wasn't more than a dozen steps up though when she felt the glass shudder beneath her.

Ever had reached the stairs. To her surprise, before he had gone three steps up, his foot slipped. As he tumbled backward, Isa caught a glimpse of the violet glow just inside his eye. And blue. There was also the glint of blue.

So that's what the enchanter was doing with her power. Anger rose within her as Isa realized Bronkendol was using her own power against her. Now, if only she knew how to break the hold.

As Ever struggled to right himself, Isa bolted once more up the steps. Whatever rage the enchanter had put Ever in must be making him clumsy. Everard was the most agile creature she had ever seen, but now his clumsiness was the only thing that was keeping her alive. Once she reached the bridge, she paused, not sure which way to go. She hadn't explored enough to know which ones would provide places to hide. Then she remembered the vision.

The green room. With the confused state Ever was in, the mirrors might make him pause. They certainly wouldn't protect her from his wrath, but the time it would take for him to find her within the room's strange reflections might give her time to form a plan.

Unfortunately, if Isa remembered correctly from the Glass Queen's vision, the room was downstairs, which meant she was running the wrong direction. There had to be someplace where Isa could turn around. With her decision made, she sprinted down the hall to her right, but she could hear Ever trailing behind her.

Please, she begged the Fortress, *I don't know what to do!* Without her strength, she was no match for him physically. Her only hope rested in knowing the castle better than he did. But when he found her eventually, which he would, what then?

She didn't want to hurt him, but she couldn't let him just kill her either. A strange sense, one that felt much like the power she used to have, warned her to look back. When she did, she found that Ever had closed much of the distance between them, and was continuing to gain on her. Desperately, she tried to choose a door, any door that might give her somewhere to hide. And hopefully, one that wasn't locked. As he drew closer still, Isa picked the closest room to her and threw herself against its door with all of her might.

To her immense relief, the door was unlocked, and she had just enough time to lock it after flinging it closed. Ever let out a shout of rage that echoed down the glass halls outside, and Isa knew she didn't have much time. Unfortunately, she realized, she had chosen what could only have been the worst room in the entire castle.

Weapons filled the room. Although the chamber was nearly the size of the servants' kitchen at home, it was so cluttered she received several nicks along her legs and arms in her hurried entrance. Hung on the walls, from the ceiling, and filling the floor in piles, there was little space to even turn around between the stacks of swords and axes, flails, and scythes. Even chains were strewn about. Some of the weapons were so ancient she didn't recognize them, but didn't need much imagination to guess how they could be used. She would never make it out of this room alive.

Then, out of the corner of her eye, she saw another door that was hidden behind a stack of pikes leaned upright against the wall. Everard had resorted to kicking the door, and it wouldn't be long before he knocked it in. Praying the door wasn't a closet, Isa crawled between the rows of razor edges that stuck out from all directions, and tried to push it open.

It seemed ridiculous that a glass door should stick in the same way a wooden one might, but this door was most definitely stuck. *Just let me open it,* she pleaded to the Fortress. But the door didn't budge. As she heard the glass lock on the door behind her shatter, Isa cried out in frustration.

To her amazement, the smallest streak of blue fire flitted from her fingers into the door. Unfortunately, it wasn't fast enough. The door behind her crashed to the ground with a sound that echoed throughout the empty castle. Isa barely managed to throw herself behind an ancient suit of armor just before he stormed in.

Because of the height of the piles, and the rage that seemed to somewhat blind him, Isa felt oddly well-hidden. As she watched Ever shouting and swinging his sword in circles, something warm dripped down her cheek. She put her hand up to her face, only to pull it down covered in bright red blood. Judging from the glass pieces all over the floor at her feet, she realized a piece must have flown out and cut her when the door had shattered.

The armor was just beside the second door, so when she thought he wasn't looking, Isa reached out and tried once more. Again, the blue glowed, but only just. This time, however, the door opened, and Isa nearly let out a cry of joy when she saw that it wasn't a closet after all. Before she could dart into the new room, however, she glanced back to see Ever standing over her, like a wolf regarding its prey. Instinctively, Isa kicked both her legs out, knocking the suit over onto him, and though her heart weighed heavy with guilt, she knew it was better than being gutted.

Scrambling through, she shut this door as well. As there was no lock, she would have to hide quickly. The room appeared as though the servants had left their work in a hurry. The room was full of bed linens. Most were folded and stacked neatly, but some had simply been tossed in a heap, most likely waiting for their washing. Just before the door behind her burst open, Isa ducked behind a tall pile, hoping it would hide her while she made her way to the room's main door.

She did no such thing though. Ever leapt to the center of the room and began kicking down piles of cloth. Isa froze, praying for him to just go away.

"I know you're in here," he bellowed. "I can see the trail of blood!" Isa instinctively put her hand up to her cheek. The cut was still bleeding. Before he could come any closer, she took her chances and bolted for the door, which put her back in the hallway once more. She didn't pause to look back this time. Instead, she dashed toward the back of the castle, where she knew the greenhouse lay.

Her strength was so spent from running down the stairs, through the throne room, and down the secret hall behind the thrones that Isa nearly gave up by the time she reached the greenhouse. The light outside was beginning to fade into twilight, and it was hard to see as she worked her way toward the back. She could hear Ever thundering down the last hall. Her progress was infuriatingly slow as she continued to bump into pots of soil and buckets for water. As she squeezed down behind a pot that grew something with thick, furry leaves, she began to plead with the Fortress.

Let him . . . But she didn't know how to finish. Let him what? Let him get confused and give up? Let me best him in swords?

Let him see.

Isa looked down at her hands in the dimming light. Though a bit of her flame could flicker, it was no more than that which might light a candle. She couldn't beat him in swordplay, particularly not without her full strength, and Ever's surrender was out of the question, unless the Fortress knocked him down on its own accord. Ever didn't give up even when he was his own self.

But how do I open his eyes? she whimpered, more out of habit than out of an expectation of an answer. The blue glow grew brighter as it moved down the hall toward her, its light already bouncing off the oddly angled windows.

Love him the way he tried to love you.

Isa gasped, nearly giving away her hiding place, when the Fortress spoke to her. How long it had been since she'd heard that voice! How she had yearned for it! *But it didn't work,* she stammered in her head. *And I can't go near him. He will kill me!*

Leave his heart to me. Just trust me and do as you know you should. I will bring about the rest.

Isa drew in a shaky breath. Ever had entered the greenroom. Just as she'd hoped, the light of the dying day cast eerie reflections upon the hundreds of concave panes, making it difficult to tell illusion from reality. She nestled even deeper into her hiding place.

"I can sense you in here," Ever hissed. "And I can smell your blood." Isa peeked out just enough to see him crouched, tightly coiled like a predator ready to strike. His face was unshaven, and his eyes burned with a hatred Isa hadn't known him capable of. Perhaps brightest of all were the blue-violet slivers at the edges of his eyes. All the courage Isa had gathered fled her again. How was she to conquer her own power?

Isa cringed as he passed her, circling the room. It was only as he walked away, still circling, that she realized that there *was* another power present besides her own and the enchanter's, one that she might use.

She would have to harness Ever's strength in place of her own. If she could hold it just long enough to slip past his defenses, there might be a chance. The Fortress *had* provided a way.

Ever had finished his first circle around the room, and was

beginning his second. If she didn't strike now, she might lose her chance. Fear made her tremble, but Isa swallowed hard and silently laid her sword on the ground. She felt around her feet until her hands found a clod of dirt. She would do her best, but everything was up to the Fortress now.

As hard as she could, Isa flung the clod across the room, where it hit the window with a loud *thunk*. When Ever flipped his head to look toward the sound, Isa jumped up from her hiding place, landing before him. She seized Ever's cloak and pulled so that his face was almost touching hers.

As was his sword.

Somehow, he'd managed to bring his sword up to her neck in the split second she had moved. He had not only evaded her trap, but had set one of his own. And Isa had walked right into it. She could feel the edge of the blade beginning to cut into her skin. Her breaths were ragged and fast, as he held her there, neither of them moving. She still clutched his cloak in both hands, unable to move even if she'd wanted to.

"You stole her from me." Ever's breath was hot on her face. "Now I will do to you what you did to me."

"Ever!" Isa squeaked, but her husband only shook her with his free hand, so hard it felt like her head was rattling.

"Ever, it's me!"

"Silence!" Pressing the blade even deeper into her throat, Ever leaned down and whispered in her ear, "Now I will do to you just as you did to her. It will be meticulous and slow." A trickle rolled down her neck, though she couldn't tell if it was blood or sweat. She had no more time. Closing her eyes, Isa reached out the way Ever had taught her to.

And felt nothing. If she hadn't been able to see the blue light in her husband's eyes, she would have thought none was there. But it was there, and she was determined to find it. Or she would die.

Again she reached out, but still there was nothing. Isa reached further. She only had a little air left . . .

It was hardly even warm at first, more like a tingle than a flame. But the more she concentrated, the more Isa remembered the feel of Ever's strength. Whereas her own strength had often felt like a stream of joy, bubbling delightfully as it danced along its banks, Ever's was more like a river that had exceeded its capacity to hold rain. Strong and swift, it moved to envelop everything it touched. And now, Isa needed it to envelop them both. After drawing in what might be her last breath, Isa pulled Ever and the blade closer.

Her lips met his, and they tasted of salt. Pain bit her neck, but Isa let it. He fought her. Instead of the predator, he was now the hunted, trapped in a net and wriggling in confusion. In her mind, Isa wove their strengths together, braiding them into a rope that could not be severed. Her weak light and his strong one. But the sword was too sharp. Too much blood was spilling down her neck.

Just when she could not hold the blade off any longer, Ever leaned in.

Dropping the sword, he crushed her to himself as he kissed her with a desperation he'd never had before. A wave of blue light exploded out from them with a *boom*, and with a cry, Ever let go and dropped to the floor, pressing his eyes into his palms.

"Ever!" she tried to scream, but her call was lost in the deafening crack that echoed throughout the entire castle. Isa hit her knees beside him, holding him as he clutched his head. Beneath them, the entire island shook.

Somehow, despite his pain, she felt Ever throw up a shield of light around them. Through the shield, Isa watched as the queen's tower gave way first. The cracks appeared in the center of the tower itself, then crawled both up toward the six-sided bedroom and down to the rest of the castle. Like the plague it spread. Even in the near darkness, splinters visibly worked their way loose from the cracks. The castle was collapsing.

Once the tower could no longer support itself, the queen's room fell. Hitting the main roof on its way down, it was as though the tower had claws, and used them to ensure it wasn't alone. Chunks of tower and rooftop and walls mingled as they sank. The castle groaned as it began to break apart.

Isa didn't have to watch the pieces plummet into the depths of the chasm that surrounded them to recognize that the cracks were moving toward them. Her ears began to hurt as larger chunks of towers and upper floors caved in on themselves.

Finally, it was their turn. Isa screamed and clung to Ever as the roof above them collapsed. The shattering glass was deafening. Isa wondered if the island itself might topple. The ground beneath them shook, and even the moon was blocked by the cloud of dust and debris as the Glass Castle crumbled. It felt as though it would never end.

Eventually, the ringing in her ears did stop. Isa dared to look up, and Ever let the shield fall. In the light of the moon, they crouched, surrounded by a sea of blue-green dust. What had been proud pillars and arches was now reduced to sparkling sand beneath their feet. After surviving myth and legend, time and spell, the Glass Castle was truly gone.

CHAPTER 45

TREADING WITH CARE

S houldn't we have been there by now? They said it would only take four days." Olivia grimaced and shivered. Despite the thick fur cloak her maidservant had brought along, she was somehow still cold. How she was still cold under all those petticoats, Launce would never know. With the vast layers of clothing women had to wear, he was amazed they didn't sweat all the time. Launce knew better than to say such things aloud though. His mother and sisters had chastised him for pointing out such truths on more than one occasion.

As the mountain road wound higher, travel had become more difficult for the carriages and supply caravans. So difficult that the trip had so far taken eight whole days. Of course, Launce had anticipated this, reveled in it, actually, and had suggested they take the longer road around the mountain in order to extend their slow trek.

"We don't have the time to dally, but it is good of you to consider such things," Rafael had gushed. "That's kingly thinking for you already. Is it not so, Your Holiness?"

"Quite so," Bronkendol had replied placidly. From the look he'd sent Launce after that, it was clear he knew what game

Launce was playing. Taking the longer road would buy Garin at least another week to prepare for what was coming. And since he'd not been able to send out any messenger birds, Garin must know by now that something was wrong. Had Rafael taken Launce's suggestion, it would have bought Garin at least three more days' time.

And yet, it was for naught. The mountain road it was. All Launce could do was pray that the caravans carrying weapons Rafael had ordered to be taken would roll back down the mountain and be dashed to pieces. Without their drivers, of course. But thus far, no such good fortune had come. Even the mirror, which Launce had hoped to dash again while the enchanter was gone on one of his many disappearances, was wrapped up tightly in bedclothes, and guarded fiercely by two soldiers. The soldiers had been added after Launce's first attempt at ridding them of the glass. Now, all he could do was pray and try to prepare Olivia for the difficulty that lay ahead.

Bronkendol's good mood had disappeared along with the last of the autumn warmth. After his last disappearance through his mirror, he'd returned with just a vestige of his easy mirth. Instead of watching Launce and Olivia with the contentment of a grandfather, he simply stared vacantly, or spoke to the stupid little mirror he kept in the pocket of his robe. Despite the unfortunate consequences this dark mood promised for Launce and Olivia, Launce found an immense deal of pleasure in seeing the mysterious bruises on the enchanter's face, as well as the way he kept an arm protectively over his side. Launce didn't know where the man had gone, or what he had done to earn himself such injuries, but Launce hoped they would hurt for a very long time. Launce also hoped they were one more sign that Everard was still alive.

Today, however, Launce had no time to dwell on such niceties. "Before we reach the Fortress, there are a few things you need to know," he told Olivia in a low voice. Olivia regarded him with a keen eye before nodding.

Thankfully, the narrowness of the mountain path had made it impossible for more than two people to ride side by side, which gave them at least a small bit of privacy. This would be the last part of the journey that would be safe enough for them to share secrets. Launce decided to make it good.

"You asked me how my sister and her husband met. Are you still interested?"

"As you can see, I am much too busy."

Launce nearly laughed aloud as she rolled her eyes at him. He sobered quickly, as the story began to bring about all sorts of memories that he would rather have done without.

"When my sister was just nine, our family went to see the annual parade that Everard and his parents were to participate in. She was shoved into the street right in front of his horse, and he helped her to her feet. My sister didn't know royal etiquette, and in her haste to thank him, grabbed his arm. He shoved her off, but didn't control his power." Launce drew in a breath, the bile rising in his throat the way it always did when he remembered. "Everard's force shoved her beneath a rearing horse. She nearly lost the use of a wrist and ankle. Then, for thirteen years, Isa lived as an outcast. He took everything from her, and he never cared to know it."

Olivia watched him with large eyes, but didn't speak. He could see from her expression that she hadn't heard this version of Isa and Everard's story before. It made him wonder how many people really knew.

"Then last year, when Ever's father, King Rodrigue, died," Launce continued, "Everard lost his temper and got drunk." The words flowed more freely the more Launce spoke, the desire to tell someone suddenly bursting forth like an overfilled wineskin. He hadn't realized how much he needed to share this story, the one that haunted him every night as he fell asleep.

"Everard ordered his soldiers to kill all the sick and crippled right where they found them, on the streets, in their homes, everywhere." The princess's eyes grew wide, but Launce shook his hand at her alarm. "His orders were never carried out."

"Why not?" she breathed.

"The Fortress cursed him, taking the very strength from his body. But not just him. Even the Fortress servants turn to phantoms, and the Fortress itself went dark for the first time in a thousand years."

A light of understanding lit Olivia's eyes.

"That's why he never chose a queen after his ball. I mean, we knew he had gone to war with Nevina, but everyone had still expected him to choose someone . . ." She stopped the train of thought abruptly and leaned forward. "So, how did he find your sister?"

"Honestly, it's still beyond me. Isa says it was the will of the Fortress." He still hated thinking about it to this day, even if it was of the Fortress. "My father was caught in a blizzard, and he decided to seek shelter in the Fortress, not knowing Everard was still living there. We hadn't heard or seen anything of the Fortress or its staff for months. But once Father was inside, Everard forced him to share all about our family. When Everard learned that my sister had a strong heart, he demanded she come to the Fortress alone, or he would send a sickness on us all."

"She went, didn't she?" the princess guessed quietly

Launce nodded. *Deep breaths*, he reminded himself. Remembering that day still made his heart race. When he was able to speak again, his voice was shaky.

"It was months before we heard from her. My father nearly lost his senses as we waited. And even after we heard that she was safe, even after she returned home, Isa was no longer ours. She belonged to the Fortress, and somehow, to Ever. But still, the curse would not break."

"What changed?"

"Everard's heart was so hardened that they nearly both died before the curse broke. In his fear and anger, my brother-in-law had decided that he knew better how to protect Destin. That decision to trust himself, rather than the Fortress, nearly cost him and my sister their lives."

"So that is the burden he carries," Olivia said.

"What?"

Olivia paused for a moment before answering, drawing her yellow cloak about her a little more snugly.

"King Rodrigue and my father were the closest of friends. I suppose you could say that Everard was always like a bit of a nephew to my father." She blushed a little. "When I was little, there was some talk of betrothing us from a young age, but Everard wouldn't have it. He always said he wanted the Fortress to choose." She gave a nervous laugh. "I was more grateful than you'll ever know. I trusted him, but the man frightened me, even from a young age. He was always so brooding . . ." Her voice trailed off as she stared up at the path ahead of them, her eyes distant.

It took everything in Launce not to think daggers at his brother-in-law, who might or might not be dead.

Finally, she shook her head and resumed speaking. "Anyway, I noticed as soon as you all arrived that there was something different about him. He was serious before, but now he stalks . . . I mean, he stalked around like a panther, guarding its prey. There was a feverish look in his eye the whole time he was there, as though he were desperately afraid of something. It all makes sense now, because he *needs* her." She nodded once to herself. Launce didn't miss the dreamy look in her eyes though. Isa had often looked the same way as a girl when she talked about true love. Launce had always scoffed at such things. Now, however, he found himself morbidly curious as to what she was thinking.

"But," Olivia looked at him, "why are you telling me all of this? I sense it is not a time you particularly like to relive."

Launce edged his horse closer to hers, hoping not to draw the attention of the others. King Rafael appeared to be lost in whatever world the enchanter kept him and the rest of the travelers in, but Bronkendol continually glanced back at the two of them.

"This scheme the enchanter has with your father is nothing short of suicide." Olivia's eyes grew wide, but she said nothing, so Launce continued. "There is a bond between Destin's Fortress and its monarchs. Isa has tried to explain it to me four or five times, and it's rather difficult to understand or talk about, but I'll do my best.

"A thousand years ago, a lower knight from Tumen happened to hear a cry for help from a woman that lived in what is now Soudain, just at the foot of the Fortress's mountain. He went to his liege and requested to bring some of his brothers with him to help the woman's family fight off the bandits that had been plaguing them. Tumen's king refused, however, as the woman wasn't wealthy or anyone of importance. So the knight said he would help her himself.

"The knight set out on his own, and nearly died helping the woman's family. But in the end, he was victorious, and when he was, others from the area began to ask him for help as well. They had been forgotten by the Tumenian king, and needed protection from the marauders who frequented their homelands. And while the king refused to assist him, even ordering him to return to Tumen's capital and to ignore the peasants, the Maker was pleased. As a reward for helping the helpless, He gave the knight his own crown, and Destin was born."

"That doesn't seem so hard to understand," Olivia said.

"It isn't. The difficult part is understanding the Fortress itself. You see, the Maker gifted the Fortress to the knight as a way to help protect the people. He imbued His own power into the citadel to aid the king and his descendants in protecting the people and providing shelter for the desolate.

"But the Fortress isn't just a place. It's..." Launce struggled for words. It didn't matter how many times Isa explained it. The Fortress was hard to comprehend. "It is as if the Maker placed a part of Himself within the Fortress stones. And not just there, but in the hearts of its monarchs as well. I hear Everard and Isa talking to it sometimes, even when they're not at home.

He paused, feeling silly for his inadequate words. "I used to scoff at the old stories, but since spending time there myself, I can't deny the feeling of power and awe that the place inspires." Olivia still stared at him, looking more confused than ever, so Launce tried another tactic.

"I'm sure you've seen Everard's eyes?"

"Everyone knows about the Fortiers' eyes."

"Well, it's said that when the Fortiers' fires go out of their eyes, they die. For those with pure hearts, who have been faithful to the Maker, it is of old age or during battle. But for those that forget whom they serve, the Maker takes them home sooner. Isa says it is because the Fortress holds too great a power for an unfaithful king to handle. If he cannot wield it correctly, the Fortress removes its light from his eyes, and the Maker takes him to eternity so the people will remain safe in the hands of the next monarch. As I said, it is not easy to understand."

He looked her right in the eyes, holding her gaze this time. "The reason I tell you this is because we are in grave danger." Olivia bit her lip, but said nothing, so Launce went on in a rushed whisper, for Bronkendol was watching them once more.

"The Fortress cursed Everard, its own son, in order to preserve the purity of its kings and queens and save the innocents of the land. How do you think the Fortress will respond when we barge in and declare we're putting ourselves upon its throne, the throne the Fortress alone has chosen for the last thousand years? Especially," Launce said, "after its queen was taken and its king was attacked." Even if Everard was still alive, Launce had no doubt Bronkendol had at least made some attempt on his life, or would soon, at any rate.

A delicate shiver danced across Olivia's shoulders. "I didn't think of that," she said in a low voice. Then she glanced up at her father and Bronkendol ahead of them. "What about them?" she whispered. "If we don't do as they say, they will do terrible things to us too."

"If there is one thing I've learned from my sister," Launce said slowly, "it's that the Fortress always knows what it's doing. The hard part is believing that, even when we can't see it."

And as much as it pained him to say it, Launce finally knew it was the truth. Isa had trusted the Fortress to see her through the curse. And it had. Now it was his turn to trust, and, he prayed, Olivia's. He didn't doubt Olivia's sincerity in the slightest. As they reached the rounded summit of the mountain, however, he hoped she could keep that faith, for he got the feeling that their current troubles were about to multiply.

CHAPTER 46

RAW

Ever's eyes felt as though someone had ripped them open. The glass dust had settled, and the sounds of shifting debris were quieting, and yet he could only clutch his eyes. His arm shook as he looked down, half expecting to see blood gushing from his face, the pain was so great. To his relief, however, there was no great flow. Only a few drops sat on his hands where the slivers had fallen from his eyes. The shards of glass themselves were gone.

His relief was short-lived, however, when he looked up at Isa. His wife knelt beside him, looking around with the same dazed expression Ever felt on his own face. Copper strands of her hair waved in the dry, icy wind. Her right cheek was smeared with dried blood, and the wound on her neck was still fresh.

Who had done such a thing? And where was Bronkendol?

The enchanter was nowhere to be seen. Only the island covered in broken glass remained. Enough of the glass had fallen over the edges of the island, into the depths of the void below, that it was possible to see some of the objects that had been inside the castle through the remaining debris. Here and there, shining green and blue in the moonlight, bits and corners of objects and furniture stuck up out of the gleaming rubble.

Joy and alarm exploded within him as he realized that the fire was once again burning within her eyes. From the guarded weariness in those eyes, a terrible feeling as to what had just transpired began to build in his stomach as well. He tried to recall all that had happened, but had to sift through the haze. He remembered rage. Hate as pure and volatile as molten steel had taken hold of his body. The more he considered it, the more he did remember fighting someone. But that had been Bronkendol ...

He filtered back through his memories, and saw only her. What had come over him? How could he have been so blind to do such a thing? Such things?

Slowly, so as not to frighten her, Ever reached out and gently took her face in his hands. She made no move to stop him, but watched him warily all the same. The wound just under the hollow of her cheek was easy enough to heal. The cut at her neck was much deeper though. Guilt roared in his ears. Had he pressed any deeper, it would have killed her.

As he worked to heal her, the blue fire thrumming between his fingers, Ever tried to come up with something to say. All he could think to ask, though, was the question that had drawn him to this forsaken wasteland in the first place. That Isa had followed him was enough to give him a shred of hope. But she wouldn't meet his eyes long enough for him to know for sure.

After five minutes of silence, Ever could stand it no longer. "Are you—"

"Yes." She still didn't look at him.

Ever longed to tuck the stray bits of hair behind her ear, but he knew better. So he focused instead on trying to keep her skin from scarring. When he was finally done, he hoped she would speak, but she simply stood up and wandered through the rubble, pushing the broken glass bits around with her foot.

When she did speak again, her voice was practiced and distant, statesmanlike.

"Did you see what he did with the mirror?" She spoke without looking at him.

Ever tried to recall. The enchanter had spoken to a little mirror before the rage had overtaken him, but he couldn't remember what had happened after that. "Not after he spoke to it."

"He spoke to it?" She finally raised her eyes to his and lifted an eyebrow delicately, but not for long.

"What did he do to me?" Ever hated feeling lost. Even more so, he hated being out of control, and that, he got the feeling, was exactly what had happened to him.

"I think," Isa spoke slowly, "he is using my power to control the hearts of others. He placed the glass inside of you so that you only saw what he told you to see . . . or feel. I don't know. But it seems that he used my power, which was channeled into the mirror, to influence your heart so that you would do as he wished."

"Of course he did." Ever groaned and placed his head in his hands. He'd been so blind. It was Isa Bronkendol had been after. And by leaving her alone, Ever had practically handed his wife over on a platter. If only he'd listened to her. "But you can feel again now, even though he took your power?"

This time, she turned and looked right at him, her eyes piercing. "Yes," she said quietly. "I can feel again."

Somehow, that was almost worse than when she couldn't.

Ever pushed himself to his feet and began to sift through the glass. He found Isa's sword, and she took it without a word. Before she could walk away again, he grabbed her shoulder.

"I need to know." He searched her midnight eyes. "Did he touch you?"

Isa's gaze softened for just a moment. "No. Not in that way."

Relief filled Ever so that he nearly felt shaky. The question had burned within him since she'd been taken. Buoyed with the knowledge, he grew a bit bolder with his questions.

"Why didn't the glass shards work on you?"

"He pitied me after he took my power, so he removed the glass before he sent me home. He promised me I would never have to suffer the shards again." Isa stopped searching the debris below and smiled acerbically up at the frigid starry night. "He may scheme to the utmost, but the man has a strange sense of honor. He could have given me more glass anytime, and he didn't." Before Ever could ask anything else, she declared their search fruitless. "He most likely escaped before the castle fell, and I know for certain he wouldn't have left the mirror behind. Let's go."

Ever followed in somewhat of a daze. That she was speaking to him at all was encouraging. But her walls were up. Ever sighed. It was their early days at the Fortress all over again.

He didn't dare speak until they had crossed the bridge, which had miraculously survived the castle's collapse, and had mounted their horses. It hurt to watch as Isa dropped her stiff formality to lean over and whisper musical tones in her horse's ear. How long had it been since she had shared that same warm smile with him?

Hugon tossed his head and rolled his eyes back to glare at his master, as though demanding to know why Ever wasn't singing to him too.

As they set out for the Fortress, back into their world and out of the nightmare of snow and glass, Ever gathered his courage to broach the subject that would either save or break his marriage. They might as well get all of the heartbreak over with at once.

"Isa, I know that you're angry with me."

"You are right." Isa nodded amiably as though they were discussing one of Cook's new dishes. "But how well do you actually know me? How many hours have you spent with me to know with any confidence what I think or feel, or why I might be angry?"

"What about the time we spent practicing?" Ever stuttered. It was like trying to grasp a fistful of water.

"There was that. It was so kind of you to fit me into your schedule so that we could fight every day."

"What is this about, Isa?" Everard pulled his horse to a halt. "I am trying to fix this! But I cannot change anything if I don't know what you want!"

"What I want?" Isa's eyes finally met his, and though the rings of fire within them were thin, they blazed with heat. "What I want to know is why you are incapable of putting me first! Why I will always come second to your weapons and your allies and your schemes. Even on—"

"A war was about to break out!"

"On our wedding night? Twelve hours, Everard. You couldn't give me twelve hours before you galloped off to meet the first cry for help that reached your ears, off chasing that next glorious feat." With that, she urged her horse into a gallop, tears streaming down her face.

Ever followed along, but more slowly. It irked him to know that his ultimate failure hadn't been the enchanter's success, nor had it even been any of his idiotic words back at the Cobrien palace. No, this pain had been brewing since the beginning of their marriage. The chink in their relationship had been there all along, beneath every hopeful smile she gave him, each time he'd put her off for a foreign dignitary, or when he'd imprisoned her in her room so he could consult with another queen. As usual, it was his own pigheadedness that had threatened to dash the thing he loved most.

"I am so sorry," he said into the wind. The words were pathetic, but they were all he had.

Isa didn't even turn to look at him.

Ever pushed his horse to catch up to her. If his heart hadn't been contrite already, it shattered completely when he saw the way she now wept. Her cries weren't silent, as they must have been for so long, but were ragged and broken. Abandoned.

Ever wanted nothing more than to draw her into his arms and hold her until her tears were all gone. He would hold her until they were gone, he decided. Reaching over, he grabbed her horse's reins. Then, after hopping off his own horse, he pulled Isa off too, ignoring her weak protests.

"We will sleep here tonight."

"It looks cold." Isa sniffled as she glared at the snow-covered ground.

"It will be cold up on the horses too. Besides, we won't be in familiar territory until tomorrow. We might as well get some rest."

Before she could argue, Ever lifted his hands to his face, palms up. He blew gently but steadily into them until a small blue flame danced within them. Then, with the flick of his wrist, Ever tossed the flame to the ground. The blue flame grew larger and flitted to the ground, surrounding them, licking up all the snow in its path. It didn't die until they had a perfectly round patch of dry ground, large enough to fit both the horses, a campfire, and enough space for the two of them to stretch out fully and lie down.

Since they had moved into the lower country, evergreen trees were scattered about. They broke the plains of whiteness in small, uneven clumps. It didn't take Ever long to find and dry some firewood in the same fashion as he had dried the ground for their camp. Soon enough, a small but warm flame blazed in the center of the circle. As he worked to prepare their supper, he watched her out of the corner of his eye.

She no longer cried, but the emptiness in her face said it all, and Ever prayed for words to tell her what he felt. If only she could see his intentions, perhaps she could forgive him one day.

"I know it doesn't change anything." He handed her a bowl

of dried cherries, honey-sweetened bread, and pork, then sat down beside her with his own food. "But I swear, I was only doing what I know best to prove that I love you." He looked at his bowl only to realize his appetite was long gone. "You had just saved me. I was eager to show you my own love in return."

Isa turned and looked up at him. The anger in her eyes had somewhat lessened, but it had been replaced with dark circles beneath her eyes, as though she hadn't slept in a week. "But you were never there. How was I supposed to know your love if you were never there?" She dropped her eyes and muttered, "I thought you were avoiding me."

"Avoiding you?" What on earth had possessed her to think that?

Isa nodded without looking up. "I hadn't fulfilled my duty to the Fortress. My fire was dying. I just thought that perhaps being gone on official duty was your way of avoiding the subject. If you were off being the king everyone expected you to be, then you wouldn't have to be embarrassed when someone asked about your inept queen."

"Is that what you truly think?" Ever put his bowl on the ground and grabbed her face with both hands, forcing her to look at him.

Isa bit her lip before nodding as tears came once again to her eyes.

Ever pulled her close, holding her as she sobbed quietly into his shirt. How had he muddled things so badly?

"Before we go any further, you need to understand something. My father rarely spent more than five minutes with my mother after I was born. The way he showed his family and the kingdom his devotion was by conquering those that threatened their freedom." Ever chuckled humorlessly. "You may think I'm gone often, but I am present much more than he ever was." He pulled back just enough to wipe her eyes with his thumbs. "I'm not strong enough to be without you for that long."

"As much as you're absent, you would never know it," Isa pouted.

"But that's what I mean! Isa, you grew up with a family that spent time together and built one another up! And thanks to you, I'm learning. But it's hard to show love in a way you've never seen it! Just because I don't know *how* to love you doesn't mean I don't love you at all." He gave her a cockeyed smile. "It just shows you what an idiot I am."

Isa let out a choked sound that seemed part sob and part laugh, and Ever was able to breathe once again. It was the first hint of a smile he'd seen on her face since she'd been taken.

He leaned over and pulled a thick blanket out of his pack, draping it carefully over them. It would be a long time before he was able to sleep, but the late night air was becoming exceptionally cold. After making sure his sword was positioned well beside him, he reached under the blanket and pulled her closer. Warmth flooded his soul as she snuggled her head in the hollow beneath his chin. *Teach me*, he begged the Fortress silently, *to show her how much I love her! I need her to know what she means to me.*

The only sounds were the snaps and pops of the fire as it slowly ate into the firewood, and the songs of the wind as it pushed through the trees and over the snow drifts. The yellow tongues of flame licked the wood, filling the air with a sweet earthy scent that rose and danced into the night, where it dissipated. A tired silence floated around them for such a long time that Ever was surprised when Isa spoke again.

"It was just so hard to be told time and time again that I was the Fortress's chosen. That I was the queen everyone had been waiting for. And then months passed. There was no child, and my powers drifted, and you were always gone. I suppose I never really felt the part of a queen after the coronation, nor did I feel like your partner. You were just so good at everything, and it felt like I could do nothing right. But worst of all, having what little power I had left ripped from my heart . . ." She shuddered. "It was like losing the air from my lungs. After Bronkendol sent me away, my heart simply decided it would be easiest to be without feelings at all."

She turned her face up to gaze into his, and Ever felt his breath catch. How he had hungered to see her look to him with that sweet adoration once more! "Forgive me, Ever?" she whispered.

Before she could say anything else, Ever had drawn her into the kiss he'd been craving for so long. It was pure bliss. There were no curses to be broken, no enchanters to defeat. Only wounds that needed to heal. And it would take time, Ever knew, to heal the wounds they'd inflicted upon one another. But that was alright. They had the rest of their lives to move past this place, and Ever swore then and there to never let her hide from him again.

He would have gone on kissing her forever, but Isa pulled away, a small frown on her face.

"I'm still not sure where to go from here. I mean," she stared at her hands, "a little of my power returned at the Glass Castle, but only just a little."

Ever placed his forehead against hers. "Honestly? I don't know. This is new for me too." He picked up her left hand and traced circles on her finger, around the crystal ring she always wore. "My father and I were close, but either he was king or I was. I've never had a partner before. And I mean it when I say I've never needed anyone so much."

He tipped her chin up, drinking her beauty in. Her hair was mussed and there were deep shadows beneath her eyes, but never had she been so lovely. "You may think I'm strong," he whispered, "but I don't know how to go on without you. I may be Destin's sword, but you are the heart. I cannot tell what the Fortress has in store for you, but you are too rare a woman for its choice to have been an accident."

For the first time, a wide, radiant smile shone from her face, and an all-too-familiar yearning filled Ever as her flame-rimmed midnight eyes stared up into his. He began to pull her in again for another kiss, but she gently placed her fingertips on his lips.

He must have looked pathetic, for Isa let out a laugh, her blue eyes sparkling.

"You can have all the kisses you want in a minute, but your queen needs something from you first."

"The king will do all that is within his power and more," he said somberly as he held her fingers against his lips and bowed his head. "For he is under your spell."

Isa giggled again, then looked as if she was trying to be serious. "If you truly mean it when you believe I was meant to be queen, I need you to trust me to be your partner. You can't keep hiding me away like a little doll."

Ever frowned. "I nearly just lost you. That is going to be difficult to do."

But Isa patiently shook her head. "I know I have much to learn, but if I'm truly meant to wield the Fortress's power, you must trust the Fortress to protect me." She sat back a little. "You also need to consider me your partner. I like Queen Kartek. She's intelligent and kind, but," Isa leaned forward with a knowing look, "she is not *your* queen, and she has said as much herself. In the future, I need for you to confide in *me*."

Ever drew in a sharp lungful of frigid air before letting out an annoyed huff. "You don't know how much you ask of me." He leaned forward also. "I can't lose you again."

"By ignoring my call, you nearly did lose me already."

They watched one another for a long time. She was right, but Ever hated to admit it. Allowing her to face evil by his side was going to be the most difficult challenge he had ever undertaken. His concentration was broken, however, when she slipped him a little mischievous smirk.

"If it's going to be that hard, I'll just have to convince you."

He started to ask her how she was going to do that, when her arms wrapped themselves around him, and her lips were suddenly on his. He pulled back enough to groan.

"That's not fair."

She smiled into his kiss. "It's not supposed to be. Now, hush. Your queen commands it." And before Ever could protest, she kissed him again.

CHAPTER 47
IMPOSTORS

Panic seized Isa as she stretched her arms out and found nothing. Where was Ever?

Bolting upright, she looked around, and relief came over her when she found him stoking the fire.

"I'm sorry," Ever said. "I was hoping you would sleep a bit longer. I thought I would get the fire warmed up before I woke you."

Isa snuggled back under her blanket as deep as she could go. Morning hadn't yet broken, but in the early gray, the gently sloping hills of snow looked much less threatening than they had the night before. As she looked around, she realized she was clutching Ever's black cloak as well as her blanket.

It was so good to have his attentions once more.

Ever's posture was as straight as always as he knelt to feed the fire. The bags beneath his eyes were even more pronounced though than they had been the day before. He must have remained awake all night to keep watch. Isa felt a prick of guilt.

"I should have taken a turn on watch. It wasn't fair for you to take the entire night."

Ever smirked at her. "You wouldn't have been able to stay

awake even if you had wanted to. Besides," his tone became more serious, "I may not know how to be attentive, but I can guard. Let me love you in the way I am able."

Isa couldn't help the smile that spread across her face. Pulling his cloak off the top of her blanket, she braced herself for the wave of cold air that would hit her as soon as she left the safety of her covers. As soon as she stood, the wind was so cold she nearly squeaked. She tiptoed to Ever as quickly as she could and draped his cloak over his shoulders before cocooning herself up again in her blanket beside him. Thankfully, the warmth of the fire soon began to grow, and as it did, Isa felt a little more awake.

There were so many things she wanted to say, an unending stream of questions she could ask. But as much as they'd redis-covered the night before, talking and laughing again in a way they hadn't in a long time, there was still a veil between them. Time would have to heal their marriage in some ways, she sensed.

"So what happens now?" She finally worked up the courage to meet his eyes again.

"We need to speak with Garin. Launce was supposed to send him word of what's been going on in Cobren."

If Isa had been sleepy before, she wasn't anymore. Shame and frustration slapped her as she remembered her callous words when Ever had first told her about Launce's dangerous intent. And yet she couldn't quite scold her husband greatly, as for several days, he had been more concerned about Launce's welfare than she had.

"I still don't understand why he had to go," she mumbled, not quite able to look Ever in the eye.

Ever appeared unruffled, however, as he handed her a warmed biscuit drizzled in honey. "If I hadn't sent him to Cobren, he would have insisted on coming along with me."

Isa shivered, and not from the cold. It was bad enough that

Launce had gotten so tangled up in their business in Cobren. She couldn't imagine him squaring off against Bronkendol in the Glass Castle. At least there were others he could turn to in Cobren. She hoped. When she looked back at Ever, he was still frowning thoughtfully.

"What is it?" she asked.

"It's nothing."

Isa gave him a knowing look. "You promised. No more hiding."

Ever sighed. "It would be simple enough to take on an army, even an army of glass men such as those Bronkendol conjured. But if everyone else falls to his power the way I did, then he won't need an army." Ever picked up a pebble at his feet and chucked into the white wilderness before them. "We won't even have a choice. Once he sees we're alive, he will set them upon us. Shedding your enemy's blood is a grim enough matter, but fighting our allies, our friends, and our kin?" He pressed his mouth into a tight line, but didn't go on.

The thought of fighting against Launce chilled Isa to the bone. The enchanter hadn't given him the glass slivers before, but what was stopping him from doing it now? No. Isa shook her head to lose the thought. She had raised her sword to Ever only to survive, because she knew he would kill her, and ultimately himself, if she didn't stop him.

But Launce wasn't the killing machine her husband was. Against her weak blocks and parries, she had known Ever would survive. Launce's self-defense skills, however, were such that he might injure himself if the enchanter told him to use a sword. Ever was right. They needed to get to Garin.

Without saying it aloud, they both knew it was time to go. As they resumed their journey, the sun lifted above the horizon completely, just in time for the eternal hills of snow to melt away, and Isa was grateful to see the signs of late autumn still upon the ground. Had full winter truly arrived everywhere, it would make the journey back to the Fortress, and then Cobren, much harder.

"How is it that I've never seen those mountains that surrounded the Glass Castle on the maps before?" Isa asked. "Shouldn't Lingea be north of us?"

Ever nodded. "I do not think it's so much of a place, as a time." When Isa frowned in confusion, he continued, "Did you notice that the castle had no dust? Three thousand years go by, and the wood of the furniture hadn't crumbled, the linens were still clean, and the plants in that greenhouse were still alive. Even the newer houses in Soudain need their wood reworked on the years where snow and rain are particularly heavy. Let's rest the horses here." He clucked to Hugon, and Isa followed him off the road and into the brush. A gurgling stream ran right down at the bank's edge.

Though the snows had not yet come to these woods, it ran deep enough for the horses to drink heavily. Isa could tell they were getting close to Destin's northern border again, as the tall pine trees were looking more familiar. Soon they would cross the desert gorges that separated Lingea, Destin, and Tumen's lands. Not that Isa had any desire to visit Tumen, but at least the desert would mean they were only a day from home.

"I have a question for you this time." Ever interrupted Isa's thoughts. He was leaning back against a tree, sharpening a dagger as their horses rested. Isa let her eyes follow the fine lines of his arms and chest. "Isa?"

"What was that?"

He gave her a cockeyed smile as though he knew where her thoughts had gone, and she felt herself blush.

"I was asking you how you knew the kiss would break Bronkendol's hold on me."

"I didn't."

Ever raised his eyebrows, and Isa shrugged.

"It was instinctive. Like the way I stopped Nevina. I knew what I needed to do, and somehow, it happened. Why?"

He rubbed his neck thoughtfully. "The Fortress gave you the power you needed both times, and yet, we continue to worry about why it isn't there. I think it's been there all along though."

"I've failed so much!"

Ever held up a hand. "Your power of the heart is different than any the Fortress has on record. Even Garin hasn't seen anything like it before." He gave her a thoughtful look. "I think it's time we stop trying to judge your strength by the strength of others. The Fortress has given you the strength to defeat Nevina and Bronkendol at the exact moments you needed it. No more and no less." A small smile began to grow on his face. "I think that when we are all through with this mess, you're going to be just fine."

"But you're strong all the time."

"And see how far I've fallen." He gave her a sad smile. That wasn't exactly what Isa had wanted to hear. And yet, they had more important problems to solve than her erratic fire.

They led their horses back to the road before she dared ask the question she feared had no answer.

"So how do we stop him?"

"Simple," Ever said. "We break the mirror."

He bent to help Isa mount her horse, but she placed her hand on his face first. Her heart fluttered as he paused, their faces nearly touching. "Together?" she asked breathlessly.

Ever began to answer, but a bush rustled to their left. Before she could move, Ever had drawn his sword, and was crouched in a ready stance in front of her. Isa felt clumsy as she unsheathed her own sword and tried to hold it out just as he had taught her. As they waited, listening, Isa prayed it was only an animal. It would be absurd for them to die now at the hand of bandits.

The men who stepped out of the trees were no bandits though. Isa heard Ever let out a sigh of relief when ten foot soldiers walked into the little clearing, all wearing blue and green. She even recognized a few of them.

"Percy!" Everard reached out to clap the shoulder of the soldier closest to them.

Isa watched in surprise as the man did not bow or salute his king, as the soldiers always did at home. Instead, he only looked at his companions, confusion on his face.

"They cannot be—"

"Don't let your eyes deceive you, Percy. He said there would be no noticeable difference."

Ever watched them in disbelief as the soldiers conversed among themselves. "Could someone please enlighten me?" he shouted.

The second soldier cleared his throat. "You are hereby ordered to appear before His Majesty in court. He and His Holiness will know what to do with such impostors."

"Impostors?" Isa repeated. "Do you not recognize your king?"

"And if I'm here, who in the blazes is 'His Majesty?'" Ever roared.

"His Holiness, Bronkendol of the North, will deal with you. Now, if you will cooperate, we can keep this from being unpleasant." The soldier looked at them expectantly, as if he actually believed they would obey him.

Isa could feel Ever tensing beside her. Heat radiated from his body as he began to lift his sword, but she grabbed his arm and whispered, "Look at their eyes!" Indeed, the smallest fractals of blue-violet light pulsed from the edges of the soldiers' eyes, just as they had done in Ever's. "They're just as much prisoners as we are," she urged him. "Let's just go with them, and no one will be hurt." Ever glared at her, so she added, "Just as you said, we cannot fight our own."

"I will take those." The guard held his hand out and nodded at their swords.

"Over my dead body," Ever growled.

"No." An arm wrapped itself around Isa's neck and dragged her backward. Isa felt herself choking as her captor continued to tighten his grip. "Over her dead body."

The fire which had burned strong in Ever's eyes now threatened to kill each and every soldier present. Desperately, Isa shook her head as well as she could from beneath the man's tight hold. She wasn't ready to bear their blood on her hands just yet. For a moment, she wasn't sure he would listen. It felt like an eternity as he held her gaze. As he did, she pleaded him with her eyes. Not yet.

Finally, he lowered it nearly to the ground. "You swear we shall remain safe?"

"We are under direct orders to bring you to the Fortress," the soldier said. "The Holy Adviser wants to meet with you himself." The young man's eyes flicked down to the slight blue floating over Ever's hands. "He said there would most likely be sorcery involved," the soldier muttered. Then he nodded at another man behind him. "Pull out the talisman."

Isa's stomach twisted violently when he held out the "talisman." Instead of a gift to ward off strange magic, as they must have been told, it was a simple hairpin, decorated only with a thin, discolored rose made of painted wood. It was Gigi's.

Anger burned within Isa, and she felt Ever watching her curiously, no doubt sensing the sudden change within her mood. She could feel the fire burning in her eyes, as thin as it might still be. The soldiers might not know what pawns they were being played for in this game, but Bronkendol surely did.

"Take us." Isa had never issued a command with such authority. She focused so hard on the soldier's face that he began to look uncomfortable. Ever said nothing else, handing over his sword once and for all. Isa felt another set of hands take her own sword from her, but she didn't care. Soon they would be back at the Fortress, where it now seemed as though the enchanter was waiting for them. And soon, he would be sorry.

CHAPTER 48
DUNGEON

Although she was perfectly aware that the soldiers were under Bronkendol's influence, Isa hoped the hard desert floor hurt their feet through their boots. Before they had left for Cobren, Isa had been planning on ordering the royal cobblers to craft boots with thicker soles for the foot soldiers, but now she was glad she'd never found the time.

At least they had allowed her to ride her horse. Her hands were bound, but it was still better than walking. Isa never would have made it through the night had they forced her to walk the whole way. Their captors seemed to be in a hurry, as they only ever stopped long enough for the horses to rest, then they were off again, riding all through the night. Isa's own muscles ached whenever she thought of how hard they were pushing Ever. He was not allowed to ride his horse. She'd overheard some arguments between the men themselves about this. One, with hair the color of the desert they now traversed, never lost his worried look.

"If we push that one too hard, His Holiness will be angry with us."

"We cannot risk his escape." Another man with a large nose

shook his head. "He might be an impostor, but that doesn't mean he isn't powerful. His Holiness said the forests would be ripe with wizards trying to take King Everard's place." And so, Ever walked.

Isa glanced back to Ever again to see how he was faring. They wouldn't allow him to come any closer to her than thirty paces' difference. They were a rather strange sight, with two soldiers riding alongside Isa and her horse in the front, and eight soldiers on their mounts as they surrounded Ever in the back. After seeing her change of countenance back in the forest, Ever had allowed them to tie and hold him with four different ropes, but the look on his face had told her just how difficult the submission had been.

Still, he walked proudly with his head held high. Isa knew him well enough, however, to recognize the exhaustion on his face. Even Ever had a breaking point. She just prayed he could last a little while longer before reaching it.

The desert seemed to stretch on forever. This was the valley, Ever had once told her, where the Tumenians' late princess, Nevina, had killed his father, King Rodrigue. Their party had reached it a few hours after leaving the forest.

Isa couldn't remember the distance feeling nearly so long when she'd ridden after Ever toward the Glass Castle. Dry, powerful winds bounced down the bare, crusty cliffs above and rushed down into the arid valley below, covering them with dust.

Just then, Isa spotted the main road that led back to Soudain. Hope swelled, as she realized they might meet someone she knew on the path, someone who might be able to find Garin, or her parents, at the very least. Rather than heading toward the main road, the soldiers turned while still in the valley. They led her horse to a sandy slope, where a path barely visible hugged the steep incline. It was their own mountain, but Isa couldn't see the Fortress from the north side, or its wide, pristine fields and gardens. Why were they going up the mountain this way?

The slope eventually grew so steep that Isa could feel her horse straining beneath her when they were barely halfway up. Again, frustration and anger warred within her. She had never forced her animal to take such difficult terrain. She made sure to whisper encouragements to him, and eventually talked her guards into letting her walk beside the animal instead. That helped, but by the time they were nearing the top of the slope, foam began to appear on the animal's silken coat.

When the path split, one side going right and one left, Isa stopped her horse and refused to go further. "I do not know what your *holy man* has told you," she snapped at the guard nearest her, "but you are going to ruin my horse if you don't allow him to rest."

"We're nearly there." The guard with the sandy hair pointed and gave her a shove as they turned up the left path.

"What is this?"

The three of them turned as Ever shouted from below, where he and his entourage still hiked the trail.

"You're taking us straight to the dungeons?"

Isa's breath hitched. She had never been to the dungeons. Not even a part of the Fortress itself, a distant ancestor of Ever's had thought it necessary to hide the prisoners where no loyal friends or hired swords would know how to find them. She'd asked about visiting once, but Ever had said there was no reason to make herself uncomfortable. Now she was to be held there.

Isa's soldiers urged her along the top of the cliff until they came to the most out of place door Isa had ever seen. It was hardly visible, carved into the side of the mountain itself, little roots and grasses sticking out of the wood where soil had gathered in its cracks. One of the soldiers gave four sharp raps upon the door. It opened from the inside with a creak, and Isa was assaulted by the stench of stale air and soured dirt.

She leaned into her horse and wrapped her arms around his neck. Never had she seen such blackness as that which was down that hole of a hall. Just higher than Ever was tall, and wide enough for three to pass through at the same time, the hole belched forth its wretched stench as though a wind carried it from the dungeon's belly. *I can't go in there*, she silently screamed to the Fortress. *It's worse than You ever were, even under the curse!*

No saving grace appeared, as each of the soldiers firmly took her by an arm and began to pull her toward the hole.

"No!" she shrieked, falling dead weight as best she could while kicking her feet. "I can't go in there! I just can't! Please!" But no matter how hard she fought, she was no match for the men who held her. *I need Your power!* she told the Fortress. But no power came, and with a little effort, they were able to haul her inside.

A single weak torch hung on the wall. The third man, who had opened the door, removed the torch and walked before them as a guide. But the flame did little to illuminate the inky blackness. Isa continued to trip over her own feet as they led her further in.

After they'd been walking for some time, she could hear Ever struggling behind her, but when she turned to see if he was any more successful than she at her attempted escape, it was impossible to see through the dark.

Deeper and deeper they walked. The air began to feel different, as though it were pressing in on her from all sides. Panic sped her breathing, and it was all she could do not to break out into hysterics. They seemed to be moving upwards, though the incline was barely noticeable. She wasn't allowed to stop until the narrow passage opened up, and Isa could feel that they were now standing in a room of some sort, though she couldn't see how large it was or any of its other details. In the light of three more weak torches hung on the wall, she could make out the silhouette of a man, powerfully built. As her eyes adjusted, she realized the lines of his face were familiar.

"Acelet!" She nearly sobbed with relief. Isa lunged forward and threw her arms around her husband's favorite general. He would set things straight.

But Acelet didn't move a muscle. He merely waited as the two guards fought to get her under control again. Only then, after they'd pulled her back, did Isa see the faint blue-violet glow from the edges of his eyes. Bronkendol had gotten to him too.

Without a word, he began walking. Isa's guards followed, dragging her with them. Isa could feel resentment and hatred rolling off the general, and decided pleading with him would do no good. Whatever the enchanter had convinced him of, using her stolen power, she would not be able to turn his heart as she was pulled along behind him.

The soft planks of wood they'd walked upon since entering the cave gave way to metal. She could feel it echo with each step as they moved her into another area that was, again, too dark to see.

She wished so much for Ever's group to catch them. Earlier, she'd heard him put up a fight loud enough to echo down the hall. But there was complete silence now. Either they'd moved him farther away, down another hall, or they had found a way to silence him. That thought rattled Isa more than anything else she had seen that day.

They came to a stop. "You will take three steps forward."

"No." She was shocked at her audacity as the word left her lips. But whatever he had in store couldn't be good.

"You will do it, or I will move you myself."

Isa glared into the darkness, wishing he could see the anger in her eyes. In that moment, she felt the slight heat of the blue fire glance her right foot. She froze, hoping for it to flare to life. Nothing permanent stayed though. It was almost as if the Fortress was telling her to trust. To go. With a sigh, she made three slow steps forward.

On the last step, her boot touched something soft, like cloth. As soon as both feet were down, the floor dropped from beneath her, and Isa shrieked as she fell into what felt like a giant sack. The cloth leapt up around her, catching her in midair. Slowly, the sack was lowered deeper and deeper. When Isa touched a hard surface, the sack twisted, and she was dumped out onto the ground. Immediately, the sack was taken right back up. Still on the ground, Isa stared up. In the distance, she could barely make out the light of a torch as a slitted metal cover was pushed over the opening of the hole she'd just been lowered into.

As she stood, trying to study the light above, Isa stumbled. When she tried to catch herself, she quickly realized that the floor wasn't even, and she tripped forward into a hard metal wall. When she finally caught her balance, Isa lowered herself to the ground again and began feeling her way up.

As if being buried deep in the mountain wasn't bad enough, the cell itself had no level surface. Even the ground was curved upwards, like a giant's bowl with sides that curved up all around her, narrowing as they moved to the top. The metal reflected dimly at first in the light of the torch, but that didn't last long. Distant voices murmured unintelligible words, but soon they disappeared, echoing footsteps carrying them away. And as they went, so went the light.

CHAPTER 49
CHOOSING A LOSS

I am sorry, Launce, but I am under strict orders to let Princess Olivia rest."

"But it's been two days!"

Gigi reached out from the doorway and patted his cheek affectionately. "I know. And you will see her soon enough." Her face grew somber then, as though she had just remembered something. "You should use this time for mourning, you know. You won't have the proper time once the coronation takes place." As she spoke, her eyes welled suddenly with tears, and Launce swallowed the frustration he needed to unleash.

"You know he might not be dead after all." He lowered his voice. "We have no proof Ever actually died." *Please, let her believe me*, he prayed. If he could get even one person to see sense, perhaps there was hope for them yet.

Gigi brushed a silver curl from her face and gave him a watery smile. "Always so hopeful. Do not lose that once you become king." And with that, she reached out and squeezed his hand before retreating back into the room that was now declared Olivia's.

Launce stared at the closed door for a long moment,

wondering what kind of chaos would ensue if he barged in and seized Olivia. He would drag her to the farthest corner of the world, where they would settle as strawberry farmers, never to be seen or heard from again. Before his dreams took him too far, however, Launce gave a weak kick to the door, then turned back to his own chambers.

Well, technically they were the king's chambers, but no amount of gold could convince him to sleep anywhere but in the corner, on the floor. Perhaps the many connected rooms would afford him somewhere to plan, without someone stumbling upon him and asking his opinion on the smoked boar, or where else to house the hundreds of horses and carriages brought along by the unexpected visitors that now filled the Fortress to its fullest capacity.

They had arrived at the Fortress two nights before, whereupon Olivia had been immediately whisked away to be "prepared" for their upcoming nuptials. Launce knew what Bronkendol was up to though. Their constant whispering throughout the journey must have made him finally nervous, for Launce recalled Isa being allowed to leave her room during the week before her coronation. But the enchanter held the upper hand, and now he played it well, for though no one else seemed to suspect a thing, Bronkendol's threat was less than subtle to Launce.

Not that the servants or other royals were good standards to judge by. In less than an hour after they'd arrived, Bronkendol had somehow planted the shards in all of the Fortress's residents as well. And like Gigi, since then, none of them had made a bit of sense. Now, as staff hurried up and down the halls, preparing the Fortress both to mourn for Everard, and also for its forthcoming double coronation, Launce refused to look at the purple and blue glow of power each servant wore.

Garin was the only exception, of course. Because Garin was gone.

As though he'd never existed, the steward was nowhere to be found, nor did anyone remark on his absence. Launce could only hope that Garin was in hiding, waiting for the right time to emerge, for it was on Garin that Launce's plan of escape depended.

"It would appear that autumn has gifted us with one last day of sunbeams."

Launce didn't have to raise his head to see who waited for him at the window across from his new chambers. "What do you want?"

"Walk with me, lad." Bronkendol turned away from the window to smile amiably at Launce. "Let us enjoy this last day of good weather the Maker has provided for us."

Launce thought about giving him a smart retort and then locking himself in his chambers. But when he remembered Bronkendol's threat to Olivia, he silently fell into step alongside the enchanter.

The visiting guests from Cobren strolled by the two of them as though nothing were out of place, and the servants carried along as well as any servants might do whose good king had died after only five months of rule. No Destinian citizens crossed their paths though. Launce could only guess news had been circulated that there was a plague or some other sort of foolishness at the Fortress. Surely Bronkendol could not have placed the glass shards in all of Soudain's citizens already. He hoped not, at least.

As they walked, it galled Launce that someone so short could hold him in such a tight grasp.

"It would be simpler for you if you stopped trying to convince your friends that Everard is alive, or that all of this is an evil plot," the enchanter said. "They will not be able to see your version of the truth no matter how hard you try."

Launce kept his eyes trained forward. "And why is that?"

"Because it's incredible how blind we can be when our

heart promises us a certain truth. Even when the facts before us point to another truth entirely."

"So you admit you're lying to them."

"I am allowing them to see the world through the lens of truth as I know it. Of course, that might demand a few embellishments here and there, but soon enough, it won't matter."

"And how is it that you've convinced them all so thoroughly?" Launce had a hunch, but if Bronkendol was in the mood to talk, he was by all means welcome. Listening could only aid Launce in the end.

"Let us venture outside, shall we? I feel the need for some fresh air."

Launce didn't argue as stepped out onto the northernmost balcony. It was an extension of the royal library. Not the sacred one in the Tower of Annals, of course. But its view was nearly as breathtaking. From where they stood on the white marble overlook, Launce could see the border deserts that began at the foot of the mountain. A thin trail he had never noticed before snaked out from some hidden spot below. When he squinted, it didn't appear the trail had any purpose at all. It simply ended midway between the Fortress and the desert floor at the bottom.

"This wouldn't have anything to do with my sister's power, would it?"

"You are sharp. I will credit you that. And yes, the power I drew from Isabelle to end her suffering is the power I harness now to keep the people from panicking while we transition here. It will make the change more palatable for everyone present. That, in turn, will make it easier for your citizens, as well as everyone else's."

Launce frowned. "I don't understand. The people are themselves . . . but they are not at the same time." So far, the enchanter had answered his questions. Launce hoped he would answer this one as well.

"Even your sister has never understood her power. In fact,

she hardly ever tapped into its true potential. And yet, it is her power that holds every new thing in place here." Bronkendol leaned over the edge of the balcony railing, and Launce noticed his eyes training on the thin trail as well.

"Everyone has been waiting for your sister's power to blossom into a strength akin to her husband's. Everard was always fast, strong, and intuitive enough to use his power far beyond his years, at least compared to those of his ancestors that I witnessed. But Isabelle's power is something else entirely, and no one has been able to see it." He placed his hand in his robe pocket, as he seemed to do often. "Not even she can see it," he murmured.

"So Isa's power hasn't been dwindling?" Launce asked. If Isa somehow survived all of this, it was something she deserved to know.

"Not in the way everyone thinks. You see, Everard was bestowed with the strength of the hand, while Isabelle was given the strength of the heart, something you knew already. But what that heart power truly entails is far beyond what even your Fortress steward could understand." Bronkendol spit out Garin's title as though it tasted sour, and Launce nearly smiled. Garin must have at least posed something of a challenge to have ruffled the enchanter's feathers so.

But Bronkendol continued. "Your sister had the ability to turn people's hearts." He eyed Launce. "She's unwittingly used her abilities on you several times." Immediately, Launce recalled the night he had allowed her to go to the Fortress without him. And then, when she'd convinced him to join her in Cobren. That had been her?

"She doesn't force others to act against their will," Launce said, unable to keep the disdain from his voice.

"Oh, but I haven't done such a thing either!"

Launce looked at the enchanter in disbelief.

"All I had to do was introduce despair into their hearts."

"But you've given them no proof!" Launce turned in disgust to leave the balcony. The view of the thin trail made him uncomfortable for some reason.

The enchanter followed, but instead of wandering the enormous round room, filled to the ceiling with books, Bronkendol passed him and strode purposefully to the first set of stairs he could find. "I've told you," he said over his shoulder as Launce flagged behind. "When someone's heart whispers truths to him, his instinct is to trust the whisperings inside above all else. Your friends may not see any proof that Everard is dead, but they don't need it. Their hearts tell them it is so already."

They walked out to the edge of the northern lawns and had come to an old gate. He stopped, fishing around in his other pocket.

"Ah, here we are." Strangely, its bolt was strong and new, not rusted like the rest of the gate. As Bronkendol produced a large brass key and opened the gate to let them through, Launce wondered at how easy it had seemed for the enchanter to get whatever he wanted. Launce had seen that key only once. It had been tied to a leather cord that hung around Everard's neck.

"Launce Marchand, you are a clever young man, and I know you're probably wondering why I have been so free in sharing all I know with you."

Launce didn't respond, but it was the truth.

"I have told you before, and I was earnest, I am excited to see all the Fortress and the future hold for you. You are kind, you have a sharp wit, and you know what it is like to suffer. Most kings haven't lived half as much as you by the time they die. But you still have a choice to make, and I fear you are running toward the wrong one."

As soon as they were through the gate, they found themselves at another door. Only, this one led straight into the side of the mountain. Bronkendol unlocked it as well. As the door swung open, a blast of rancid air hit them, making Launce want to choke. A small torch hung from the wall before them, and just inside to the left, a set of narrow, stone steps led down into a darkness Launce had never before imagined. He wanted nothing to do with such darkness, but for now he decided to follow the enchanter. There must have been a reason the enchanter was bringing him to this horrid place.

Launce had to breathe deeply as they descended, to remind himself that the world wasn't caving in upon him. The stairs twisted and turned in different areas, to the point where Launce couldn't recall what direction they were traveling in. All he knew was that they continued to climb down.

After what seemed like an eternity, he felt the stairs give way to steel floors. He followed Bronkendol's torch, but he noticed that some areas beneath his feet sounded hollower than others. Bronkendol soon came to a stop, and a soldier appeared out of the darkness. After the enchanter whispered something to him, the soldier nodded and led them even further into the depths.

Finally, they stopped in a small corner. Again, the torch was lowered, but this time, Launce could see a large circle carved into the steel floor they walked upon. About four feet across, it had bars slitted through the middle. Bronkendol nodded at the floor, so Launce bent down to look through them. There, at the bottom, the form was nearly invisible against the blackness. But it was one he would know anywhere.

"Isa!" he shouted. His sister's name echoed throughout the wide steel chasm they stood in, but his sister's sleeping form didn't stir. Launce glared up at Bronkendol and the silent soldier that guided them. "What's wrong with her?"

"Nothing serious, just some sleeping herbs. She hadn't slept well in days."

As Launce leaned back down to try and see her as best he could in the dark, he knew exactly why the enchanter had brought him here, why he had been willing to tell him so much.

"Everyone has a choice to make in this world, even if he claims to have none." Bronkendol's lilting voice echoed off the stone walls that surrounded them. "Your sister and brother-in-law made theirs. If you choose rightly, however, I can spare your sister from her choice."

Fury heated his face as Launce stood and stepped as close as he could to Bronkendol. If he had only been as strong as Everard, he could crush this little man like the parasite he was. "I would hardly call extortion honorable."

"I'm showing you how dire this situation is."

"You mean how dire you've made it!"

"When you've lived as I have, then you can tell me what is and is not dire!" Bronkendol's shout echoed through the underground tunnel. Neither of them spoke for a long time, only glowered at one another in the dark. Finally, Bronkendol sighed, and when he spoke again, his voice was ancient.

"I promised you I wouldn't place a shard inside of you. And though I may bend the rules in other ways, I always keep my promises. But I needed you to see what is at stake here."

Launce's fist burned as hot as his face, and he longed to do nothing more than beat the enchanter to death. Where he had once abhorred Everard's ease with violence, he now hungered for it like a man on the brink of starvation. Launce racked his memory for something, anything he could do to make the man uncomfortable. Anything that would cause Bronkendol a portion of the pain and misery he was bringing down upon everyone else.

"Launce, look around you. You speak of doom and wrath, but the Fortress has not shown any sign that we are not welcome. There have been no more earthquakes, and no one has died since we arrived. No one has even been injured. Surely you can see that the Maker is with us, rather than against us. It should serve as a comfort to you."

Launce didn't answer. As he continued to search for the

words to express the depths of his loathing, the soldier replaced the metal grate and led them back to the winding set of stairs. Neither Launce nor Bronkendol spoke again until they reached the top. As the enchanter locked the gate behind them and they stood on the Fortress grounds once more, Launce turned and said softly, "You cannot move through the Fortress's glass, can you?"

Bronkendol froze, the key still in the gate. "Why would you think that?" The words were casual, but Launce felt satisfaction wash through him as he watched the enchanter struggle. Finally, he had found a weakness.

"That's why you had to bring your own mirror. The Fortress will not let you travel within its glass. In fact, I will venture to guess that you've even tried on more than one occasion, but after you had failed enough times, you had to come up with an alternative plan." When Bronkendol still didn't answer, Launce allowed himself an acerbic smile. "You think you know the Maker's will, and you think you know the Fortress. But the Fortress never chose me. And, it would seem, it never chose you either." With that, Launce stalked away.

CHAPTER 50

BRUISES

As soon as Launce was able to leave Bronkendol behind, he hurried to the king's quarters. Frustration swelled inside of him as he knew he only had a few minutes before the enchanter sent someone to either interrupt or keep an eye on him.

Everard had to have blank parchment in his room somewhere. He was too preoccupied with his work not to have writing materials somewhere at hand.

After a minute or two of tearing the room apart, Launce finally found some parchments tucked behind a pile of books on the large desk in the corner. He snatched up the nearest quill he could find, but his hands shook at he tried to sharpen it, breaking the nib off completely. Disgusted with his clumsiness, Launce grabbed another quill and began to sharpen this one also, more careful this time.

He still wrote too quickly, smearing the ink beneath his hands as he held the paper, but at least his words were legible. After writing only the salutation, however, he stopped. He would have to choose his words with care. If this letter fell into the wrong hands, Bronkendol would not leave his family unpunished, of that he was sure. It would have to read like a letter any absent son might send his family. And yet, his parents would need to understand that something was indeed wrong.

Dearest Mother and Father,

Please accept my apologies for staying away for so long. I've had a series of unexpected, and yet delightful happenings that have gone on as of late. I am not at liberty to discuss them now, but I can promise you, they will be spectacular.

I must admit, however, that I am most sorely homesick. While on the way to Cobren, I was talking to Isabelle, and we were laughing about our old escapades. We were wondering, though, if you could resolve a disagreement between us. Father, do you remember the place Isabelle used to hide in when she was small, each time you would return from trading? She believes that they did not bother to fill it in, but it has been my impression that the spot is now paved, and completely useless. If you can, end this disagreement we've had. Isabelle desires greatly to clear it for a place to picnic. I have told her, however, that such an idea is worthless if the place is no longer in existence.

Alas, I must remain absent for a little while longer. I am needed here at the Fortress. Isabelle has taken a bit ill, but we have high hopes for her recovery, so Mother needn't worry. The Fortress has been closed off from visitors until the sickness is gone, as it seems quite catching. It is midday as I pen this, but we hope by tonight's highest moon for Isabelle to be in better health and spirits. You know Everard will have her on her feet in no time.

Your devoted son,

Launce

THE LETTER WAS RUBBISH, of course. Launce never called his sister by her full given name, nor in his wildest dreams would he have ever penned anything with the words *delightful* or *spectacular*. The Launce his parents knew would not have given Everard so much credit, even when it came to healing. At least, not in writing or aloud. And while there truly was a spot on the side of the road where Isa had liked to hide as a little girl, it would have made a ridiculous spot to picnic.

But Bronkendol didn't know that.

Launce just hoped his father would understand the hidden message, where Launce begged him to meet at Isa's hiding place so he could ask for advice. He was desperate for someone, anyone to talk to who wasn't bound by the enchanter's power. Had Garin been present, he would have been Launce's first choice, but at this point Launce would have gladly consulted even with Everard.

If his father could understand the meeting place and time, just before midnight, when Isa was supposed to be in better health and spirits, Launce could have just a few moments alone with him. Ansel might not have unique healing powers of Everard, or generations of experience with the Fortress like Garin, but he was the best man Launce knew and his heart was pure. Ansel would help him sort things out.

Launce went back to the door and peeked out into the hallway. To his relief, the enchanter was no longer hovering about outside of his door, at least for the moment. And to his surprise, no one else was there either. With the parchment folded neatly in his pocket, Launce began to walk toward the servants' quarters.

He wasn't sure who he might send. Everyone he saw had been touched by the enchanter's powers. The violet glimmer in their eyes signified that. But surely there had to be *someone* who had escaped!

After scouring the kitchens, the stables, and even some of his childhood friends' quarters, Launce had nearly given up when he spotted a small, barefooted girl playing in the tomato garden, just outside the servants' kitchens, and he gave a sigh of relief. If anyone was likely to have missed the glass shards, it would have been her.

Launce had seen her enough times during his time spent at the Fortress that he'd taken a liking to her, perhaps because she reminded him a bit of Isa. The first time they'd met, Yasmina had placed a burr on his chair at the dining hall. Her mother had been horrified, but since then, Launce and the child had taken to trading pranks whenever he would visit. He prayed now that she wouldn't think this was a game.

He pulled a sugar lump from his pocket, the kind he often kept there for his horse. It wasn't the best payment, but perhaps for a child, it would do. As he stepped outside, he could see that again, to his relief, she was alone. He would have to be fast.

"Yasmina," he called softly. It took a few tries before she heard him, so deep was she immersed in whatever game she was playing in the mud. When she did finally turn and see him, her brown eyes lit up without any hint of a violet glimmer, and she bounced over immediately. "I have a job I need you to do for me," he said, holding up the sugar cube so she could see it in his palm.

Her eyes grew wide, but then she blinked and shook her head. "No. That's not nearly enough."

Launce frowned as he dug his hand back into his pocket for another lump. Was he truly negotiating with a child for the balance of the kingdom?

She looked at his new offering and pursed her lips for a moment before reaching for the treats, but Launce closed his hand.

"Hey!"

"You can have them, but I need you to agree to accept my job first. Only good workers get paid two sugar lumps. Do you understand?"

Impatiently, she nodded and reached for them again, but Launce kept his fist closed.

"I need you to deliver a letter to my parents back in Soudain. Do you know the way?" She raised an eyebrow, and he had to laugh. Of course she did. All children raised in the Fortress knew the way to Soudain. In his own childhood, his friends had shown him a number of ways to sneak in and out of the Fortress without even having to use the gates.

"Their names are Ansel and Deline Marchand, and they have a mercantile in the city square. If you get lost, just ask for the queen's parents."

"I know," she said with a dramatic sigh, tossing her stringy blond hair. "I've been to their shop before."

"Good. This is very important." He bent down to look her straight in the eye. "I mean it," he said in a softer voice. "This is so important that I need you to promise me you'll give them this letter. But you can't tell anyone else!"

When she had promised, he finally handed her the sugar. She tucked the parchment into her apron, and he watched her as she sprinted off toward the forest.

He allowed himself half a smile. No child ever used the road to reach the Fortress or the town when traveling between the two. He'd never questioned the oddity of children being able to come and leave the Fortress at will, when many adults tried and failed in the same way. But now that he was older and more familiar with the Fortress, Launce wondered if the children were given special permission by the Fortress itself, simply because it loved them. It appeared that way at least, which was why he had chosen a child to be his messenger in the first place.

"You've certainly been busy since we last spoke."

Launce jumped at the sound of Garin's voice. Turning, he found the steward leaning against the wall with his arms folded, as if he'd been there the whole time. Never had Launce been so relieved to see anyone in his life.

"Where have you been?"

"A certain someone sent me an invalid queen and her cheeky personal guard." Garin raised an eyebrow. "Apparently, sending a travel party was easier than simply sending me a messenger bird."

"I'm sorry. I tried, but Bronkendol wouldn't let me get near the birds. I'd hoped Kartek and Apu would explain what he was up to but . . ." Launce shivered. "I didn't know he had planned for us to come here."

Garin nodded once. "I had thought as much." He straightened himself and gestured toward the trees. "Come. Let's not linger where they might see you."

"See *me*?" Launce laughed, but he followed Garin anyway. "And where might you be?"

Garin only gave him a sly grin before heading quickly up the brown fields toward the edge of the Fortress land. Of course. Launce should have known Garin would be hidden from others. Little the steward did surprised him anymore.

They walked until they were deep inside the trees that edged the Fortress's back lawn. A wide assortment of fruit trees had popped up here, which, according to Garin, were due to the pieces of fruit Everard had loved to toss on the ground as a boy. Now, the two men settled under a grove of orange trees. The branches were bare, but the trees themselves were thick enough to shield them from prying eyes up in Fortress tower windows.

"I hear you will be gaining a new title soon," Garin said.

Launce blanched. "I have told Bronkendol repeatedly that I want no part in this!"

"And yet," Garin raised his hand, "here you are." The steward's tone was conversational, but Launce knew there was a purpose to Garin's visit. He hadn't sought Launce out to chat about orange trees.

"They have Olivia . . . Princess Olivia, from Cobren. My

family is still in town, that I know of. And just this morning, I found out that Isa is being kept in the dungeons."

A flash of something dangerous crossed Garin's eyes at the mention of Isa, but he didn't interrupt.

"I need to be here for them. I need to do *something*. I just don't know what that something is." He sat down on a large boulder. "I know you aren't like Everard, but can't you just . . . make them go away?"

Garin laughed. "No, my power isn't like his. However, I do believe that *you* have a decision to make."

"What do you mean? I've already told you I won't accept Bronkendol's offer."

"So if this coronation I've heard about is still on by tomorrow, you'll refuse?

"What am I supposed to do, Garin?" Launce was exasperated with the steward and with himself as the truth came spilling forth. "If I refuse, my sister, my family, even Olivia could die. If I accept, I will be defying the Fortress." Launce stood and began to pace.

"I think you know what you should do," Garin said quietly. "But your fears are telling you otherwise."

"Look, I am trying. I even sent Yasmina with a letter to my parents to ask my father to help." Launce paused, suddenly worried. "You'll make sure no one harms her along the way?"

"The Fortress will see to that. You have no reason to worry."

Launce let out a deep breath, greatly relieved he hadn't just sent a little girl to her death. He stopped pacing and looked up to ask Garin another question, but the steward was gone. Annoyed, Launce trudged back to the Fortress to wait for the night.

Perhaps his father would have some advice that was a little less cryptic.

❆

391

Launce pulled the borrowed cloak tightly around him as he waited for the bells to ring the hour. Using Everard's clothing was hardly ideal, but Launce's cloak wasn't nearly as thick, and the night felt as though it would be exceptionally cold.

Just a little longer and he would be with Ansel.

Launce's years might have made him a man, but at the moment all he could do was think of how safe it would feel to be in his father's fierce embrace once more. Sometimes it would be easier to be ten than twenty.

Steps approached his room, and someone pounded on his door. Before he could answer, the door was kicked in, and Sir Absalom tossed a large bag into the room with a *thump*. The look he gave Launce was cruel, and though the purple and blue light glimmered in his eye, the hatred in Absalom's glare was real.

They stood there, the large bag laying between them for a long time. Finally, without saying a word, the awful knight left.

Launce considered looking at the bag's contents after he met with his father, but a rustling inside of it caught his attention. He stared for a moment, wondering if he should find some gloves or a weapon, just in case the bag contained something that might bite. There was no telling what strange prank Sir Absalom had played on him while he wasn't under the enchanter's direct orders. When another sound came from the bag, this time a very human groan, Launce didn't hesitate. Loosening the drawstring with fumbling hands, he threw it open.

Inside, Ansel's face was covered in dark, sticky blood, and his eyes were swollen shut. Launce's chest constricted as he struggled to yank the rest of the bag off of his father's limp, battered body. As soon as Ansel was free, Launce fell beside him and cradled his father's head in his lap. Tears made it hard to see as he tried with shaking hands to wipe the blood from his father's face.

"Father? Father, can you hear me?"

Ansel couldn't quite open his eyes, but after a few moments, swallowed weakly and opened his mouth.

"Launce?" When his voice finally worked, it was raspy.

"I'm here, Papa!"

But his father could say no more. His chest rose and fell in shallow bursts, and he could hardly open his eyes. The hands that had held, disciplined, and instructed Launce now trembled like an old man's.

"I'm sorry," Launce whispered, trying to keep the tears from blinding him entirely. "I'm so sorry." Part of him was dying, screaming to find a healer, anyone, even Gigi, who might know how to help his father. But with Bronkendol in charge, there was no assurance that anyone he asked would help him at all. The helper might harm Ansel even further if he or she was under orders.

Without the slightest knowledge of how to care for someone so wounded, Launce lifted his father from the floor as gently as he could and laid him in the king's gigantic bed. The thick, wide mattresses might be too much for Launce, but his father deserved the best.

A clean cloth and fresh water had been laid in one of the two porcelain basins for Launce to use before bed. He took the cloth and wet it so that he could try to get the worst of the blood from his father's face. Then he checked for stab wounds and broken bones. There appeared to be no punctures, but from the way Ansel cried out when Launce had lifted him, there was a good chance he had broken a few ribs at the very least.

Once he was done with that, Launce sat on the edge of the bed and watched his father. It was impossible to tell if Ansel slept or not, but he did stop trying to move as much. As he watched, Launce wanted to kick himself for ignoring the field wound treatments Everard had tried to teach him. What he wouldn't do to have his infuriating brother-in-law here now.

But, a small voice of hope whispered, someone else was nearby that might know how to help. As soon as the thought was in his head, Launce was off of the bed, and plowing ahead toward Olivia's room, barely remembering to lock the room and bring his key in the process. He couldn't have anyone else entering to hurt his father further.

Launce sent up a prayer of thanks as he met no one in the halls. Not even servants or guards were to be seen at the late hour. It struck Launce as odd but, he decided, it must be the Maker finally moving events in his favor. That revelation buoyed him on even faster until he reached her chambers. Once there, however, he slowed. The thought of entering a young lady's room without escort, or even knocking, heated his face. But he couldn't risk being discovered and thwarted by Gigi or any of the other women who constantly hovered nearby.

If the enchanter has his way, he thought, *you'll be sharing chambers soon anyways*. This thought made him flush even more, and he hurried to banish it as quickly as possible. His father's life was at stake.

Launce snuck into the room as quietly as he could. It only took him a moment to find the bed, and when he did, he was overjoyed to realize there were no other women sleeping in the room as well.

The moon spilled through an open window and onto the girl's face as she slept, her face more peaceful than he had seen it since they had met.

"Olivia," he whispered as loudly as he dared. She stirred but didn't wake, so he tried again. "Olivia! I need your help!"

"Launce?" she mumbled. Slowly, she rolled over and sat up, rubbing her eyes. When she did, however, he froze, panic squeezing his chest.

"Launce, what are you doing here?" She pulled the covers up higher against her chest, suddenly more awake. "This is highly improper!"

Launce struggled for words as he stared at the blue and purple glimmer in the corner of each of her beautiful, almond eyes.

"I..." He swallowed, not sure what to say. He could hear footsteps approaching in the hall, so he had to try. Perhaps her feelings for him would show her the truth. "My father was injured! I need your help to take care of him!"

"Master Launce!" Gigi stormed in, holding a candle and looking quite shocked. "You must leave this room and return to your own chambers at once!"

"Please, Olivia!" Launce yelled, not caring anymore who heard him. "My father might be dying!"

At this, Olivia's eyes softened, and a look of compassion came over her face. Maybe, just maybe she had heard him, even through the enchanter's lies.

"I'm sorry, Launce," she said gently. "But it's better this way."

Shock paralyzed him and rendered him powerless as Gigi fussed and pushed him from the room. Olivia's cruel words echoed in his mind as the door was shut in his face. Deep down, he knew the words were not Olivia's, but the enchanter's. Still, his hope of swaying her heart with his affections had been dashed. Launce had failed, and because of him, his father might die.

Somehow, Launce made it back to his room, although he couldn't recall actually directing his feet to carry him there. Curling up at the edge of the bed, he allowed himself to weep, holding his father's limp hand as tightly as he dared.

He didn't realize he had nodded off and let most of the candles die until a light knock sounded at the door. Sitting up, Launce rubbed his eyes as a shadow stepped in to the edge of the room, light from the torches in the hall spilling through the gap.

"I'm sorry this had to happen." Bronkendol's voice was low

and soothing. "I told you, though, that you need to think care-fully about your choice."

"You think you're helping the world," Launce snapped, wishing desperately that tears were not running down his face as he spoke. "But everywhere you go, only pain and death follows!" He stood and began to stalk toward the short figure in the corner. He was going to kill this evil little man. There would be no one to hear him scream if he shut the door first.

"Your sister will be at the coronation tomorrow."

Launce froze.

"You should also know that I cannot be so forgiving next time." The shadowy figure crossed back into the light, but before he stepped out, turned back once more. "If you cross me again, I swear to you that there will be death. And it won't be yours."

Launce collapsed on the ground and beat his fists against the stone floor until they were bruised. Angry hot tears drenched his face.

How dare this man threaten and hurt his family? And how dare the stupid guests do his bidding? He didn't care if they were under a curse. He hated them all.

But most of all, how dare the Fortress allow such evil to endure?

"I tried, Garin," he choked out into the darkness, wondering if the steward was near enough to hear. Part of him hoped he wasn't. "But I can't lose anyone else."

CHAPTER 51
THAT NO PRISON CAN HOLD

There now, some of this will do you good. Drink up."

Isa tried to open her eyes, but they felt stuck. And so did the rest of her body. When she tried to move one arm at a time, she found she could barely wiggle her fingers. What was wrong with her? She felt as though she'd been sleeping for years. And why was it so dark?

"There you go," the voice said. "Now swallow."

Isa did as she was told, and a hot liquid slid down her throat. As it moved, her body began to remember itself, and her memories began to return one at a time.

A broken glass castle.

Ever's promise.

The dungeon.

Isa opened her eyes wide when that memory returned. Wildly, she looked around, but after a moment of blinking the sleep from her eyes, she realized she was still there. Instead of being down in the metal pit, however, she was laying on the metal floor beside a large hole. In the dim light, she could see Bronkendol leaning over her with another spoonful of what looked to be soup. He held the spoon out even closer, but she resisted, licking her lips instead.

There was another taste on her tongue, and it wasn't from the soup. It was older, as drops of it had dried on her mouth. First, she tasted the sweet tang of a nectar, but very quickly recognized the subtle bitterness beneath. Isa couldn't remember the name of the plant that made such a wine, but she did remember learning that it could put a full-grown horse to sleep in minutes.

"How long have I been asleep?" she asked, rubbing her head, which felt as though someone had laid a pile of bricks on top of it.

"Just one day and night, my dear. You were distressed, and I didn't want you to hurt yourself."

Ah yes. Despite the impossibility of escape, Isa vaguely recalled trying desperately to do so. She had even managed to work the bindings on her hands loose somehow. It had felt as though the walls were closing in around her, and the voice of reason that usually resided in her head had snapped. Then the enchanter had come with his drink and forced her to sip it, and suddenly, her unbound hands had made no difference as she had been lowered, unable to move, back down into the pit.

"Please, eat a bit more," Bronkendol said, pushing the bowl toward her.

Isa lifted the bowl and sniffed the soup. It smelled like any chicken soup, but how was one to tell whether or not he had hidden more herbs?

As she hesitated, Bronkendol sighed. "I promise, it's just soup."

Isa studied him, refusing to let go of her suspicion. How could she know for sure that she wasn't under the influence of the glass slivers even now? What if he had placed some inside of her while she'd slept? She touched the outer corners of her eyes, but felt nothing unusual. Still, would she be able to tell if he had hidden them there?

Isa came to the conclusion that the only way to know whether or not he had her under his influence was by asking herself one question. How did she feel about him? After a moment of thought, Isa decided with satisfaction that she still loathed him. The fact that she was still imprisoned and desired to escape only further convinced her that he was telling the truth.

Reluctantly, she began to feed herself. He smiled a bit, his boyish grin reminding her of why she'd been so taken in at first by his sweet, enthusiastic ways. How things had changed.

"I've come to ask for your help."

"My help?" Her voice sounded like a bullfrog's. She took another sip.

The enchanter nodded. "I want you to know that though your power is gone, you're still more valuable than I can express." He took a deep breath and looked her in the eyes. "The people love you. You could still be great."

"And why would I help you? You turned my husband against me. You've imprisoned me beneath my own home. You even threatened those I love!" Strengthened by the food, her voice began to rise as the familiar anger returned. "Why, for the love of goodness, would I want to help you?"

"In just a few hours, I will be crowning your brother king of the Fortress. I—"

"You can't do that!" Isa jumped to her feet, every ounce of energy returned. "The Fortress hasn't chosen him! He'll die!"

Bronkendol stood, too, so that they were nearly nose to nose, and his voice was no longer patient.

"You've been queen to a holy place that rejected you after only a few months, and you think you have enough understanding to tell me what is not acceptable?"

His words stung more than Isa wanted to admit, but if there

was any truth, any knowledge left in her, she knew without the shadow of a doubt that Launce would die if he accepted that crown.

"For our world to move on from these wars and disagreements," Bronkendol continued, his voice quieter once more, "we must learn unity. I pray to the Maker that you choose rightly." He snapped his fingers, and two guards appeared. Each took one of Isa's arms, and though she fought them, they managed to wrestle her back into the giant sack once again. As they began lowering her into the pit once more, Bronkendol's curly head appeared over the hole's mouth. "I am ready to make difficult decisions. The question is, are you?"

Isa didn't answer as she went deeper, only watched until the light disappeared again. Once she was at the bottom, she folded herself up in the most comfortable position she could find and buried her head in her hands.

Was there a chance the Fortress might accept Launce? He had a good heart, and he'd spent enough time around the Fortress with her that he wasn't a complete stranger to its unusual ways. Perhaps it would overlook the insubordination of those who were pushing him to accept the position, and focus only on the young man himself.

But what about Ever?

Bronkendol was too much of a schemer to have killed Ever yet. By using her to ensure his cooperation, the enchanter had a great deal of power at his hands, even more than usual. Of course, the enchanter could work the other way too, threatening Ever to gain Isa's cooperation. And as much as she hated to admit it, the tactic would probably reap significant results. She knew better than to make any deals, but a tiny voice inside of her wondered all the same whether she would be strong enough to withstand his threats.

Was there a chance that her agreement to help Bronkendol might ensure her husband's freedom? He would hate that so much. But Isa had lost him too many times already. She really didn't think she could lose him again.

Tears rolled down her cheeks as she pressed her face against the cold metal beneath her.

"Why are You allowing this?" she sobbed softly. "What are you telling us that we just can't hear?"

But no one answered. There was no friendly breeze ruffling her hair. There wasn't the slightest bit of a whisper. But the truth already in her soul was nearly deafening inside.

If the boy hadn't pushed her, she never would have fallen in front of Ever's horse. If Ever hadn't injured her, she would have married Raoul instead of Ever. If the curse hadn't been cast, she never would have known the strength the Fortress had given her at birth. If the enchanter hadn't given Ever the slivers of glass, they never would have moved past the brokenness that had been haunting their marriage from the start. If she had conceived as early as all of the other Fortress queens did, her baby would be in grave danger now.

As Isa lay huddled at the bottom of the dungeon, she didn't feel strong, nor did she feel brave. And yet, she knew what she had to do.

CHAPTER 52

LETTING GO

Isa awoke to the scraping of the metal cover being removed from her pit. As usual, the light was low, though she was getting used to it now. A rope with knots and a loop at the end was lowered until it hit the bottom of her pit with a soft thud.

"Get on," a man ordered from above.

Isa obeyed, not caring who waited for her at the top. Whether it was friend or foe, she would be out of the pit. Staring into the darkness, wondering whether or not she would die there, feeling helpless to save the ones she loved, had been maddening. Once she held on tightly and had her foot through the loop, the rope began to rise.

Still, she wondered, who was pulling her out? Her heart leaped before she could quell the hope. Had Everard somehow escaped? Could Garin have staged an escape? As the circle of light neared, she strained to see who was awaiting her. Disappointment set in though when the enchanter was the one who appeared over the edge.

"How did you sleep?" he asked, as though he was the host and she were his guest. Isa decided not to answer, but he carried on as if she had. "Have you thought about my proposition?"

Isa glowered at him in response, and he nodded.

"I see. Well, your mother will be disappointed."

Even if Isa had wanted to talk after that, it would have been impossible. She was too busy trying not to imagine her mother's face. Traitorous tears rolled down anyway.

The guard who had pulled her up took his torch from the wall and set off to their left. It was the direction opposite from which they'd entered the first time. Or at least, that's what Isa thought. She wasn't able to recall just where they had come from or how much time had passed since she'd been imprisoned. All she knew was that any time spent in this hell had been too much time. And amidst all the more important worries, what she wouldn't have given for a bath.

Her legs felt wobbly after so many hours of sitting in the cramped, bowl-shaped pit. Walking quickly was impossible, so she was forced several times to stop and stretch her legs. Bronkendol waited patiently each time, though the guard sounded a bit irritated. She wondered where they were going through such a maze of tunnels, but she refused to ask and give Bronkendol the satisfaction of having the answers. So she simply walked. And stopped. And walked again.

On and on they went, through the halls, and up more flights of winding stairs than Isa could count. Finally, they came to a door, and the enchanter removed a golden key from his sleeve. Isa recognized it immediately as one that Ever never let out of his sight. He'd even worn it to bed each night. The only person it had ever been entrusted to was Garin, whenever Ever left the Fortress.

So if Bronkendol had the key, where was Garin? This thought brought her more apprehension than she'd thought possible.

"Are you quite sure?" Bronkendol paused, his hand on the

door and the key in the lock. "Even if it meant possibly saving your husband?" This time, Isa couldn't help but meet his eyes. Even in the dim light, she could feel them probing her, hoping. And with good reason. Was there a chance that she could save him? It had been five months ago, but Isa remembered how her heart had torn as she watched him breathe his last to save her. The Fortress had brought him back then. But what about now? Isa knew the response she *should* give, and yet, she couldn't get her tongue to utter the words.

What would Everard say?

The whisper floated through the air. But even without the Fortress's prompting, Isa knew the answer.

"I have nothing more to say to you."

"You don't know how sorry I am to hear that. I'm also sorry that I must do this then as well." He passed his hand over her face, and in turn, something cold and hard began to grow over her eyes.

Isa rubbed her eyes until they hurt. She could still see, but it felt as if she were looking at things from a distance, as though there was a window between herself and the world.

"I thought you said you weren't going to give me the slivers!" she protested.

"I won't. But if you refuse to be a part of this new world, I can't have you confusing those who need to enter it as well." He reached into his cloak and removed a large, round glass pendant. It was a deep red, the color of wine, and he placed its gold chain around her neck. Bright flashes of light emanated from the glass, but Isa couldn't feel any deep power from it. It was just a trick. But what for?

Before she had time to wonder too much, Bronkendol had also removed a knife from his robe. He stepped back and studied her for a moment before grabbing her messy braid and cutting it off just below her shoulders. Then he gave her one more thorough look up and down before turning the key and opening the door.

Isa gaped at the length of braid in the enchanter's hand as she stepped into the sunlight. The locks that had reached nearly to her knees when loose and unbraided, now swung carelessly from the enchanter's hand, glinting copper in the sun's rays. Ever had always loved her hair. He'd even admitted once that though he had first hated her while they were under the Fortress's curse, he had always thought her hair was beautiful. A new anger heated her cheeks along with the morning sun, strengthening her resolve all the more.

She would die before Bronkendol had her allegiance.

ONCE THEY WERE OUTSIDE, two more guards joined them. Bronkendol handed Isa off to them before taking his leave, and Isa was herded through another gate that led onto the northern lawn of the Fortress, and then into the Fortress through a side door. She could tell that careful attention was being paid to keep her hidden from sight, which meant someone was here that wasn't under the enchanter's thumb.

As the guards pushed her along, Isa spotted a mirror hanging on one of the walls ahead. She managed to stumble just in time to pause before the mirror as she stood back up, and when she did, she understood what Bronkendol had done in the dungeons. Her eyes were no longer a deep blue, but blood red. He must have placed colored glass inside of her eyes to alter her appearance. Even her own mother would have been frightened.

She didn't have time to dwell on the change in her eyes, because her escorts didn't let her rest until they were standing just outside the throne room's main doors. Before she could get too comfortable, something passed over her head, and Isa's throat tightened as she reached up to find a rope, nearly as thick as her braid had been, that now sat loosely around her neck. She turned her head just enough to see a hooded guard holding the end of the rope in one of his hands, and a tremor snaked through her as she recognized the executioner's hood. Another guard, who was also hooded, roughly slipped another, thinner rope around her wrists.

Where are you? she thought to the Fortress. But the only sound she heard came from inside the throne room doors. Hundreds of voices drifted in and out, and Isa wondered exactly who the enchanter had invited to witness this horrendous occasion.

How she wished for her sword!

A ruckus drew her attention as a clump of guards approached from her left. Surely they weren't for her. But when she saw the terrifying figure they led, Isa understood her own noose and bindings.

Ever had never looked more like an animal than he did now. His eyes had been made blood red as well. He wore a thick black cloak with a heavy hood, and an even larger red glass amulet around his neck. Thick black lines had been traced with charcoal around his eyes, the way dark sorcerers blackened theirs for incantations.

He had been walking along with the guards submissively until he saw her. His eyes widened as he took in her noose, and Isa could see him struggling with himself. She knew he could have taken those guards in a fight without question. Why didn't he?

Before Isa could say anything, however, she winced as the rope tightened just slightly around her throat.

That was why he didn't fight. Again, they were using her as a safeguard to make sure Ever cooperated. Isa wished more than ever that she, too, could have colossal strength. Then neither of them could be used against the other. But she had little time to wish, for the crowd on the other side of the throne room doors hushed, and the herald began to speak.

"Presenting King Rafael of Cobren." The herald interrupted her thoughts.

"Welcome," Rafael's voice boomed. "Most of you know who I am by title, but I doubt most of you know that I considered your king as a part of my own family. He and the late King Rodrigue, may the Maker eternally guide his soul, came to our assistance many times, and for that, I will always be grateful." Then Rafael sighed so deeply that Isa wondered if he truly thought Ever was dead. When he spoke again, his voice was gentle.

"Everard was just and fair and good. And he loved your queen with the tenacity of a thousand men." A sob broke through, and Isa glanced at Everard. To her surprise, however, he wasn't looking toward the door, or even at the guards surrounding them.

He was looking at her. And despite the frightening intensity of the ghoulish red in his eyes, the tenderness in Ever's face was unmistakable, deeper than she had ever seen. Unable to look away, Isa drank it in like a soul dying slowly in the desert. Never had she needed him more. Never had she loved him so much. If given the chance, she would do it all over again. Every single day. Every single hour, Isa would love Ever until the last breath had left her body.

"Only the most unrighteous of souls could have stolen two such gems from our world," Rafael continued, his voice growing steadier and more determined with each word. "And I take it upon myself to see them brought to justice! Bring in the impostors!"

Gasps broke out as the doors were opened, and Isa and Ever were prodded down the aisle like cattle ready for the slaughter. The fear in the room was palpable, and Isa wondered how many would see through the impostors' work, if any. If neither the glass amulets that hung about their necks weren't persuasive enough, nor was her shorn hair, the terrifying, crimson-eyed man beside her would surely do the job of convincing everyone in that room that they were indeed impostors.

Rafael stood at the front of the raised steps, a few feet in front of the gilded thrones. Bronkendol stood close to the back, partly in the shadows. Soldiers were everywhere, some even on the steps of the dais itself. But where was Launce?

When they had reached the front of the room, Isa and Ever were turned to face the crowd. Isa scanned the people to see who was there. The kings, queens, and nobles who had been visiting Rafael's court hissed and shouted for the impostors' deaths. The Fortress nobles and servants openly wept, but there were faces from Soudain that showed neither anger nor sorrow, but rather frightened bewilderment. Friends and acquaintances looked back and forth from Isa to Ever. They had no purple light in their eyes, and their uncertainty was clear. Isa wondered if Bronkendol would be able to fool everyone without the use of his shards. From the looks on the Destinians' faces, it seemed highly unlikely, and Isa suppressed a smile.

"These sorcerers infiltrated my castle with their dark powers," Rafael said. "They took it upon themselves to imitate your king and queen, before brutally murdering Everard and Isabelle in their room at night, even after I had helped Isa recover from her illness." Another gasp went up from the crowd, and several more people started to weep. Still, most of those from Soudain continued to only look confused.

Finally, one man stood. A cobbler. Isa's mother used to take Launce to him for shoes because he was the only cobbler who could keep up with the feisty young man. He was also on the city council with her father. Twisting his hat in his hands as he spoke, the poor man looking everywhere but at Rafael himself.

"The king and queen were strong . . . The Fortress made them that way. I don't . . . I don't think they could be killed so easily." He swallowed. "Besides, if these two were strong enough to overtake our king, then how is it that you have them captured here?"

Isa both rejoiced and feared at the same time. Would Bronkendol or Rafael punish the cobbler for such questions?

"Good questions, good sir," Rafael said in a kind voice. "That brings me to my second announcement. I want to introduce you all to the holy man who has succeeded in subduing such villains."

Bronkendol stepped forward. Unlike when he went to visit Isa in the dungeons, he now wore a silk robe of ice purple. It was an unusual cut, but it reminded Isa somewhat of the ancient statues in the gardens, the earliest ones of the first Fortress kings. Without speaking, he merely gave a slight smile and bow to the crowd, before flicking his wrist. Glass spikes grew up around the two of them until the spikes reached two heads taller than Ever, imprisoning them both. Exclamations broke out, and the crowd shifted uneasily. Bronkendol moved his wrist once more, and the glass spikes disappeared.

The cobbler, visibly shaken, said nothing more and sat down.

"Because Everard was so dear to me," Rafael said, taking control of the situation once more, "I feel as though it is my responsibility to bring a new king to Destin's throne, as there is no heir. He is new and young, and yet, not an unfamiliar soul. One I believe your late queen could not have approved of more. And by his side, I present my own daughter." Looking back with a proud smile, he raised his hand.

Isa looked back as well, and her heart fell as Launce and Olivia stepped forward. She hadn't seen them in the corner before, but now they were impossible to look away from. The Fortress's ceremonial robe was too big on Launce's thin shoulders, and his face was a sickly pale, but he stood beside Rafael nevertheless. Olivia was dressed in Isa's ceremonial gown, but her eyes also showed her to be under the enchanter's control.

Despite her resolution to wait, Isa felt like screaming inside. *Don't allow him to accept*, she begged the Fortress. *Let him know You're watching! Please don't let my brother die!*

"Your queen's younger brother, Launce Marchand of Soudain, has proven himself a worthy successor in my own country at my daughter's betrothal ceremony." Looking back once more, he smiled indulgently.

In a movement so small she nearly missed it, Isa saw Bronkendol place his hand inside of his robe pocket at his side. Something small and silver glinted from inside, and as soon as he rubbed it, Isa knew what it was.

She had to get that mirror.

As soon as Bronkendol's fingers touched the mirror, Rafael's expression changed back to one of ceremony.

"And so, to bring justice to the needless deaths of King Everard and Queen Isabelle Fortier of Destin, your future king shall be the one to put these traitors to death."

Bronkendol stepped forward once more and handed Launce a sword of pure glass. Launce looked at the weapon in his hands with wide eyes. The two hooded guards reached out and turned Isa and Ever roughly so they faced the dais.

No. No, no, no. Surely the Fortress would not allow this. Being slaughtered with her husband as criminals was a fate harsh enough. But to expect Launce, her gentle-spirited brother, to be the one to spill their blood? What kind of hold did the enchanter have on her brother? Who had he threatened for Launce to be considering such a sin?

"And who has authorized such a change?" Ever's voice was loud and strong. Launce froze and stared at them, but Bronkendol glided forward and answered in a steady voice.

"Who can speak for the Maker? For the Fortress?" Then he turned to the crowd. "My power may not be as impressive as your former king's was," the enchanter said in a calm voice, "but it is a power from the Maker no less."

"And I suppose that is what you told the holy men in Lingea?" Ever threw off his robe and broke his shackles in the same movement. Hushed whimpers sounded from some in the crowd, but Ever stared only at the enchanter, his red eyes flashing even without the blue fire that was hidden beneath them. Several of the guards pulled their swords, including the hooded guard nearest Ever.

"Ever!" Isa squeaked as the rope tightened around her neck.

But Ever kept on. "All ten of them, found dead in a field with glass spikes in their hearts! What did they do to earn such horrible deaths? Did they dare question your claim to the Maker's words?"

"And what proof do you have of this?" Bronkendol asked in a cool voice, his hands folded in front of him.

Ever reached into his cloak and drew out a glass spike the length of a grown man's arm. How had he gotten such a thing? Isa wondered. Hadn't he been stuck in the dungeons as well?

"How did this find its way into one of my messengers?" Ever hurled the spike at the enchanter's feet, where it shattered. Bronkendol stared at the broken pieces below him, while the crowd began to make uneasy sounds. Isa turned as well as she could in the noose, and she could see the people moving about as though they were wishing to run.

What was Ever up to? Clearly, he thought he had the upper hand. If so, then why was he waiting so long? And, Isa thought, why hadn't he freed her yet?

"They discovered you, didn't they?" Ever shouted. "When you traveled between realms, the true holy men saw through the tear in the worlds. And you saw fit to silence them before they could leak news of your little secret to others. What you forgot, however, was that the Maker does not look lightly upon the murder of His children. And you, sir, have more blood on your hands than any of my ancestors ever had!"

Then, as Bronkendol shifted uncomfortably throughout Ever's rant, Isa saw the glint of silver in his pocket again. The mirror. That was why Ever hadn't struck yet. He needed to get the mirror to free the others from the enchanter's grasp. She recalled his words on the road, about how hard it would be to fight friends and loved ones who were under the direction of their enemy. It would be a blood bath. Ever was stalling.

"Launce," Ever called up to her brother. His voice was kinder this time. Launce, who was still gaping at the glass weapon in his hands, had to be called three times more before he looked up to meet Ever's eyes. "I know he's threatened your family. But you must trust the Fortress. Do not commit a sin that will haunt you forever. No matter what he's promised you."

Once more, the rope tightened around Isa's neck, causing her to make a small choking sound. Launce watched her with fearful eyes.

"Launce," Ever's voice had a warning tone to it. "Remember what happened to me when I tried to shed innocent blood!"

But Launce didn't answer. Closing his eyes, he gripped the hilt of the glass sword until his knuckles turned white. Isa watched in horror as her brother walked slowly down the steps toward her husband. *Please!* she pleaded. *Don't let him do this!*

As she cried out inside, a movement caught her eye. Her hooded guard had moved up so that he was beside her, and Isa was able to glimpse just enough of the face beneath the hood to recognize Garin's slightly cleft chin. He gave her the smallest ghost of a smile before turning his attention back to Launce.

As Launce continued to move forward, Bronkendol walked forward as well, staying in line with the young man, and Isa decided not to wait and find out what would happen next. She didn't know what Ever and Garin had planned, but she was done watching her brother try to kill her husband. Whirling around, Isa knocked the rope from Garin's hand and stumbled into Bronkendol. She clutched the bottom of his robe.

"Your Holiness!" she begged as pitifully as she could, clawing at his robes. "Just let him be! Don't make my brother do this! I beg you!" She allowed herself to collapse at his feet, sobbing.

Bronkendol bent down and whispered, "You had your chance. Now let him have his." With that, he motioned to Isa's guard, and Garin hurried forward to take charge of his prisoner. Isa went willingly, but wanted to sing and dance with rejoicing as she tightened her fingers over the little mirror in her hand.

In one smooth movement, Garin's hood was thrown back, and he tossed Ever's sword over Isa's head. At the same time, the hooded guard keeping watch over Ever threw his hood back as well. Apu, Queen Kartek's personal guard, maneuvered to cover Ever's back. Garin grabbed a stunned Launce and Isa, who was still bound, and the group of five began to run toward the doors. Launce paused. Isa guessed he was looking for Olivia, but she was nowhere to be seen in the chaos that suddenly erupted from the crowd.

Unfortunately, even without the mirror, it seemed the enchanter's orders were still in effect. The soldiers, and even the kings and nobles from the other lands took up their weapons and gave chase. Isa ran as fast as she could, but the question plagued her even as they moved. How would they destroy the mirror?

"Isa!" Ever's shout came just in time. Isa ducked, just missing the swipe of a club from above. Men, and even some women, came from every direction, and somehow, they had all found weapons. Ever's blue fire was a blur as he moved from side to side. Apu wasn't much slower. Even Garin fought with increasing speed. Launce and Isa stood between the other three, although Isa wished to the heavens that *someone* would give her a sword.

"We can't stay here forever," Garin called out over his shoulder. They had been shoved up against a marble column, their progress stalled as the three men tried to hold off their attackers without drawing blood. "Where are we going, Everard?"

"To the tower!" was Ever's reply. He stepped out just enough for Isa to move behind him. In that instant, she saw the clearance to the stairs. Miraculously, there was a break in the waves of men, and Isa took it. Ducking beneath Garin and around Apu, she grabbed Launce's hand and dragged him toward the stairs. He fought her though. When she looked back, she could see him staring above the chaos at the room where Olivia still stood.

"We can't help her until the mirror is gone!" she shouted at him. When he didn't respond, she yanked on his arm. "Launce!"

As if waking from a dream, Launce slowly nodded and began to follow her. It was just in time too, for the brawl was nearly to the base of the tower stairs.

If they could destroy this accursed mirror anywhere, it would be in the Tower of Annals.

CHAPTER 53
SHATTER

Launce finally awoke from his stupor and grasped her hand tightly, even surpassing her as they ran up the winding stairs of the tower. Ever, Apu, and Garin were following after them, but as Isa and Launce left them behind, she could hear from the men's terse exchanges that the fight wasn't going well. Angry shouts echoed from further down the tower stairs as they ran, and her heart ached. Whose blood would be shed first? Her husband's? Apu's? Or one of their friends being used by the enchanter?

Isa stumbled a few times in the darkness of the tower, as did Launce, dropping the glass sword somewhere along the way. But the sounds of clashing metal behind them left no time to stop and look for it. And so they ran. For the first time, Isa questioned whether the tower really needed to have been built so tall.

They didn't reach the top until Isa's lungs felt like they might collapse, and her vision was spotty. Launce was first to reach the top. He yanked her into the tower behind him and then immediately shut the door. Isa stood beside him, waiting for the others to come through the door, but Launce locked it instead.

"What are you doing?" Isa darted back to unlock the door, but Launce grabbed her and held her tightly so she couldn't move.

"They're too far behind. If we let them in, the others will follow! Isa! Isa, look at me!"

Isa stopped struggling, and she stared up at her brother. Launce's hair had been cropped short for the coronation, and his eyes were lined with a stress she had never seen before. He looked older, and for the first time, to Isa at least, like a man.

"You know this is what Everard wants."

Once she was still, he carefully let go, and she stepped back. He was right. This is what Ever would want.

Which meant they had no time to waste. Isa raised the mirror as high as she could and threw it down upon the floor with all her might. Instead of cracking, it just rolled away. Isa grabbed it again and brought it down hard against the edge of the table this time. But the table only dented.

"How do we break it?" Isa cried, racking her memory for something that might stand a chance against the enchanter's magic. She searched the room desperately for something sharp or heavy. Books would do them no good, and the furniture was too heavy for her to lift.

"Hurry!" Launce had his ear to the door. "They're coming!"

Isa spotted the rack of swords that hung above the fireplace. Four of them were displayed against black velvet, the fourth one looking as if it were just low enough to reach. She hopped on a chair and leaned over the mantle, trying to pull it from the bottom rung. As her fingers touched the sword, Isa's boot slipped from the arm of the chair she stood on, and both Isa and the swords crashed onto the stone hearth.

Her left elbow came down painfully upon one of the stones, but when Isa opened her eyes, she was amazed to find that nothing was bleeding, and only two of the swords had broken. She grabbed the two remaining weapons and ran over to Launce.

"Here!" She handed him one sword and then moved back to the center of the room. Placing the mirror on the floor, Isa raised her sword above her head. Before she could bring it down, she was distracted by the sound of splintering wood.

The door shuddered as something beat against it from the outside. Launce adjust his grip on the weapon Isa had given him, and Isa realigned her sword with the mirror. But she couldn't focus enough to aim. Her breath was coming too fast, and her palms were sweaty, so the sword kept slipping.

"That's not Everard." Launce looked back at her.

They stared at one another for a long moment. If one of their enemies was here, where were Ever and the others? Cold panic pooled in Isa's belly. Had Ever's fear of killing his friends allowed him to be overcome? Had Bronkendol killed him? *Fortress*, she thought, *where is my husband?* The only answer she heard though was the hacking at the door.

Isa shook her head and tried once again to steady the sword. *Please let it break!*

The swords above the mantle had belonged to the first kings, Ever had once told her. That meant they would have been forged within the Fortress walls, imbuing them with the Fortress's power and strength. If any weapon could stand against the enchanter's charms, it would be one of these. Isa swung the sword downwards, but just as it hit the ground, the hilt slipped from her grasp and missed the mirror. Frustrated, Isa wiped her hands on her dress and raised the sword to try again.

"Isa."

She stopped and looked up at her brother. He wore a torn expression. "When he gets through, I will have to take him."

"No!" Isa immediately shifted into a ready position, mirror

all but forgotten. This was what Ever had trained her for. "I can hold him longer than you can. If we can just wait until—"

"They're not going to make it in time."

"No! Don't say that!" Isa tried to run to his side, but Launce held out his sword to stop her. Isa began to protest again, but he interrupted, and when he spoke, his voice was resolved.

"I made the wrong choice by not trusting the Fortress before. Now please just let me make this right."

"By killing yourself?" Isa shouted. As if in agreement, the edge of a glass axe made its first hole all the way through the door, sending chunks of wood flying toward them.

"No." Launce gave her a small smile. "By trusting the Fortress will help you stop him."

"But how? I can't break it!"

Launce stared in frustration at the mirror on the ground, before a look of understanding lit his face. "Maybe you don't have to."

"What?"

Launce spoke quickly as the axe gnawed away at the hole, making it larger with each blow. "Bronkendol told me that your strength isn't like Everard's, that it's not like anyone else's! He said you have the strength of the heart, not the hand."

"What is that supposed to mean?" Isa tried to dart toward Launce again, but Launce held his sword in front of the door once more. "I can't let you do this!" Isa protested, her voice breaking at the end. "You're my baby brother!"

"Then don't let me die in vain. Let me be the hero, just this once."

As he spoke, the rest of the door gave way enough for Bronkendol to drop his axe and step through. His silver curls were matted, and sweat rolled down his face and neck. He pointed the glass sword straight at Launce's heart.

"Give me the mirror, Isabelle. This sword is poisoned, and though I don't want to kill your brother, I will if you don't give me what's mine." He held his left hand out to Isa as his right forced Launce against the wall with the glass sword.

Isa looked at Launce, then down at the mirror.

"Don't do it, Isa! The Fortress gave you the mirror for a reason!"

"Give it to me, or he dies! None of your Fortress's power can heal the poison this weapon was forged in!"

Isa looked back and forth between the mirror and her brother. How could she destroy it even if she had all of Ever's strength? Even now, away from its master, the mirror's power pulsed through her hands to a rhythm, like the beating of a heart.

"I don't know how," she mouthed to her brother, tears streaming down her face. Without hesitation, Launce launched himself off of the wall. Isa cried out as the sword bit flesh. Even Bronkendol stared in horror.

"Now you have nothing to lose," Launce gasped as the enchanter stepped back. "Do what you were made to do!"

Panic and sorrow clouded Isa's mind as she stared once more at the mirror in her hand. If only Ever were here!

Who is holding the mirror, Daughter?

The familiar voice Isa had waited so long to hear whispered now.

I am, she cried. *But I don't know how! I'm not my husband!*

A memory flashed before her eyes. Nevina, lying unconscious upon the floor before her. *How did you know what to do then?* the voice prodded.

I didn't! I just knew . . .

That she belonged. That she was wanted. That she was the Fortress's. That she had been chosen.

I chose you then, and I choose you now. And I didn't give you strength of the hands, but strength of the heart.

Isa could somehow feel the Fortress smile.

Now use it.

Without thinking, Isa lifted the mirror to her mouth.

"No!" Bronkendol lunged for her. "I took your power! You have none left!"

But Isa knew her power wasn't gone. It had never been hers to begin with. It was the Fortress's, and she was merely the heart to hold it, a vessel. Isa closed her eyes and focused on what she knew within. Not on what she felt, but on what she knew in her heart to be the truest of truths.

"Peace," she whispered.

CHAPTER 54

AN OATH FULFILLED

Hundreds of voices cried out in agony as the glass shattered between Isa's hands. Their shouts of pain echoed all the way up to the tower, where Launce laid on the floor bleeding and Bronkendol stood, a look of disbelief on his face. It didn't last long though.

"Do you know what you have done?" He raised the bloodied glass sword and began to stalk toward Isa.

Before he made even three steps, however, he stopped. A choking sound gurgled from his throat and his eyes bulged before he slid limply to the ground.

Behind him, Ever stood, his own sword bloodied as he let the enchanter fall from it.

"I swore I would kill you," Ever snarled.

"Ever!" Isa thrust herself into his arms, and held him with all the strength that remained in her worn, ragged body. He drew her in and silently stroked her short hair. She hadn't lost him again after all. As he rocked her from side to side, Isa caught a glimpse of her brother.

"Launce!" She tore herself from Ever's arms and collapsed on the floor, wrapping her arms as gently as she could around her little brother. Ever quickly joined her and turned him so that he was facing up. To Isa's dismay, his face was pale, and his eyes were lifeless, staring blankly at the ceiling. "You have to heal him, Ever!" Isa said frantically. "You have to stop the poison!"

Ever inhaled and laid his hands upon the young man. Isa held her breath as the blue flames licked Launce's wounds. But as seconds passed, nothing changed. Ever set his jaw and pushed hard. When still nothing came, however, Isa lost patience.

She placed her own hands on Launce as well, but before she could try her own strength, Ever shook his head and gathered her in his arms.

"It's too late for me to help him," he murmured into her ear. "I'm so sorry, Isa." Isa was about to protest. He had given up too easily, she wanted to shout, when another voice spoke.

"I might be able to help him though."

Isa looked up through tear-blurred eyes to see Kartek standing at the door. Her sun-kissed face was paler than usual, and she held one hand over her side protectively, but she gave Isa a weak smile.

"Garin." She turned to the steward, who had just walked up behind her. "Can you take this young man to a dark, quiet room?"

Garin stooped and lifted Launce's long, thin body as though he weighed nothing. The steward's hair was mussed, and his clothes were torn in several places, but aside from some sweat, dirt smudges, and the fact that he was wearing the executioner's uniform, he looked as much like himself as he ever did. As he turned to leave with Launce's body, Isa leaped up to follow, but Kartek held out a hand.

"I am sorry, but I will need to be alone for this. I will call for you when I know his fate." The queen's brown eyes softened, and she kindly took Isa's face in the hand that wasn't holding her side. "Do not despair, young one. The Maker's gift to me might yet bring him back from the dark."

Ever pulled Isa back to him as Garin and Kartek began down the stairs, and Isa let him, drinking in every second as though he'd never held her before. The warmth of his arms, the familiar smell of leather and the forest were as intoxicating as a fine wine. Isa gazed up at him and shuddered at the thought that she might have lost him again.

"What happened?" She frowned and reached up to touch the red gash just above his left brow.

Ever made a face. "An earl managed to throw a frying pan at me. I must have blacked out long enough for them to think I was dead, and for Bronkendol to slip by me." He shook his head. "Fighting in battle is nothing new, but not fighting my friends and those who have sworn to serve me . . ." his voice trailed off, and he looked away from her.

"How many?" She could hardly hear her own voice.

"Too many." He closed his eyes, but they glistened at the corners. "A few dozen of my own men, three servants, and a Cobrien duke." He opened his eyes, and a tear escaped as his face crumpled. "I tried so hard just to hold them off, but—" A ragged sob escaped him, and his chest heaved violently.

Isa felt tears running down her own cheeks as she reached up with both hands and gently pulled his face down against hers. In turn, Ever took her shoulders in his large hands and leaned against her as the sobs came faster and harder. Isa ached for him as he wept in her arms. Ever was always in command, always had a plan to fix what had gone askew. It was wrong for him to be this broken, as if the sun had risen in the wrong part of the sky.

She couldn't tell how long they stood there as he let her hold him, but it was, in a strange way, the closest to healing she'd felt in a long time.

"You don't always have to be so strong," she whispered to

him as she wiped the tears from his face, ignoring those on her own. He opened his eyes and looked into hers. As he did, she realized that the red glass was gone, and wondered if her own eyes were clear again as well.

"But if I'm not—"

"I will be." She smiled and caressed his cheek. "I made that vow before the people, this Fortress, and you. I'm not about to break it now."

Ever stared hard at her for a long moment before wrapping his arms around her and kissing the top of her head.

"This is going to take a while to clean up," he said in a hoarse voice. And Isa knew he wasn't just talking of Bronkendol's doings.

"It will be worth it in the end."

"Yes. Yes it will."

ALL TOO SOON, it was time to face the chaos that awaited them below. Ever shed the ludicrous, heavy garb Bronkendol had forced him into, and Isa changed into a practical gown that wasn't tattered and grimy. It was difficult to look in the mirror and see her hair so ragged, but at least its new length would keep it out of the way as they worked.

Garin had directed the servants to gather everyone to the throne room so Ever could address them, but it took a little longer than usual, as most of the servants were recovering from the enchanter's influence as well. The enchanter's power had taken a toll on many, and some of even their most reliable servants needed assistance.

When they were finally all gathered, Isa stood tall and proud beside her husband. The timidity she'd known was gone now. She was done comparing. This was her place, and these were her people. This was her Fortress, and never again would she doubt its love for her.

The kings, queens, dignitaries, and other guests of high standing were all unhappy to have been manipulated so easily, but they listened to Ever with respectful humility. Isa watched as Ever explained the enchanter's wiles. In the middle of his speech, Isa caught the eye of Lady Jadzia, but the woman refused to hold her gaze. Isa didn't miss the little daggers Jadzia still sent her throughout Ever's speech, when Isa pretended not to pay her heed. Would the woman ever give up?

After the address was made, Isa was standing beside Ever, when she spotted Jadzia primping herself before beginning to walk toward them. Anger flamed inside her, and her hands grew slightly warm as she felt her power rise within her. Before Isa could say anything, Ever surprised her by grabbing her around the waist and kissing her with such a passion that Isa felt her cheeks flush.

"Um . . . thank you?" Isa breathed when Ever finally let her go. He gave her a mischievous grin and wiggled his eyebrows.

"Perhaps Lady Jadzia will think twice next time she's tempted to try and play for a married man."

Isa turned, and sure enough, Lady Jadzia was staring at them, open-mouthed with a look of shock on her face. Isa allowed herself a wide grin for the woman.

So Ever had noticed. The thought made her nearly giddy.

LADY JADZIA and her father finally left a week after the enchanter's death, along with a few of the other royals. Progress was slow, as most of the servants and guests were still recovering, so Isa suggested that they bring in some of her old friends from the village to help, a suggestion which Ever readily agreed to.

Isa was glad to make the trip down the mountain alone. She didn't even mind the guard that trailed loosely behind her. While she had spoken the truth about calling on old acquaintances for help, there was a visit she needed to make. As soon as all of her requests for assistance at the Fortress were made, Isa wound her way through the main marketplace to the familiar little shop that sat on the northeast corner of the square.

Megane squealed when Isa walked through the front of the shop into their kitchen, and Deline was overjoyed as well. But there was one face in particular that Isa had come to see.

Ansel's face broke into a wide smile when she let herself into her parents' room. It hurt to see his eyes and cheeks still mottled and purple from Bronkendol's cruel orders.

"How are you?" She sat at the edge of the bed and looked anxiously at his legs, which were covered by his blankets.

Ansel shrugged as though it were nothing. "The healer says he's not sure if I'll walk again, but—"

"Father!" Isa cried. "Why didn't you tell me? I'm sure Ever can help you somehow!"

"Considering the chaos of that place after your enchanter died, it was good of the servants to simply bring me back here." When Isa continued to glare at him, he gave her a placating smile. "But perhaps I will, in time. For the time being, though, I would feel more comfortable if that husband of yours stays right where he's at."

Isa sighed and sat back down. Her father was right, as usual. Ever was busy, but he never failed to check on her brother whenever he had the chance. Kartek and Apu had gone home finally, so Ever was the main physician of the Fortress.

"It is up to the Maker now," Kartek had told them. "I am sorry I cannot do more, but now the best medicine will be for you to wait." And so they'd waited. Ansel, Deline, and Megane from the city, and Ever and Isa from down the hall at the Fortress.

"Your Highness," Isa's guard called from behind the door. Isa and her father looked at one another in surprise. Isa's guards always waited outside. "The king has sent a messenger to request that you return to the Fortress. It's about your brother."

Isa was off in a flash. As soon as she was on her horse, they flew up the mountain road until the incline made it impossible to run. Isa's heart pounded with impatience as they plodded along. Had Launce awakened? Had he taken a turn for the worse?

She didn't even pause to unbridle her horse at the stables. For once, she would let the servants take care of that. Once she had vaulted herself off the horse, she sprinted through the Fortress, not stopping until she reached Launce's room. As she approached, Ever was just shutting the door behind Princess Olivia and her escort. The princess curtsied, but didn't meet Isa's eyes.

"I cannot express how sorry I am for playing the part I had in all of this," she said. Isa could hear the tears in her voice. "We tried to hold him off, but it was just too much—"

Despite Isa's need to see Launce, she could only assume he was improving if Ever had brought the princess to see him. Isa didn't let Olivia go any further, wrapping the young woman in her arms and giving her a good squeeze.

"You did well to hold out for so long," she whispered. Then she laughed. "You have seen more of the Fortress at work in just a few short weeks than most Destinians see in their lives!" She pulled back to look the girl in the eyes. "The Maker has given us a new day. We've mourned the past. Now let's not dwell on it any longer."

Princess Olivia pulled back and gave her a tremulous smile. "Will you come visit me sometime? I should like to know you more without an enchanter trying to take over our kingdoms."

Isa laughed told the girl yes, giving her one more quick hug.

Then Ever placed his hand on the small of her back and gently pushed her toward Launce's door. In spite of Ever's reassuring smile, Isa felt her heart pound as she entered her brother's room.

Launce was propped up against a mountain of pillows, which somehow made him look even scrawnier than usual. His head was leaned back and his eyes were closed as he lay there, but as she approached, he slowly lifted himself up to see her.

"Launce," was all Isa could say. The young man before her looked like her brother. And yet he didn't. There were thin lines of exhaustion at the corners of his eyes, and his skin was unusually red, as though it were thinner than usual. He looked as though he might faint at any minute, and yet she could still see a bit of life in the half smile he managed to give her.

"So you did it," he croaked.

Isa rolled her eyes. "As much as it pains me to admit it, you were right."

"I don't think I've ever heard that one before." His dark eyes gleamed with mischief. "I will be sure to bring that up now whenever you doubt me."

"I'm sure you will." Isa stuck her tongue out at him, then sighed. Even their childish games were difficult when he was lying in bed looking half dead. "But truly, how are you?"

Launce looked down at himself. "Everard seems to think I will be at least a few months in recovery. Apparently, Bronkendol's poison has proved to be the most difficult healing Queen Kartek has ever attempted. Still," he paused, "it seems I should be well enough to travel by summer."

"Travel?"

Launce looked down, studying his hands with sudden interest. "King Rafael has asked if I am willing to consider being Cobren's next king."

"And . . . you're accepting?" Isa frowned. "You hate court life."

"Of course I do. But I spoke with Everard and I think . . ." He drew in a deep breath and blew it out before finishing. "I can see a little better why your husband makes the choices that he does. The Fortress has given him many lives to be responsible for. And now, Cobren has lots of healing to do as well. Olivia thinks I can help with that somehow."

Isa smirked. "Ah, and the truth comes out."

Launce grimaced at her. "You know what I mean. It's just that I feel like the Maker, for whatever reason, has put me in this place now. I don't fit into the life I had before, thanks to you." He swatted Isa's arm, then doubled over in pain. "I keep forgetting about that," he grunted. "Anyway—Ouch!—I think it would be best to give this a try. They think they need me, and I think I need a new start."

"I still don't understand this life entirely either," Isa said. "And to be honest, I don't know if I ever will. However," she scooted closer so she could take his hand, "I do know that you and I make a terrific team. How about we just enjoy being lost together for a while?"

Launce smiled back. "Sounds good to me. Just don't go running into any horse thieves or glass enchanters or evil Fae until I'm walking at least."

"I will try." Isa grinned at her brother. "But I'm not making any promises."

CHAPTER 55

NEW BEGINNINGS

Yasmina, please hand me that spoon." Isa smiled as the little girl handed her the spoon with a shy look. "Then as soon as your mother is done eating, I think we're going to brush your hair."

"My hair doesn't need brushing," the little girl said, holding her stringy blond hair up for Isa to see.

"Oh, that it does," her mother said. Then she smiled at Isa with tired eyes. "I can't thank you enough, Your Highness. I couldn't stand watching her run around like that for one more day." The woman laid back into the pillows and sighed slowly as she rubbed her temples. "How are the others?"

"You're all getting along quite nicely." Isa reached out and squeezed the woman's hand. "I suppose that in a way, it was best that you were all down here to begin with. You would have gotten the glass too, had you been working in the upper levels with the others." The thought of the invalids under the orders of the enchanter made Isa shiver. There had been too much blood shed at the Fortress as it was. No, it was better that the infirmary had been forgotten, even if it meant more work for Isa and the few other women who were well enough to help.

"It has been two weeks." The woman shifted uncomfortably. "When will you be relieved? Surely the other servants will be recovered soon enough to return to their duties."

"Some are, but many of them were injured in the fight, and others are grieving . . ." They were silent for a moment, reflecting on their losses, before Isa cajoled the woman into eating. "You need to keep up your strength." Isa nodded at the woman's burgeoning belly. "Soon enough you will have two to keep up with."

Isa couldn't help the slight jab of envy as the woman smiled and rubbed her belly. And yet, Isa was the closest to feeling content that she had felt in a long time. The desire was still there, but at least she now saw a purpose in the wait. She sighed as the woman ate. The Fortress had known what it was doing all along, even though she hadn't seen the purpose at the time.

As soon as the woman finished her meal, Isa chased down the little girl, and was just finishing with her hair when Gigi came in.

"There you are. I'm sorry for interrupting, my dear, but the king has requested you meet him at the stables."

Isa patted the little girl's head once more before standing and gathering her things. "We were just finishing anyway." She gave the room another look before she was satisfied that things were in order. Hopefully, the woman and her daughter would be back in their quarters before long anyway. As she walked up the steps from the bottom levels to the main floor, Isa glanced at the other rooms along the way, making a list in her head of the items she would need the next time she came down.

"My mother saw her yesterday," she told Gigi, "and she says the child will come any day. The man in the next room over, though, will need to stay quite a while longer. His leg will take longer to heal than her convalescence will last." Isa sighed. "I wish we had more rooms down here, instead of having to keep so many in the greeting hall. Ever suggested using some of the guest rooms, but they're too far apart to see to everyone's needs."

"You leave those worries to me and the healers." Gigi took Isa's arm and guided her elbow so that they were heading toward Isa's own chambers. "You have done far enough and more than what could ever be expected from you."

"It was a nice change from Bronkendol's chaos. Now, what exactly am I doing? I thought we were going to the stables."

Instead of answering, Isa was hurried into her own chambers. Two voices sounded from the connecting sitting room, and it was impossible not to overhear.

"Do you think she'll need any looser clothes?" A young woman's voice gushed with hope, and Isa felt her cheeks turn pink.

"Of course not." Cerise's words were sharp. "They'll only be gone a week. Now please focus on what you're doing. You've just rumpled that gown."

"Are we nearly finished?" Gigi let go of Isa's arm as they rounded the corner to find the two young women filling a travel bag with Isa's things. Isa didn't miss the look of rebuke Gigi sent the younger servant.

Before she could get a better look at what was in the bag, however, Cerise dragged her over to her mirror, where she was bathed and dressed in a new riding outfit. The gown was trim and easy to move in, and there were only a few layers of petticoats beneath the skirt, something Isa would have liked for most of her gowns. The deep green was exactly the color of the rose stems in her favorite garden, and her boots were new as well.

"When did you have time to make these?" Isa was in awe.

"We didn't." Gigi grinned. "I had them made five and a half months ago."

"Whatever for?"

"For the night that should have been ours." Ever's deep voice came from the door. When she turned, Isa caught her breath. Ever walked toward her, also in a new outfit of dark red and brown. Red was a color he didn't wear often, and Isa thought it looked quite dashing on him.

"You were right when you said I chose others over you." He came to a stop just before her, and took her left hand in both of his, examining the blue crystal ring that burned brightly from her finger. "I cannot change our first night, as much as I'd like to, but I can offer you a new beginning in its place."

Was he being earnest?

Ever seemed to sense her doubts and fears. With a small smile, he pulled a delicate bracelet from his cloak. Isa gasped as he placed it on her wrist. Purple stone roses glittered from a gold chain. In awe, Isa looked up to thank him, and to her surprise he reached up and gently tilted her chin back. Before he could lean all the way in, Gigi squeaked and pushed them apart. "There is a reason your horses are loaded down with clothes and food and wine. Now go, before you forget where you are!"

Ever sent Gigi a scowl before leaning down and kissing the top of her white head. Then, in a flurry of people and horses and last-minute instructions, Isa and Ever somehow made it down to the stables, where Garin was waiting with their horses' reins in hand.

Isa hadn't seen much of the steward in the last few weeks, with the exception of quick exchanges about Launce. It was good to see him looking less harried and back to his typical calm.

"Thank you, Garin." Ever helped Isa up onto her horse before climbing astride his own.

"You'll watch out for Launce, won't you?"

Garin smiled knowingly. "Of course, my queen. Now, both of you, go!"

Finally, they were on their way. Isa was bursting with questions, but Ever was strangely silent, so she decided to hold back. Besides, it was too beautiful a day to clutter the air with words. The first powdery snow of the season had fallen the night before, and the wind was nowhere to be heard. Scarlet cardinals sat on bare branches, and the sun glistened off the snow until it nearly hurt to open her eyes. There were few sounds, aside from an occasional seasonally late chipmunk.

Isa wondered how Everard knew his way without the visible trail, as they had seemed early on to veer from the usual road, into the forest itself. But Ever rode confidently, as usual, so she didn't ask. Although the more she studied him, the more she realized he looked . . . nervous. Every few minutes, his eyes would dart to her, but they wouldn't remain long enough for her to catch them.

After about an hour of riding, they came to a little wooden cabin that looked like it was dusted in sugar.

"It's beautiful!" Isa exclaimed as Ever helped her off of her horse. When he didn't respond, she turned to find him staring at her. A strange mix of emotions swirled about in his fiery, gray eyes. And Isa stared back. What was he thinking? Was he sorry they were away from the Fortress after all? But she didn't ask as he returned to unloading the horses in silence, confusion and sorrow and curiosity lingering in his eyes.

Still, Isa's patience had nearly worn out by the time he'd finished putting the horses away. Before she could say anything, however, his face broke into the most beautiful smile she'd ever seen. After throwing their supplies over his shoulders, he bent and lifted her so that his arms were beneath her shoulders and under her knees. Isa squealed with delight as he carried her over the threshold and into the cabin itself.

The inside was just as idyllic as the exterior. A wooden headboard carved with roses and ivy overlooked the bed that took up nearly half of the room. Across from the bed was a large hearth with a fire already lit, two plush chairs, and a small table with four books stacked on it. Two windows filled each wall except the one the headboard stood against, and each window had twelve panes, which could be covered or uncovered with curtains of red lacy gauze. Even the planks of wood were a light, cheerful maple wood.

"Oh, Ever!" Isa sighed. "It's perfect!" Then she laughed. "You can put me down now."

"I don't think I want to."

Isa laughed again at his ornery expression. "How did you find this place?"

"It's a little-known secret that Fortress kings and queens need rest too. My great-great-grandfather had this cabin built so he and his wife could escape for even just a few hours from time to time." He finally set Isa down, and she began to wander.

"Do the others know where we are?"

Ever made a face. "If the kingdom decides to go up in flames, Garin can find us, but I will wring the first person's neck who seeks us out with a declaration or a treaty that needs sign-ing." He shrugged off their supply bags. "I also knew I could never convince you to stay away from your brother for too long."

Isa, who had been walking slowly through the little room, touching things to try and convince herself that this wasn't a dream, walked back to him as though in a daze. He placed his hands in hers and led her over to the warmth of the fireplace.

"I need to tell you again how sorry I am." He shook his head, a look of disgust on his sharp features. "The Fortress continues giving me chances to learn, and I continue to throw them away by thinking I know best."

"Ever, you really needn't—"

"No, I mean it. If I had allowed you to develop your own strength instead of trying to force you into mine . . . who knows how much sooner we might have stopped Bronkendol?"

"You weren't the only one." Isa placed her hand on his chin and lifted his face so he had to look at her. "I thought the same." She chuckled, although there was little humor in it. "Can you imagine me doing all of that running while pregnant?"

Ever's eyes flashed. "That's not funny."

Isa just shook her head and smiled. "But the Fortress knew better. It knew what I needed, and it pushed us so that we *had* to learn. You had to see that I was meant to be beside you, not behind."

"And what did you have to learn?"

"That Garin was right."

Ever smirked as he played with a lock of her short hair. "He usually is. But about what?"

Isa pressed Ever's shoulders down so that he sat in one of the chairs, then she sat in his lap and wrapped her arms around his neck. "I had to learn that it doesn't matter what I *feel*. Whether I feel like the queen or not is insignificant. What is most important is *knowing* the truth. I think that was why my fire disappeared. At least, from our sight. It was there all along, but as I lost faith in my place, my fire dipped lower and lower, until only the Fortress could convince me to believe I belonged once again."

To demonstrate, she held out her hand, and a small tongue of blue flame sprung up inside her palm. Gently, she placed her palm over his heart. Ever's mouth dropped and his eyes widened as the flame moved into his chest.

"What was that?" he asked breathlessly.

"Bronkendol was wrong about many things, but he was right about my power. That means that my power works in ways I'd never even imagined. I just took the love I hold for you in my heart, and I sent it straight to yours." She paused, watching him carefully. "Now you cannot doubt how much I love you. I promised to love you forever, and even if we don't always feel it, the love is still there, waiting."

"Do you know that I love you?" Ever's voice was suddenly throaty, and his breath came faster on her face.

"I don't know." Isa grinned and looked deep into the fiery rings inside his eyes that burned with a sudden intensity. "I might need some reminding."

"And how would I do that?" His lips brushed hers as he spoke, and his hand was buried beneath her hair, bringing her face close to his.

"As everything good and worthy is best begun."

"Which would be?"

"Simple," Isa whispered. "With a dance and a kiss."

Ever didn't answer. He was too busy following her advice.

Beauty Beheld

A Clean Fairy Tale Retelling of Hansel and Gretel

"ACELET," Isa called out to the general, who rode ahead of her, "how many at last count?"

As he thought, the general rubbed the back of his neck, which was probably stiff, Isa guessed, from the furious pace Ever had set since leaving the Fortress that morning. "My scouts brought in reports last night of two hundred and six, but I believe it might be higher than that."

"Why is that?" she asked.

"The woodland towns haven't reported losing any children, but I'm assuming they've had children go missing as well. They just don't like to send messengers up our way very much. The fools would rather handle their problems themselves." He looked at Ever. "And they don't much like you, Your Highness."

Ever gave him a sardonic look. "I think I shall survive."

Acelet smiled wryly before turning back to Isa. "Anyhow, I simply think there are a number of children who have probably gone missing and their parents have not come to us to tell of it. Hold now, is this it?"

They had come to a stop, and Ever was too busy studying the forest before them to answer, so the party simply waited. Isa had never been to this part of Destin before, and now that she was here, she was rather sure she hadn't missed much. The forests weren't thick and tall the way they were in the woods closer to home. Rather, the trees rose out of the ground like long, thin snakes with their heads turned toward the skies. The ground itself was wet and resembled a marsh much more than a forest. Isa was suddenly also sure that it probably hid an assortment of animals she would prefer not to meet. As she drew quick breaths in and out, the sickly, moist air clung to her lungs and made breathing more labored. No, Isa decided, she did not like the southern forest at all.

But it was better than staying at home to face Launce and Olivia's constant looks of guilt and pity.

"We'll walk slowly from here," Ever said as he dismounted and took his horse by the reins. "There is a source of power nearby. I can feel it."

"Thank the Maker," Isa heard one of the young soldiers behind her remark to one of his comrades. "I was going to puke if we ran another mile at that pace."

Isa didn't mind the speed that resulted from Ever's use of his power to hasten their travel. What should have been a three-day journey had taken place in less than one. And the view had been incredible. Isa had seen everything in one day, from their own mountain to valleys and plains to a great chasm of dark blue granite, which could only be crossed using a bridge wide enough for one horse to pass over at a time. But now that they had arrived, the sobering reminder of why they had made such a journey settled upon her once more.

"So many broken hearts," she murmured.

"What was that, Your Highness?"

"Oh," she shook her head, "only that I can feel the heart-break." She looked up through the trees into the gray sky over-head. "Even here, the sorrow of their parents is thick in the air." Ever had been right. They were getting close.

At such a statement, an air of solemnity filled the group, and they passed on quietly, following Ever as he led them forward. Isa tried to focus, but as they moved deeper into the forest, and the despair of the many families wrapped about her like a hot, stuffy cloak, Isa's thoughts turned, as they had so often of late, to the child that by past Fortier standards she should have had by now.

If all had gone as tradition had led them to believe it would, Isa would have conceived the month they had been married. It would have been a boy, as all the Fortiers had boys first, and he would have been three years by now. She knew what he would have looked like, too. His eyes would have been the same shade of stormy gray-blue as his father's eyes, and his hair would have been darker than Ever's, probably with just a hint of her own copper red. He would have had his father's stubborn jaw and might have ended up being even a bit taller than his father.

Not that any of that mattered. What mattered was that whether he had golden, red, or even white hair, he wasn't there for Isa to kiss to sleep at night. There were no chubby arms or legs or cheeks to squeeze and no little hand to hold. And though Isa knew the Fortress made no mistakes, she couldn't help feeling that she had been robbed of something very precious, for her arms were still empty.

And so were the arms of hundreds of other parents, Isa scolded herself. Now was not the time for a good cry, though she suddenly wanted very much to have one. Even the thought of her imaginary son being stolen from her in the dark of night angered Isa to a place of danger, and if she couldn't have a child of her own to keep safe, Isa swore to herself, she was going to do everything in her power to return these children to their families. No one should have to suffer such a terrible fate as to live wondering where a child had gone and what had become of him. Then she felt it.

"Wait!"

Everyone stopped and turned to look at her, but Isa only dismounted her horse and handed the reins to one of the soldiers nearby.

"Isa?" Ever asked warily. When she didn't respond, he drew his sword and began to follow her, but Isa didn't stop. Her fingers and toes and even her chest felt alive, humming like a hive of bees. Never had she felt such a powerful pull before, and without knowing where she was going, her feet carried her toward the source. Heartbreak. So much heartbreak. Loneliness, curiosity, and terror. The terror was thicker than any other feeling Isa could sense in the air. But this terror was different from that of the parents that she had felt earlier. Unable to utter a word, so filled was she with the need to find the children who were producing such emotions, Isa broke into a run.

"Isa, slow down!"

But Isa couldn't slow down. The feelings were too strong for her to ignore or break away from. It was as though they had stitched themselves right to her own heart and were pulling her in without her permission. Ever had been right. She was too wrapped up in this struggle. It was too personal. She should have stayed behind. And now she was letting her heart lead her rather than her head. Still, the vine-like trees continued to fly past her as she raced into the heart of the sickly wood.

Until she came to the house.

"Here," she said breathlessly as Ever came to stand beside her. "The children are here."

"All two hundred and six?" Ever cast a doubtful look at the ramshackle little cottage.

Even with the second story, there couldn't have been more than three rooms in the entire house, certainly not enough space for a quarter of so many children. And yet, the pull of terror was stronger than ever.

"Do you smell that?"

"Smell what?"

"It's sweet," she said, approaching the house. "Like... the scent of sugar." For a brief instant, a vision flashed through her mind, and instead of the crumbling stone house that stood before her, Isa saw a house made of every kind of candy imaginable. Red-and-white striped sugar stick columns supported the roof, rather than the collapsing wooden beams she had seen just a moment ago. Bright lemon drops, dark green mint drops, and even brown honey drops made up the walls, rather than gray, round stones. Roses made of chocolate, a rare delicacy Isa had only tasted after she'd come to the Fortress, lined the path up to the door, and unfamiliar blue truffles were arranged alongside them. Dozens of other sweets unknown to Isa made the house into the most lovely and inviting sight she had ever seen.

But then the vision was gone, as was the scent, and Isa was left touching one of the dirty rock walls. "Whoever did this lied to the children." She turned to Ever.

"Lied to them?" Ever frowned at her.

"I think... I think I know what they saw!" she exclaimed. "The thief used an illusion of sorts to draw them here, making them think the house was made of sweets."

Ever looked at her as though she'd lost her mind but said nothing as he moved closer to the house to examine it for himself. "Perhaps that would explain why no one saw these children leave," he said. "If the thief had the ability to create such a grand illusion, perhaps he had the ability to also cover the children with an illusion while they walked here." He turned to Isa, the blue rings of fire burning intensely in his eyes.

"They must have walked for days," he said, wonder and horror mixing in his voice. "Some of the children were reported missing from near the border of Tumen, and others from the coast!"

Isa was about to respond when another wave of fear crashed through her. Again, she felt the immediate, driving need to find its source. As she began to open the cottage's door, Ever blocked her path.

"Isa, I know you are excited about this, but you need to take care," he said. When she didn't respond, he grabbed her arm. "I am serious. You need to unsheathe your sword and walk cautiously, or I will pack you up myself and send you home."

"You wouldn't—"

"I would, just as I would do to any of my soldiers unfit for duty. Something is very wrong here. Now, I need you to focus—"

"Mummy!"

The cry had come from inside the home. It was a little girl's cry, and the sorrow and fear within it touched Isa in a way no other voice had moved her before. In a moment, she had torn away from her husband's grasp and had burst through the slanted front door. She could hear Ever shouting to his men behind her, but there was no time to wait. The cry came again, and Isa darted deeper in. As she did so, however, her foot caught on a loose stone, and sent her sprawling across the dusty ground, where her head came down on the floor with a very painful crack.

Continue Isa and Ever's happily-ever-after in their third and final book, *Beauty Beheld: A Clean Fairy Tale Retelling of Hansel and Gretel.*

Dear Reader,

Thank you so much for continuing Isa and Ever's journey with me. I hope you found the magic you were looking for. If you enjoyed it, please help other readers find this story by leaving a review on your favorite online retailer or Goodreads.com.

And if you want free, exclusive stories about Isa and Ever, visit BrittanyFichterFiction.com. By joining my email list, you'll get free access to exclusive secret chapters with more Ever and Isa, sneak peeks, book updates, discounts, and more!

About the Author

Brittany lives with her Prince Charming, their little fairy, and their little prince in a ~~sparkling~~ (decently clean) castle in whatever kingdom the Air Force has most recently placed them. When she's not writing, Brittany can be found chasing her kids around with a DSLR and belting it in the church choir.

Contact Brittany:

Subscribe: BrittanyFichterFiction.com
Email: BrittanyFichterFiction@gmail.com
Facebook: Facebook.com/BFichterFiction
Instagram: @BrittanyFichterFiction

Publisher's Note: This is a work of fiction. Names, characters, places, and incidents are a product of the author's imagination. Locales and public names are sometimes used for atmospheric purposes. Any resemblance to actual people, living or dead, or to businesses, companies, events, institutions, or locales is completely coincidental.

Blinding Beauty / Brittany Fichter. -- 1st ed.
    Edited by Katherine Stephen and Mark Swift